LAST WOMAN STANDING

ALSO BY AMY GENTRY

Good as Gone

LAST WOMAN STANDING

AMY GENTRY

Houghton Mifflin Harcourt
Boston   New York
2019

For information about permission to reproduce selections from this book, write to trade.permissions@hmhco.com or to Permissions, Houghton Mifflin Harcourt Publishing Company, 3 Park Avenue, 19th Floor, New York, New York 10016.

hmhco.com

Library of Congress Cataloging-in-Publication Data
Names: Gentry, Amy, author.
Title: Last woman standing / Amy Gentry.
Description: Boston ; New York : Houghton Mifflin Harcourt, [2019] |
Identifiers: LCCN 2018017517 (print) | LCCN 2018021380 (ebook) | ISBN 9780544963870 (ebook) | ISBN 9780544962538 (hardback)
Subjects: LCSH: Psychological fiction. | BISAC: FICTION / Suspense. | FICTION / Thrillers. | GSAFD: Suspense fiction.
Classification: LCC PS3607.E567 (ebook) | LCC PS3607.E567 L37 2019 (print) | DDC 813/.6—dc23
LC record available at https://lccn.loc.gov/2018017517

Book design by Chloe Foster

Printed in the United States of America
DOC 10 9 8 7 6 5 4 3 2 1

For AJZ, a very wise woman

NANCY: I oughta go to you for plots.
SYLVIA: You oughta go to someone.

—*The Women*, 1939

1

"Next up, *Daaaaana Diaz!*"

A few hands clapped as I stepped up onto the wooden platform stage, picking my way around the PA system. Under the lights, I tugged my shirt hem away from the waistband of my jeans one last time, cleared a strand of dark brown hair from my lip-glossed smile, and palmed the mic, carefully unwrapping the cord from the stand. No point in losing two minutes wrestling it down to my level—five foot four in the four-inch heels I am rarely without onstage.

"Hello, everyone," I said. "I'm Dana, and I will be your brown person for the evening."

I waited for the uncomfortable snicker, but there was only the dim, offended pause of a bar in which the music had been turned off, followed by a hacking cough. I forged ahead.

"And don't tell me to go back where I came from. Amarillo is the pits." Silence again. I toyed with the mic stand. "Have we got anyone here from Amarillo tonight? No one?" There was no hoot. "It's okay, I wouldn't cop to it either if it wasn't my job. Well, hobby."

I'd been back in Austin a little over a year, performing as many open-mics and guest spots and showcases as I could force myself to show up for, and I'd earned my slot in the Nomad Third Thursday lineup fair and square. But nothing was landing lately, and I wasn't sure why.

I pressed on. "There's not a lot to do in Amarillo. I mean, the second-largest employer in town is a helium plant. When I was in high school, we used to hang out behind the Seven-Eleven and—" I mimed sucking on a Mylar balloon, then made my voice high and squeaky: "Hey, dude, stop bogarting the *Happy Birthday from Sponge-Bob and Friends.*"

Blank stares. If my pothead voice has never been too convincing, it's because my weekends in high school were actually pretty clean. Jason and I saw what drugs did to his big brother and wanted nothing to do with them. I made a mental note to work on my funny voice and kept plowing through the set. "My mom worked at the helium plant when I was a kid. For the longest time I thought she was a birthday clown." Beat. "Take Your Daughter to Work Day was a real disappointment."

Scanning the seats closest to the stage for a friendly face, I saw only dull-eyed drunks and bad Tinder dates. I let my mind drift into the depthless glare of the lights. It was Jason, my writing partner and best friend since we were fourteen, who'd told me long ago to find the friendliest face in the crowd when I was bombing and focus on telling all my jokes to that person alone. Jason's trick rarely won the audience back, but I'd bombed enough by now to know that didn't matter as much as showing the audience you were doing just fine up there, thank you. Nothing is more cringe-inducing than watching someone flail onstage. Privately, I had a name for this rule: *No blood in the water.*

I could feel myself fidgeting to the right and left, straining my voice to sound bigger. After four years in Los Angeles, it was a struggle to relax in this too-easy town. I missed the grind. The crowds in L.A. had been tough, but they'd made me tougher too; here in Austin, indifference was the killer. By the time I left L.A., Jason was barely talking to me, so I didn't bother telling him what I told everybody else: I needed a break, just a short one, and then I'd return. But it was harder than it sounded. Last time I'd made the move, I was five years younger, and I wasn't alone. Everything had been easier with Jason, who knew where we'd come from and how important it was to keep moving forward so we'd never slide back.

So much for that. After four years away, it felt like I was just starting out in Austin all over again, except the comedy scene was more crowded and the beer more expensive. The rent on my crummy apartment was going to skyrocket when the lease came up in a few months, my take from the tip jar barely covered a pint after the set, and I was still paying dues in flop sweat at dive bars and coffee shops. Twenty-eight might not be old, but it was too old for this.

"I'd like to thank my mom for giving me the initials double D." I stared pointedly down at my chest and was rewarded with a handful of snickers. Ah, boob jokes. Comedy gold. "That made junior high a real blast."

"Nice tits!" someone called from the back of the club.

"Bobby Mickelthwaite, is that you?" Without missing a beat, I shaded my eyes with my hand as if trying to see past the spotlights. "You haven't changed a bit since seventh grade." I squinted. "Except —what is it? Oh yeah, you're a lot uglier."

Undaunted, the voice shouted, "Take off your top!"

"Same razor-sharp wordplay, though," I muttered and made to move on.

"Show us your tits!"

A few people booed. One yelled, "Shut up!" I felt the thrilling tang of the audience's anger but knew that if it got out of control, the heckler would succeed in wresting their attention away from the stage permanently. I suppressed a tickle of panic. *No blood in the water,* I thought. *Show them you can take care of yourself.*

I sweetened up my voice until it dripped saccharine and said, "Who hurt you?" Then, in my normal voice: "First and last name, please. I want to know who to PayPal to make it happen again." The audience laughed uncertainly at the suggestion of violence. "And again. And again."

The heckler subsided into drunken mumbles, but only a few people laughed. "I'm just kidding, guys!" I said, spreading my arms wide. "I don't make that kind of money. Maybe we can set up a GoFundMe?"

Mixed laughter and boos, though I couldn't tell whether the boos were meant for me or the heckler. The bouncer was finally making his way over to the guy, so I picked the set back up where I'd left off, transitioning into a bit about my day job. My adrenaline was up and so was the crowd's, but it wasn't a good feeling. Since they hadn't been with me before, the heckler had only condensed the toxic energy in the room into something tangible. *Don't close your eyes,* I told myself, *Don't blink until you've got them back.* But black dots began to multiply in my peripheral vision.

I heard her savage bark of laughter first, and then I spotted her: the friendly face. The woman sat at a table near the wall, a green neon beer sign lighting up her shaggy blond hair. I caught a glimpse of large eyes set far apart in deep-shadowed sockets, sharp cheekbones, white teeth clenched in a grin. I wondered why I hadn't noticed her earlier — either she hadn't been under the light before or she hadn't been laughing. Now she was nodding like a dandelion in the breeze, an oasis of rapt approval, and I felt myself relaxing. I memorized her face and for the rest of my set, I looked at the crowd as usual but told my jokes solely to the dandelion woman, who intermittently let out a guffaw. The ten minutes went by mercifully fast, and then I stepped off the carpet-covered dais, out of the lights, and back into the ordinary darkness of a grimy bar.

"Give it up one more time for Dana Diaz!" Fash, the emcee, shouted to limp applause as I stepped over the amplifier cords and skirted the edge of the room heading toward the bar. "Up next . . ."

Up next was Toby, a hipster from Minneapolis who was about to move to L.A.—"So let's give him a warm sendoff!" (Scattered applause.) After him would come Kim, aka the Other Girl, with her heavy blond bangs and Courtney Love slipdress, then James, who wore suspenders and played a ukulele. Last of all, Fash Banner, the emcee and organizer, who'd placed third last year in the annual Funniest Person in Austin contest. I didn't have the heart to watch them all succeed or fail, one after the other. I wanted my drink in the other room, and tonight it needed to be on the strong side. "Whiskey soda," I said to Nick, the Thursday bartender, over the sound of Toby launching into his set.

"Let me get that for you," a voice said at my elbow, and someone slapped a credit card down and pushed it across the bar. I turned and saw the woman with the friendly face.

"Thanks," I said. I was in no position to turn down a free drink, and I felt a lingering warmth toward the stranger for helping me get through a bad set. I surveyed the blond woman standing next to me, or rather towering over me—though it doesn't take much to do that—and could see, close-up, that her mess of wavy hair was bleached in big chunks that had grown out around dark blond roots. The mandarin collar of her beat-up biker jacket gave her a faintly priest-like look.

"One for me too," she added in Nicky's direction, and I realized she meant to sit down and have a drink with me. It was too late to stop it now, so I picked up my whiskey soda on its damp cardboard coaster, gestured toward Toby on the stage to indicate we should quit talking, and started walking to the other room to see if she'd follow.

In less than a minute, she appeared in the doorway of the side room with her drink and glided toward my table. The PA system was quieter here, the hum of drinkers more subdued.

"I'm Amanda," she said, sticking her hand out. "I thought you were amazing dealing with that drunk guy, and I wanted to buy you a drink."

It was as I had suspected; she had watched the whole set but started caring only during the heckling incident. It cast a bit of a pall on the free drink.

"Dana," I said, shaking her hand. "And thanks. It didn't win me any Brownie points with the crowd, though."

"People don't always like hearing the truth," she said. "But guys like that need to be taken out."

Guys like that. It was almost sweet. "You don't see a lot of comedy, do you?"

Amanda smiled. "No," she admitted. "I just moved here a few weeks ago." Whether she meant it as a justification of why she hadn't seen much comedy or as an explanation of why she'd decided to come tonight, I couldn't tell.

"Well, Amanda," I said, "'Show me your tits' is like heckler pre-school for a female standup. If you can't deal with that . . ." I shrugged.

"So you get harassed like that all the time?" Her eyes were wide and unbelieving. "And you just have to take it?"

"Hecklers go after everyone," I said uncomfortably. "It comes with the territory. It's not really that bad, though. Honestly—" I laughed. "I mean, better a heckler than a creepy comment from the emcee."

"That happens?"

"Or a bunch of rape jokes in the set before mine. Or, my favorite, when an audience member comes up to you afterward and says, 'You're funny—for a girl.'" I'd long since tired of these old "women in comedy" chestnuts and tuned it out when I heard other female comics griping. It wasn't that they weren't true, it was just that there was no point in focusing on them. But now, perversely amused by Amanda's shocked expression, I found myself relishing them.

"You must develop a thick skin," she said, shaking her head.

"Sure. I used to be a size two," I cracked. The joke flew past her, which I found oddly endearing. My mother didn't get my jokes either, but I could never be sure how much of that was the language barrier and how much was a defense against being reminded of my wisecracking dad, who was long gone. Sometimes she chose what she did and didn't understand.

Amanda was looking at me expectantly, waiting to hear the rest of the story, and with a large sip of my whiskey soda, I resigned myself to explaining further. "All I mean is, you get a knack for dealing with hecklers pretty early on. Otherwise you get derailed."

"I can't imagine thinking up an insult that fast."

"It's not really about the zinger. It's about getting through the moment so you can move on with your set. Showing him"—I corrected myself—"no, showing the *audience* that he's not getting to you."

"Really? You didn't enjoy it even a little? Smacking that guy around just now, making him feel small?" Her eyes narrowed and she smiled conspiratorially. "Come on."

The whiskey warm in my stomach, I laughed. "Maybe a little," I admitted. In the moment of zinging the nice-tits guy, there had been a tiny spark of pleasure in imagining him getting hurt. The thought made me uncomfortable. There was something indecent about it, though a lot of comics indulged the impulse. It was time for a change of subject. "You said you just moved here? Where from?"

"Los Angeles," she said. "I was trying to be an actor."

Rather than surprise, I felt a wave of recognition. Her combination of naïveté and poise reminded me of certain women I'd met in acting classes, frail women with striking features who'd been spotted in laundromats or plucked out of drugstore lines in their hometowns while waiting to buy cigarettes. Groomed for girl groups and minor roles on soap operas, they seldom made the cut. They had too little imagination and too much reality for acting, and they eventually slipped back into the beautiful scenery of L.A. or moved on.

"I lived out there for a while too," I said. "Maybe we have mutual friends."

"I was only there a year," she said, swizzling her drink. "I hated it there."

"Yeah, me too," I lied, suddenly thinking of a pilot idea: *Failed actress opens community theater in her hometown.* Waiting for Guffman *meets* Crazy Ex-Girlfriend. I fiddled with my napkin, wishing I'd brought my pen. "You probably got there right before I left. Let's see . . ." I began running through an inventory of places we might have bumped into each other, listing improv theaters, acting workshops, networking events, even the Culver City diner where I'd waited tables. At every name, she shook her head. We'd just missed each other, although as I listed potential sources of connection, the familiar feeling strengthened rather than weakened. "Who *did* you hang out with there?" I asked.

"No one, really. I lost all my friends when I lost my job in tech." She saw my questioning look and elaborated. "I was a programmer for Runnr."

Even I, a borderline technophobe, had heard of the errand-running app that had pushed all the others out of business, though in this gig economy, more of my friends had worked as runners than used the service. My face must have betrayed some of the surprise I was feeling, tinged with shame over my assumptions—girl groups and soap operas!—because she gave me a wry grin. "Yeah, I know. I don't look like a software engineer. Any more than you look like a standup."

I flushed. It was true that my appearance—short and brown-skinned and shaped like my mother minus the control-top pantyhose—did not prepare most people for my extracurricular activities. "Sorry."

"It's okay," she said. "Let's just say none of the guys I worked with thought I looked like a programmer either. They made that abundantly clear." She took another sip. "And that was *before* my supervisor started sending me dick pics."

"Gross," I said. *Guys like that.* "Is that how you lost your job?"

"Yeah." She finished her drink, holding the straw to one side and draining it. "Like an idiot, I actually went to HR with it. Two years in the trenches of a sexual-harassment suit got me a little pile of settlement money, sure. But it also got me the cold shoulder from every startup in Silicon Valley. And then there were the trolls—someone on Reddit guessed my name from a news spot. It couldn't have been hard to figure out. There weren't tons of female programmers at Runnr."

"So how'd you end up in L.A.?"

"It seemed like the best place to disappear." She looked down into her empty drink. "One of them swatted me—you know what that means, right? They sent a SWAT team to my house. I woke up in the middle of the night to a bunch of dudes armed to the teeth pounding on my door. After that, I was a nervous wreck. I scrubbed my online profile so they couldn't find me again, went to the dark side of the internet. And got out of town in a hurry."

"Why acting?" I said.

She shrugged. "I was looking for something as far from the tech world as possible. I thought, *Fine. Let's see what it's like being a pretty face.*" I had to admire the way she owned it, plainly and without the standard self-deprecating gestures. "To tell you the truth, I sucked, but I kept getting auditions because of my looks."

At this I couldn't help feeling a twinge of bitterness. I raised my glass. "Must be nice."

"It was okay," she admitted. "Until I met my ex. He killed any chance I had at getting anywhere with acting. He was insanely jealous. Freaked out if I stayed late at a party or, God forbid, talked to a man. Which—everyone you need to know is a man, right? But that's a whole other story." She sighed and rattled the ice in her glass. "Once we moved in together, he started hiding my phone to keep me from going to auditions. Spying on me. Threatening me." She watched me closely, almost challenging me to react. Her wide-set eyes were, I could see now, greenish gray, and what I had mistaken for frailty in them was something else, some hunger I couldn't name.

Then she said, "He didn't hit me, if that's what you're thinking."

Unsure how to respond, I fell back on irony. "Sounds like a prince."

"He did other things. Locked me in a soundproof room." She shuddered. "He would have hurt me bad someday. If I'd stayed."

"I'm glad you didn't stay," I said.

A burst of applause from the other room signaled that Toby had finished his set, more successfully than I had mine, it sounded like. The Other Girl was being introduced, and I couldn't help wondering whether the nice-tits guy would turn up again. I pictured him lurking just outside, waiting for a woman's voice to come over the PA system.

I held up my empty glass and said, "Why don't I buy the next round?"

The next round blurred into the next one after that, and too late I realized I was getting hammered. What clued me in was when I started talking about the Funniest Person in Austin contest.

"It's stupid," I said. "Not to mention a total long shot."

"I'm sure it's not," she said, elbows slipping drunkenly on the table.

It really was, though. I would never have brought it up this way —sloppy, hopeful—with my comedy friends, because we all wanted it and all felt stupid for wanting it. But comedy was a foreign country to Amanda, and I was her only guide. There was relief in spilling my pathetic dreams to someone who wouldn't realize how far-fetched they were.

"It's this big competition at Bat City Comedy Club every year. Every standup in town does it. There's prize money." The winner got five thousand dollars, enough to move back to L.A., maybe even with a little left over to shoot a comedy special on the cheap. Or a pilot, if I could just come up with the right idea. If I won, a small but insistent voice said in my head, maybe Jason would take me back as a writing partner, and we could write the pilot together. "I was too late to sign up last year," I went on. "But this year—" Amanda's face lit up, and I rushed to say, "It's impossible. All the comics in town, everyone I know, is competing." I gestured toward the other room, where James was strumming his ukulele and wailing. "The judges are a bunch of industry people from L.A. and New York and Toronto, though, so even if you only make it to the finals . . ." I trailed off. People I knew had landed managers and agents, festival invitations, even spots on sitcoms after placing in the competition. It seemed unwise to name the possibilities.

She must have seen the raw look on my face. "Why did you come back here in the first place?"

There had been lots of reasons for leaving L.A.—our rent was climbing, and my job at the diner was wearing me out—but the final straw had been my disastrous solo meeting with Aaron Neely. Neely was a one-time comic's comic with a self-destructive streak who had, after the usual stint in rehab, made the unusual move of putting aside his own career at its height to produce up-and-comers. In four years, Jason and I had come close to breaking through a handful of times, but when Jason snagged the pitch meeting with Neely through some minor miracle of networking, we thought this was really it, the big one. We had each vowed never to take a meeting without the other person—we were not *those* L.A. people—but when Jason was a no-show at the smoothie bar where Neely was waiting, I couldn't bring myself to pass up the opportunity. After checking my phone one last time for a text from Jason, I went in, fearless in my fake Prada heels and fake Diane von Furstenberg wrap dress and fake Marc Jacobs bag, to pitch our pilot alone.

What followed was almost comically surreal. The smoothie Aaron had waiting for me at his private table, a maroon swirl of kale and beet pulp with a chalky aftertaste that I forced myself to exclaim over enthusiastically as I choked it down. The way the tall stool had seemed to tip under me halfway through the meeting, the walls around me sliding downward. The loud whispering noise that seemed to come from the ferns shielding us from the rest of the smoothie bar, gradually drowning out every sound but his voice saying, "You look terrible, please, let me take you home."

And then, of course, there was Neely himself, a comedy hero of mine with a ruddy, pitted nose and the hands of a giant. Larger than life. Later, in the black-upholstered back seat of his SUV under black-tinted windows, merely larger than me.

When he finally dropped me off at home, unsteady on my feet but relieved to be walking at all, I found Jason sick too, hunched over the toilet in misery. The look he gave me was so awful, so full of betrayed confidence and disgust, that I knew we would never talk about what happened. And some part of me didn't want to, feared being pulled down into the quicksand of memory in the back of Neely's car. It was enough to know that we never got a follow-up call on the show. I had evidently flubbed the pitch.

Amanda was still waiting for a response.

"Sometimes dreams just don't work out," I said after a moment's pause. "But you can't dwell on it. You have to go back to square one. Try again."

Amanda fixed me again with her long stare, which seemed to flip from naiveté to knowingness and back effortlessly, as if they were two sides of the same thing. "Admirable," she said, finally.

I'd never been good at being friends with women. I couldn't get the hang of the transactional nature of female friendship—you give me this secret, in return I share my deepest insecurity. Rinse and repeat. Even as a child, I was never interested. In fifth grade, it became clear that some girls were going to get tall and pretty, and others were going to make straight As, and others were going to act boy-crazy, and still others were going to do all these things in Spanish, which I don't speak, even though I look like I should, and understand only when it's my mom talking. Being funny didn't get you into any of the cliques. When Jason appeared a few years later with his fart jokes and *SNL* recaps, I was grateful to be rescued from the elaborate pas de deux of girl talk forever.

But feeling Amanda withdraw slightly now, I knew enough to offer up an ersatz confession. I took a stab. "Actually, I'm kind of blocked for material right now," I said, looking for something that wasn't true and realizing, even as I said it, that it was. "Everything in my set feels kind of dead. Sometimes I feel like *I'm* dead." Damn those whiskey sodas.

Amanda leaned forward, suddenly fierce, and wrapped her skinny fingers around my wrist. "Listen, Dana," she said. "I know what it's like to be driven out of town, lose your livelihood, your self-respect, everything. I let my ex lock me up and tell me I was worthless. He wasn't even good-looking." She chuckled, but it was a grim, unpleasant sound. "I would never have given him the time of day if I hadn't felt dead inside. But I'm not dead. I'm still here. And so are you." Her eyes burned drunkenly, and her knuckles pressed into my wrist bone. "Whatever happened to you in L.A., you're not dead. The person who did it to you is the one who should feel that way, not you."

"Nothing happened to me in L.A.," I said, and gently pried her fingers loose.

She released me and drew back a little, seeming to come to herself. Then she looked at my wrist, which I was rubbing with my other hand, and laughed, that short bark I'd heard during my set, like a fox. She settled back into her chair.

"Right," she said, grinning. "I'd just like to know who Nothing is, so I could find him and break his knees for you."

Score one for the literal-minded. "I could tell you, but then I'd have to kill you."

"I'll take my chances."

The tension suddenly drained out of me, and I felt tired of pretending. "I've got a better idea. How about if while you're off breaking Nothing's knees, I go find your ex-boyfriend and kick his ass?"

"That'd be a start," she said. "But I warn you, if you're looking for asses that need kicking, I've got a long list."

"I'll show you mine if you show me yours."

"Deal."

I raised my glass. We clinked and swallowed in tandem. In the other room, I could hear Fash wrapping up his set, and the comics who had stuck around to watch were gearing up to head somewhere together—probably Bat City for the late-night open-mic. Any minute, one of them would be poking his head around the corner and asking me to come along. If I wanted to avoid introducing Amanda, now was the time to go.

"Hey, it was really nice meeting you," I said. "That set was rough. And now I feel . . ." I put my hand over my heart. "Much more wasted." She laughed. "But really, thanks." Remembering something I was always supposed to be doing to help my comedy career, I said, "If you want to know when I'm performing around town, follow me on Facebook."

"I stay off social media," Amanda said. "Call me paranoid, but after working at Runnr, I know what they use that information for. Could I get your number instead?" She pushed a napkin over and handed me a pen.

I hesitated only an instant, then said, "Sure." I jotted down my number and stood to go. As I handed the pen back, I thought of another pilot idea: *Failed comic creates Instagram for fake lifestyle guru. Account goes viral. Comic must pretend to be sincere for rest of life.* I started walking toward the door.

"Good luck in that contest next week," she called after me.

"You mean break a leg," I said reflexively.

"Only if it's someone else's."

I recognized her second attempt at a lame joke and chuckled in return. It seemed possible at that moment that she might become, if not a fan, something I needed even more: a friend.

2

Waking up late with a hangover the next morning, I hustled to Laurel's Paper and Gifts for my opening shift and nearly smacked myself on the forehead when I saw all the cars in the parking lot. I'd forgotten about the early staff meeting. I used my key to get in and hurried past the display shelves full of stationery and gilt-edged notebooks.

When I first came back from L.A., I'd dropped into Laurel's as a customer, hoping one of those fancy notebooks might inspire me to start writing again, though in the end I wound up buying the same old pocket-size Moleskine I've used since they first appeared by the cash register in Amarillo's sole Barnes and Noble. But Laurel herself, a squat, hippie-ish woman in her late fifties, happened to be managing the store that day, and I made her laugh as she was ringing me up, and then we got into a long chat that ended with her asking if I'd like to work there. It was the easiest time I've ever had getting hired for anything. Back then, it reinforced my idea that Austin was not only an easy place to be, but the perfect place to recover from L.A.

People say retail is boring, but I didn't mind. After having waited tables for so long, I never wanted to see another apron again, and the days seemed to pass at an unimaginably luxurious pace in this store full of inessential luxuries. The trifling nature of the merchandise appealed to me, as did the way customers drifted around, looking for a vague something, a housewarming gift, maybe, or a stack of thank-you notes. No one ever rushed through the door needing anything more urgent than a birthday card.

Unfortunately, Laurel's stray-dog approach to hiring had recently plagued us with Becca, a trod-upon twig of a woman with eyebrows tweezed into a perpetual look of surprise, and her boyfriend, Henry, a self-described "retail identity therapist" with sleeve tattoos and careful stubble. Henry knew how to throw serious charm at a woman in her late fifties and had rapidly edged his way into a consulting position to upscale the store. The new items he had ordered and placed among the older journals and cards were objects that, in his words, "told a story about their own creation." The right kind of story called to mind ease, but not luxury; difference without hostility; poverty, but never disaster. Items that qualified included colorful place mats hand-woven by Indonesian women (actually nuns, but Henry said religion was a downer) and heavy stone cubes that, according to the display card, represented the *thing-in-itself.* Minimalist bowls in dull, hammered silver were filled with scarves of braided and distressed twine. It went without saying that it was all prohibitively expensive. The jokes practically wrote themselves. (*Pilot idea: Enchanted gift shop where all the gifts can talk, but they're even bigger assholes than the humans.* Wonderfalls *meets* BoJack Horseman.) It was the way the whole city was headed, and I could only assume the rising rents that had driven out the store's old-Austin neighbors were making Laurel, who'd owned the little shop for as long as I'd been alive, antsy. Or perhaps all this talk of authenticity appealed to her hippie soul. Either way, Henry was a loathsome addition to a job that was otherwise perfect for getting writing done on a little notepad I kept under the counter.

When I opened the door of the break room, Henry was already holding forth, looming over a table that was barely big enough for the rest of the staff, all women, to squeeze around it. A powerful smell of bacon and eggs reminded me of my hangover in ways both positive and negative, though from the crumpled paper bag and empty salsa cups scattered around the table, I gathered that I'd missed the break-fast tacos.

"Oh, hello, Dana," Laurel said as I maneuvered myself around the door to close it. "Henry was just saying how we're going to be more than just a store. We'll be an—um—" She looked at him uncertainly.

"Aspirational lifestyle brand," Henry filled in airily. "Which starts with everyone on the team committing to punctuality."

I restrained an eye roll as he continued talking. Henry's objects, with their obsessive authenticity, grossed me out. I found the idea of Indonesian nuns and Japanese ceramicists and San Salvadoran peasants sitting in their faraway countries making them unutterably depressing. As the staff members dispersed, I found myself hoping the stories behind all of these items were fabricated and they were actually mass-produced in China. Now, *that* would be funny.

"Flimflam artist," Ruby muttered to me as I was taking the note later. She stood at my elbow behind the counter, her eyes on Henry and Becca fighting in the parking lot as she vindictively yanked the white paper price tags off of fountain pens to make way for the new, Henry-mandated linen tags. "I can smell it a mile away."

Ruby fascinated me. Some ten years older than me, she came to work every day in a stylized version of a fifties secretary costume: sheath dresses with string bows at the waist, pencil skirts and Peter Pan–collared blouses, emerald-green cat's-eye glasses on a chain around her neck. Her shellacked curls were short and red, and it took me a long time to figure out that she wore a wig. One day she took a pencil from behind her ear and I saw all the curls shift at once, just a few millimeters, in unison. "I just got sick of bad haircuts," she explained when she noticed me noticing, and I waited until she went to the back and scribbled it down verbatim.

"Frankly, I don't know what Becca sees in that creep," Ruby was saying. She leaned over and whispered, "Do you think he hits her?"

The idea jolted me out of my reverie. "Why do you say that?"

"I don't know, I just get a vibe," she said. "Have you ever noticed how she always has bruises on her arms?"

"No," I said.

"Well, that's because she wears long sleeves. Even in the *summer.*" She raised her penciled eyebrows meaningfully.

"It's still spring," I pointed out, and Ruby shrugged. She was a hopeless gossip and paranoid to boot, but the conversation brought Amanda to mind again. Where a moment before I'd been thinking disdainfully about Henry's objects, I now found myself imagining the tall, rangy woman from the night before standing at the displays in her leather jacket, picking things up and putting them down, swinging the little Japanese ceramic pendants in front of her face and weighing the votives in her palm. Something about her made me think she'd be able to listen to their stories. I blushed.

"Last night I met this kind of strange chick at Nomad," I said. "She came up after my set."

"Sounds like you've got a new number-one fan," Ruby said. "Watch out."

"I'll be sure to hide my sledgehammer," I said. "No, she was nice, actually. We had a lot in common, it turned out."

"People must come up to talk to you after shows all the time."

"Only a dozen or so per set," I said with a straight face. "I can usually handle it." I went back to doodling in my notebook.

Ruby jerked at another tag and looked at me. "What was strange about her?"

"Huh?"

"You said she was strange."

"Did I?" Ruby looked at me pointedly, and I backtracked. "It was what you said about Becca that reminded me." What was it exactly? "This woman was telling me about her ex-boyfriend, and she said, 'He didn't hit me.' Just out of the blue."

"He definitely hit her," Ruby said sagely.

"It just seemed like a weird thing to volunteer to a total stranger."

"Sounds like she has boundary issues. I used to have major boundary issues because of being molested as a child." I'd grown accustomed to upsetting revelations like this from Ruby, but I never knew where to look. I kept my eyes trained on my notebook. "My therapist says I cope by controlling what I can. Like this." She pointed at her fake hairdo, and I nodded as if it made perfect sense to me. "You have to be careful, though. They can really change your personality. This one wig I used to wear, kind of a Louise Brooks–type bob, made me really mean . . . She was bad news . . ."

My note-taking fingers were itching, but Ruby droned on until my phone buzzed under the counter. I had a sudden presentiment that it was Amanda calling, as if I had summoned her with my thoughts. Superstitiously, I let it vibrate and listened for the shudder of a voice message before glancing at the screen.

I suppressed a mild disappointment. It was Kim, the Other Girl in the Thursday-night lineup. To the extent that every girl comic has a schtick, hers was familiar: blond and skinny and kind of dirty-sexy, with a high-pitched baby voice and a foul mouth. At shows like this I was always the only brown girl opposite some Kim or other. I didn't take it personally. It was better than when I'd left, but ironically, that was part of the problem. There had always been a strong Latinx comedy scene in Austin, but it was dominated by men. Besides, as a half-Mexican, half-Jewish woman without a word of Spanish, I'd never quite fit in there. My mom had given me her last name but failed to teach me her language, venting her anger at my dad without sacrificing her ambitions for my perfect assimilation and eventual departure from Amarillo. It had worked; I'd left. And the mainstream comedy scene run by pasty white men had worked for me too—probably because I was best friends with one. While I was in L.A. the scene had grown more diverse, but with my clumsiness for such matters, I'd somehow managed to leave Austin at exactly the wrong time to benefit from it. Missing the chance to build connections on the way up, I'd reaped none of the rewards of the new scene, just stiffer competition from a glut of newcomers.

Staring at Kim's text—she told me to break a leg in the contest and offered herself as a practice partner if I needed to try out new material—I realized, not for the first time but with a fresh throb, how lonely I was back here in Austin. I kept my distance from comics like Kim, avoiding the preshow beers and the postshow hangouts. That went double for the guys. They were fine, all more or less like Fash. But if I didn't want to sleep with them, and I didn't, I knew the best I could hope for was to become a mascot, their short, cute, brown girl-buddy, great fun to pick up and swing around when they were drunk. No, thanks. I missed Jason too much to want to play that role for anyone but him.

My mom always said I must have gotten my sense of humor from my dad, and I had vague memories of him as a hairy, elfin jokester who was always winking at me and taking off his thumb to make me giggle.

Still, it was my mom who bought me my first joke book sometime after he'd left. She'd taken to shopping the Saturday-morning garage sales, waking up at the crack of dawn to scoop the neighbors, and often came home with stacks of worn, dog-eared chapter books for me. Included in one of these stacks was a flimsy orange paperback called *101 Wacky, Hilarious, Totally Crazy Jokes for Kids Ages Eight to Ten.*

Most of the jokes were god-awful puns, but there was one that always stuck with me. It went something like this:

A moth walks into a psychiatrist's office and lies down on the couch.

PSYCHIATRIST: So, why don't you start by telling me a little about yourself?

MOTH: Well, Doc, I've got a wife, two kids, and a nice house in the suburbs with a two-car garage.

PSYCHIATRIST: And how does that make you feel?

MOTH: Okay, I guess.

PSYCHIATRIST: Any problems?

MOTH: Nope.

PSYCHIATRIST: So you're saying you're perfectly happy with your life?

MOTH (thinks): Yes, I think so.

PSYCHIATRIST: Then what brought you in here today?

MOTH: The light was on.

I can still close my eyes and see the cartoon illustration, down to the last pen stroke: the moth, standing upright in a cartoon fedora, holding a briefcase in one of his hairy insect legs and shaking the psychiatrist's hand with another, the mysterious couch looming in the background. Everything I learned about joke structure, I learned from that pathetic moth. Setup: two things that don't go together (moth and psychiatrist). Heightening: the middle of the joke, lines that make you forget he's a moth. Punch line: a sudden remembering.

There are a hundred different versions of the moth joke, I later discovered. The moth goes into a bar, but he doesn't order a drink; the moth walks into a gym, but he doesn't lift weights; the moth strolls into a dealership, but he doesn't buy a car. Eventually someone asks him why he's there, and the moth always says the same thing: *The light was on.* The joke lulls you into believing that *this* moth, *this* time, is different. But he never is. In a way, it's a joke about comedy itself. Comics aren't happy people. We crave the light, and we don't know why.

When I started putting together my own set, I tried to picture the author of *101 Wacky, Hilarious, Totally Crazy Jokes for Kids Ages Eight to Ten.* I imagined some poor guy sitting in a bleak New York apartment with a typewriter in front of him and a stack of paper napkins on which he'd made his drunk friends write down their favorite jokes, but they were all too dirty for a kids' book. So in the end, past deadline—with a whole batch of these joke books he'd committed to churning out—maybe he went down to the library and checked out a stack of slightly older joke books, where he found the hoary old moth joke. And somehow, the hour being late and having just watched a Woody Allen movie with his girlfriend and maybe even had an argument with her afterward, he set his version of the joke in a shrink's office, despite the fact that one of society's most fervent desires for children ages eight to ten is that they should have little to no idea what a psychiatrist does.

I didn't even know how to pronounce the word, much less what it meant. But I knew this: No matter what the moth claimed, things like *wife, kid,* and *two-car garage* didn't make anybody happy. I knew because my dad had had all those things, and he, too, had gone off looking for a light, leaving me alone in Amarillo with my mom.

Alone, that is, until Jason came along.

We met in American history in the eighth grade. We'd both been absent the day a big project was assigned, and everybody else was already in groups, so we got stuck working together. I was annoyed at first, because I could see right away that I would be doing all the work—the researching and writing of facts about Geronimo, the neat lettering on posterboard—while this dark-haired, gangly boy with glasses sat hunched over his notebook, silently doodling. But when I peeked over his shoulder at what he was drawing, a thrill went through me: David Letterman, his flattened-out, Neanderthal brow and *gotcha* smirk recognizable even in cartoon form.

Jason looked up, noticed my expression, and waggled his eyebrows. "What do you think, Paul? *He-hee!*"

It was such a perfect impression of the Letterman giggle and so incongruous with Jason's glasses-and-acne face that I almost cracked up. Instead, I put on my best Paul Shaffer and said, "Pretty good, Dave, pretty good."

We went back and forth a few times before we both lost it.

"What's your favorite Stupid Pet Trick?" I asked.

"I don't know yet, I'm not finished."

"Finished?"

"I'm watching recordings of every episode. I'm only up to 1987." He misinterpreted the look I gave him. "I'd be farther, but I keep having to stop and look up stuff from the monologue."

"Wow" was all I could say. "Who else do you like?"

"Conan."

"Duh. What about from now? Sarah Silverman?" His face soured. "Maria Bamford?"

"She's good. I'm studying the classics first, though," he said importantly. "The big late-night hosts. So I can get into a writers' room someday."

"Why not be the host? That's what I want to do."

"Girls never do late-night." He said it like he was sorry to have to break the news to me.

"So I'll be the first."

"You're humble," he said. "I like that about you, Dana Diaz."

That was how it started. Of course, in school, we couldn't hang out without accusations of the boyfriend-girlfriend variety, but we knew who we were and what we had to offer each other. The summer after eighth grade, he started inviting me over to watch comedy specials DVR'd off of late-night cable, and I found any excuse to go. Luxuries like cable and DVRs had become rare after my dad left, and they disappeared entirely when my mom was laid off from the newly privatized helium plant. Jason had the TV mostly to himself in Mattie's old room, which their dad had converted to a game room with a pool table and a Nintendo.

Mattie was the one dark spot. Jason's older brother was a high-school dropout who lived at home. He looked like a version of Jason drawn from memory by someone with no particular artistic talent: black hair hanging limply over a narrow forehead, blue eyes that squinted unevenly over a broken nose. Not much bigger than Jason, really—in fact, Jason may have had an inch on him—but he was broader in the shoulders, or carried himself as if he were. He picked on Jason, but it was his unpredictability more than anything else that cast a pall over the house. Mattie spent most of his off-hours walking his big, scary German shepherd, Kenny, and lifting weights in the fume-y, stuffy garage apartment their dad had grudgingly fixed up for him when he got off drugs and got a job driving a forklift at the meatpacking plant. But every once in a while he would suddenly appear in the doorway of the TV room—"Oh, hi, *Gay*-son, I didn't know you were home"—and Jason would seem to fold up in his presence. Whenever he saw me, he stared pointedly at my chest, and I had to concentrate hard to keep from crossing my arms.

Jason stole glances at my chest every now and then too, and I thought for a while that he was going to ask me out. But he never did, and soon I didn't expect him to, which made me feel less guilty lying to my mom about the mostly adult-free situation at Jason's house. I'd bike over while Jason's dad was still at work—his mom, like my dad, was long gone—and we'd go straight to the TV room and settle in side by side on compressed beanbag chairs in the flickering half-light of the TV. Like any good moth, I told myself the light was the only reason I was there.

3

Bat City Comedy Club's undignified location in the elbow of a strip mall north of town belied its centrality to the Austin comedy scene. Shadowed by an overpass and flanked by fabric stores and dance studios, it celebrated the inherent ridiculousness of the whole enterprise of standup with a certain bravado that included neon signage, a bar decorated in primary colors, and a banquet room swathed in acres of comedy-and-tragedy-mask novelty carpet. You could argue it wasn't the most appropriate carpet for a comedy club, but I'd spent enough time staring down at its nauseating pattern of ribbons and grimaces while waiting for my open-mic slot to have internalized its sobering lesson. It was a kind of memento mori of standup: *Remember, you must kill.*

On the night of the first round of the Funniest Person in Austin contest, I pulled my bumperless Honda Civic up to the closed businesses at the opposite end of the parking lot, as per e-mailed instructions, wishing I'd been confident enough to sign up years ago when the terrain wasn't so crowded. I'd recognized only about half the names scheduled to compete tonight—though among them, I'd noticed with a pang, was Fash Banner, last year's second runner-up. There was room for both of us to advance, but if the newcomers were any good or if I bombed as badly as I had the other night . . . I tried not to think about it. When I'd first come to Austin from Amarillo a decade ago, lured away from the self-pity and stagnation of my mom's house by Jason's tales of all-night diners and plentiful open-mics, the contest was still small and clubby, just a week or two of performances by friendly rivals who hooted and slapped each other on the back after their sets. Now there were a staggering number of preliminary rounds—night after night for weeks—and a full week of semifinals.

Of course, I had been more easily intimidated back then. Jason's college friends had been welcoming enough toward his funny little hometown sidekick, but I was shy and self-conscious around them, painfully aware that I was in community college because I hadn't gotten into UT, where they all went. And although Jason dragged me out to open-mics and told me over and over I was better at standup than he was, it was a long time before I believed it.

I'd always liked standup best, but, like everyone else in the Austin scene back then, I'd sampled everything. With few opportunities to perform, we took improv classes, wrote sketches, moonlighted in local theater productions, until eventually we settled into our spots like the many-shaped blocks in one of those baby puzzles in a doctor's waiting room. The optimists stuck with improv, not caring whether they became famous, *yes-and*-ing their way through life in a sickeningly good mood. The delusionals went with sketch, holding out hope that someday, someone would come along and cast them in *SNL*. Some people would say it was the masochists who went for standup, but I'd argue we were just realists. If you bombed, at least you knew who to blame.

I was very much in a realist mood as I sized up the contestants pacing nervously under the awning. I hoped for a gaggle of newbies— anyone could sign up for prelims—but they all just looked like comics to me, smoking cigarettes and trying to ignore one another as they practiced their five-minute sets. The stage order pinned to the door gave me my first good luck of the night: I was slotted for the second half of the show, but not, thank God, the last slot. And Fash—poor Fash!—was first. I began to relax.

Avoiding the pacers, I settled myself at the bar inside and endeavored to stay calm with the help of headphones, a gin and tonic, and a chair pointedly angled away from the TV monitors streaming the main-stage competition. One by one, starting with Fash, the comics before me finished their sets. The ones who did well hovered around the bar, pecking at drinks and each other; the ones who bombed slunk out into the parking lot, avoiding eye contact. One tall guy I recognized from a coffee-shop open-mic slammed the chrome panic bar on the double doors with both hands on his way out, uttering a curse I couldn't hear through my upbeat Beyoncé mix.

Fash, who had recovered from his set early and was seated at a bar table nearby, raised an eyebrow and gestured for me to remove my earpiece. He pointed toward the door, which was still bouncing from the impact. "Hey, all that matters is we're having fun up there, right?"

"You keep telling yourself that, Fash."

"Just trying to ease your mind!" he said. "I mean, not everyone goes in knowing they're already the third-funniest person in Austin."

"What happened to one and two, again?" I said, furrowing my eyebrows. "Oh yeah, they moved to L.A. I guess that doesn't happen for thirdsies."

He snapped and pointed at me. "Zing. Truly. Consider me zung."

I smiled and returned to Beyoncé. There was no reason to let Fash psych me out. My material might not be fresh, but I knew it like the back of my hand. I'd seen comics bomb because of a clenched jaw, a flickering eyelid, a brow that kept a straight line while the mouth grinned manically below, but nerves weren't my problem lately. My problem was sleepwalking through my set. Here, the whiff of potential fame in the air was waking me up, the adrenaline of the competition digging into me like the sharp edge of a knife. By the time it was my turn to go onstage, I was ready.

Under the lights, I breathed in the smell of sweaty metal off the dented microphone and woke up all the way. I hadn't expected such a large audience for the preliminary rounds, but the rows of banquet-style tables were crowded. I'd rarely performed in front of so many people. I avoided looking at the judges' tables to the left, focusing instead on the unexpected energy of the crowd. They were well primed, buzzed on the club's two-drink minimum.

"So I'm originally from Amarillo—" I began, and someone hooted in solidarity from the audience. "Did someone just 'wooo'?" I interrupted myself. "Did you really just 'wooo' for Amarillo, Texas? Examine your life." I got my first laugh, and the stage lights transformed into a clean, solid wall of support, flaring gently in rhythm with the crowd's laughter. I segued easily into my opening jokes, the crowd meeting me at every punch line, and kept them coming at a good clip, rushing only enough to keep the audience on its toes. By the time I got to the bit about my chest that had brought the heckler out last time ("Got these when I turned nine. Worst birthday present ever"), I felt so safe that I ad-libbed a few extra lines, teasing it out fifteen or thirty seconds longer than usual, buoyed by laughter all the way. This was going to be easier than I'd thought.

The blue light on the back wall came on, piercing the veil of the stage lights and bringing me a message: One minute to go. One minute of coasting downhill into the applause that would send me to the semifinals, which could send me to the finals, which might even send me, I was beginning to think, back to L.A. I silently thanked Austin, the so-called "velvet coffin," for having been there when I needed a soft landing place. Even as I wrapped up my set—forty-five seconds; I could feel the rhythm of the time draining down—I was thinking about getting a subletter to cover the rest of my lease, just as I'd covered someone else's when I first moved in. *Goodbye, Austin.* Behind the curtain of stage lights, I could almost feel the walls of the comedy club dissolve and transform into a vista of palm trees and smog. Thirty seconds to go.

It must have been thoughts of L.A. that made me glance involuntarily toward the judges. Perched behind a long table to the left of the audience, they were far from the spotlight's glare, and at first I could only see silhouettes. Then something in one of the silhouettes caught my eye—a tuft of beard sticking out just under the ear in a way that made me look again, a fraction of a second longer this time. Long enough to notice the shape of the part and the glisten of sweat on a high, round forehead.

It was him. Aaron Neely was at the judges' table.

The lights turned ice cold. Then they turned red, then black. I stopped my last joke midsentence. In the darkness, I heard my lips open and close, amplified by the mic. A wave of dizziness passed over me, and for a moment the floor felt as if it were pressing up hard against my feet. I blinked furiously to clear the black fog and said, "Um."

The lights came back with a rushing sound. I blinked again.

The joke, the joke! I reached for it, but it was gone. So, I saw, was the audience. Chairs were creaking impatiently. *Blood in the water.* "Thank you," I said and left the stage to uncertain applause.

I made my way up the aisle and through the bar, past the other comics. On the way out, I hit the panic bar on the double doors as hard as I could, hoping the *chuh-kung!* noise was loud enough to make Fash spill his drink.

· · ·

Of course Neely was in Austin. Of course he'd followed me to the place I felt safest, the place I felt sure he was too much of a big shot to ever grace with his presence. The irony being, of course, that while I was in L.A., Austin had become just the kind of scene a guy like Neely liked.

What Neely liked. I shuddered. What he'd liked was humiliating me in the back of his SUV, showing me how small and insignificant and utterly disposable I was to a man like him and, by extension, to the industry whose highest ranks he represented. He'd shown me, in a stretch of time that felt like an eternity but probably took no more than five minutes, that I would never be in a position to make jokes, not for men like him. Because I *was* the joke. Setup: me, woozy and sick from whatever I'd come down with at the smoothie bar, laughing nervously as he unzipped his pants because I didn't realize, at first, what I was seeing. Heightening: still me, now frozen in shock against the safety-locked car door as understanding dawned. Punch line: me again, blood rushing to my face, a visceral, writhing discomfort intensifying in the near silence until it felt like actual physical pain.

I was the joke, and I wasn't even a good one. I was just something to do for fifteen minutes, a way to kill time in the back seat of his car between appointments. He hadn't touched me while he did it, just the edge of my dress. I'd dropped my eyes, confused, and waited for him to finish, which took long enough for tears to start rolling down my cheeks and falling onto my lap.

The tears were falling again now as I stalked across the parking lot to my car, and I felt the surge of shame take me over and shake me from the inside. Why hadn't I said something? Why had I just sat and cried, like an idiot, like a moron? It was just what he'd wanted me to do. And now I knew it wasn't the stomach bug that had kept me riveted quietly in place, weeping, while he jerked himself off. After all, I hadn't been sick tonight, and I'd reacted the same dumb way, with frozen, self-sabotaging terror, like a deer in the headlights. For all my bravado, in the end all it took to shut me down and drive me out of town was one obscene man I'd mistaken for a mentor when he didn't even think I was funny—at least, not funny enough to outweigh the temptation of jacking off to my double Ds.

And didn't that prove he was right—the fact that I couldn't take it, that I'd run away, that I was back here in Austin instead of in a writers' room in L.A.? For the millionth time, I thought, *Nothing happened, he didn't even touch me,* words that had first echoed through my head in the half hour after he'd finished as we sat side by side in L.A. traffic—him, unbelievably, making small talk. I'd repeated the words like a mantra to myself to drown out his insipid chatting until I was home safe. And after all, it was the truth. It wasn't as if he'd attacked me. It wasn't rape. I, of all people, knew the difference. What was it, to cause me such shame?

When his car finally stopped in front of my house and the automatic door lock clicked, Neely himself told me what it was, with the unanswerable authority of someone who could take a joke, who was, in fact, in charge of deciding what constituted a joke in the first place. As I scrabbled at the door handle and stepped down to the curb, the last words I heard him say were: "Come on. This is a funny story. You'll be able to use it someday."

There was someone following me across the dark parking lot. Someone tall, because the footsteps behind me—how long had they been there?—punctuated by the rhythmic creak of boots suggested a lengthy stride. Passing under a lamp, I watched my shadow spring out ahead of me, and in the few feet before the circle of light faded completely, I could see another shadow trembling just under my right heel. I squeezed my eyes shut for a millisecond to clear them of tears and tried to push down the thought of Neely. He couldn't have left the judges' table early—could he? I strained to catch a glimpse of my car in the narrow alleys between Suburbans and jacked-up pickup trucks. Without slackening my pace, I fumbled in my purse for the keys. When I found them, I slotted each jagged key between my fingers, then squeezed the key ring until it bit my palm. My Honda emerged into view. I increased my pace and heard the footsteps speed up behind me. I was almost there.

Just as I was reaching to unlock the door, I felt a hand on my shoulder and whirled around. A tall woman stood in front of me, her shock of hair backlit by the long-necked street lamp: Amanda.

"Jesus, you scared me to death!"

"I'm so sorry," she said. "I was just trying to catch up. I wasn't trying to freak you out."

"Mission not accomplished!" My heart was racing, the tension of the past few minutes releasing all at once. "What is it this time?" Snapping at someone, anyone, felt amazingly good. My rage at what had happened onstage was almost overpowering, and I was coldly aware that Amanda was the perfect person to take it out on. A random stranger I'd only just met, new in town, she existed completely apart from the rest of my life, was barely a person to me. I remembered Ruby's "number-one fan" remark and felt a new surge of irritation. "Why are you suddenly everywhere I look? What are you, pumpkin spice?"

She fell back half a step, stunned into silence. "I—I'm sorry," she said again. "I just saw your name in the paper, in the listings for—"

"And, what, you want to tell me some more sob stories?" I said nastily. But it was me who was on the verge of tears.

Amanda noticed. She had regained her composure, that eerie, wide-eyed stillness, as if she were waiting for my next move. "You've been crying," she said. "What happened in there? You think you messed up?"

"I did terrific, thanks," I said reflexively. "A regular king of comedy. Anyway, learn your terms. It's called bombing."

"You didn't bomb," she said. "You were the best of the night." I stifled a sneering comment as she went on. "You choked a little at the end, but trust me, it wasn't that big a deal."

"Thanks, Coach," I sneered. Then, suddenly, just like last time, my defenses came tumbling down without warning, and I found myself telling her the truth. "Look, I didn't finish a joke. Even if the rest of the set killed, there's no way the judges will let me through on that mess." The danger of tears eased up as I explained the situation, but my next thought threatened to bring them back. "And even if by some miracle I did advance to the next round—" I broke off. I wasn't going to come back to get judged by Neely again. I couldn't stand in the spotlight and have him stare at me the way he'd stared at me in the back of the SUV. What if he came up to me after the show, tried to talk to me?

Amanda's eyes narrowed. "Is this something to do with what happened to you in L.A.?" She saw my expression. "I know, I know, nothing happened in L.A., right? Absolutely nothing. Just like nothing happened in there." She jerked her thumb back toward the neon sign in the distance. "Listen, I get it. You don't want to tell anybody. But I'm not anybody, am I? Nobody important, anyway."

It was so close to what I'd been thinking only a moment before —that Amanda was nothing to me, no one, and therefore it didn't matter what I said to her—that it startled me.

She saw me waver. "Let's just go somewhere and have a drink and talk."

The adrenaline lessening, I felt exhaustion setting in. "It's stupid," I said. "It's nothing to get this upset over."

"But you are this upset."

She was right. I was this upset, and there was nobody in my world to talk to about it. Who was I going to tell—Kim? Fash? I couldn't even tell Jason right after it happened, and he'd been my best friend. He'd already been so mad that I took the meeting alone, I'd thought he might blame me. But even worse than that, on a level that was itself embarrassing to admit, I'd been afraid Jason would laugh—that *anyone* I told would laugh. Afraid everyone would see it like Neely did: a dirty joke with me as the punch line.

Looking at Amanda, I knew she wouldn't laugh.

I unlocked the car door and gestured for her to come around to the passenger side. She opened the door and got in, and I slid behind the steering wheel. Once the doors were closed, the silence of dead air cocooned us. I glanced around anyway, just in case, looking into the darkened cars that seemed suddenly menacing. No one was around, and we were all the way across the parking lot from Bat City, where the last few comics were shredding their fingernails under the awning as they waited their turns.

So I told Amanda what happened in L.A.

"That's disgusting," she said. "He really did that?"

I nodded my head. "It got on my dress. I threw it away when I got home." It had been my favorite audition outfit, an exceptionally flattering wrap dress. I almost gagged remembering how I'd gotten up in the middle of the night, worried that Jason might see, and stuffed it all the way to the bottom of the kitchen trash can, under used paper towels and greasy takeout containers and half a leftover rotisserie chicken that had been in the refrigerator for two weeks. Back in bed, I'd tossed and turned, and finally I got up a second time to dig it out and take it outside to the dumpster in the back alley.

"He assaulted you."

"I don't think it counts as assault. Does it?" I laughed weakly, but Amanda looked deadly serious. "Honestly, I think the reason he did —*that*—was because it's so absurd," I said. "I mean, who could I tell? The police? He jerked off in front of me. He didn't steal my wallet." I had wanted to see this exact look on Amanda's face—the *Guys like that* look — but now that it was happening, I felt somewhat ridiculous. "I survived."

"Surviving isn't living," she said shortly. "These guys — Aaron Neely, my shithead supervisor, my asshole ex-boyfriend — *they're* living. Believe me. They're not losing any sleep over it. They're not wondering if it was assault or not, worrying about whether they'll bump into you someday. They can go anywhere, do anything. *That's* living." She clenched a fist. "Neely may not even remember you. He's probably done it to a lot of women."

That hadn't occurred to me. I'd been thinking of the incident in the back of the SUV as something specific to me, something to do with my particular shape and size, the plunging neckline of that particular wrap dress, or maybe even the events in my particular past. As if Neely could tell at a glance what had happened to me long ago.

"It doesn't matter anyway, because I'm out of the competition. There's no way I'll advance now."

"I wouldn't be so sure," she said shrewdly. "If he does remember you, he might want to keep you in the competition just to see you squirm. Guys like that" — there was that phrase again — "it's the power trip they get off on."

She was right. Even with my flub, he'd have enough sway on the judging panel to advance me. The rest of the judges would be locals; they almost never snagged celebrities and industry types for the preliminaries, which dragged on for weeks. I wondered if he was scoping the city for a longer-term project. I put my head in my hands. If Neely was planning to cast and shoot something in Austin, the nightmare could go on indefinitely. He'd be here semi-permanently, showing up at open-mics and showcases, surrounded by Fash and other comics currying favor, impossible to avoid. *Pilot idea: Woman hides in mascot costume to avoid local dirtbag, zipper sticks. She's stuck in giant armadillo outfit forever.* I could almost hear the velvet coffin slamming shut.

A text rattled my phone. I pulled it out and took a look. It was from Kim. "Oh my God," I said. "You're right." I slowly turned it around so Amanda could see all the exclamation points.

"I told you it was a good set," she said, unfazed.

"Or it's what you said—he just wants to fuck with me." I groaned. "What am I going to do? I can't go back in there."

"Send a text," she said slowly, with a thoughtful expression. "Get her to tell the people in charge that you're not feeling well." I looked at her skeptically. "What? It's not a lie."

"But I can't do the semifinals next week," I said in despair. "Not with him in there. Next time I won't even make it onstage."

Amanda nodded. "Don't worry about that now. I'll take care of it."

"What do you mean?"

"Programmer. I've got skills, remember?" she said, wiggling her fingers like a magician. "Just leave it to me." She opened the car door and got out. "And Dana? Don't contact me for a few days."

She was gone before I remembered that while she had my number, I didn't have hers. Not that it mattered. Neely wasn't going anywhere, at least not because of anything Amanda did. She might be a genius programmer for all I knew, but she had no idea how my world worked.

I had to text Kim something, though, and it couldn't very well be the truth. I stared down at my phone and typed, *Bad shellfish, talk tomorrow.* I added three puke emojis, pushed the green arrow, and peeled out of the parking lot. I couldn't wait to be home in bed.

4

For a few days after the prelims, I kept my head down, skipped the open-mics, and focused on showing up at Laurel's on time. I was sure now that I would need this job for the foreseeable future, and it wouldn't be a good idea to lose it with my upcoming rent hike. I dug up the lease renewal from the pile of papers on my filthy kitchen table—though I made a point of being coiffed and heeled in public, my house was a mess—and scanned through it again. There was a fifty-dollar rent break if I paid first and last on signing. I studied the numbers in my checking account, trying to figure out how much I could conceivably save in the next month by cutting all bar tabs, eating only rice and beans, and curbing my Zappos habit. It was time to set a real budget, like an adult. I wished I had asked Jason about the software he used to keep track of the grocery budget when we lived together. I hated computers.

I hadn't yet decided what to do about the semifinals, but at first, the mere fact of having told someone about Neely made me feel almost as if the problem had been solved. Austin was in full spring mode, the perfect crystal-blue days strung one after another like beads on a necklace, each one seventy degrees Fahrenheit with just enough breeze to ruffle the crape myrtles. It was easy weather to love and feel loved by. March had already slipped by, and April was about to do the same. With the weight of secrecy lifted slightly, I wanted to enjoy myself at last. At times it felt as if I had dreamed it all up—not just Amanda, who seemed unreal when she wasn't right in front of me, but even Neely himself. I'd been sick, after all, which had made the whole thing feel like a nightmare. How likely was it that what had happened had *really* happened, at least the way I remembered it?

Of course, I knew perfectly well that everything with Neely had happened just as I remembered, and that the feeling wouldn't last. But the temporary relief was so welcome that I indulged it for as long as it lasted, responding graciously to the handful of well-wishers texting me congratulations and pretending to all and sundry, including myself, that my surprise advancement in the contest was good news and only good news. I even banged out a few scenes for the lifestyle guru pilot, feeling momentarily unblocked.

After a day or so, though, the relief wore off, and a half shade of brightness leached out of the spring days. When I glanced at my text messages, I couldn't help wondering whether any of them would be from Amanda, though she'd made it clear, in her conspiratorial way, that we wouldn't be in touch for a while. What could she possibly have meant by "I'll take care of it"? Now, after almost doubting her existence, I caught myself fantasizing that any minute I'd get a text from her saying it was done, whatever it was, and Neely wouldn't be at the semifinals. This was nonsense and I knew it. Still, I wished I had Amanda's number, so I could call and find out what she had meant.

But I didn't have Amanda's number, and she didn't call or text, so I kept polishing brass bowls and folding linen napkins at Laurel's, and then it was the weekend before semifinals. I began to feel less worried about Amanda than about the upcoming competition. Would I be able to perform or not? Could I even trust myself to walk onto the stage at Bat City, much less make it through an entire set without glancing Neely's way? A stray thought about him while I was on the mic could bring on another embarrassing stutter at best, total silence at worst. Whenever I woke up in the middle of the night and couldn't go back to sleep, I anxiously tested myself, rehearsing the situation mentally again and again with my eyes squeezed shut. I'd imagine myself making my way through the parking lot, running the gauntlet of the other comics, checking the list by the door, settling down to a drink at the bar. But when the emcee called my name to go onstage, I'd always blank out and fall back into a deep, black sleep.

The answer hit me during a busier-than-usual Saturday shift. I'd just sold a three-hundred-dollar antlered recipe stand and was dusting the essential-oil display while Becca took over with customers. I remembered what Ruby had said about Becca's arms and noticed that today, as always, they were sheathed in long sleeves despite the fair weather. I wondered if she, too, had a secret. If so, it seemed like a stupid and destructive secret to keep.

But wasn't I being just as stubborn?

Telling Amanda had brought instant relief. But Amanda didn't matter—even she knew that. Once she'd faded into the background, the relief had faded with her, and I was left alone to anticipate another confrontation with Neely. What if I just needed to tell someone else? Not my mom, who would freak out, or Ruby, who would gossip about it, but someone closer to my world, who would understand?

Kim, for instance. After prelims, Kim had checked in with me to ask after my imaginary illness. She'd even offered to bring me soup and Gatorade. It wasn't the first time she'd made friendly advances, and I wasn't quite sure why I'd never responded to them before. Okay, it annoyed me that she played up the sexy-baby thing onstage, and maybe she really would laugh at the idea of Aaron Neely, *the* Aaron Neely, masturbating furiously at me in the back of an SUV. Maybe I needed someone to laugh, to break the spell of it, at least for long enough to get me through the semifinals. Anyway, hanging out with Kim would give me something to do other than dread Neely and wonder about Amanda.

I finished up the oil display and got back to my phone, which was tucked under the counter in my purse. I had just enough time to send a text to Kim—*Ran out of puke, all better now. Hang out before shows?* —before the next wave of customers. I heard the buzz of a text, but I didn't get a chance to look until the shift was nearly over. Kim had replied, *Meet me at the lake @6?*

I'd been thinking more along the lines of happy hour than exercise, but since I was supposedly recovering from food poisoning, it wouldn't hurt me to play along. *See you there,* I texted back, trying to remember if I owned a single pair of walking shoes.

"The lake" was Ladybird Lake, which I still thought of as Town Lake, the homelier name it had worn when I first moved to Austin. By either name, it wasn't a lake at all but a fat stretch of the Colorado River running through the heart of the city just south of downtown, flanked on both shores by hike-and-bike trails and kayak-rental places. Since coming back to Austin, I'd spent more time sitting in my car in traffic on the bridges over the river than down among the annoyingly healthy trail runners and dog walkers. But no matter how backed up the bridges were, the broad, rippling surface of the water, glinting at rush hour in the slanting sun and dotted with paddleboarders like gondoliers, made for a pleasant view.

That said, parking by the river was a bitch. Already late from having stopped by my apartment to change into a more walkable outfit, I maneuvered the car up and down the clogged one-way streets and cursed the no-left-turn signs until I found a spot a quarter of a mile away. I texted Kim I was on my way and hustled toward the trail under the powerful six o'clock sun, marshaling the last vestiges of bounce in a pair of ancient tennis shoes I'd found buried in the piles of heels in my closet. I was already pouring sweat when I got to our agreed-upon meeting place, where Kim, clad in a threadbare Eagles T-shirt over a lime-green sports bra, was executing an isosceles downward-dog in a sunlit patch of grass. She sprang up when she spotted me, her cheeks perfectly flushed, like an actress in a movie about working out. Panting, I waved in lieu of saying hello.

"Hey, late-ass bitch," she said.

"Namaste, slut," I said, still catching my breath. "You're looking very white-lady today." The snarky greetings among comics used to throw me before I accepted them as just part of the job. Remembering that I was supposed to be convalescing, I added, "You're lucky I came at all. If I die out here, I'm suing you."

"You want to walk or run?"

"Did I stutter?"

"What, you mean at prelims?" she said with a nasty grin, and I bowed sarcastically. "No, seriously. Congrats, though." She steered us toward the path, at this hour a slow-moving river of people and bicycles and dogs swathed in a low cloud of reddish dust.

"You too," I said. Kim had placed in her preliminary round the week before mine. "But the prelims are old hat to you, right?"

"Yeah, this is my third year," she said with a quick sidelong glance at me, like I'd touched a nerve. She'd never placed at finals.

"Third time's the charm, they say," I said, to make nice.

"It's so fucking exhausting."

"Skip it," I suggested. "Go sailing."

"Are we even allowed to do that?" I knew what she meant. Since Funniest Person had gotten so big, standups in Austin referred to it as the "comedy tax." It ate up months every year. "Let's just bitch about it and pretend we don't care who wins instead."

"Sounds like a plan."

"I mean, it's going to be the same dudes who place every year."

"And the Funniest Person in Austin goes to . . . a guy with a handlebar mustache!" I said in my announcer voice.

"Second place . . . a guy with a slightly smaller handlebar mustache —and a neck tattoo!"

"Third . . . some woman, so nobody can accuse us of sexism!"

"I'll take it," Kim said. "I'm your token, right here." I wondered if I should make the next joke but Kim took the words out of my mouth, cocking an eyebrow at me. "Maybe they'll double their money and put a Latina comic in third."

"I fully endorse that idea, since I'm the only one in town."

"May the best token win . . . third, that is. If they even throw us a bone this year. I mean, last year it was three white dudes." She smirked. "Speaking of that, I want to buy a drink for whoever gave Fash firsties last week. He nearly pissed his pants when he saw the order."

"May the first slot always go to a white man." I cast my eyes heavenward.

"Amen."

We walked for a little while in silence. I watched the dogs trotting along the path and imagined what they were thinking. A golden-haired collie: *I'm trying to spend less time on Instagram and more time really living.* A pit bull running next to a septuagenarian in butterfly shorts: *I love this man, and when he dies, I am going to love eating him.* A chow chow: *Sometimes I pretend I'm a cat. What, you don't have any kinks?*

"Someone told me if you don't get to L.A. by twenty-six, you're never going," Kim said suddenly.

"I heard it was twenty-three," I said, not asking Kim's age. I didn't feel like reminding her I was two years past the expiration date. "But then, I also hear you have to spend six years out there to make it. So if you do the math, it's really seventeen."

We had reached a shaded part of the path bent around a stagnant outcropping of the river. The overgrowth blocked out the sun, but it also shut out the breeze so completely that it felt like an airless room. We weren't walking fast, but I was drenched, and Kim's forehead was beading up at the hairline. She pulled a strand of sweat-darkened gold off her temple and fanned her cheeks with her hand. "Sometimes I think I'd rather off myself than keep slogging through it year after year."

I didn't know what to say except "Yeah."

"Well, anyway," she said with a short laugh. "I said the same thing last April, and the April before that. But it's April again and I guess I'm still alive, so." She shrugged. "April, man. Funniest Person, South by Southwest, Moontower . . . all those festivals. It's just fucking . . ." She trailed off.

"The cruelest month?" I said. I'd had one good class in college, and it was modern poetry.

"Totally. The fucking cruelest."

We emerged from the overgrowth and shared a moment of silent enjoyment as the breeze dried the sweat off our skin.

"Anyway," Kim continued, putting her game face back on. "I got to talk to Aaron Neely after prelims."

My blood froze in the full sunshine. Surrounded by people on every side and distracted by the exercise, I had almost forgotten why I was there and what I'd wanted to talk about.

"Oh, really?" I said cautiously.

"Yeah, he was great," she said. "I've heard he has some weird thing with female comics, but who doesn't? Anyway, he liked my set, and he said he wanted to talk shop sometime."

A panicky feeling started up in my gut. I had to tell her. At the same time, an equal and opposite force was telling me to keep my mouth shut, not to insult her by suggesting that she and I were in the same category, that what Neely had done to me, he was planning to do to her. Maybe he really did like Kim's set. And even if he did give her the Aaron Neely special on the car ride home—would she care? Kim was one of the cool girls. Half her set was about awkward stuff that happened during sex. Maybe men did this type of thing to her all the time, and she knew how to laugh it off. Maybe I really was the only one who couldn't take the joke.

We stepped onto a large pedestrian bridge that hugged the underbelly of the street bridge, a shaded breezeway suspended by concrete pillars like massive tree trunks over the glistening river. From here, even the noise of cars passing overhead felt calm, a soothing whoosh of white noise that complemented the sounds of rustling branches from the riverbanks. I struggled with what to say until we reached the very center of the double-decker bridge. The long, low sun stretched all the way across the bridge between the twin layers of concrete. From this vantage point, we could see up and down the whole pewter-and-gold span of the river, crisscrossed with graffitied railroad tunnels, pedestrian walkways, and log-jammed traffic bridges. The hoods and windshields of the cars suspended over the river looked like they were on fire in the slanting sun. We both paused involuntarily and then drifted to the railing, taking in the view.

Kim had stopped talking and was staring out over the water. It was now or never.

"Kim," I said.

"Don't get too jealous." She sighed. "It's not actually going to happen."

"I'm sure he liked your set," I said, and I was drawing a breath to say *But* when she cut me off.

"Yeah, well. He's gone now, so it doesn't matter."

"What?" I swiveled to face Kim, whose forehead was crinkled up in the glare.

"Neely took off all of a sudden. Nobody knows why. Family emergency or something? Or maybe he just got bored with Austin. God knows I am." She plucked a leaf out of her hair and threw it over the railing.

My eyes went wide. Neely was really gone, and not because of any family emergency. I felt certain that Amanda had done what she'd set out to do. A tidal wave of relief hit me. Neely was gone, and I was free.

I saw Kim's face and checked myself. "That's—wow, bad luck," I said, trying to sound normal.

She turned toward me, still dejected. "It just sucks to feel like you're so close to something, you know? And then have it yanked away."

In my giddy state, I had to stifle a laugh. *Yanked* was the appropriate word in my case. "Yeah, I know what that feels like."

"He gave me his card, though. With his direct line. Maybe I'll get out to L.A. this year after all, while he still remembers who I am." She laughed shortly.

I didn't trust myself to answer. The urgency of warning Kim and unburdening myself had passed, and I was now consumed by the desire to see Amanda. Maybe I would still tell Kim about Neely—but later, after I found out what was really going on. In the meantime, she was in no danger of being trapped in a back seat by him any time soon.

And me? I was going to the ball.

5

I begged off shows for the evening and stayed home to watch TV and monitor my cell phone obsessively, waiting for Amanda to contact me. Around one o'clock in the morning, just as I was drifting off, a text woke me up.

Come over. With an address.

Before I was fully awake, my thumbs started moving in a reply. Then I glanced at the address again and stopped typing. It was somewhere downtown—not exactly where I would have expected Amanda to want to meet at one in the morning on a Saturday. Maybe a degree of caution was in order. I typed, *Just checking, who's this?*

It's me. I have something to show you.

Show me?

A link to a video appeared in the next text. If this was some creep from Tinder or a heckler stalking me . . . but I was getting paranoid. I checked out the thumbnail, squinting and bringing the screen close to my eyes. Most of the picture was covered by the play arrow, but behind the triangular icon, I could just make out a familiar face.

I followed the link.

At first it was hard to tell what was going on. The screen was a grainy blur of bad lighting and beige walls. There was a knock and a lot of rustling and thumping, and then the beige went the color of a bruise as a door opened. The dark outline of a bald guy appeared in the doorway, backlit by a ceiling fixture that temporarily flooded the frame with white glare before receding again behind the figure's head.

"Come in, come in," the silhouette said in a muffled but familiar voice, and there was more rustling as he stepped back into what appeared to be a hotel room. He was wearing a bathrobe.

Next came a woman's voice that I recognized as Amanda's, much louder, presumably because it was closer to the mic. "Where would you like me to set up the table, Mr. Neely?" The camera moved forward into a spacious hotel suite, and Neely disappeared from the frame temporarily.

"Let me get the—" Sound of a door closing. "Next to the bed, please. Thank you. Do you need any help with that?"

The camera moved jerkily through the suite toward the king-size bed. Amanda's voice came through her heavy breathing, as if she was carrying something large. "No, thanks, I've got lots of practice."

"Of course." Neely's voice sounded nervous and tinny off camera. "It's a big table, ha-ha." The screen went black for a moment and there was a clacking sound. Neely's voice in the background said, "You sure you don't need anything? How about a glass of water?"

"A glass of water would be nice," Amanda said. The picture came back, veered wildly for a moment, then settled into an angle and stayed there. A strip of white appeared at the bottom of the frame, out of focus, as if the camera was sitting on a bedspread. In the middle of the frame, a thin, tall woman in a red polo shirt was visible from the shoulders down setting up a massage table. When she bent over to tuck in the sheets and adjust the legs, she was careful to turn her face away from the camera, revealing the back of a red baseball cap and a flash of wavy blond hair.

Neely came back into the frame, also cut off from the shoulders up, carrying a glass of water, which he handed to Amanda. "Thank you," she said. "And now I'll just step into the other room, Mr. Neely, and if you could just disrobe and lie face-down under the sheet. I'll knock when I'm coming back in to make sure you're ready." As she spoke, she walked out of the frame with the water, her voice growing fainter until the last few words were swallowed by the click of a door closing.

"Great," Neely called in a loud, somewhat strangled voice. He fumbled with his bathrobe, still headless and partially blocked by the massage table, and the robe opened, revealing a massive, hairy chest flushed nearly brick red. Letting the robe fall open but not taking it off completely, he swung one hammy thigh up on the massage table, then the other, something unmistakable flopping between them.

Even I, who had seen Neely's fat red worm of a penis in uncomfortably close quarters, couldn't suppress an involuntary gasp at the intimacy of all that naked flesh. The left robe flap rode farther up as he wriggled into position, exposing one fleshy white buttock squished flat on the table and a deeply creased overhang of white side belly covered with straggling hairs. He reclined back, leaned onto his left elbow, bent his right leg into a triangle for stability, and tilted his lap a few degrees toward the camera, almost as if posing for it, though it was obvious he didn't know it was there. Last of all, his face appeared: a giant moon shape, dappled and flushed, with an expression that was at once anxious, eager, and revoltingly childlike.

My stomach flipped over as his features became fully visible to the camera eye, surreally recognizable, like all celebrity faces. Once that face was onscreen, juxtaposed with that body—all in dramatic close-up and lit with improbable artistry by a bedside lamp—I could almost feel the shock waves rippling through some invisible crowd, as if the video had already gone viral and I was only a single viewer among millions.

From the background came a quiet knock. "I'm coming in, Mr. Neely," said Amanda from offscreen in her gentle, breathy massage-therapist voice. "Are you ready?"

"Ready," he replied, dick in hand.

The video ended. It was less than three minutes long. I stared in shock. I had almost forgotten where I was and that I was alone.

A text came, reminding me that I wasn't alone at all. Not anymore. *You can probably guess where it goes after that.*

Then: *Trust me now?*

I grabbed my keys.

Downtown on a Saturday night at last call was never my favorite place to be, and tonight was no exception. The days of stumbling down a piss-soaked stretch of Sixth Street with Jason and a couple of comedy buddies drunkenly mocking the drunk girls in platform heels and micro-minis who tripped over the curbs were long past. Now I felt that anyone who chose Austin's miniature version of the French Quarter, cordoned off on weekends to create a dreamscape of hammered pedestrians, tour buses, and Bible-wagging street preachers, was equally perverse. After paying what I felt to be sufficient dues at the notoriously rough open-mic at Fondue Freddy's, I'd avoided downtown clubs whenever possible.

The dreamscape was in full effect tonight. Though the Red River venues had quieted after midnight, per city ordinance, the bar bands and jukeboxes of Sixth Street still sent out a soup of clashing beats audible several blocks away. Taxis, their windows rolled down to air out the sodden drunks inside, blared world music at every stoplight; even the loaded pedicabs emitted strains of jam bands and hair metal, rhythms to keep their stoned drivers mashing the bicycle pedals. I had no trouble finding a place to park; there were never enough cabs and always plenty of drunks vacating their parking spots at this time of night. Eager to avoid sharing the streets with them, I took the first open spot I saw and walked toward the address Amanda had given me.

As I approached, I recognized the area, an urban living district whose paved pedestrian walkways were lined with olive oil boutiques and manicure places I could afford only with a gift card. Just a few blocks from the squalid circus of Sixth Street, it looked like a different world. Amanda's building had gone up before I left, during the first big tech boom. Its copper siding had at first been visible from almost any part of town, a blinding pinkish-gold beacon in daylight. In the five years I had been away, the siding had tarnished to the respectable auburn of a Lincoln penny, but it still looked like money to me. The single people I knew lived in rundown student apartments—mine was a converted nudist compound from the sixties whose walls always felt uncomfortably moist—or divvied up dilapidated cottages in the five-year floodplain. I wondered just how Amanda paid the rent here, her own tech job more than a year gone. The security guard buzzed me in without looking up, and I took the elevator to the eighth floor and knocked.

Amanda opened the door in a T-shirt the mottled-gray color of botched laundry, looking not just wide awake, but wired. Without a word, she waved me in, and I stepped past a narrow kitchen with a granite bar. The living room, half swallowed by the black night outside the curtainless floor-to-ceiling glass windows, was just large enough to hold an entertainment system and an L-shaped sectional sofa. Everything was in perfect order, from the coordinating throw pillows to the perfectly straight rows of Blu-rays on the shelf above the TV—mostly rom-coms and action movies, to my surprise. Outside, a wraparound balcony glowed with a ghostly concrete pallor, and the pale pink lime-stone of the capitol's dome reared up in the distance.

She shut the door behind me. "Amanda—" I said, but she was already talking.

"Shall we celebrate?" she said. "I have some nice wine I've been saving. I wish I had champagne."

"But how—"

"Neely's gone for good." Her back to me, she rummaged through the cabinets in the narrow kitchen, calling over her shoulder, "I knew he'd go slithering back to L.A., but I wanted to wait until I was sure before I contacted you."

"How did you know?"

"I have my ways." She produced two wineglasses from the back of a cabinet, blew into them to clear the dust, and set them down on the bar in triumph. "Anyway, it was only a matter of time, once he saw what I had on him." She closed the cabinet. "What *we* had."

"The video? How did you—" I was still standing awkwardly in the middle of the room, unwilling to take my seat until she came out of the kitchen.

"Isn't it perfect? Once I figured out that he likes to order up a massage whenever he's in a hotel . . . I just knew he would try something. I knew his MO, you know?" She reached up to a wine rack on top of the refrigerator, pulled out a bottle of red, checked the label, and put it back. "As a matter of fact, a lot of people do. You just have to be in the right online forums, understand the coded language. Nobody wants to call him out in public because he's so universally adored." She rolled her eyes. "But this guy, trust me, he does this all the time. Like, every chance he gets. And service workers are less motivated to keep it quiet than comics are." Having pulled out a few more bottles of wine, she finally located one that pleased her and set it on the countertop next to the glasses. Then she said, "Corkscrew, where are you?" and started opening and closing drawers with the same jittery energy.

She eventually found one. "Give it to me," I said to get her out of the kitchen faster. I opened the wine and poured it, then swiftly grabbed both glasses so she'd follow me to the sofa. "Now sit down and tell me everything. From the beginning."

"Okay." She perched on the short side of the L as I took a seat on the long side. "But first—" She leaned forward, brandishing the wineglass. "To having each other's backs."

"To having each other's backs," I said, trying not to betray my impatience as I clinked my glass to hers and drank. "So . . . entrapment. I'm more of a lead-pipe woman myself. In the study." I laughed nervously at my own joke.

"I should really be toasting my former employers at Runnr," she said, ignoring me. "These Silicon Valley types pride themselves on large-scale vision, but they have poor day-to-day management skills. And shockingly short attention spans." She giggled. "It took the admin ages to get around to changing my passwords and revoking my access."

"Access to what?"

"Everything." She raised her eyebrows. "User data, code—half of which I built from scratch, by the way. Eventually I had to turn over my laptop and sign mountains of nondisclosure and noncompete agreements—proprietary tech and IP theft is what they care about." She took a big gulp of wine. "But by that time, I'd already gotten into the code and left a number of back doors open for myself—along with a few bugs. After I left, they were too busy putting out fires without the help of their best programmer to double-check the metadata. Particularly the user database. There is a lot of information in there, my friend."

"So Neely uses Runnr?" I said, finally catching up.

"Everyone uses Runnr," she said, then looked at me. "Well, everyone whose time is worth more than the Runnr fees. Which are dirt cheap, because it's ridiculously easy to get signed up as any kind of runner, even the ones you supposedly need to have a license for."

"Like massage therapist."

"Right. You should see all the garbage they let slip through the cracks. You know they don't even do background checks? They don't advertise that, but it's been in the news. People just don't care enough to stop using it." She laughed. "If they knew how few runners actually make a living at it, they'd care. I mean, how do you trust someone who just turns up at your door and says she's a massage therapist when she's only making, like, twenty bucks for a two-hour massage?"

"Yeesh." I made better money hawking hand-stamped stationery at Laurel's.

"Well, to be fair, I programmed an auto-bidder to make sure I got the run, which drove the price down. Usually female runners make more because there's a higher demand for them. Imagine that." She rolled her eyes, then shrugged. "Anyway, it was no big deal getting in with the camera. After that, Neely did the rest."

I replayed the ghastly intimacy of it, the greedy expression on his face, his hairy flesh looking somehow more naked for being half covered by the robe. "It's perfect," I agreed. "But what if you'd actually had to do the massage? And what if he'd—tried something else?" Now that I was talking about someone else's safety rather than my own, I suddenly realized what it was that had paralyzed me in the back of the SUV that day. It was the inarticulable fear that if I made the wrong move, or any move at all, the situation would turn from mere humiliation into something else entirely.

But Amanda was shaking her head. "He was too impatient to sit through a massage. You know the water he gave me? I'm ninety percent sure he put something in it. I didn't taste it, of course, but it smelled funny. I think part of the game is some kind of sedative. Just to get you a little woozy, so you don't move as fast. He's a total coward."

I felt a surge of nausea, and bile rose in my throat. The smoothie with the chalky aftertaste. I had been so sure Jason and I had the same bug, but I never threw up, just got dizzy and slept for twelve hours afterward. Amanda didn't say anything, but from the way she was looking at me, I could tell she'd already had the thought, probably when I first told her the story. I took a moment to catch my breath. So I'd been roofied in addition to being . . . whatever you called what he'd done to me.

"So where are we going to post it?" I said finally.

"Post what?"

"The video. Or do we send it to a news site anonymously? Or what about those comedy forums you mentioned? Let him be the butt of the joke, for once."

"We're not showing anyone this video, Dana."

I stared. "But — isn't that the whole point? Show the world? Show everyone what he really is?"

"It's worth way more to us hanging over his head."

"Blackmail?" I stood up, and my voice rose, just as it had when Amanda had followed me out of the comedy club. I hated losing control, and talking about Neely, even thinking about him, brought me too close to the edge. "Are you doing this for *money?* Because I don't want his money. I don't want anything from him. All I care about is that it doesn't happen to anyone else."

"It won't," she said. "Trust me. Neely doesn't know who we are, but he knows we have this video. We know everything about him, and we can get to him at any time. That's why he turned tail and ran back to L.A. I've got ways of knowing what he's up to, though — not limited to Runnr, by the way." She looked pleased with herself. "Besides, I think I got my message across. After this, he's going to be too para-noid to pull his signature move on anyone for a long time."

"But why not just release it?"

She looked at me pityingly. "Out in the world, the video is falsifi-able. His PR reps will make up stories, spin it for the press. And in the meantime, since we'll have done all the damage we can do, he won't be afraid of us anymore. He'll hire investigators to find us. Trust me, you don't want that. You don't want to be the lone woman standing up against a celebrity with an accusation like that."

"But there's proof," I said, losing steam.

"If it ever went to court, they'd find a way to get the video thrown out. That's what rich people have expensive lawyers for." She shrugged. "But nobody enjoys spending their money that way, and nobody wants the publicity. As long as we keep our fingers hovering over the but-ton, he's going to do everything in his power to keep us from going nuclear."

There was a moment of silence as I processed this. "Okay, so we don't go nuclear," I said. "Even though—I wouldn't be in it alone, right? If something went wrong."

"No. You wouldn't. If it came down to it, I'd be right there beside you, in court or anywhere else. I promise."

I sat back down on the sofa and took a long, warming swallow of wine.

"So," she said, tapping her fingers together with excitement. "Are you ready?"

"Ready for what?"

"It's your turn."

"Ha-ha," I said, after a long pause.

"I got your back," she prompted, her voice level. "Now you get mine."

"Funny joke." But I knew she wasn't joking.

"I've got a name for you."

I was starting to panic. "I never asked you to go after Neely, Amanda."

She gave me a long look, and the excitement slowly drained from her face. By the time she turned toward the window, her gray-green eyes had gone perfectly flat and opaque. For a moment I thought she might cry.

Instead she got up from the sofa, opened a glass door, and stepped out onto the balcony.

She didn't ask me to follow, but after a few uncomfortable minutes passed, I did. I found her sipping her wine and staring out into the night sky, which had cleared of clouds and was now glittering with stars. To the right, far down, I could just see the Congress Avenue Bridge, a garland of streetlights over the dark river. I stepped toward her and looked up at her profile, lit from below by the balcony lights. No wonder she kept getting auditions. Her cheekbones could've won an Academy Award all by themselves.

"Great wine," I said. "Really, uh, jammy." I took an overly enthusiastic sip and choked.

"Look, you don't have to do it," she said wearily. "Obviously, you don't have to do anything. When we were talking the other night, I just thought—" She stopped abruptly. I opened my mouth to reply, but she started again, more forcefully this time. "I thought we understood each other. But if you think I enjoyed watching Aaron Neely jerk off in that hotel room—if you think I got off on playing his victim, even for a minute—"

I felt stricken. "Of course I don't think that."

"He's a huge guy. Like you said, he could have turned on me any time. It wasn't exactly fun."

"I know," I said. "And I can't thank you enough."

"Not nearly enough," she said, whirling on me. "But I didn't do it just for you, Dana. You never see the big picture, do you? You don't read the forums or listen to the stories, so you don't get it. The problem is so much bigger than what happened to you. These guys do the same thing, over and over again, until somebody finally stands up to them. You have to find a way to hurt them more than they can hurt you."

I took it in silently. I'd said that what mattered to me was that it wouldn't happen to anyone else. But what had brought me over to Amanda's apartment tonight? What had filled me with joy on the bridge with Kim earlier today? Wasn't it just that Neely wasn't my problem anymore?

"Anyway, you got what you wanted," Amanda said, as if she could read my guilty thoughts. "Buy me a drink sometime, I guess."

"What do you want me to do?" I said, exasperated. "Go find your ex-boyfriend and get revenge? He's kind of far away, isn't he? Believe me, if I could be in Los Angeles right now, I already would be."

"If he lived in Austin, you'd do it?" she said, looking out over the city.

"Probably," I said. Then, struck by a sudden impulse to firm up the lie: "Yes. Yes, I would."

"Doug Branchik, my old boss from Runnr." She took another sip. "He lives here now."

"In Austin?"

Amanda uncurled her index finger from around the bowl of the glass of wine and slowly extended her arm. "There. He lives right there."

6

"What?" I said, ducking instinctively. "Where?"

"Across the street. The balcony with the orange deck chairs."

"Amanda——" The slender ledge of concrete we were standing on suddenly felt unbearably exposed.

"If you're going to ask did I know he lived here——of course I knew," she said, ignoring my discomfort. "After I got fired, they transferred him to Austin to help start up the new office here. You know, the *well was poisoned* for him at the home office. Or maybe it was damage control from on high. Either way, I wouldn't waste too many tears on Doug Branchik." She said his name so loudly that I winced, looking across at his balcony. "I'm the one who's blacklisted. He's doing fine."

Unspoken: She knew how he was doing because she could watch him from her window. "Did you——"

"Come here because of him? No. Just a happy accident." I must have looked skeptical, because she laughed, lightly annoyed. "Believe me or not, I don't care. Tons of people move from L.A. to Austin every year. The way people complain about it here, you'd think we were a plague of locusts." She whirled and went back inside, and I followed her, relieved. "Anyway, he's not going to be there much longer. That's a Runnr-owned crash pad. They're just putting him up there until his wife finishes decorating the six-bedroom mansion on Lake Travis."

I glanced over my shoulder at the window. "Aren't there some blinds you could draw or something?"

"Come on, just listen. I've got it all worked out." She cracked a grin. "And the beauty of it is, you'd never even have to see his face."

I didn't say yes, but I didn't say no either.

The next day was the Funniest Person semifinals, but I couldn't concentrate on prepping my set. Memories of the grainy, sordid video haunted me all day. When evening came, I walked through the door into Bat City with some trepidation, wondering if a guilty shadow would hang over my performance. In the waiting area, I kept my headphones on with the sound turned off, bopping my head to imaginary music while comics all around me gossiped about Neely's absence. The replacement judge was rumored to be Cynthia Omari, one of my favorite comics and the host of a hugely popular podcast. As I stepped up onto the stage to start my set, I glanced toward the judges' table, expecting—what?—dust motes where his shape had been? Ominous music?

Instead, there was only the exhilaration of relief. The set did not feel particularly inspired. It did not feel uninspired. It happened almost without me.

That was how light I felt, how free.

I remained in this floaty state of oblivion for the rest of the night, right up until the emcee announced my name as one of three comics moving on to the last round of the competition. As the crowd roared, I looked at my fellow contestants, and the words *I made it to the finals* ran through my mind. I felt my real life turning on with a click.

I stumbled through the bar, past the comics reaching out their hands to congratulate me, and into the women's restroom, where I locked myself in a stall and pulled out my cell phone. The screen still showed Amanda's last text from the night before.

Trust me now?

"Trust me, this is going to be epic."

Our senior year in high school, Jason tried to get me to help him steal Mattie's truck.

Mattie still scared the shit out of me, though I did my best to hide it from Jason. Kenny the German shepherd had run away and gotten hit by a car the year before, so at least I no longer had to worry that the giant dog would come bounding through the dog flap in the garage apartment and put his massive paws on my shoulders and growl, which was the way he'd been taught to greet everyone but Mattie. But Mattie himself had only grown more menacing. I felt him looking at me all the time now.

As practical jokes went, the truck caper seemed to me both incredibly juvenile and nowhere near what Mattie deserved. I never knew what exactly Mattie had done to inspire it, but whatever it was, Jason seemed to have snapped. Maybe he just couldn't take Mattie's ribbing about his manhood anymore, and with Kenny gone, he had no excuse not to try something. At any rate, Jason had decided that it would be hilarious to take the truck in the middle of the night while Matt was sleeping off a payday bender, drive it three counties over, and leave it in the middle of a field, roughed up, as if it had been stolen by a local kid for a joy ride.

"It has to look like something some methed-up punk would do," he'd explained when he saw my expression. "He'll get it back. The tires'll be slashed and it'll need a new paint job, that's all. And I'll rig up the steering column to make it look like it was hot-wired. I found a book at the library with instructions and everything."

"Why don't you just hot-wire it for real, then?" What I didn't say out loud was that if he hot-wired the truck, he wouldn't need me to get the keys. Mattie kept those keys on him at all times. As far as I could tell, the only two things he'd ever cared about were Kenny and the GMC. When Jason insisted I was the only one who could fit through the dog door in Mattie's garage, I was flattered, but skeptical; Jason had filled out in the shoulders that year, but I'd been filling out more or less continuously since the third grade. Moreover, the idea of crawling through a dead dog's door at night and stealing keys from the pocket of a drunk's dirty jeans while he slept a few feet away nauseated me. I told myself that would be true even if that drunk were someone other than Mattie.

But Jason was getting defensive. "Because this is a prank, not a crime." He snorted. "I'm not a *criminal*."

"Oh yeah. Grand theft auto, totally legal."

He'd started on an angry retort, then caught himself and laughed. "Okay, okay," he said. He ran his hands through his hair, and I could see that his palms were sweating from the damp trail they left in his bangs. "Maybe I'm also a little worried I wouldn't be able to pull it off. I nearly failed shop."

"So that's why you got mono last year."

"Saved my GPA," he admitted.

My own GPA was in free fall. I'd already guessed I wasn't going to UT with Jason next year and wanted to spend as much time with him as I could. In the end, I had agreed to do it for the same reason I agreed to everything Jason wanted: because he wanted it.

I was supposed to set an alarm for one a.m. and sneak out of the house, and I went to sleep early but full of adrenaline, sure that I would roll out of bed at the first beep. Instead, I awoke to a desperate tapping on my window sometime in the early-morning hours, still dark but way past one. Lost in a thick waking haze, I couldn't tell if I actually saw Jason standing outside my window in the bushes, pale and shivering, or just heard him furiously tapping. But whether awake or asleep, I knew that I would never crawl through that dog door and steal Mattie's keys, much less follow Jason to a field three counties over and watch as he banged up Mattie's truck so I could drive him home afterward. I told myself I wasn't really awake, and the tapping sound followed me into my dreams.

I caught up to Jason the next day in the cafeteria. Standing in the nacho line, he couldn't get away from me, but he wouldn't look at me either.

"Okay, top ten reasons I didn't do the plan last night," I said. "Number ten: It was a stupid fucking plan."

Wrong move. He stared resolutely at the floppy cardboard boats under the heat lamp, their tortilla chips stuck together with greasy cheese, then slid one onto his tray.

"Number nine: Dreamed I was helping; woke up in the bathroom trying to shift the toilet into third gear."

Nothing. I swallowed.

"Number eight: I'm a rotten friend." I touched his sleeve and, in a different tone, said, "Jason, I'm sorry. Really."

As if he hadn't heard me, couldn't even feel my hand on his arm, he mechanically heaped sour cream and guacamole onto his nachos.

"Fine, skip to number one," I said. "I chickened out, Jase. I didn't want to tell you, but I was scared."

Eyes still fixed on his tray, he slowly grinned, then chuckled. "You should have seen the look on your face when I was telling you about it." He tossed the guacamole scooper into the hot-water tin with a splash. "It was like hurdle-jumping day in gym class all over again."

I beamed, relieved. "In my defense, I still don't think you should have to have a doctor's note when you're obviously a midget."

By the end of the day, we were acting like it had never happened. Jason never brought up pranking Mattie again—although he took up smoking shortly afterward, which seemed related somehow—and when his girlfriend dumped him right before prom later that year, he gave her ticket to me. Standing next to him in a pile of silver balloons for the picture, my red column dress looking slightly silly next to his Texas tux, I felt thoroughly forgiven.

Deep down, though, I knew I had lied about the reason I'd stayed in bed that night. It was true I was scared of Mattie, but I wouldn't have let that stop me from helping Jason out. The number-one reason I hadn't helped Jason steal Mattie's truck was that he couldn't admit he was too scared to do it alone. We both pretended he'd have gone through with it if only he'd had the keys, but he wouldn't have. And that was ultimately why I couldn't join him in crossing the line. He needed me too much.

Trust me now? The question still hung unanswered in the little speech bubble on my screen.

Amanda had crossed the line without me, unhesitatingly, on my behalf.

I do, I typed into the text box, and pushed SEND.

7

Absolutely not." I glared at the red cross-front apron full of spray bottles that was lying on Amanda's sofa. "You said I'd be a runner. You never said anything about a maid."

"It's the only Runnr service he uses regularly!" Amanda protested. "Think of it like a part."

"I don't do maids." One of the reasons I'd stopped scouring the audition boards years before I left L.A. was that I got sick of showing up to read for the best friend and getting handed sides for the cleaning lady.

"It's just a costume," she said, seeming genuinely bewildered. "And you won't be wearing it long. Once you get inside —"

"I know, I know." I took a deep breath and reminded myself that I was a finalist for Funniest Person in Austin. "Just shut up and give it to me." Amanda dropped the apron into a shopping bag, and I stalked out to the car with it wedged under my arm.

Once home, I donned the cleaning outfit as quickly as possible, to get it over with, and forced myself to look in the mirror. The red

Runnr apron aged me ten years, and the half-empty bottles of cleaners in the pockets along the front forced my shoulders into a heavy slump. I thought of my mother hustling off to work in heels every day, her shoulders thrown sharply back. Even after getting laid off from her secretarial job at the helium plant, she had refused to return to the housecleaning work she'd done when she first came to Texas. "I don't clean up messes anymore," she'd insisted. "Not your father's, not yours. Not anyone's." I pulled my own shoulders back, straining against the apron straps, and even attempted an old acting-class trick of inventing a walk for the character. But in the end, my waddle more or less invented itself, an attempt to minimize the sloshing of the bottles as they bounced off my belly. *Pilot idea,* I thought, then stopped myself. Too depressing.

I checked my phone for activity on the app. For a regular weekly job like this, Amanda had explained, Branchik would get a notification on his phone to approve the run before it went out on the app. It was part of the company's philosophy not to allow standing gigs to go to the same runner week after week. That might foster an independent relationship between user and contractor, encouraging them to drop the middleman altogether.

"The Runnr philosophy is based on the fungibility of labor," Amanda explained, and then she saw my blank expression and clarified. "Price, speed, and quality are the only variables that are supposed to matter to the algorithm. The way Runnr sees it, familiarity breeds wage inflation and tolerance for mistakes. You get to know someone, you learn their kids' names, suddenly they're a person. The Runnr customer is supposed to be able to order up human help like an appetizer, at the spur of the moment, without worrying about that stuff."

Just then, the notification arrived with a ding. The words *We have a Run for you!* popped up on my screen, a shower of confetti raining down behind them. I tapped DETAILS and watched as Doug Branchik's address came up with the specs for the cleaning job; bathroom, kitchen, laundry, all boxes checked. At the bottom of the screen, the bidding price Amanda's program had auto-generated to ensure I would win the run: $16.79.

Unbelievable. If this were a real run, my percentage of the take would barely cover round-trip bus fare. And the bus was, unfortunately, a vital part of this plan, so my car wouldn't be seen downtown on the day of the strike. I tapped the ACCEPT icon and stormed out the door.

The bus arrived at the stop by my apartment complex ten minutes late. Climbing aboard, I was already sweating heavily, feeling at once ridiculously conspicuous in my uniform and angry at how invisible it made me. By the time I reached Branchik's door and typed in the key code that had been sent via the app, I was already sick of the whole thing.

Looking around the condo, however, I felt a fresh surge of inspiration. I'd thought *I* was messy. Branchik's floor was wall-to-wall dirty clothes and empty takeout containers. An overturned juice bottle labeled POWER PULP lay on the gray sofa next to a greenish splotch. Boxer shorts lay twisted up on the carpet and draped over the elliptical machine in the corner of the living room. This was the cleaning job Branchik expected some faceless runner to perform for $16.79? An anarchic spirit of rage swelled in me as I surveyed the scene. I'd show him "fungible labor." I crossed the squalid living room and drew the blinds with a brief glance up at Amanda's balcony—she was on lookout duty—before peeling off the apron and kicking it viciously into a corner. Then I took off all my clothes, pulled the blond wig out of my apron pocket, and slipped it over my hairnet. It was time for my close-up. Naked except for the wig, I put my phone's camera in selfie mode and started clicking.

The wig was Ruby's. I'd told her I wanted to borrow it for my act. She had a closetful of them, and this one was a relic of a long-ago attempt at Betty Grable—a miserably failed attempt, since its platinum locks drooped and wouldn't hold a curl, but it was perfect for my purposes. The goal wasn't to look natural—nothing about the radioactive blond against my olive skin looked natural—but simply to hide my face from shots that might inadvertently reveal it.

The trashiness was a bonus. The minute I had it on, it transformed my nakedness into a costume far more lurid than fetish lingerie or stripper heels. Like most female comics who weren't a size 6, I had an arsenal of defensive jokes about my body for the mic, but as I warmed up to the selfie shots, I gained a new appreciation for how well my body photographed. The girl I saw in the pictures was sexy—slutty! —her generous curves pillowing out into pornographic landscapes, wisps of the plasticky blond wig contrasting against brown nipples. It was exhilarating.

So exhilarating that I almost lost track of what I was doing. I needed incriminating shots. The décor in Branchik's company-owned apartment was generic, and even the mess was largely an anonymous mess, the kind someone might leave in a hotel room. Hoping to capture a few recognizable pairs of boxer shorts in the background, I rolled around in the nests of dirty laundry—another act that would have seemed unthinkably disgusting to me when I had clothes on but that bare-ass Betty seemed to relish—but it wasn't quite enough. I needed a backdrop that was unmistakably identifiable as Branchik's apartment. I got up, dusted the crumbs of some bachelor meal off my back, and picked my way into the bedroom.

Bingo.

On the bed, by the nightstand, stood a framed wedding picture. It was shot at sunset on a sparkling beach under a hazy Instagram filter, the bride's slender gown of tiered lace in the rich hippie style accessorized with a flower-crown veil; she had the whitest teeth I'd ever seen. Laughing vividly, as if caught in a candid shot, Branchik's new wife nonetheless looked a touch rigid, a gleam of manic anxiety in her eye. Knowing what I did about her husband, I might ordinarily have been at least a little moved by her plight, but wearing the garish Betty wig, I thought it was hilarious. In any case, it was the perfect background detail. I plopped myself on the bed and began clicking selfies at virtuosic angles, photographing my mountainous breasts in extreme close-up and then twisting around to capture my ass half entangled in sheets. I contorted myself for crotch shots, experimenting with more and more explicit angles, always careful to keep the photo of Mrs. Branchik's desperately grinning face in the background.

I was so absorbed in this task that when the first text came, it took me a moment or two to look away from my own image and read it.

DB's car in garage, get out

I jumped off the bed in a panic, but the texts kept coming:

He's walking into lobby get out NOW

He's in the elevator OUT OUT OUT OUT GET OUT OF THERE NOW

I ran for the pile of clothes in the living room, grabbed my jeans, and started yanking them on. I'd gotten one of my legs in when I heard a tiny *ding* coming from the hallway outside. The elevator. I tripped trying to get the other pants leg on and had to finish lying on my back on the floor, legs in the air. Footsteps creaked outside the door as I frantically threw my T-shirt on, braless, and jostled the apron full of bottles up my arms onto my torso. There was a metallic key-chain jingle followed by the swipe-and-click of a keycard as I jerked the strings into a knot behind my back and stuffed my bra down between the bottles in my pocket. A moment before the door swung open, I remembered the wig on my head and yanked it off. There was no more room in my apron, so I crammed it down my shirt.

I didn't wait to get a good look at Branchik but instead began yelling indignantly in Spanish cribbed from my mother's long-ago rants about my room: *"¡Sucio, sucio! ¡Es muy sucio!"* I stalked back and forth, flailing my arms wildly to indicate the debris on the floor, the mess of takeout containers on the table, the general state of filth. He began to protest, but I yelled over him, *"¡No habla ingles!"* and *"¡Sucio!"* until he took a few steps into the room, clearing the doorway. I ran past him and stomped out of the apartment without looking back, bottles rattling on my thighs. The elevator doors were still open, thank God, and I darted around the corner and pushed the button, praying that Branchik wouldn't care enough about his failed Runnr experience to take the stairs down after me. I had run through all my Spanish fit for the occasion.

Amanda screamed with laughter.

"It's not funny!" I said, barely able to get the words out between heaving breaths. I stood in Amanda's apartment, hands shaking, hair plastered down with sweat — I'd ripped off the hairnet and apron as soon as I was out of Branchik's building — thighs quaking from the effort of getting myself across the street and back up into her apartment without attracting undue attention. Leaning back against the safely locked door, conscious of staying as far from the window as possible, I tried to stop my heart from hammering in my chest. "It's not —" I tried again but found my gulps of air turning into sobs of laughter. A moment later I was sliding down the wall, my legs collapsing under me, still laughing. "It's not funny!" I gasped from the floor, tears oozing out of the corners of my eyes. "I almost got caught!"

"You're right, not funny at all," Amanda said, regaining her composure for a moment only to crack up again a moment later. "No kidding, I heard you from all the way in here. *¡No habla ingles!*" She giggled explosively.

"Hey," I said, catching my breath and wiping my eyes. "That was some top-notch improvising. Probably the best scene work I've ever done. Apparently the secret is fearing for your life." I trudged forward on my hands and knees, not bothering to get up, and made my way to the sofa. Sitting on the living-room rug, I propped myself up against the sofa near Amanda's legs.

"It was closer than it should have been," she agreed. "What happened in there anyway?"

"I guess I got carried away," I said. "Here." I passed the phone to her, photo app open.

Amanda squealed as she started swiping through the pics. "Oh my God, these are amazing! You are so good at this." She lowered the phone and looked down at me. "You have a gift for sexting, my friend."

"I learned on the job."

"You should consider working for Pornhub." She turned her attention back to the screen. "How did you manage to keep the photo in the background so clear? The depth of focus is like an Ozu film." She squinted. "There's a lot of detail in your, uh, foreground too."

"Look close. I think you can see all the way up to my tonsils." Now that my adrenaline was beginning to ebb, a wave of exhaustion hit. "This had better work," I said, "because my DNA is all over that apartment."

"It's going to work," Amanda said. "After this, he's not going to want to call anyone. Not a private detective, not the police. And definitely not"—she grinned—"another housecleaner."

"What if he's complaining to Runnr right now?" I said. "I didn't exactly deliver five-star service. And it's his company."

"That's exactly why he won't complain," she said. "The system is supposed to sort out the bad apples on its own. If the app says you're a five-star runner, you're a five-star runner, end of story. And Branchik's the one who fought hardest against background checks." She frowned. "He might try to look into it on his own, though he's too dumb to get far. But believe me, by the end of today, his lousy maid service is going to be the last thing on his mind. He'll be on his hands and knees scrubbing the floors himself, getting rid of the evidence for us."

I snorted. "If he cleans anything in there, it'll be a first."

"You'll have made such a difference in his life. Brenna should send you a fruit basket."

"Who's that?"

But Amanda had already grabbed her laptop from the coffee table, attached it to my phone with a USB cable, and started typing. I leaned over her shoulder and saw that she was uploading a few of the choicest pictures to the comments section of a blog called *From Cali Girl to ATX Mommy*. The banner photo of the site showed a pregnancy test lying next to a Mason jar full of Texas wildflowers.

"Brenna Branchik," she said, still typing. "Duh. You saw her wedding photo."

"ATX Mommy?" I said. "She's—"

"Pregnant, yes," Amanda finished. "And very bored. Picking out furniture for the Lake Travis house doesn't take up nearly enough time to keep her busy. She spends her days at the local spa, getting expensive blowouts and taking yoga classes." Amanda was still concentrating on the pictures. "She's especially chatty after bikram. That's when she told me about her blog."

"You *spoke* with her?" I felt a thread of alarm. "What did you do, pretend to be her friend?"

"Anyone can go to a yoga class," Amanda said lightly. "It's not like I lied to her. Most people are so eager to talk about themselves, they'll tell you what you need to know before you ask. Especially someone as lonely as Brenna Branchik." She smiled. "Her blog has eleven followers so far."

"And you're one of them." It made me deeply uneasy. I read what

Amanda was typing under the photos, username Homewrecker: *Ur hubby showed me his so I showed him mine.* "A little on the nose, don't you think?"

"Don't worry, I use a dummy IP," she said blithely. "Anyway, I'm sure Brenna knows all about Doug's little habit. She's gone deep with the herbal supplements and healing gemstones. Self-medicating."

"If she already knows about him, then why are we—going nuclear?" I waved at the screen. And more to the point, why hadn't Amanda told me this part of the plan?

"Brenna's very concerned about her baby's future." She finished typing with a flourish. "That's where we're going to be able to apply the most pressure."

"Pressure? We're not going to hurt her, are we?"

"No, Dana." She sighed impatiently and turned away from the screen toward me for the first time. "There wouldn't be any point. Men are like dogs—they misbehave, you roll up a newspaper and bop their noses. It's all they understand, all they respond to. But women learn to live with violence early on. They spend their whole lives learning how *not* to respond. You of all people should know that." I flinched. "So getting at a woman like Brenna isn't as simple as a tap on the nose. You have to find something she cares about."

"But—she didn't do anything!"

"Exactly." She raised her hands in the air, exasperated. "She doesn't do anything. She knows her husband is out there harassing women. You look at her face, you know she knows. But she doesn't care whose life he ruins. She doesn't divorce him, she doesn't expose him. She just goes to the spa and gets an extra hour of vaginal-rejuvenation therapy." She saw my face and rolled her eyes. "Okay, okay, calm down. Yes, we're going to use her to get to her husband. But we won't hurt a hair on her blowout, I promise. Much less her fetus."

"How are we going to use her?"

"Well, the first thing is to make sure she freaks out, good and hard," Amanda explained, pushing a scraggly lock of hair out of her face. "She'll be getting out of spin class right around now, and she'll want to blog about it. When she sees this, she'll flip out and start texting him ultimatums. He'll check the IP address, which I set up with a pretty easy-to-spot dummy that redirects to a *second* dummy—one that'll point straight to St. Catherine's."

I just looked at her.

"St. Catherine's, aka the Exeter of Westlake, aka the most exclusive K-through-twelve private school in Austin?" She smiled gleefully. "Brenna Branchik already has her unborn sweetheart on the waiting list. The dummy IP belongs to the girls' dormitory. Where the boarders live. All of whom are underage."

I was catching her drift. And starting to smile, despite myself.

"So now Branchik's got a real live Catholic schoolgirl sending kiddie porn to his wife from inside the sacred walls where his own daughter is expected to matriculate. And if Brenna finds *that* out"—she smirked—"let's just say he'll do anything to make this go away. Promise her the moon and stars. We'll be doing her a favor, in a way."

"Surely he would know if he was sexting teens."

"How could he be sure? Guys like him cast a wide net on Tinder and Snapchat. How about if one of his swipe-rights just happened to be a sweet seventeen-year-old—or, better yet, a fourteen-year-old—and she's eager to reciprocate?"

"I do *not* look fourteen," I said indignantly, my concern for Brenna Branchik already fading.

She shrugged. "Kids grow up fast these days."

One thing still bothered me. "If all that matters is the IP address, why couldn't we just send her the dick pics you already have?"

"I'm pretty sure he'd recognize those, since they were the subject of a formal complaint." She gestured toward the screen. "Anyway, this is so much better, don't you think? The wedding picture! This is definitive proof you were in his apartment. *Recently.* He'll have to figure out something to say about that."

So would I, if anyone found out. But the exhilaration of being in Branchik's apartment, crossing the line — the thrill of the sultry, faceless pictures — and even the pleasant terror of nearly getting caught hadn't worn off completely.

Amanda continued to crow. "Plus, he knows you can get in any time you want. You got him once. You can get him again. I'm not naive enough to think he's going to stop sending dick pics altogether. But I want him to be very, very scared every time he does it. I want him to fear his own desires."

8

The week leading up to the finals night of the Funniest Person in Austin contest was relatively calm. I'd been too wrapped up in the Branchik strike to pay much attention to the rest of the semis but was happy to see that Kim had made it. Fash had too, unsurprisingly.

I knew I should be stressed-out, if only because I was going to deliver the same set for the third time in the competition. Plenty of comics did it, but there was something discouraging about parading the same five minutes' worth of material past the judges—especially when one of them was Cynthia Omari. *The Bestie Cast* had five hundred thousand Twitter followers and regularly featured interviews with comics who would otherwise have been stuck playing bit parts with incomprehensible accents in second-rate Hollywood comedies; the podcast had even launched some of their careers. I wished I could show Omari something more exciting than my usual set. But I was still blocked for new material, and there was no point in trying to sharpen up jokes for the finals that I hadn't even thought were good enough for the preliminaries.

Yet I felt surprisingly mellow, and I knew it had to be because of the Branchik strike. Once the roller coaster of adrenaline and exhaustion had run its course, I'd woken up feeling refreshed, as if I had gone to the gym and then eaten a huge but healthy meal.

At first I'd waited excitedly for blowback, though Amanda had deleted my Runnr account instantly, scrubbing the metadata so that no trace of me remained. She'd also convinced me that there was no way Branchik could see into her apartment from his, a fact I'd confirmed for myself when I was there but that did little to ease the feeling of exposure when we sat outside on the balcony drinking glasses of wine.

But within a few days, Branchik had vacated the apartment entirely, piling some boxes into a U-Haul and driving away.

"Looks like someone's going to live in the hills where wifey can keep an eye on him," Amanda said with satisfaction. "I think we can rest assured she'll put a damper on his photography habits for a while."

It did feel good to see him go—and not just because it made the balcony a more comfortable place to hang out. As when Neely had gone back to L.A., there was a palpable sense of having driven someone off our turf. I liked the feeling of taking up space. I wondered once again whether Amanda had deliberately found an apartment close to Branchik, but even if she had, it didn't seem as outlandish a move as it had before. After all, why should he be able to go where he pleased while she had to work at avoiding him? She had come to Austin and staked her claim, and the fact that he was already there didn't make a difference. That was living, not just surviving.

I'd felt the thrill myself when I donned the Betty wig, infiltrated Branchik's apartment, and rubbed my scent all over it like a bitch in heat, claiming it for my own. I remembered what Ruby had said about the wigs changing her personality, the "mean" wig she wouldn't wear anymore. I'd thought it was just Ruby being Ruby, but wasn't that just what the Betty wig had done for me—changed me into a different person? Or at least given me permission to let out a side of my personality I'd never acknowledged before?

One evening that week, after I came home from Amanda's place a little drunk, I tried on the Betty wig before I went to bed, just to see what she looked like in the mirror. When she wasn't naked, Betty was an ordinary girl with platinum-blond hair—petite and tan and not exactly dripping with class, but laid-back. She looked uncomplicated, fun, and none too intelligent. Nonthreatening. A girl who didn't have to work extra hard to smile, who never had to worry about people thinking she was prickly if she was quiet, aggressive if she was loud. She could look at her phone in the line at Starbucks and the barista would assume she was checking Instagram, not being rude. She could yell as much as she wanted on game day, even get drunk and throw a beer can in the street, and people would just think a white girl had had too much to drink, and wasn't that kind of cute? The type of bouncy, fluffy girl that men treated like a pet, picked up and carried around over their shoulders for a joke, egged on when she was drunk with the words *Go get 'em, tiger.*

I reminded myself to put the wig in my purse so I'd remember to take it to work on my next shift. I'd promised Ruby I would return it to her, but for some reason I kept forgetting. The thought of losing the wig made me ever so slightly depressed, as if I were giving back some of the space I had won. I began to wonder whether there would be a next time for Amanda and me. Her list was long, she'd said. Mine was too.

"Go get 'em, tiger," I told Betty.

The night of the finals, I stood in the Bat City bar watching Kim on the monitor.

"Destroy everything in your path," I'd told her with a quick hug before she walked out, and she was doing a bang-up job, her sleepy drawl more animated than usual. The audience was following her down every nook and cranny of her decidedly blue set and went wild during her deadpan imitation of a male orgasm.

I smelled stale cigarette smoke and turned to see Fash, who was up next, standing beside me. He, too, was watching the monitor.

"Take a good look," I said. "That's who you have to beat tonight."

"More like beat off to," Fash said with a deliberate leer.

I made a gagging noise. "You think you could save that thought for private time?"

"Sorry, didn't see you there." He grinned under his mustache and turned toward me. "You're so short."

"And you're so full of shit," I said. "But unfortunately I can still hear you."

"Feisty!" he said, and I rolled my eyes. "Jealous? Don't worry, I can beat both of you at once." He sucked his teeth. "I promise you'll like it."

But now the audience was clapping and Kim was exiting the stage, which meant Fash was up. I noticed a greenish tint to his face under the red bar lights and smiled widely at him. "As long as we're having fun up there, that's all that matters, right?" As he started down the hall toward the stage, Kim came out through the swinging door on the other side. I high-fived her, but we watched Fash on the monitor with a certain grimness. He was on tonight, undeniably. And I was up next.

Feeling a little green myself, I ducked into the women's bathroom to touch up my makeup. Under the fluorescent lights, I caught a gleam of blond peeking out from my purse, like the telltale lock of hair sticking out of a trash can on an episode of *Law and Order: SVU*. I'd managed to lug the wig to work and back several times now without giving it to Ruby, and here it was, throwing little tendrils over the side of my bag like an octopus trying to escape a tank.

I fished out my makeup bag and reached for the zipper pull to close my purse. But I couldn't do it. I had the absurd thought that the wig was alive and needed to breathe. I pulled it from my bag and shook it out. The blond shimmered in front of the mirror. I smoothed it against my chest, then reached for the bobby pins that were collected in the inner pocket of my purse. I pinned the elastic cap in place and shook the plastic hair down over my shoulders the way I'd done in the mirror at home. In natural lighting, it looked even more fake, but then, it didn't need to look real; onstage, everything is fake, whether it's real or not.

I emerged from the bathroom in the Betty wig, and Kim didn't even turn her head when I passed; I was evidently unrecognizable. Betty's bouncy strut propelled me down the hallway, where I nodded at the photos of past winners on the wall, and toward the banquet room, whose back half had been unroped for the finals. The swinging door gave, and I threaded my way through a packed house toward the stage as the emcee reeled off my introduction. Stepping onstage, I faced the largest crowd I'd ever seen.

My hand flew up to the wig. What on earth was I doing? I couldn't do my Amarillo opening with this blond opossum stuck to my head, but I had prepared nothing else. I cleared my throat and opened my mouth.

"I'm Betty," I said in a girlish soprano. "I'm so excited to be here." I breathed slowly and loudly into the mic, my eyes stretched wide and wild. "I have to tell you about this great guy I just punched in the face."

There was a confused pause and then one sharp laugh from the audience.

"I know what you're thinking. Every time Betty punches a new guy, she always thinks he's *the One*. But what can I say?" I paused and drew my breath in through my teeth slowly, making a liquid sucking sound into the microphone. "There was a real connection."

The audience had fallen silent, understanding at last that something strange and uncomfortable was happening onstage. Ordinarily this type of reaction would have prompted me to amplify my voice, exaggerate my gestures to fill space, and perhaps cut the rest of the jokes in the bit. But this wasn't a bit. This was a story. And I knew I wasn't going to cut anything. Once Betty opened her mouth, she wouldn't close it until she had said every word she wanted to say. The audience knew it too. I heard the shifting of weight in chairs, felt the strain of people wanting to get up and leave, but it only made me want to draw things out more. I kept my eyes wide and let the silence gather into a large, empty pool. The oxygen felt thin, but I let it continue, saucer-eyed. Slowly, keeping my gaze fixed on the audience, I turned my head to the right and held the pose for ten long, silent seconds.

A man in the front row let out an explosive laugh. I stayed rigid, my eyeballs bulging with the strain of looking as far left as I could while my head lolled to the right. Another man chuckled, then a few women. The mood broke. I relaxed my eyes without blinking them, flickered my eyelids slightly, just enough to telegraph my control over the situation. A wave of relief swept the crowd. A few people even clapped.

"Do you want to hear about it?" I said, keeping my face as motionless as possible.

Cheers and applause were my answer.

What followed wasn't really standup, at least not in any way I'd ever performed it. It was some kind of performance art. It wasn't coming from me; it was happening to me. My face felt like a mask, and I had no idea what I was going to say next. The words that came out of the mask, accompanied by grotesque contortions, didn't require effort or forethought. Betty was unsettling and weird, and I was as transfixed by her as the audience was. Blond and pretty and ugly, all at the same time, she was pure, terrifying id, amoral and animalistic, a stunted half human in a state of nature. She made earrings out of real ears. She drank out of the toilet. She thought a manicure was a cure for men, and a pedicure was an abortion. She was alternately petulant and brash, vulgar and cute, Baby Jane and the Bad Seed rolled into one.

When the blue light came on to signal one more minute in the set, I pulled her story back around to the part about punching the guy, and it felt like tugging a large, mean dog to heel. As long as she had an audience, Betty would want to keep talking and talking. It took all the discipline I'd acquired as a performer to keep the last minute building in a direction, but finally, she came to a line I recognized immediately as her catch phrase, delivered with a bit of what they call in improv "space work"; holding an invisible kitchen knife in one hand, I mimed grabbing something at crotch level with the other. "So I took matters into my own hands!"

The audience burst into shouts and applause, and I pulled the wig off my head, said, "Thank you," into the mic, and walked offstage, relieved to be me again.

I'd always hated nastiness for the sake of nastiness. Dirtbag characters, insult comics, and even excessive brutality toward hecklers made me itch. I would have hated Betty's material on paper. But it didn't really matter. When you kill, you kill. And Betty killed.

"Second runner-up goes to . . . Kim Rinski!"

To my left, Kim gave a yelp and jumped up and down. I squeezed her hand and whacked her on the back as she stepped out of the line of comics and clopped up the steps in her chunky heels to accept her medal and five-hundred-dollar check.

I held my breath. I was definitely making the top three. And now I knew I wasn't third.

Behind the emcee, a woman in heels and a short sequined dress, probably some put-upon Bat City employee hoping for her own break in comedy, held the winner's red robe and crown aloft. From where I stood at the base of the stage, huddled shoulder to shoulder in the line of twelve comics who'd performed that night, I could see one of her high heels stepping on the hem of the robe. I realized I was feeling guilty in advance for what would happen when the winner was announced, as if it would be my fault if she pulled the robe out from under her own feet and gave the audience an eye-level peek into her gynecological mysteries.

"Stay onstage, Kim, right there," the emcee said, gesturing her to one side. "Next up is the second-funniest person in Austin, our first runner-up, and I think you'll agree with me that it's well deserved this year . . . *Dana Diaz!*"

I launched myself up the steps to the stage in a daze, made my way to the microphone, and let the emcee hang the medal around my neck, where it immediately slithered into my cleavage. Digging it out, I almost forgot to accept the check that went with it and had to be gestured back toward the emcee.

"Don't forget your prize money, Dana! It's great to see the ladies doing so well this year, isn't it? And now, the moment you've all been waiting for . . ."

Numb with disappointment, I didn't need to listen to the rest. I stared at the check in my hand. Fifteen hundred dollars. As the emcee announced the inevitable winner and the crowd went wild, I occupied myself with catching the robe bearer's eye and pointing toward her high heels until she caught my drift, looked down, and stepped off the hem. When she lifted her arms to drape the Funniest Person in Austin robe over Fash's back, she would not become a joke. At least I could control that.

But offstage, the reality that I had just won second place my first time in the competition began to dawn on me. Several people pressed cards into my hand, saying, "Do you have an agent?" and "Do you have a manager?" I smiled dumbly and thanked them all and then observed the crowd parting before a tall black woman, her braids gathered in a low, thick bundle, her face radiating the same kind of surreal quality of celebrity Aaron Neely's had. She was smiling broadly as she leaned over and grasped my hand.

"Hi, Dana, I'm Cynthia Omari," she said unnecessarily. "You were great up there." She continued talking over my stammered thanks. "You know what, Dana, we're always looking for guests on *The Bestie Cast*. I'll have to hook you up with my producer Larry to get you booked, but I'd love to have you sometime."

"I—I love *The Bestie Cast*" was all I could manage.

"You're sweet!" she exclaimed, looking around us at the rapidly emptying banquet tables. "This is so much fun, I don't know whether to send Aaron a get-well-soon card or a thank-you note." She leaned over and said in my ear, "By the way, if it was up to me, you'd have won first place. But I'm so glad I got to meet you, at least."

"Me too," I said stupidly. "I mean, I'm glad to meet you too."

Then, wonder of wonders, she handed me, not her card, but her phone, with a new-contact screen open, and told me to enter my number and e-mail address. When I'd given it back to her she said, "Good. We'll get you on the podcast soon. Now go celebrate!" and whirled away, quickly becoming obscured by the mob of people around Fash.

Kim walked up, grinning wildly, her cheeks streaked with mascara tears that made her look more like Courtney Love than ever. "Victory party at Chacha's, everyone's coming, you in?" she said, and given Cynthia's parting exhortation, I didn't feel like I could say no.

It was always Christmas at Chacha's, a dive bar a few blocks from Bat City festooned year-round with silvery tinsel, paper bells, and strands of blinking vintage lights. Sitting in the disorienting glow, sipping drink after drink purchased by well-wishers and hangers-on who'd followed us to the bar, I started getting fuzzy fast. Fash held court by the Christmas tree in the corner, his bulbous gold crown and fake-fur-trimmed red robe giving him the look of one of those old-world Santa figurines advertised in *Parade* magazine around the holidays. Surrounded by friends and the finalists who cared about looking like good sports, he brandished his scepter, a glitter-filled Toy Joy baton with an Austin-themed snow globe duct-taped to the top, swirling with tiny black bats instead of snow. A flash went off; a reporter from the *Chronicle* had also followed us over from the club, perhaps hoping for an alcohol-fueled feature story to break the monotony of the same postcompetition write-up he had to do every year.

Ruby and Becca had surprised me by showing up briefly at the bar to represent the Laurel's crew. Nobody at work had ever come to one of my shows before. Ruby looked exultant in her forest-green wasp-waisted frock, turning every once in a while to someone nearby to say, "That was my wig up there."

"I knew that blond one was lucky," she said, stirring an unseasonal mug of hot cocoa with a peppermint stick. In fact, she'd lent me the Betty wig grudgingly, with a set of instructions for its care that I had so far completely ignored, but I gathered that she felt well compensated in reflected glory. Through the descending fog of alcohol, I thanked her profusely.

"I can't believe you came," I said, sincerely moved.

"Of course! I wouldn't miss my wig's debut. You hang on to it for as long as you want. Just thank me when you win an Oscar with it."

"I think Travolta has Best Wig on lock, but thanks anyway," I said, and was rewarded with a sympathetic nod. "Anyway, now you know what I'm working on all the time in that notebook."

"Oh, I know. I read it whenever you go to the bathroom." My smile went rigid on my face as I remembered all the notes about Ruby I'd jotted down, but she rattled on. "Don't bother saying goodbye to Becca, she won't hear you. Henry's been blowing up her phone all night demanding to know who she's really with. Did you look?" She raised her eyebrows meaningfully and gestured toward her upper arms, and I noticed that Becca was wearing a sleeveless shirt for once.

"I don't see any—" I said, and she cut me off.

"Makeup," she said behind her hand. "Spray tan." She grabbed Becca, who was hunched over her phone, oblivious, and moved off toward the door.

After I'd waved goodbye, I found myself stranded between Fash's adoring mob and Kim's friends from her bartending job. With Ruby and Becca gone, I suddenly felt the absence of friends who'd come just to see me. I finished my drink more quickly than I intended to, bought another, and, with no one to talk to, downed it fast. I half expected Amanda to show up, the way she had for the first round of the competition, but since the swap, she'd insisted it was a good idea for us to keep away from each other, at least in public. It was obviously the right thing to do, but the irony it created felt especially acute now: the one person who was willing to do the most for me and for whom I'd done the most could not be seen in my company. I was beginning to depend on Amanda, but when she wasn't with me, she felt disconcertingly like an imaginary friend.

The reporter, perhaps seeing that I was alone, seized his moment to pounce. "Dana, you placed second your very first year in the competition. What do you think won it for you?"

"It's an honor even to compete," I said, irritated to find myself slurring my words. "Austin's got a great comedy scene. Everyone did really great out there tonight."

"I saw your semifinals performance," the reporter said. "Your material tonight was different and very provocative. Is it risky to debut new material in the finals?"

As I readied another canned response, he raised his camera and started snapping pictures. The flash made me dizzy, and as I gesticulated with my drink, I got the impression he wasn't really listening to my answers.

"And what do you think about another white male comic taking home the big prize?" he said between clicks. "Is it time for a change in Austin?"

Still safe behind his camera, the rat bastard, and clicking away. I had just said, with spiteful tact, "Austin is changing, all right," when Fash sidled up to me, the flash having finally lured him from his throne to see who could be stealing his press.

"Why don't you ask him yourself?" I said. "What do you think, Fash? Is it time for someone other than a white dude to win Funniest Person?"

"What's important is that we're all having fun up there," he said, wrapping an arm around my shoulder and squeezing.

"How about a picture with the runners-up?" the reporter said. "Stay right there." He took a few steps over to Kim's table.

Fash stayed glued to my shoulder. "Kim! Kim!" He leaned over me to shout and got so close I could smell his mustache oil. His eyes were watering sentimentally, I noted with distaste. As I shrank away, he mumbled sorrowfully, "You don't like me, Dana. Nobody really likes me."

Conscious of the scene we were making in the middle of the bar, I said, "Everybody likes you, Fash. That's why you won."

"Yeah, they do, don't they?" He brightened up momentarily, but soon darkened again, shaking his head. "But now that I won, they're all going to hate me." To my horror, the rims of his eyes grew even redder, and I found my eyes prickling sympathetically from sheer proximity. "I want you to like me, Dana. Why don't you like me?"

Just then, the photographer returned with Kim. At the sight of the camera, Fash snapped his head up as if it were attached to marionette strings, his maudlin mood disappearing so completely I found myself doubting whether I had seen it at all. "Kim! Third place!" he shouted. "Last year I got third. That means you're going to win next year."

"So you've said," Kim said. "Several times."

"Last year I was third and look at me now!"

"Congratulations, Fash." Kim sighed and positioned herself to my right, putting her arm around my shoulders. "Take the picture?" she pleaded with the photographer.

"Winner in the middle!" Fash shouted. "King of comedy in the middle!"

"I'll get a few different shots," the reporter said diplomatically. The bulb flashed a few times, and then he tapped Kim's shoulder, gently shepherding her over to Fash's left side. She grimaced visibly but submitted, and Fash, now between us, wrapped his other arm around her shoulders. Her own arms hung limply at her sides. "That's good, that's good," the reporter said, backing away with his camera in front of his face. "Hold it."

"It's good to be king," Fash said, squeezing us to him roughly. He moved his hand from my shoulder to my back a few times, then quickly wriggled his hand along the band of my bra to my armpit and dug his fingers into the side of my breast. I went stiff.

"Hold it, hold it," the reporter was saying. "Smile, everyone!"

I forced a rictus onto my face, Fash's fingers still maintaining their death grip on my side-boob. The flash went off five or six times, the fingertips wiggling up and down slightly.

"That's enough," Kim said abruptly, and she pulled away. "I gotta pee."

I broke free of his other arm, but he didn't seem to notice. "Hey, Kim, wait!" Fash called after her, the desolate look flashing across his face again for just a moment. I started to follow her to the bathroom, but Fash stayed glued to the reporter. As I walked away, I heard him say, "Third place kind of sucks, to be honest," and I knew that the look had disappeared again as quickly as it had come.

In the bathroom, Kim was leaning over the sink, splashing water on her face. When she looked up and saw me in the mirror, she said, "Fash is so disgusting."

"I take it he did the boob thing with you too?" I said.

"It's pathetic," she said, yanking a handful of rough paper towels from the dispenser and rubbing them all over her face. "I mean, you can't really be surprised," she said between swipes. "He's been pulling that shit since he first came to Austin."

"When was that?"

"Oh, I don't know, a couple years after me." She tossed the soggy paper towels in the trash. "We took level one together, if you can believe it."

Among comedy performers, "level one" means one thing. "Improv? That doesn't seem like your scene."

"I was really into it for a while." She was rummaging through her purse for something. "Anyway, you know how it is. People are so nice in improv—it's all that *yes-and* crap—and when Fash came around, everybody just adored him, you know? And I thought since people were acting like they knew him, they, you know, *knew* him. Like, vouched for him. So I was nice too. Aha!" She found the eyeliner pencil she was looking for and pulled off its cap triumphantly.

"What do you mean, nice?"

Kim was leaning forward, pulling at her lower lash line and reapplying the black crayon liberally under her eyes. "I mean, apparently he did it to several women in the scene. It wasn't just me."

"It?" The stuffy bathroom was making me feel a little dizzy. I leaned against a stall and felt the whole structure shudder under me.

"You know. You're hanging out after a show with a bunch of people at his place, and then everybody else leaves. And he keeps saying, 'Hey, you can crash here.' And you know it's stupid, and you just want to go home, but you're so drunk. And cab service sucks here." She finished one eye and moved to the other. "He keeps insisting that you can take the bed and he'll take the couch *because he's such a fucking gentleman,* and you're finally just too tired to argue. And then you wake up and he's next to you under the covers . . ." She snapped the cap back on abruptly and mimed an obscene gesture with her hips.

"Oh my God. Really?" For a moment I smelled tequila, felt the brutish, awful weight on top of me, saw the black outline against glowing TV static. Then I pushed it out of my mind. "What did you do?"

"I mean, don't get it twisted. He was pretty easy to fight off. Like I said, pathetic." She dropped the eyeliner back in her purse. "He started crying like a baby." Fluttering her eyelashes up and down in the mirror, she flicked a few stray dots of eyeliner off her cheeks. "Eventually someone caught on and word got around, and he got banned from a couple of theaters. That's why he doesn't do improv anymore."

"Neither do you," I pointed out.

"I guess I wasn't that into it after all," she said in a way that signaled the conversation was over. She gestured toward the stalls. "Did you have to go?"

"Yeah. Will you wait for me?"

"Yeah, bitch. Go."

I didn't have to, but I was suddenly overwhelmed with the urge to get in touch with Amanda and didn't want to text her in front of Kim. The feeling had been growing all night, a kind of restless itch, scratched temporarily by my set in character as Betty but now back with a vengeance. Gradually, over the course of the night, I had come to understand what—who—was causing it.

I closed the stall door behind me and had already pulled out my phone when Kim said, from the other side of the stall door, "Dana?"

"Yeah?" I stopped texting.

"You're, like, good friends with Jason Murphy, right?"

It was so unexpected that I just said, "Yeah." In a hurry, before I could think too hard about whether it was still true or not.

"I mean, you were roommates in L.A.?"

"Yeah."

Her voice sounded funny, but since I couldn't see her face, I couldn't tell exactly what kind of funny. "No hard feelings, right?" Before I could respond, she said, "I thought for a while when you came back, maybe you had something against me? I mean, I don't know what he would have said—"

"He didn't say anything about you," I said truthfully, suddenly wondering why I'd never realized Jason and Kim had gone out. Jason had leveled up his dating game in Austin, and when I joined him I was often intimidated by how improbably blond and beautiful his girlfriends were. But they never lasted long. They'd always had to reckon with me, the best friend who'd known him longer than they had. Eventually Katie or Jenna or Bella or Rose would exit stage left, and I would still be in the spotlight with Jason. I'd been only dimly aware of Kim's presence in Austin five years ago—she was, as she said, mostly doing improv back then—but it didn't particularly surprise me that she'd been one of the parade of skinny, button-nosed blondes in the background.

"Oh. Well, that's good," Kim said. I realized I had been silent for a while. "I mean, it was a long time ago."

"No hard feelings," I said. "None at all." I flushed the john for appearance's sake and opened the stall door. She was leaning against the opposite wall. "I'm glad we're friends now."

"Yeah, me too," she said. "One of us should really have won first place tonight. On the bright side, maybe Fash will move to L.A. and get hit by a cab."

"Or eaten by a shark," I said. "I hear they have those there." When we were out of the bathroom, I realized I'd been too distracted by Kim's questions about Jason to finish my text to Amanda. "I think I'm taking off," I said with only a quick glance at my phone.

But Kim noticed. "Secret boyfriend?"

For the second time, I was taken aback. "No!"

"You're so mysterious these days." She winked. "I thought maybe you were texting someone in the stall just now."

"I was just looking at the time," I said lamely. "I didn't realize how late it was. I have to work early."

"Gotcha." She looked amused, and I dropped my phone in my purse and gave her a hug.

"Congrats again."

"You too. I like your new bit," she said gruffly. "Drive safe, you."

I nodded. I'd thought better of texting my next name to Amanda —too risky—and instead asked her if I could come over. I spent the car ride home imagining us sipping wine on the balcony and discussing how to rid the Austin scene of the scourge that was Fash.

9

Hmmm, Fash Banner. Tricky."

"What's tricky about it?" I was stalking back and forth by Amanda's giant windows, daring someone to see me. I knew I wasn't thinking clearly, but I didn't want to lose momentum. What Kim had told me in the bathroom about Fash had been burning a hole in my brain.

Amanda was sitting cross-legged on the sofa, laptop open, sipping her habitual glass of red wine. "Well, since he just won, he's fairly high-profile right now—"

"Higher-profile than Aaron Neely?" I said in disbelief.

"No, no, of course not." Amanda looked mildly irritated. "But far more directly connected to *you*. Nobody knew about your meeting with Neely."

"Just Jason," I said. "But what about Branchik?"

"People at Runnr know about my connection to Branchik, but they don't know I'm anywhere near him. *He* doesn't know I'm anywhere near him." She paused, frowning thoughtfully. "I'm not saying we can't do it. But it's going to require more care. A different approach, maybe."

"Can't you just break in and smash his record collection or something?"

"Look, you want him gone," she said, and I nodded. "But the problem is, he's just won five thousand dollars in a contest, plus offers of management. Opportunities." I winced. "I don't think losing a few hard-to-find LPs is going to set him back much. And anyway, you don't just want him to leave, right? Because he's probably going to do that anyway. He'll go to New York or Los Angeles, and he'll succeed —if anything, he'll have a whole new group of people who don't know what a predator he is. He will have been rewarded for his behavior, not punished."

I could see the wheels turning, but I felt like this wasn't the time for equivocating. "Okay, well. I don't think it's going to be easy to catch Fash in the act. And blackmail is out; as far as I know, he doesn't have a girlfriend or anyone who'd really care if they found out." It was one of the things about him that was easy to pity, if you weren't careful. Until you heard him onstage using his loneliness as an excuse to justify sexualizing the women around him and, as I'd now experienced, groping them. "And anyway, I don't think he's still doing it, at least not the worst of it."

"You mean the assaults?" She narrowed her eyes. "Didn't your friend Kim say that happened just after he moved to Austin, four or five years ago?"

I nodded. "Yeah. He's already been frozen out of the improv scene for that stuff." Reluctantly, I allowed myself to consider a possibility I'd been pushing to the back of my mind since last night. "Maybe he's learned his lesson."

Amanda scratched her nose. "That guy? Not likely. Oh, I bet he hasn't actually crawled into bed with any passed-out girls in a while. I would guess he acts out more in a new environment, when he's insecure or stressed-out. Which, by the way, he will be in L.A. Success can be just as stressful as failure." She chewed her lip, absent-mindedly tugging on a curl. "I wonder if he has a clinical diagnosis."

"While you're wondering, he's probably packing up his car and looking for a subletter," I lamented. Then I snapped my fingers. "That's it! You could show up to see his apartment, pretend you want to sublease, and then . . . I don't know . . ."

"Relax, Dana," Amanda said. "I've already got a few ideas. I just need to do some research, that's all. This one is not going to be quite as fast, but I promise it'll happen." She looked at me. "Have I ever let you down?"

I stopped in my tracks and shook my head. Amanda might act slightly nuts, but she had her own way of doing things. She was secretive, sometimes excessively so, and relished her conspiracy theories. It was as if, having rejected the Silicon Valley world so thoroughly, she had burned its mentality deeper into her psyche. All the same, I trusted her absolutely—if not to tell me everything, then at least never to lie. She maintained a kind of scrupulous adherence to the way things were that felt brave, admirable. And in such a short time, she'd opened my eyes. Was she really paranoid, or was I naive? After all, I'd been so quick to assume the Neely episode was an isolated incident, just a nasty one-off. Amanda, with her statistically inclined mind, had immediately intuited that it was a pattern and, moreover, she'd known just how to capture hard proof. That revelation had already changed how I took in new information. Kim's story about Fash —if she had told me that same story just a couple of weeks ago, might I have shrugged it off? She herself was quick to minimize it. I thought of Branchik's wife. Why were all of us so ready to lie to ourselves? Was the truth—that we were hemmed in on all sides by the Fashes and

Branchiks and Neelys of the world, that we let ourselves be herded out of some arenas and penned into others by their behavior—just too horrible to contemplate?

"You'll do it," I said. "I know you'll do it. I'm just—" I reached for words to describe my feeling of powerlessness, knowing that all around me these acts were unfolding. "Impatient."

"Well." She smiled like she had a present for me. "How would you like something to do while you wait?"

Amanda wasn't kidding when she said her list was long. She showed me her spreadsheet of men who'd harassed her on the internet, their online handles listed along with the names and addresses she'd found for some of them. They lived all over the world. There were three in Texas, including one in Houston and one in El Paso. RadioMacktive666 was just the lucky one who lived in Austin.

The bulk of the harassment had come almost two years ago, right after the news item in which she'd been anonymous but identifiable, and most people had forgotten her quickly. But a tenacious few had held on until the day she erased her online identity. She opened a file full of screencaps of comments and e-mails, all scrupulously saved with notes on the trolls who'd sent them. They were mostly rape threats embroidered with varying degrees of obscenity, but RadioMacktive666 had been particularly creative, sending horrific GIFs altered to look like the violent acts in them were happening to Amanda. I looked away from these quickly.

"What's the plan?" I said, disgusted.

"He's a Runnr user, naturally," she said. "He likes to pay people —preferably women—to get him Thai food, though sometimes he splashes out and orders one of those fifteen-dollar burgers with the fried egg on top. Username Carl M. I'm not giving you his real name, because the less you know, the less tempted you'll be to look him up online and give him a way to trace you. This guy's a lot smarter than Branchik. He could find you and dox you in a heartbeat."

I looked over her shoulder at a screen full of numbers. In the left-most column, there were six digits, then a space, then four digits. Dates and times. "Are those his runs?"

"Yeah." She grinned. "See if you can figure out the pattern."

It seemed self-explanatory. "Once a week?"

"Yeah, but what about these shifts in the pattern? These gaps here? Or here, where they come twice weekly for a while?"

I looked harder, tried to think in patterns, like Amanda. "It's the same day of the week for about three months at a time, then it changes." I pulled up the calendar on my phone and checked. "The most recent dates are Thursdays. And it looks like he did ten Sundays in a row last year . . . wait a minute." I looked at the times again. "Nineteen thirty, nineteen forty-five . . . that's right before eight o'clock. They're all TV shows." I started chortling. "And that one's got to be—"

"*Game of Thrones*," she finished. "The new season premieres Sunday."

"Sunday," I said. "That soon?"

"If we want to take advantage of a sure thing, yeah," she said casually. "There's no way he'll miss this. And he'll be hungry."

I tried to get used to the idea. "What am I going to do once I get there?"

"Malware," she said, holding up a flash drive. "This is a program I'm particularly proud of. The first thing it'll do is send screenshots of his most questionable online activities to everyone in his e-mail contact list, including his boss, his coworkers, and, I'm guessing, his mother." She smiled. "He's too savvy to open a link, but if you can upload this to his computer, we can do some serious damage."

"So I have to get all the way in?" I frowned. "Won't he be there?"

"It's definitely more dangerous," she said, fixing me with a level gaze. "I'm in charge of software, but you should bring some hardware."

I looked at her blankly.

"You're hardly a giant, Dana. Remember what almost happened last time. You're going to want some protection." She clicked on a tab and started scrolling through a website. "Think of it as a tool, nothing more."

I glanced at the screen and felt myself pale. Handguns, row after row, little oblique angles of destruction. "Good thing we live in Texas," she said. "This should be a piece of cake."

I looked for a joke but for once came up blank. Instead, I just said, "I can't." Amarillo was lousy with guns, but there were none in my house growing up, and I had been taught to stay as far away from them as possible. Jason's dad hunted with rifles, but that was different. And even that had frankly creeped me out. This was one line I just couldn't cross.

Amanda and I argued about self-defense for some time. In the end, I solved the problem by Googling *Runnr driver self-defense,* which turned up a harrowing array of stories from runners who'd been attacked on the job. As I skimmed articles with titles like "The Five Things That Could Save Your Life on a Bad Run" and "How to Tell If a Run Is a Trap," I realized Amanda's talk of the company endangering customers by not doing background checks on the runners had blinded me to the dangers the runners themselves faced. Just another peril of the gig economy. No wonder there were fewer female runners than male ones.

A few veteran runners suggested bringing a handgun on every run, but stun guns were by far the preferred mode of self-defense, since they were less likely to escalate tensions in a bad situation. Moreover, and this is what clinched it for Amanda, I could get my hands on one without registering it, leaving no traces to clean up afterward. Relieved, I agreed to procure a stun gun before Sunday's premiere and left Amanda's apartment feeling surreal. The last thing she said as I walked out the door was "Be sure to wear that awful wig. He likes blondes."

It was only after I was out on the sidewalk and headed toward my car that I remembered I had gone to Amanda's to talk about Fash and left with every intention of procuring a weapon.

I was still in bed the next morning when the call came.

"Hi, Dana. Larry Green here." I racked my brain for a Larry Green I knew, but before I could answer, he said, "Look, I know this is last-minute, but we had a guest drop out of the taping this morning. Cynthia threw your name out as a replacement."

Cynthia. Larry. I was talking to the producer of *The Bestie Cast*. "Wow," I said, finally catching up. "Thanks for calling, Larry. So when—"

"We'd want to get you on as soon as possible to get the podcast up at the usual time," he said. "We're already behind schedule. How's nowish?" I stammered out something affirmative. "Great, I'll call you back in fifteen. Be ready." He hung up without saying goodbye.

Three minutes later I was fully dressed and perched on the edge of my sofa with my cell phone in hand, not even daring to look at it lest I run the battery down from its 91 percent charge. It rang at five minutes after ten, and I answered on the first ring.

"Dana Diaz?" Larry asked, as if it were the first time we had spoken. He continued in a smooth, well-worn version of the gruff voice I'd heard a few minutes before. "This is Larry, producer for *The Bestie Cast*. We're so excited to have you on the show. I'm going to patch you through to Cyndi in just a second. You'll hear her talking for a few minutes before anyone can hear you, then she'll say hi, and then Bob's your uncle, as they say." He chuckled.

"Oh my God," I said before I could stop myself. "This is really happening."

"Relax," he said. And then added, with profound cruelty: "Just be funny."

And suddenly, I was hearing Cynthia's plummy, melodic voice on the line, midsentence: "With breakfast tacos! So, paradise on earth, right? I was recently down there judging the Funniest Person in Austin competition, a six-week-long, elimination-style battle of the local standups. That's how I met our next guest, Dana Diaz, who placed second in the competition with an act I can only describe as, well, intriguing. Dana, are you there?"

I spent a few agonizing seconds trying to figure out whether to call her Cynthia or Cyndi, but in the end all I could come up with was "Yes, hi."

"You're on *The Bestie Cast*," she said. In a voice of mock reproof, she added, "I need you to sound like my bestie, Dana."

"Oh, sorry." I laughed feebly. "Hey, girl, what's up?" It felt horrifyingly stiff, even after she answered me in kind. For the first few minutes, I could feel her trying to loosen me up—not that the effort showed in her voice—and I tried desperately to loosen. We chatted about our parents; I told a story about Amarillo that, without a roomful of people to laugh at it, sounded so flat I felt sure no one anywhere would ever laugh at it again. She gave me opening after opening for the kind of soft-serve autobiographical anecdotes I usually trimmed out of my sets, B-material that would give me some room to spread out and show my personality. But without the energy of an audience to feed off of, I could feel myself slipping off the thin, taut wire of funny, fumbling at the trapeze Cynthia kept tossing my way as I flailed over the void.

After a few minutes of this, even Cynthia's calm voice began to betray hints of irritation. "Tell me about Betty, a character you sometimes do in your sets."

"Betty came to me, kind of, kind of all at once," I stuttered. "I borrowed the wig from one of my coworkers—"

"Great, great." Cynthia cut me off before I could start rambling about my day job. "What if you got into character for a minute and just answered some questions as Betty? I definitely have a lot of things I'd like to ask her."

"Sure," I said, so eager to please I didn't quite understand what I had agreed to until it was too late.

"Okay, so my first question is: How'd you get so *basic,* Betty?"

One second. Two seconds. Three seconds. The excruciating sound of dead air ticked by as I ran with the phone into my bedroom, quickly located the wig on my dresser, and smashed it crookedly down on my head, ruffling it over my bangs. "Basic?" I said in Betty's high-pitched squeak, glancing at myself in the mirror. "I'm salt of the fucking earth, bitches."

Cynthia laughed, relieved. "Betty! So glad you could join us today. Just don't give Larry anything else to bleep, okay?"

I garbled out a long streak of curse words, one after the other, that devolved into croaking toward the end. "How's that?" Surrendering to Betty, I stopped trying to connect with Cynthia and started connecting with the invisible audience. Instinctively, I knew her listeners would love to hear their beloved podcast host needled—as long as it was by an imaginary character who would disappear at the end of the episode.

Cynthia rewarded my instincts with easy laughter. "That's great, Betty. You know, Larry's already had a rough night, this could break him. For a minute there, he was worried you weren't going to show."

"And miss *The Betty Cast?* No way."

"That's *The Bestie Cast.*"

"That's what I said." Betty could ride the corniest material with absolute confidence. If Dana's rule was *No blood in the water,* Betty's was *Pull out your tampon and get busy splashing.*

"Now tell me the truth, Betty. You're wearing the wig, aren't you? I heard you put it on. Listeners, we are dealing with a true artist here. Like Kaufman."

"I'm not coughing, I'm just out of breath from running," I quipped facilely. "And if we're talking about wigs, I have a good story about Cynthia's—"

"Do not even go there!" Cynthia faux-warned. "You know what, Betty? You are really lacking in social graces."

"That's what my psychiatrist said, only he said it with more words. Let's see, how many words is *antisocial personality disorder with homicidal tendencies?*" I pretended to count but gave up at three. "Well, anyway, it's a lot, but back then it was easier for him to talk. Because he had lips. And a tongue."

"What happened?"

I settled onto my sofa, stretched out my legs, and held the phone in place with my shoulder while I picked at my nails. "I'm so glad you asked, Cynthia. It all started the other day when I got my dog Blister certified as a therapy animal so I could sneak into retirement-home kitchens and soak in the creamed-corn vats." I snorted indignantly. "Who knew biting even one senior gets you kicked out of those places?"

"Wait a minute," asked Cynthia, playing the straight man. "Why would you soak in a vat of creamed corn?"

"How do you think old people get such soft, smooshy skin?" I said. "I can tell you, though, it doesn't taste as good as it looks, so don't bother."

"Creamed corn?"

"Old-people skin."

"It was you biting the seniors?" she said in disbelief. "What about Blister?"

"Blister's been dead six years," I said. "Turns out that's another thing that's against the rules. Now shut up and listen, bitches, Betty's talking."

For the next hour, as Betty rambled and Cynthia pretended shock, I lived in a double world. The apartment all around me seemed to have gone semitransparent; I could see through it to a world beyond that smelled like chlorinated pools and salt water and leather sandals and success. Finally, when I'd maneuvered Betty into the psychiatrist's office and supplied her with an arsenal of weapons straight out of an old Warner Brothers cartoon, Betty yelped her punch line—"So I took matters into my own hands!"—and she was out.

Cynthia thanked me for the worst hour of her life, which I recognized as a compliment. "You've got to come out to L.A., Dana. Any plans to?"

"Definitely, definitely," I said. My fifteen hundred dollars from the competition would pay for at least a short trip. The swimming pools seemed so close, I could almost dive into one. "Thanks for having me on *The Bestie Cast*, Cynthia."

"It was *The Betty Cast* today. And thanks for being my bestie for an hour. See you!"

And then she was gone, and Larry the producer was back on the line, saying, "Thanks so much, Dana. You did great. The episode airs tonight, and then it's available on the website immediately afterward, so just keep an eye out on social media."

As I thanked him once more, the line went dead, and with it, my connection to the world beyond my apartment walls. My furniture, the television, everything went opaque again. Even the daylight coming through the drawn curtains looked dingy. In the new silence, the air conditioner rattled on and started to whir.

It was still too early to go to work. Instead, I got out the stack of business cards I'd been handed at the finals and sat down at my laptop. It was time to send out some follow-up e-mails with a link to the *Bestie Cast* website in the signature. If I was going to make an L.A. trip sometime soon, I would need representation.

That night the episode came and went while I was wrapping up my shift at Laurel's, and when I went to bed, it had been shared on Twitter only a few times. I woke up unprepared for the deluge of agent and manager e-mails that had hit my inbox overnight. Overwhelmed, I spent the morning on the phone fielding offers of representation, allowing a handful of agents to believe I was on the point of moving to Los Angeles. The feeling of being wanted was too intoxicating for me to bother with details. My contest winnings wouldn't get me far, but maybe they would at least give me time to start looking for a day job out there.

Which reminded me: I was late for my shift. As I wound through the midday traffic on the east-side streets, I thought about day jobs, the ultimate costume for comics, our way of pretending to be normal people just like everyone else. We seldom allowed ourselves to dream of life without one, but we'd stick with each minimum-wage or tip-sharing job for a year or two at most. Then we'd get restless, decide our day jobs were holding us back, and quit, announcing on social media we were making more time for art, for ambition, in our lives. Then, suddenly, one day, we'd reappear in an apron on the other side of town, and you'd know, once more, we hadn't made it.

Having spent the past twenty-four hours in the oasis of daydreams, the luxury career of comedy stretching out before me, I spent more time looking around Laurel's store than I had in a while. Something occurred to me.

"How come I never see men in here?" I said to Ruby, who was

straightening the linen tags on a display of necklaces. "We're a gift shop. Don't men have to buy gifts for, like, their wives or girlfriends or something?"

"Men don't know how to buy women gifts," Ruby explained. "That's what flowers are for."

I was jotting it down—I didn't bother hiding my notebook anymore—when, as if on cue, a new text lit up my phone. When I saw the sender, my heart leaped into my throat.

Heard you on Omari!! Let's catch up sometime

That was all. Two sentences from the person I used to care about most in the world, the best friend who had never once checked in with me as I faded out of his existence and retreated back to home base. The breezy double exclamation points, the lack of an *I* in the first sentence, as if he'd grabbed a minute to text between commitments, and the missing final punctuation all left it so that I would have to interpret and respond without further information. If there had been a period, an exclamation point, or even an ellipsis at the end —if he had so much as written *soon* instead of *sometime*—I would undoubtedly have gone on break early and called him right then.

But he hadn't. Which meant I would have to content myself with a soft lob back over the net. Something casual and preferably funny. I'd have to come up with words that were not *Jason, I have missed you. I am only half myself without you.*

I stared at my phone and texted nothing.

That night I skipped the open-mics and went to bed early, drained by hours of pretending to care about tiny baby cacti in glazed ceramic pots and other Henry-curated crap. Rather than bringing Los Angeles closer, Jason's text had caused it to recede again, ever so slightly. In its place, the Carl M. strike loomed. I needed my rest.

10

Carl M.'s two-story apartment complex consisted of twin rows of doors and windows facing each other, motel-style, across a pitted parking lot, the windows glowing yellow or blue to signify the private worlds enclosed behind diseased-looking venetian blinds.

I parked on the street around the corner. As I walked toward the parking lot, I went over the plan, fumbling nervously in the pocket of my red Runnr hoodie for the key elements: gloves, thumb drive full of malware, and, of course, the stun gun. Although I was relieved to have talked Amanda out of a firearm, the conversation had shown me how easy it was to purchase one. Now, in the dark, I couldn't help wondering what good the stun gun would do me if my client was packing heat. I tried to come up with a joke—*Did you know food trucks are now more heavily regulated in Austin than assault rifles? But at least murder by vegan taco is way down this year*—but it didn't help. Walking between the rows of apartments with the bag of Thai food swinging by my thigh, I looked at every window and tried to picture the guns that might be hiding in each apartment like malevolent Easter eggs. Was this the way Amanda saw the world—evil possibilities lurking just beneath the surface, glinting out of the darkness? Feeling suddenly conspicuous in the parking lot, I ducked between the cars to the awning on the left-hand row of apartments and hurried up the concrete stairs to the second floor.

Carl's apartment was all the way at the end, his window completely dark behind the grin of sagging blinds. Was he even home? I was ashamed at the flash of hope I felt at the thought that he might be out. Maybe he'd dashed to the corner store for a six-pack. Or, better yet, decided to attend some viewing party where half a dozen tubby Jon Snows and a single Daenerys Targaryen would be clustered on a sofa arguing their fan theories. Of course, he had placed his usual order—I readjusted my sweaty grip on the plastic-coated Runnr bag full of Thai food—but maybe he'd forgotten about it. As I was resolving to leave it on the doormat and run, a light came on along with a burst of music so loud that, even muffled, it made the concrete walkway shudder under my feet. I hesitated for a moment in the twitchy glow emanating from the blinds. Then I raised my fist.

Knock-knock.

The door opened faster than I'd expected, and I almost took a step back. Carl, in defiance of my internet-troll stereotype, appeared relatively normal. Just a guy of stooped but medium height, on the skinny side, with auburn hair and a weak chin. His maroon T-shirt had a grease stain just over the left nipple. Could this possibly be the same person who had sent Amanda mocked-up GIFs of her being decapitated, among other things? Close-up, he looked startlingly human. The only thing that made him seem slightly shifty was the way his eyes kept darting to the right, toward the television, which was blaring out a montage of ads for HBO shows. It was almost eight o'clock, and he could barely peel his eyes away from the screen.

"Carl? I'm your runner, Betty." I held the red thermal Runnr bag just over the threshold. "Thai Kitchen?"

"Right," he said, reaching for the bag automatically. His thumb brushed the tip of my third fingernail, and I felt something like an electric shock run through me. "Thanks," he said, already closing the door.

"Um, hey," I said. Then: "Never mind, have a great night."

But the door halted with a tiny squeak. Carl squinted at me through the crack, giving me his full attention for the first time. "I'm sorry, did I—I already paid with the app, right?"

"Oh yeah, you're all paid up. I was just—" Here it came. My big moment. It was for this I had driven all the way out to Buda yesterday and dropped part of my winnings in the mega-hardware store; for this I had fed the tail of the Betty wig through the snap-back opening of the Runnr cap and fussed with it until I looked as much as possible like a short little girl with a tan and a blond ponytail, the kind who could easily wheedle favors out of strangers. I took a deep breath. "Is there any way I could just use your bathroom real quick? I'm, like, dying." As Carl's expression ran through hesitation and doubt, I added, "My next run is a twenty-minute drive out to the suburbs. Please?"

In the room behind him, a grim-voiced announcer intoned the words, "Previously, on *Game of Thrones*." Carl winced visibly and looked toward the screen.

"I promise I'll be superfast," I said, shifting from one foot to the other expressively, trying to project an urgency on par with the impending arrival of an army of undead in Westeros.

The sound of a dragon screeching on the television seemed to make the decision for him. Anything to get rid of me and back to the *previously*s. "Yeah, that's fine," he said, taking a step away from the door and jerking his head over his shoulder to indicate my path without once taking his eyes off the TV in the living room.

"Oh my God, thank you so much!" As I scooted past him, stepping off the square of linoleum in the entryway and onto the seedy hall carpet, I could see Carl standing in front of the sofa, transfixed by something on the screen that made a bone-crushing sound, followed by a shriek of pain.

I slipped on my gloves as I walked into the hallway. Just in case he was listening, I pushed the bathroom door open as far into the tiny bathroom as it would go—just far enough to see the mold on the shower curtain and shudder before retreating back into the hallway—then I pulled it firmly shut and kept walking. In the bedroom, I could see two large screens set up on a desk. I reached into my pocket and grabbed for the flash drive so hurriedly that it almost bounced out of my hand, but I caught it just as, on the television in the other room, a woman screamed, "No!"

Amanda had given me some idea of where to look for the USB port, but the bedroom was dark, and I didn't have much time. I glanced over my shoulder toward the living room and saw the bump of Carl's head over the sofa back—unable to resist sitting down, a good sign he was getting sucked in. I went back to searching the side of the monitor, but the gloves made it hard to distinguish between the different holes. Then I bumped the desk a little too hard, and, to my horror, the monitor came to life.

The screen grew bright, and a flicker of movement started up in the browser window. My hand flew to the keyboard to turn the display button off, but then it hovered there instead. Perhaps it was only the sudden thought that with the monitor light on I had a better chance of finding the USB port that made me look at the screen a moment too long, but once I recognized what I was seeing, I couldn't look away.

It was a five-second video clip on loop—a GIF, RadioMacktive666's specialty. The man's face wasn't visible; the video had been shot over his shoulder to give the viewer the sense of participation. All you could see of him was his back and his forearm across the woman's shoulder and collarbone, holding her down. After a moment, I recognized the woman, her face contorted in pain and horror, as a famous young actress who had recently delivered a speech on women's rights at a global summit. Fighting to stay calm, I saw that her screaming face must have been lifted from one of her films — a horror film, by the looks of it — and transposed onto another, grainier video clip.

As the video looped, I stared. What was happening to the woman in the GIF had happened to me. It had happened a long time ago, in the dark, on a couch in the TV room, Mattie's old room, at Jason's house. In a way, it had been looping in my memory, just like the GIF, for ten years.

I noticed a string of letters in the address bar: nsfw_gifsound.

Not safe for work was an understatement. But what really got me was the word *sound*. A pair of noise-canceling headphones lay on the desk, connected to a jack in the monitor, and I slipped them over my ears as if in a trance. They were heavy but comfortable, still warm from their last wearer. The sound immersion was unlike anything I could have afforded. The cries of protest synced to the opening of the woman's mouth sounded real.

Feeling oddly detached, I let my gaze drift down to the comments section, which was full of compliments on Carl's technique. *Wish I could do this,* one guy wrote. *I mean the animation AND her!*

Under the numbness, I felt a quiver of nausea, but I tried to push it down. I told myself that the clip that had been pasted over was probably lifted from amateur porn, not footage of a real assault. But if something could look this real and feel this real — if it could thrust me suddenly back onto the couch in the dark TV room at Jason's house my senior year of high school, render me powerless, terrified, and numb — Mattie silhouetted in black against the television snow,

his drunken pressure forcing me down—even if it was a reconstruc-
tion, a fantasy, a fake, I knew it was at least as real as I was.

I'd never told Jason what his brother did. I told myself it was to
protect Jason; I made up all kinds of stories in my head about how he
would try to defend my honor and wind up getting his face bashed
in. But the truth was, I couldn't have told Jason even if I'd wanted
to, because even while it was happening, I had made sure it wasn't *me*
that it was happening to. I had peeled myself away from my body and
watched from a safe distance, just like I was watching the GIF now.
And afterward, I had gone on living in the me that it didn't happen to,
which meant choosing to live in a world where it had not happened
at all. That, I thought, was strength. That was moving on. Neely and
Fash and even Amanda had failed to drag me back into my body, back
into what had happened to it that night. Where they had failed, the
video in front of me, with its repetitive twitch of violence, had succeeded.

The day unfolded again in slow motion. Jason and I went to his
house after school as usual and headed straight for the TV room.
Mattie had come home while we were watching something on DVD
—*Strangers with Candy*. He leaned against the door frame, staring at
us silently, an open bottle of tequila dangling from his fingertips, until
Jason got up the guts to tell him to get lost.

"Whatever, Gay-son," Mattie had said. Then he pointed drunkenly
at me. "You—Diaz—I'll see you later."

"Sure, Mattie," I'd said, pretending to be absorbed in the show.

That night we finished binge-watching one show and started another, letting each episode blur into the next so we wouldn't have to
talk about the third presence in the room, invisible but stifling. It got
later and later, darker outside, darker in the room. I'd come home late
from Jason's house many times when my mom was already in bed, but
I'd never before spent the night. This time the inertia was overpower-

ing. During the closing credits of a *Fry and Laurie* episode, my eyelids got heavy, and I was already half asleep when Jason tucked a blanket around my feet and tiptoed out of the room.

I awoke in the dark, a strong hand clapped over my mouth, barely able to breathe under the pressure, a cloud of sickly sweet alcohol fumes making my head spin. The fuzzy light of the television, still on in the background, just enough to trace Mattie's outline but not his features, so that I couldn't even tell whether he was smiling or snarling. I squeezed my eyes shut, and the rest happened in blackness.

A hand grabbed my shoulder.

If I'd been frozen that other time, this time every nerve in my body leaped into action at once, responding to the past scene that hung superimposed over the present moment. Feeling Mattie's hands on me again, I grabbed what was in front of me—the keyboard—whirled around, and, *wham*, smacked it across Carl's face. I felt his nose buckle under the plastic side of the keyboard, but it wasn't enough. He was already coming back up, yelling something I couldn't hear with the noise-canceling headphones on. It looked like his mouth was moving around the shrieks of protest in the GIF. The effect was grotesque.

I yanked off the headphones, and the full flood of noises came rushing at me. "What the hell," the man who had grabbed me was saying between coughs, but much louder came the throb of the theme music to *Game of Thrones*—*duh* duh duh-duh *duh* duh—and I brought the keyboard crashing down on the top of his head with the next *duh* and then tossed it aside because it was too light to do any real damage. My hand fumbled around the desk until it reached something tall and spiky with a heavy base, a trophy, maybe, and I smashed it across his face. He crumpled to the side, and I reversed the statuette and swung the heavy base into his groin. He dropped to the ground.

"Ungh." He was struggling to form words, emitting a kind of gurgle, but time had slowed down, and there was blood on his face, and

I could hardly understand who he was, much less what he was trying to say.

I squatted by his crumpled form, and the voice that came out of me was Betty's.

"What?" she said. "I can't hear you. Too much noise." The credit music launched into a soaring bridge; out of the corner of my eye, I saw flames on the TV screen. "You should really turn the TV down. Your neighbors hate you."

"What do you want?"

I thought about what I wanted for a moment, but his hands were cupped over his corduroy-clad groin, so Betty swung the base of the trophy into his lower back instead. He jerked and gasped on the floor like a fish, and I remembered waking up unable to breathe from Mattie's weight and tightened my grip. "Shhh, it's okay," Betty told him, like Mattie had told me that night. The smell of tequila had turned my stomach ever since.

Even distracted by this memory, I noticed immediately when the rhythm of his writhing shifted slightly and his right hand started inching toward his left hip pocket. It reminded me what I had in mine. Betty pulled out the stun gun and leaned over and poked him with it. He went rigid with a choking noise.

"Nope. You don't get to call 911. Sorry." I brushed his hand, now stiff and shaking, away from his pocket. No shock of contact, now that I'd shocked him first. I hooked my gloved fingers into his pocket, past the corduroy bib and down into the cotton lining, and wiggled them down past the crease with businesslike efficiency, past the hipbone that had ground so sharply into mine it had left a bruise. I'd ignored the stiffness in my hips the next day as I drove the hour and a half to Lubbock in search of a pharmacist who would sell an underage girl a morning-after pill. My fingers closed on Carl's phone and I slid it out of his pocket and dropped it into my own. "See, I didn't get to call 911. So you don't get to either."

"Who are you?" Carl gasped from the floor.

"I'm Batman," Betty said in a low, growly voice and then exploded with laughter. Carl flipped onto his stomach and started scrambling down the hall, trying to pull himself along the carpet.

Still howling, Betty turned toward the video that was playing on the screen and swung the base of the statue until there was almost nothing left on top of the desk. Hiding behind the monitors like an animal crouching in fear was an external hard drive.

"What do we have here?" Betty yanked the cords out of the hard drive and stuffed the whole thing in her hoodie pocket. There was room now that the stun gun was out and about.

I followed Carl into the den. He was moving at an excruciating pace. Not in peak physical condition.

"Please don't hurt me," he said, backing up against the sofa and scrabbling his bare feet under him for purchase, trying to get to a standing position. "What do you want, I'll give you whatever you want."

"Already got it!" Betty cried, grabbing the hard drive through my hoodie pocket and wiggling it lewdly back and forth. "But thanks anyway."

"I never did anything to you." He coughed. "I don't even know you."

"That's okay, I didn't know my attacker very well either," I said. "And I certainly hadn't done anything to him. But I have a feeling you've done something to someone sometime. Or maybe you just talk a big game—make funny GIFs to scare women and watch other rapists do what you wish you could. Either way, I'll find out." I patted the hard drive like it was my unborn child. "I mean, maybe the police won't care. Maybe you haven't done anything illegal. But I bet your mom will care. I bet your employer will care. Your girlfriend—if you have one, you pathetic loser—will care."

Betty swung the statue up over her shoulder like a baseball bat, and he cringed.

"So call the police if you want. But if you do, the first thing you'll have to tell them is that you got beat up by a girl." I squatted, careful to stay out of reach of his flailing arms. "And then you'll have to tell them why I did it. And I did it because of what's on this." I patted the drive again. "So if I were you, I'd focus on being very, very good. Because if what I think is on here gets out, I bet it'll ruin your life."

Betty stood up again and swung the statue into his ribs and watched him crumple onto the floor. Everything in the room smelled like pad thai. I leaned over and righted the Runnr bag, which had been knocked over in the struggle.

"And I do want your life ruined, Carl," Betty continued. "But I don't want it ruined *that* way. I want it ruined—how can I put this? —more like mine has been ruined. Not thrown-in-jail ruined or fired-from-your-job ruined or mocked-on-the-internet ruined. I want you to *feel* like you're in jail because someone could do this to you. I want you to quit your job because of PTSD, lose your friends because you're too afraid to tell them, disconnect your internet because you might accidentally see me on a mutual friend's Facebook feed and go into shock all over again. I want you to know that I'll be watching you. Don't ask me how, but I will. I want you to be scared of being alone with strange women, like I'm scared of being alone with strange men."

I leaned forward and he rolled over onto his face with a moan, curling his hands around the back of his head.

"Except you, Carl. I'm not scared of you anymore."

But it wasn't Carl I was talking to.

I wedged the statue under my armpit, pulled his phone from my pocket, took his hand—he gasped in pain but didn't try to jerk it away—and placed his thumb gently on the unlock screen. Then I stepped back, straightened up, and opened the Runnr app on his phone. I found my name—Betty B., for Betty Bare, Betty Badass, Betty Batman—and hovered my index finger over the little circle.

"Hmm, how would you rate this run, Carl M.? Food got here pretty fast." I shrugged. "On the other hand, revenge. So maybe just four stars for Betty B.?"

Face-down, motionless except for the gentle rising and falling of his shoulders, he looked like he was asleep.

"You know what, Carl? I feel like you'd round up to five." I pushed the fifth star, then wiped the screen clean and tucked it gently back into his pocket. "That's just the kind of guy you are."

The credits were rolling as I opened the door to step out. At the last second I realized the statue was still under my armpit, and I pulled it out and looked at it. It was not a trophy at all, I could see in this light, but a twenty-inch statuette of Black Widow, the Marvel character, in a clinging costume and back-wrenching pose that showed off her boobs and butt simultaneously. "You go, girl," I told her and tossed her onto the sofa. Then I left and closed the door behind me.

I floated down the stairs and through the parking lot in a dream, my mind suspended and quieted in a soft, warm cloud. Behind me, the window that hid Carl's apartment from the world flickered like a forest fire.

11

Keeping a firm grip on the hard drive in my pocket, I pulled the red hoodie off over my head as I walked around the corner to my car. The Runnr cap and Betty wig came off, too, and I rolled all of it up into a thick bundle under my arm. Then I slid the surgical gloves off inside out and balled them up so that the blood-slicked surface was on the inside. The drive home was a blur. The next thing I knew, I was standing in the parking lot outside my apartment, holding the balled gloves up to a streetlight so that they looked like some kind of reptile egg, the blood at the center dulled under layers of translucent plastic.

I threw them in the dumpster and closed the lid.

In an apartment complex like mine, there was really no unusual time to do laundry. I let myself into my place and started gathering a bundle of clothes large enough to make the red sweatshirt and cap less conspicuous. It was easy to do. Dirty clothes spilled out of the hamper across my floor. It wasn't quite to the Doug Branchik level yet, but I hadn't been taking good care of my apartment. Too much time spent in Amanda's airy condo, with its clean lines and modern spaces that looked barely lived in, and I was starting to feel as if it were my place. By contrast, my apartment was dark—not the glittering dark of the big night sky outside floor-to-ceiling windows, but the dingy dark of dusty curtains and light fixtures with one burned-out bulb apiece.

Having gathered an armload of laundry, I stood by the kitchen counter for a long time, staring at the laminate floor. I'd never really noticed before how the laminate was notched to suggest individual boards rather than a single millimeter-thin layer of shaved wood fused to particulate plastic. The surface of the floor was sculpted with a network of tiny plastic trenches and reefs calibrated to offer gentle traction, simulated evidence of irregularity. Compared to Amanda's hardwood floor, it was obviously fake. How could something so fake have fooled me for so long?

I pulled the hard drive out of my hoodie pocket and set it on the counter, where it seemed to brood. A large rectangular paperweight that knew things, even though its tiny green eye had gone dead.

It took a few minutes to find enough quarters for a load of wash, but I found them and headed down the hall to the laundry room to erase the bloodstains.

What do you want

I'd intended to head straight over to Amanda's with the hard drive, but now I had to wait for a load of laundry. I lay down on my bed and stared at the skeleton of a hanging plant I'd purchased a few months ago in a moment of optimism and hadn't watered since. I propped my feet up on the wall, pointing my toes toward the dried tendrils and thinking, *I should really paint my toenails.*

Who are you

The lightness, which had been so calm and cloudlike, seemed to whiten and swirl around my head, and I felt a surge of something coming up. I squeezed my eyes shut and rubbed them with my hands. Giant red blotches bloomed in the blackness like diseased flowers. When I opened my eyes again they wouldn't blink away.

Please don't hurt me

I don't even know you

I rolled onto my side just as the shuddering began. An icy cold took me as I threw up everything in my stomach all at once. I lay on my side holding myself and shaking all over with the cold.

When the shaking subsided, I balled the comforter up around the vomit and walked it down the hall to add to my load of laundry.

What had I done.

I'd crossed a line I didn't even know existed. It wasn't just that I had made someone bleed by hitting him over and over again. It wasn't just that I'd aimed especially for his face, as if I wanted to obliterate his identity, make him the same as the man who'd hurt me facelessly in the night. It wasn't just that I had no idea who Carl M. really was and what he had really done, if anything, to deserve this.

I'd enjoyed it, and I wanted to do it again.

I grabbed the hard drive. I had to get it over to Amanda's tonight, tell her what I'd done, ask her what to do next. I'd come back and finish the laundry later. On the way to the door, I saw the Betty wig lying on the floor where I'd dropped it, white-blond hair curling luxuriously, its elasticized interior like a glimpse of dirty underwear. I kicked it under the sofa and left.

As always, Amanda was home and wide-awake, tapping away at her laptop on the kitchen bar. I walked up and thunked the hard drive in front of her on the counter, like a cat dropping a half-dead rat at its owner's feet.

"Here," I said. "Go nuts."

Her eyes widened when she saw what it was. "Oh my God," she said. "That wasn't in the plan."

"Yeah, well. A lot of things weren't in the plan," I said. "And actually? I'm starting to think that the plan kind of sucked." I opened the refrigerator without asking, located a bottle of white wine, unscrewed the metal cap, and took a long swig. The cold, sweet wine hit my empty stomach with a lurch and then spread a welcome warmth up my esophagus.

But Amanda wasn't listening. She already had her hands on the hard drive, running her fingers greedily over its smooth, metallic surface. "This is amazing, Dana. I can do so much with this! How did you manage to—" Then she stopped, picked with a fingernail at a smudge of brownish red on the hard drive. She brought it closer to her face and examined it. Then she looked up at me. "Dana," she said, realization dawning in her eyes.

"He snuck up behind me. I was looking for the USB port and he caught me and I just—" I swallowed a sob of panic. "I lost it."

Slowly her look of shock transformed, her lips turning upward and stretching into a wide, incredulous smile. "You're incredible, Dana. You're like a superhero."

I thought of the Black Widow figurine and suddenly started laughing, noiselessly, faster and faster, until tears masked my vision.

Amanda saw me crying and wrapped both arms around me in a hug. It was the first time we had touched since she'd grabbed my hand at Nomad. Her arms felt rail thin but wiry strong wrapped around my shoulders, and I let myself be restrained by her, the only thing stopping me from flying apart.

Keeping her grip on my shoulders, Amanda drew away from me, a concerned look on her face. "Dana, are you okay? Did he hurt you?"

"No," I whispered.

"Thank God."

"I hurt him. A lot."

"Good."

"No, no, you don't understand," I said. "I lost control. I—I don't know what happened. I—" I saw his bloody face in front of me, his arms clutched to his ribs as he slouched against the sofa, as if for the first time.

Amanda led me over to the sofa and sat me down. Then she went to the kitchen and filled a glass of water and brought it to me. She watched me drink it, studying me.

"I know what happened."

I stared at my jeans, picking a loose thread.

"You have one more, don't you?" she said.

I didn't need to ask, but I did anyway. "One more what?"

"One more name."

I looked down into the glass of water I was holding and nodded dumbly.

"Someone did something to you." Her voice was steady as she sat down next to me. "A long time ago."

I nodded again.

"It's worse than Neely. Worse than Fash. And it came back, didn't it? It came back and you were right there. Like it was happening to you again."

I could barely nod. Now that the sobs had stopped, a single tear was working its way out of my eye and down my cheek.

"I thought so. I knew there was someone else."

I waited for her to put her arms around me again, to comfort me, to ask me who it was, what had happened. I wanted to tell someone about the night I fell asleep on Jason's couch and woke up with Mattie crushing me. For so long I'd been trying to forget the details. Now I ached for them to come spilling out, the way the Neely story had that night in the Bat City parking lot. What would life look like on the other side of that confession?

There was a long pause. When, finally, I raised my head to look into her eyes, I saw that she was staring at me, her green eyes burning.

"That's good," she said. "Because I have one more name too."

I stood up off the sofa so fast the water sloshed out of the glass onto my feet. "Are you fucking kidding me? You want me to do it again? This is—do you understand what happened tonight? What could have happened?" I scrolled back through the events of the evening, trying to put the pieces in order, trying to understand the extent of what I had done. What I could have done by accident, with just a little more rage, a slightly heavier weapon. And then the reality hit me. "Oh my God, the police."

"He won't call the police," she said. "He's okay, right? You didn't do any permanent damage? How about internal injuries? Let me guess—mostly the face?" She seemed to take my sickened stare for agreement and nodded sagely. "He won't call."

"How can you say that?" I sputtered. "What do you—do you have experience with this kind of thing?"

She was silent.

"Oh my God," I said, realization dawning. "You do."

Instead of answering, she turned slowly to her laptop, pulled up an encrypted file, entered a series of passwords. Opened up a video.

I had seen the video before but never all the way through to the end. She advanced it a little further than the three-minute mark, past the absurdly comedic spectacle of Aaron Neely pleasuring himself in fast motion, to the point where the tall woman in the Runnr uniform slid a long red steering-wheel lock out of her massage bag. She raised it over her head. I squeezed my eyes shut, pressed my hands over my ears to block out the sickening sounds.

"Turn it off, turn it off!" Wine fumes ate at the back of my throat, and I felt ready to throw up again.

The sound went off, but when I opened my eyes I saw she had merely muted the video. I jerked my head away from Neely's face, a blotch of red on the grainy video, only to be confronted with its reflection in the tall black window.

"Grow up, Dana." I could see Amanda in the reflection, watching me. "This is how the sausage gets made."

"Is he okay?" It came out a snivel.

"He's fine—as fine as he needs to be, anyway." Her reflection smirked. "I hear he hasn't left his house since it happened, and all his projects are on hold indefinitely. Which should keep him out of trouble for a while."

"I can't believe this."

"You just did it to someone yourself, sweetie," she said. "It doesn't get more believable than that."

"I didn't want to. I didn't mean to."

"But I bet you liked it," she said, and my stomach lurched. "Remember what I said about the rolled-up newspaper? You just gave him a little bop on the nose, that's all. Now he won't forget the lesson."

I had to get out of there. I swallowed hard and said, "I'm leaving town for a while."

She didn't look alarmed, but I could see a glint of something cold in her eye. "Where will you go?"

"I don't know. I'll tell work it's a family emergency." I remembered Kim saying those words about Neely and flinched. "Something."

"Sure, go," she said, her voice pitched just high enough for me to hear the effort with which she was keeping herself calm. "But you can't run away from this forever. You have one more name, Dana. And so do I."

"I just need some time to think." I wondered where the steering-wheel lock was now, how many other tools of the trade she had stashed in this apartment. Then I caught sight of my reflection in the window. Tools of the trade, all right. I was looking at one.

"Sooner or later, you're going to have to face the truth, Dana."

"That's what I'm doing," I said. And walked out.

12

The eight-hour drive to Amarillo always affected me like a trip backward through time. Heading northwest into the Panhandle meant leaving behind all the cities nonlocals had heard of, abandoning the rolling hills of central Texas, skirting the majestic emptiness of the mountains and desert to the west, and heading straight into the color brown. Driving up I-27, I began to see brown plains spreading uninterrupted in every direction, brown towns laid out in squares around ancient oil-boom banks, now all but deserted, and brown cattle trampling cattle-cropped grass, giving off a thick brown reek. Even the sky was stained brown at its margins, the horizon obscured by a low-lying cloud of dust and cattle pollution that never cleared.

I loved it.

The color brought back childhood memories of writing on manila paper that came in giant rolls with soft-lead pencils whose erasers left marks. Climbing jungle gyms on a brown playground, falling one day from the highest bar onto a pile of wood chips, lying on my back staring at the brown sky. Driving back home on holiday weekends, my trunk full of laundry so I could save a few bucks in quarters, feeling the slender rope that tethered me to Austin stretching thinner and thinner, the world of skinny college boys who drank too much and stayed up all night studying in twenty-four-hour diners becoming less and less plausible until the rope snapped, eaten away by the brown landscape. As before when I'd made the trip, that moment of sever-ance—let's call it Lubbock—yielded a deep welling of relief as I let go of everything I wanted so urgently and let myself tumble back into the past.

Which, after all, mostly meant my mother's house, also brown. When I pulled into the driveway, she was already waiting for me at the back door, having heard or sensed the car approaching. I parked the car, jumped out, and ran over to her. I couldn't help it.

"Mama." I closed my eyes and hugged her.

She hugged me back. "You hungry for dinner yet? You stop along the way?"

I shook my head. "I came straight here." I thought I caught a whiff of the braised chicken she used to make sometimes on my weekends home.

"I'll put the lasagna in the oven."

Frozen, from Costco. I'd had it before. It was a weeknight, and she was still in her work clothes. As a matter of fact, lasagna was a lot of trouble for a night when she'd most likely have nuked a TV dinner for herself. I squeezed her shoulder. "That sounds great. Thanks, Mom."

I waved off her attempts to help me get my luggage from the car, holding up my one bag. I'd taken only a few days off work. "I'm sorry it's going to be so short."

"That's okay. You're a busy lady," she said. I followed her into the house. She still wore high heels to work, clip-clopping gracefully along in them at breakneck speeds, but when she wiggled her feet out of them at home, peeled off her pantyhose, and eased into a pair of slippers, she walked with a gentle lurching motion, as if her hips were uneven. She rocked her way to the counter, where a disposable aluminum casserole pan with an aluminum cover and a collar of icy rime sat waiting to be put in a preheated oven. When she had set a timer, she said, "Come talk to me while I change," and, just like I had every weeknight I'd spent at home since my dad left, I followed her through the living room to her bedroom.

The house looked the same as always. Recliner by the television. A sofa patterned with big half-bloomed roses, the subject of fierce prohibitions throughout my childhood. The plastic slipcover had come off once my dad and I were both out of the house, and my mom was finally able to enjoy not sitting on it in peace. Two ficus trees and half a dozen shiny-leaved houseplants sat around the living room in tubs. These, too, were old enough for me to remember their provenance —she had rescued them from the alley behind her office at the helium plant, where they'd been put out for trash because they were infested with tiny black insects. "No need to waste all these just because of a few bugs," she'd told me when I recoiled from the squirming soil, and she soon got rid of the infestation and nursed the plants back to health. When the industry privatized, those castoffs seemed to me like an omen of her fate. But once again, she'd attacked the problem methodically and wound up snagging a receptionist position at the helicopter company that opened up in town the next year. She was nothing if not resourceful.

In her bedroom, the smell of her hand lotion dominated. She was already unbuttoning her work blouse, her caftan lying in wait on the bed.

"How are you doing, Mama?"

"I'm fine. I keep plenty busy."

"Would you ever consider moving out to Austin?" It wasn't the first time I'd asked, though I'd never had the guts to bring up a move to L.A. I knew the answer to that in advance.

"Why would I do that?" she snapped. "This is where I live."

"But it's so quiet here," I said. "You must get lonely sometimes."

"I miss you, *mija*," she said. "But it's not the same thing as lonely. I have plenty to keep me occupied." She looked at me shrewdly. "It sounds to me like you're the lonely one."

I waited a long time before answering. "I guess so."

She snorted. "You never used to be lonely. It's that boy."

Jason had always been a sore point between us. When I was in high school, she didn't understand why I would hang around with a boy I wasn't dating. Her suspicions seemed to be aroused as much by the possibility that we really weren't as that we secretly were. My contention that we liked working on projects together did not impress her in the slightest; she had, after all, been my father's secretary at the plant when they met. If you could fall in love with someone in the time it took to go over the phone messages every day, you could damn well fall in love with him watching TV and writing comic strips or whatever it was we were doing. When I moved into the house in L.A. with Jason, it was the last straw. For my mom, living with a man was living in sin. She didn't care about separate bedrooms, his girlfriends or my boyfriends, what we did or didn't do at night. "He's not a gay, right?" she had once pointedly asked, and as I wailed, *"Mama,"* she'd followed up with "Then it's not right." And yet my moving out of our shared abode hadn't endeared him to her any further.

"What happened to that boy anyway?" she said now, and I detected a note of carefully downplayed concern.

"He's still in L.A., I think," I said, adding the qualifier so that she wouldn't know I'd been keeping track.

"Making your TV show without you?" She sounded peevish,

although she was leaning over to pick up the skirt she had just stepped out of, so I couldn't see her expression.

"No, Mom," I said. "He's probably working on something else. I don't know, we don't talk."

"Any new boyfriends in Austin?"

"The only people who ask me out are other comics, and they're literally the last people on earth I want to date."

"Jason was a comic."

"How many times do I have to tell you, Jason and I were just friends!" I exploded, although at the same time I was perversely pleased that she'd been forced to say his name. "Why didn't you ever like him?"

"He was fine," she said in a tone that meant the opposite from the depths of the caftan that was descending over her head in a cloud of silk. When her face appeared again, she said, "I just didn't like you hanging around over there so much." For the hundredth time I wondered if she had intuited, on some level, what had happened to me at Jason's place that night. But she was already going on with her spiel. "You didn't think I knew about that house, with the mom never around and the father out drinking all the time. But I knew. I just wanted you to be happy, *mija*." She shook her head. "And now that no-good brother is in Clements. That whole family—"

It hit me a moment late: Clements Unit. "What? Mattie in prison?"

She nodded, eyes wide. "Armed robbery. Maybe drugs were involved, I forget. Anyway, he's been making trouble around here for years." She gestured vaguely toward the window, as if the state prison were just on the other side of the abelia hedge. "You can't blame me for being worried . . ."

All I heard was that after ten years, my rapist was in prison. My mother didn't know about Mattie, and so I couldn't put into words what it felt like to know I wouldn't be bumping into him at Jason's house or at the corner store or at the Sears where I'd worked for a year after graduating. That night had ruined my senior year, sent me sleep-walking through the halls, dropping off at my desk in the afternoons, sometimes even in the middle of a test. When my GPA plummeted so low that I fell out of the top 10 percent of the class and thus out of the University of Texas's automatic-admission pile, it was too late to apply anywhere else. I took it as a sign that I was not, after all, intended to leave the Panhandle and go to college. That I belonged with the Matties, not the Jasons.

I would not have said it was Mattie who did all this to me, because there was a fog obscuring what he had done, a vague placeholder for the feeling that I had done something wrong, attracted the wrong kind of attention from the wrong kind of person. Only now that he was locked away did I know that I had been in prison for ten years. The door had just cracked open, and a sliver of light was shining through.

"You want to know why you never had a boyfriend, *mija*?" My mother was still talking, and I tuned back in, bracing myself. I must have seemed far away, because she sounded hurt, and she had the determined look of someone shedding her usual reserve to say something she'd been holding back for years. "That Jason boy chased them all away. They could see they never had a chance with you as long as he was around." She started to say more, then paused and looked suddenly sad. "And he loved it."

"I had plenty of boyfriends in L.A.," I said abruptly, not bothering with the finer points of terminology in the Tinder age. She didn't need to know anything about that. "Besides, I don't know why you're so eager for me to date these days. When I was in high school, you couldn't keep me far enough away from boys."

"That was when I was trying to get you off to college," she said. "I didn't want you distracted by that boy or anyone else. Now you have plenty of time on your hands. Too much. It's time to get married."

"Why don't you get married, if you're so hot for it?"

She straightened her caftan with an air of finality. "I've been married," she said. "I know whether I like it or not, and I didn't like it."

You didn't like Dad cheating on you, I thought, but I was not nearly stupid enough to say it. "I probably wouldn't either."

"Nonsense. You're not like me, Dana. You're needy, like your father. You should always have a man."

I almost laughed out loud, but something stopped me. It was the thought of Carl's face, blood gushing from his nose, clotting his hair on his forehead, dripping from a gash on his cheekbone. I needed something, all right.

"Are you okay, *mija*? You're not looking well." The hurt tone had gone out of her voice, and my mother was back to tending to me, a calm hand on my forehead.

"I'm fine, Mom," I said. "Just tired out from the drive."

She tsked distractedly, and I let myself be shepherded into the mint-green master bathroom to soak in the bathtub while the lasagna finished cooking. As I lay naked in the hot water, staring at the tiled wall over the chrome faucet, I imagined the dirt of the past weeks sliding off me onto the soapy surface, evaporating into the steam. Vengeance. That was the game I had been playing with Amanda. It had nothing to do with justice and even less to do with preventing future misdemeanors by petty offenders. It had been vengeance, plain and simple. Of course, it wasn't just Mattie I'd wanted to destroy. It was every reminder of why he thought he could do it. The gropings and wolf whistles and insults, what Neely had done to me, what Amanda's ex had done to her. The only way to bear it all was to ignore it, because once you started trying to make someone pay for every reminder that you could be held down and raped by any man who decided you were worth the energy, it was like playing whack-a-mole. The more you hit, the more you saw, and you could hit harder and harder, and faster and faster, but you'd only wear yourself out.

And now Mattie was in prison. Not just any prison, but Clements —notoriously harsh, rife with abuses. If there were ever a place where I could be sure my attacker would be hit over and over, harder than I could ever hit him, it was Clements.

I wasn't sorry he was there. I was only sorry I hadn't heard the news months ago, before Amanda had come into my life with her offer of the retribution I didn't know I was craving. If I'd found out in time, maybe I would never have had to discover my own taste for violence. Carl's face, my own face in the mirror afterward—more things I could never unsee.

But at least I was free.

Amanda had accused me of running away, but it turned out I had driven straight to the heart of my problem and found it miraculously solved without my intervention. Now Amarillo looked less like a time capsule and more like a crossroads. I could stay here for a few days, then turn around and drive back to Austin, return to my day job and Amanda and being the second-best standup in town. Or I could keep heading west. Moving forward. I could sign with an agent, a manager. Meet Cynthia for lunch.

The hardest part would be telling my mom I was staying for only one night.

I woke up at four o'clock in the morning and was on the road by four thirty. I'd told my mom not to get up and see me off because I would be leaving early, but she had obviously only half acceded to my request; on the counter, under an inverted bowl draped in a towel, was a plate with two hash-brown patties and a pile of eggs scrambled with chorizo. Nearby, an insulated travel cup full of coffee with a sticky note on it: *Keep the cup. Safe travels,* mija. I took a sip; it was sweetened with condensed milk, my favorite.

The plate was just barely warmer than room temperature. She must have gotten up to cook breakfast in the middle of the night and then slunk back to bed. I stood by her door for a moment, but the light wasn't on, and I could hear her rhythmic breathing, the deep, heavy gasps of her sleep. I ate as quietly as I could and cursed myself for having parked in the driveway instead of on the street, praying the engine wouldn't wake her when I started the car.

As I neared the on ramp to I-40 heading west, I passed the street that led to Jason's dad's house and my old high school. I felt a strong urge to turn off and drive by, feel the weight of Matt's menacing presence lifted firsthand. But what would be the point? It was too dark to see anything. Instead, I drove on, farther and farther from my mom's odd, half-present comfort, her unsittable sofas and silent conversations and the plates full of food that she put herself out to make but did not stick around to watch me eat. It was her way of teaching me to be self-sufficient, I'd once thought, but now I suspected she was simply operating at the very limits of her capacity to live with another person. It had left me with a craving for closeness coupled with a need for infinite space.

Wasn't that what comedy was? A kind of intimate distance, a way to get a response that you could predict and even, in the best of circumstances, control? When it was working, it was like getting a warm hug and at the same time staying perfectly safe from anyone's touch, the cone of the spotlight as cozy as a bell jar. I supposed it was that love of half silences and pregnant pauses that had made hanging out with Jason feel so comfortable to me.

As a teenage girl who'd never had a boyfriend, I'd had a puppy crush on Jason. All those late nights we'd spent side by side on the beanbag chair in his TV room, leaning on each other; how could I not have had a crush on him? But after Mattie, the feeling had deepened, perversely and defiantly. I was not going to let Mattie ruin things between Jason and me. The thought helped me stave off a terror that might otherwise have paralyzed me. In a way, I think I even fell in love with Jason, really in love, on purpose, *just to prove I still could*. I knew we weren't going to be together. I knew he didn't love me, not in that way, anyway. If his failure to make any overtures hadn't told me that, his parade of blond girlfriends communicated it loud and clear. Each one was a message: *You're not my type. We're just friends.*

I stepped on the accelerator and merged onto the empty freeway heading due west. My knuckles tingled. My thighs tightened. Morning was hours away, but I could feel the sun at my back, waiting just below the horizon to rise and scorch the world.

I occupied myself on the drive by making phone calls. First I called one of the agents I'd spoken to over the phone and told her I'd like to sign with her and that I was heading into town soon. Then I screwed up my courage and called Larry Green, who, though grumpy at being used as a receptionist, agreed to pass on a message to Cynthia that I was in town for a few days and would love to meet her for lunch.

I crossed into California at 3:30 p.m., an hour before I'd anticipated, the magnetic field surrounding L.A. drawing me in. I forced myself to keep checking the speedometer, but despite my efforts, the needle on the dashboard kept creeping up, as if it, too, were elated by the feeling of being in the right state at last, with a purpose, a mission.

A mission. I almost blushed. Out here, suspended in the dazzling desert air between Austin and L.A., I felt a twinge of shame that I had let things go so far with Amanda. It had been childish of us to believe that we could punish people more than they could punish themselves, an overcompensation for a lifetime of denial. What had happened with Mattie had violated my deepest sense of order in the universe.

Somehow I had known that if I looked too closely at the trauma, if I accepted that it had happened to me, I would become a grotesque, like neurotic Ruby or hunted-looking Becca. The swap with Amanda had started out as just another way to avoid the truth. I'd thought that by trading attackers, I could get some sense of closure without ever having to face how deep that violation was.

But the infection had passed to me all the same. The night in Carl's apartment had proven it.

The next few hours passed like a longer kind of minute, and then, far in the distance, I saw the sign along the roadside that I'd been waiting for. I put on my blinker and made my way to the I-15 exit.

There was one last person to contact. I waited until I was stopped in traffic outside L.A. I pulled out my phone and texted two words to the most recent number that came up.

I'm done.

The answer came almost immediately. *We have one more X to finish.*

I replied, *I don't owe you anything.*

Don't be stupid, D. You have one more name and so do I.

But I didn't have a name to give her, not anymore. Maybe it should have happened differently—maybe Matt should have been punished for what he'd done to me, not for armed robbery. But he was serving time in a state prison with a rough reputation, worse than anything Amanda and I could have inflicted and, I had to admit, far more just. I was glad it was some state's attorney and not Amanda who had caught up to him. I wouldn't want to owe anyone a debt that great.

My phone was ringing now. I didn't have to look at who it was. I turned it off.

I didn't have a plan for seeing Jason, but I didn't have a plan for not seeing him either. In the end, I drove the familiar route to our old house because it was where I knew to go, where I had been last; it was as if I were excavating for memories, and the ones at our old house lay closest to the surface, just under the soil. I pulled up to the familiar bungalow in Palms and saw his car in the driveway and felt that nothing could be more natural than to park on the street in front, walk up the cracked concrete pathway without even stopping to stretch my legs, and ring the doorbell.

The door opened, and Jason was there. Jason—taller than I remembered, his hair shorter, and traces of something sprouting on his chin that could be a beard or could be neglect, I wasn't sure. Jason, wearing the same T-shirt and jeans, his big smelly feet in flip-flops sticking out under the frayed cuffs. Jason, hands shoved in his pockets, shifting from side to side, opening his mouth to say something.

"What are you doing here, Dana?"

"You said we should catch up sometime," I said. "It's sometime."

He leaned over and wrapped his arms around me, and I was engulfed in a scent I would never be able to describe but that would always smell like home to me.

"It's sometime, all right. I missed you."

"I missed you too." My mouth was pressed against his shoulder, so the tremble in my voice was, I hoped, inaudible. A moment later, the hug was over, as we both endeavored to be the first to pull away.

"Wanna grab something to eat?"

A wave of hunger rolled through me and I nodded. And, like we had done a million times before, we got into his car and drove to the R & R Diner. It was only five minutes away, but nobody walks in L.A.

13

The R & R Diner in Culver City had been one of Jason's and my favorite places to eat until I'd made the classic mistake of deciding that it would be a fun place to work as well. Jason would still come in sometimes late at night and sit in my section drinking a bottomless cup of coffee and riffing with me over every refill, but of course I could never get any writing done there again, so we'd moved our mutual work spot somewhere else. Now, walking through the doors, I willed the smell of frying eggs and Reuben sandwiches to remind me of late-night writing sessions, but instead it tickled my nervous system with sense memories of hauling ice buckets to the wait stations and rolling silverware in the chemical heat of the dishwashing room. As we waited for a booth, I looked around for people I'd worked with, but in a year the turnover had been complete. It was a bit of a relief. I felt confused enough just standing next to Jason again.

Noticing me looking around the restaurant, he said, "You miss working here, I can tell. Ask the hostess for an application, I'm sure they'd take you back."

"Ha-ha," I said with a fake glare. "Actually, I was just thinking it'll be nice to get *my* coffee refilled, for a change."

"I guess you wouldn't need a day job if you moved back out here." He watched me out of the corner of his eye. "After all, you're besties with Cynthia Omari now, right?" I didn't answer, just rolled my eyes, and he moved on, catching me up on some of our mutual acquaintances — who was booking what jobs where, who'd moved back to Detroit to care for an ailing parent, who'd gotten really into Scientology and disappeared for a while, only to reappear with straightened teeth in a plum role. But after we were tucked into a booth with food in front of us, he returned to the topic that was obviously on his mind.

"So, are you?" He kept his eyes on the syrup he was squeezing over his plate of pancakes. "Moving back, I mean."

I dipped a triangle of grilled cheese into a bowl of tomato soup and said, "I don't know." Chewing, I marveled at my ability to sound as if I were considering it for the first time. "I guess it's within the realm of possibility."

"What are you here for, an audition or something?"

In fact, as my head began to clear of Amanda, all my reasons for being here rose up to take her place. Cynthia's assistant had called me back while I was on the road, and, to my wonder, we'd set up a lunch the next day. "A meeting," I confessed, and then I added, "I don't want to get into the details until it's over."

"Oho, big shot!" he crowed. "When I heard you booked *The Bestie Cast,* I have to admit, I was jealous. My agent's been trying to get me on that show for months." He gestured toward his face. "I have straight-white-male disease, I guess."

"Boo-hoo," I said.

"Come on, don't I get even a little bit of sympathy for being out of fashion?"

"Every time you think I have it easy, just repeat these words to yourself: *Even J. Lo had to play a maid.*"

"But she got to bone George Clooney in *Out of Sight.*"

"And Ben Affleck in *Gigli.*"

He hissed. "Oof. You win. But bringing up Affleck in a conversation about white male privilege, now, that's just playing dirty."

I shrugged and ate a fry from my grilled-cheese basket. Jason used to say stuff like that to get my goat, just to watch me get irritated. Now it seemed like a joke, not on me, but on him. Sitting across from Jason's smiling face, surrounded by the sights and smells of our favorite diner, I found it easy to believe in my own success.

"So tell me what you're auditioning for. Or is it a writing job? Come on, somebody in L.A. called you after that podcast. Who was it?"

"Not you," I said pointedly. "Though you did text, which was nice, considering you've been ignoring me for the past year." The ease with which this conversation was happening amazed me. So this was what it felt like to have the upper hand.

"Look," he said. "I've been meaning to talk to you about that. I know I was a jerk to you before you left, and I'm sorry." He picked at his pancakes. "This is hard to admit, but—I was still mad about Neely."

The name dropped between us like a brick. It was the first time either of us had said it out loud to the other since the meeting. The ghost of Neely's bloodied face in the video floated up, but I pushed it back down, trying to focus on what Jason was saying. He'd never apologized to me before, at least not for anything more substantial than forgetting to call me back or borrowing my car and leaving the gas tank empty. I didn't want to be distracted from this conversation by something I wasn't even supposed to know about, hadn't known about until recently. And anyway, I had Amanda to thank for one thing: I wasn't afraid of Neely anymore, even though I was back in the same city with him. That was something.

Jason heaved a sigh. "I just couldn't believe you took that meeting without me."

"I know. I shouldn't have." If there was one thing I was sure of, it was this.

"No, I've thought about it a lot since then, and I don't blame you."

"You don't?"

"If I'm being honest with myself, I probably would have done the same thing," he admitted, and I couldn't help thinking that if he had, the consequences would have been very different. "But then, when you came home sick, and he didn't call, I thought—"

"You thought I'd ruined the meeting somehow." He looked miserable. "It's fine, you can say it. Anyway, it's basically true, isn't it? He never called."

Jason looked more and more embarrassed. "Well, actually," he said, and he took a break from sawing bits off his pancake stack. "Actually, he did."

"What?"

"Yeah. I should have told you, but . . . you'd already moved back to Austin. And the call was for me." He put another bite in his mouth. "I mean, just me."

I couldn't believe it. For a year now, I'd been feeling guilty about ruining Jason's chance to work with Neely. And it turned out all that needed to happen for Jason to get his big break was for me to leave.

He saw my face and nearly choked trying to swallow his bite faster. "Wait, wait, wait." He held one hand up in front of his mouth and waved the other back and forth. "Before you get mad. It was more of a mentorship kind of thing. He never gave me a steady job. He had me doing punch-up on a few shows he's producing. Nothing big, nothing you would have been interested in. They cut half my jokes. Mostly I just hung out with him at his house."

"I bet it didn't help your career at all," I said with a grim laugh, thinking, *Oh, to be a man among men*. "Did he take you to his Buddhist retreat?" It was something we'd joked about, how we'd know we'd made it when he invited us to his converted ranch property in Montana.

"Once," he said, embarrassed.

"Did you meditate together?" The thought of Neely's bulbous torso twisted into a pious pretzel of contemplation made for a dark joke.

"Come on, Dana, cut me a break. Put yourself in my shoes."

Put myself in *his* shoes? Thinking of what had happened in the SUV, I folded my arms in front of my chest.

"After all these years of shunning the spotlight, he told me he was gearing up for his own show. Produced by and starring Aaron Neely. He was out scouting locations and everything. It was really going to happen." He leaned forward in the booth, suddenly intense, pointing his fork at his chest. "And I would have been in that writers' room. Do you know what that would have been like, being on the ground floor for a Neely show? I mean, writing side by side with him, seeing him deliver my jokes—it would be like writing for the *Larry Sanders Show* or *Curb Your Enthusiasm*. You'd be making history."

"Sounds awful," I said, raising an eyebrow.

He sank back in his booth and put down his fork. "Right, well . . . about a month ago, he canceled it. Just like that, out of the blue. Not interested. And not only that, but nobody's heard from him since. I've tried calling, but my calls get forwarded to his agent now. Or, rather, to his agent's assistant. Assistant's assistant." He picked up his fork again and started jabbing at the flabby bits of pancake he'd sliced into bites, collecting them from where they'd fallen apart on the plate. "So now you know why *The Bestie Cast* would have helped. I've been doing standup, working on my set, circulating scripts, but it's not like anyone's beating down my door. Dropping his name is getting me nowhere. I get the feeling Neely pissed some people off or something. I don't know."

I knew, and I almost laughed from the irony. A month ago, Neely had exposed himself to a massage therapist, had his face bashed in, and walked away knowing the whole thing had been recorded and could be released to the public at any time. So I *had* ruined Jason's chances with Neely, in a way. But if Neely was lying low, why had his reputation suffered? Were rumors beginning to circulate? Had the video appeared somewhere? Was Amanda blackmailing him after all?

"Don't look so worried," Jason said. "We've all been through ups and downs out here. It's part of the ride. The maybes, the almosts. The could've-worked-out-buts . . ." He sighed. "I guess that's why you went home in the first place."

I just looked at him, trying to pull my face together. Finally, I said, "I guess so."

"Well, I'm glad your career is going better. I really am." He went back to his stack of pancakes, which, as it shrank, had gradually deteriorated into a sticky pile. "Sometimes I wish we had stuck it out as a team."

"Me too," I said.

"And you look great," he said, assessing me slyly through the hair that swung over his eyes whenever he looked down. "I mean it. Success agrees with you. You look amazing."

With a quiver of anxiety, I moved to derail this line of conversation. "You keep talking about my success, but nothing's happened yet. I swear."

"Well, if it hasn't, then I bet it will soon," he said with undisguised envy. "Because—I mean, here you are."

"Here I am." I waved my grilled cheese with a flourish meant to take in all of L.A. as well as our booth and the diner around us. For a few seconds, we listened to the buzz of conversation and the clink of dishes.

"When's your top-secret meeting that you're not going to tell me about?"

I smiled. "Tomorrow at noon."

"You have a place to stay?" he asked, busying himself with more syrup.

"I have a motel reservation," I said. "But I haven't checked in yet." It was a concession to him, after all the talk about my success, to tell him that I had driven straight to his door without even getting settled in a motel first.

"Hey, do you want to take a walk around the old neighborhood?" he said. "I mean, if you're not worn-out from driving."

It wasn't even nine o'clock, and despite feeling dead tired, I was also wired. "Sounds nice."

He grinned widely, as if he'd been genuinely unsure if I'd say yes. "Great. Now I can keep spying on you." He gestured toward my bag. "Find out who's blowing up your phone."

I looked down quickly. I'd turned it back on in silent mode so I could get calls from Cynthia and her assistant, and now the screen was lit up, flickering rapidly, as if new messages were appearing on it every few seconds. I felt a momentary queasiness. Amanda was not happy about being left behind. "Hang on a second," I said with an apologetic smile. I hurriedly pulled up Amanda's number and blocked it.

The waiter dropped the check, and I put Amanda out of my mind as best I could. "I'll get this," I said. After all, I had my contest winnings to spend. "Since I'm the big shot now."

The vegetation in Los Angeles got me every time, the Seussian jungle of cacti and palm trees and tropical flowers, trailing vines clinging to dense shrubbery and crawling up metal gates. We strolled past fat agave spikes and jasmine, hibiscus with their veined pink petals curled up tight for the night and spindly yucca bobbing in the breeze. The Austin spring was full of blooming things for only a few weeks before the summer sun came out and fried everything to a crispy brown color. By contrast, the L.A. night was cool and the plants stayed lush year-round, fed on massive quantities of water diverted artificially into the desert. I loved it.

"We should've kept in better touch," Jason said for the hundredth time. He'd lit up an American Spirit as soon as we were outside the restaurant, and although I wanted to disapprove, had pestered him to quit a million times, I privately enjoyed the old familiar smell on the breeze. "How's your mom these days?" he said, politely holding up a branch that leaned out over the sidewalk.

"I just saw her, actually," I said, ducking under the branch with a nod of thanks. "I stayed with her on the way out here. She's fine. Same as always. How about your family?" I avoided Matt's name and kept my eyes on the uneven cracks in the buckled sidewalk.

"My dad remarried recently." He glanced sideways for my reaction. "Yeah, I know. It was a surprise to me too. And that's not even the biggest news." He took a deep breath. "Mattie's in prison."

I kept my expression carefully neutral, manifesting only the normal amount of concern. "My mom mentioned that when I saw her."

"It's the talk of the town," he said with a scowl. "Robbed a convenience store. What a fuckup. The gun was for show, he never intended to use it—the clerk was already reaching for the till when it went off and nicked a customer who was coming out of the bathroom. It's just Mattie's luck the customer happened to be a firefighter. Did you know they can sentence up to twelve years for assaulting a cop or a firefighter?" I shook my head. "But then, it wasn't his first offense." A small purple flower brushed up against his shoulder as we passed, and he made a grab for it. "Sometimes I think people were just sick and tired of Mattie's attitude. He was always such a jackass to everyone."

"I'm—I'm sorry, Jason."

"Don't be. He was the biggest jackass of all to me."

I nodded. I could still understand the truth of this, even with what Matt had done to me. After all, it wasn't personal. I was just an opportunity, a warm body he'd happened to have access to. He hardly grunted two words to me the whole time I knew him, before or after the incident. Whereas he had always made sure Jason understood exactly how much he was hated, and why. By Mattie's warped standards, Jason wasn't a man and therefore didn't deserve respect. It was easy to see how living under that dark cloud had shaped Jason's personality, his way of skulking under the radar, avoiding conflict at all costs, deflecting intimacy with a joke. "How's your dad doing with it?" I asked, hoping to sidestep into less painful territory.

"Honestly? I think he's just relieved to have Mattie out of the house. He got married pretty quick." He paused, fiddling with the purple flower, as if deciding whether to go on. "I think he'd been dating this woman for a long time. I think he was hiding the relationship on purpose, so—" He broke off abruptly and threw the flower away.

I watched it flutter sideways into the street. "So Mattie wouldn't find out?"

"Yeah," he said shortly. "So they'd never have to meet."

A shudder ran through me. Did Jason know—if not what Mattie had done to me, then at least what he was capable of doing? What an awful suspicion to have about your own brother. A suspicion as toxic, in its way, as Mattie's poisonous taunting.

Spontaneously, I reached down and grabbed Jason's hand and gave it a squeeze. He squeezed back, and we walked to our place—his place—for another ten minutes in silence, still holding hands. When we reached the door, he let go of my hand to get his keys out of his pocket and I took a deep breath. The desert air had cooled substantially while we walked, and my teeth were almost chattering with exhaustion and chill.

"Come on in," he said, and there it was, the beige stucco walls hung with kitschy Goodwill portraits on black velvet, the dingy rug, the sofa we'd bought at Ikea together our first day in town and that he'd paid me half the cost of, against my objections, when I drove back to Austin with an empty car. I sat on a cushion, now threadbare and sunken at its center, and waited while Jason put a kettle on to boil in the narrow, pink-tiled kitchen.

"Everything's the same," he called, as if he could hear my thoughts.

"Except that's a new TV, isn't it?"

"Yeah, well. As you know, my ship came in for about five minutes." He rounded the corner carrying two mugs. "I thought it was a good idea to invest in the medium. Put something on, if you want. It'll be just like old times."

"Sure," I said. "What do you want to watch?"

"I don't know, let's see." He sat down on the sofa, set the mugs on the battered coffee table, and picked up the remote. Then he put it down again without turning the TV on, scooted over next to me so that our thighs were touching, and leaned his head on top of mine.

Like old times.

We sat like that for a few minutes. And then I drew back.

"What's wrong?" he said.

"Nothing." I yawned elaborately. "I guess I'm finally getting tired."

"Hey." He picked at the knee of his jeans. "It's late. You want to just crash here tonight? There's still a bed in your old room." He affected an old-person voice. "Your mother and I haven't changed a thing, all your old debate trophies are still in there."

I ran with the bit, grateful for the shift in tone. "Debate trophies? God, I was really a geek."

"That's why we used to give you so many swirlies, kiddo."

"Okay," I said. "Sure. I'll stay."

We walked down the corridor, and Jason cleared his throat apologetically as I looked inside. I knew he had been joking about not having changed things, but I hadn't expected quite this much change. The room was entirely black, the walls lined with black paneling, the windows covered with plastic sheeting, electronic equipment stacked in the corners. "I thought I was supposed to be a geek, not a goth."

"After you left, I decided to turn it into a recording studio," he said sheepishly. "I thought I might try doing my own podcast. I mean, as long as I'm not getting any gigs. I've heard it works out for *some* people." He glanced sideways at me. "But don't worry, the mattress is still in the closet."

"Does this make me your first podcast guest?"

Jason, who had already disappeared into the closet, grunted as he reemerged pulling the bare mattress out behind him. "Split the rent, and you can be my cohost," he said, tipping the mattress onto the floor. "Now I just have to remember where I put the sheets."

In a few minutes I was lying on the mattress on the floor, staring up at the light fixture I'd never thought I'd see again, letting sleep pull me under.

I woke only once in the night, when I dreamed of missing a step on a staircase and falling with a lurch. As I struggled awake, the sensation in the pit of my stomach merged with a vague awareness of being in the wrong time, as if I'd slipped through a wormhole into the past. A tall, dark figure loomed over me, and for a moment I thought it was Jason. Then I saw Carl's bloodied face bearing down on me, his teeth chattering with an awful, rhythmic kind of moan.

I jerked fully awake, forcing my eyes all the way open. The dark form reshaped itself into a cluster of music stands, and I pressed my hand over my heart, feeling silly.

The teeth-chattering sound, however, continued. After a moment, I saw that my phone screen had flickered on and was vibrating rhythmically from its place on the floor by the mattress. I picked it up and saw a stream of texts from a series of unknown numbers, all different but unmistakably from the same person:

We need to talk. It's an emergency!!

Do NOT freeze me out, D

I thought we were friends

"Damn it." I turned the phone off. I felt wide-awake, but I couldn't have been, because it took only a few moments to fall back asleep to dreams in which past and present were all mixed up in places that seemed both familiar and strange: a children's museum, a cruise ship, a furniture store where Henry babbled on and on about honest coffee tables and purposeful futons. After that, I slept heavily until morning.

Too heavily. My phone wasn't on, so my alarm didn't go off, and when I woke up, the sunbeams coming through the curtains were suspiciously short on the floor. My body remembered before my brain what that meant: ten o'clock, at least. I groaned and rolled out of bed.

Jason was already up, finishing a cup of coffee at the breakfast table while he scrolled through the news on his laptop. "I was just wondering whether I should wake you up," he said. "You seemed really tired, so I let you sleep." He didn't meet my eyes.

"Thanks. I'm going to go ahead and take a shower and get out the door."

He nodded, and I hustled through my shortened morning routine, trying not to be late. I slipped on my interview outfit, which, ever since the tragicomic loss of my wrap dress, had consisted of dark jeans with heels, a loose top, and a statement necklace for extra coverage above the neckline. As I walked out the door, heels clicking on the linoleum entryway, Jason wished me luck curtly, no doubt thinking of the last meeting I'd gone off to without him.

As I pulled into the parking lot at the studio cantina where I was meeting Cynthia, I, too, was comparing my current situation to the one just over a year ago. Then, as now, I'd been alone, preparing for a meeting with someone considerably more important than me, fully aware that my career hung on the outcome. But this time, there was no question of my having stolen the opportunity from Jason. I'd earned it strictly on my own — though I didn't like to think about exactly how.

I took a deep breath and walked into the cantina. Cynthia spotted me from across the room and waved me over. When I reached her table in the corner, she stood up and leaned over to give me a hug. With my heels on, I came up to her nostrils.

"Dana!" She seemed sincerely delighted to see me, as if we really were friends. "Sit down, sit down. I've already ordered some snacks for us, they're on the way. Do you want anything to drink? They have great smoothies here."

My stomach roiled, but I managed to smile as I shook my head. "No, thanks, I'm not a smoothie fan. Thank you so much for taking the time to meet me on such short notice. You must be insanely busy."

"Oh, please, I'm just thrilled that you made it out here." She sat down. "But you're right, I am busy, so let me cut to the chase, Dana. What are you first, a writer or a performer?"

I opened my mouth, then shut it again. It wasn't the question I was expecting. But before I could even begin to process my response, she continued. "I know, I know, you're both. You just want to make people laugh, right? But you've got to know, in this business, what it is you're selling. You've got to know your brand."

What was my brand? I nodded eagerly to signify that I was on the point of delivering the answer. But I was saved from having to decide on the spot what it was because she wasn't finished.

"Now, I'm putting together a little pitch for a sitcom." I abandoned my search for my brand as rapidly as I'd adopted it. "Look, I'm going to level with you, we don't even have a script for the pilot yet. I mean, it's early. But I'm looking for talent like you."

Like me. I didn't even know what that meant, but she had finally paused, so I mustered the best response I could. "Really? Like me?"

"Bright, motivated, not too attached to the past. You know? Not bound by ideas of what a show like this should look like." She hadn't yet dropped a hint of what the show was about, but I wasn't about to interrupt her to ask. "I'm working with some really stellar people on the pilot right now. And we think if we could get you in the room, maybe even give you a character on the show—"

"A character?" The wind was almost completely knocked out of me or I would never have cut her off before finding out who "we" was. "On your—"

"We start you out small in the pilot. The receptionist, maybe, if we end up setting it in the dermatologist's office. Or the intern, if we go with the magazine idea. Just let you play with the character, see how you work in the writers' room, develop some chemistry, and see where it goes from there."

"Wow. I can't even—wow." My brand was turning out to be stammering idiot. I tried to collect myself enough to ask a relevant question. "Would I be—"

"Don't say yes or no," she interrupted. "I know you don't have your agent with you. You need to talk to your money people." As a matter of fact, I didn't technically have an agent yet, but I resolved to get the contract she had sent me over e-mail signed and returned by the end of the day. As for money people, no one in my life had earned that distinction thus far. "But here's the deal, Dana." Her voice dropped, and I leaned as far forward as I could across the table. "I need to know that you're as committed to performing as you are to writing."

Trying to look as if I were really thinking this over, as befit her tone of gravitas, I wrinkled my forehead and nodded slowly. "And that if the series gets successful, you're not going to use that success to take off in the middle of it to do a standup tour, like that asshole from *My Peeps* did last year."

I opened my mouth to deny that such a thought would ever cross my mind, but she waved her hand to stop me. "Don't promise anything. This is all hypothetical. I'm just gauging your interest level."

"My interest level?" The waitress showed up with a few small dishes, her patter about house-made cornichons and free-range ox-liver pâté giving me a merciful moment to reflect on what I would say next.

Cynthia popped a cornichon into her mouth and chewed, waiting.

"My interest level is high." I felt a little dizzy with the effort of finding words that wouldn't necessitate another interruption.

"The minute I saw Betty up there onstage, I knew you had commitment," she said. "And I knew that was exactly what I wanted for the show."

"Commitment?"

"Betty," she said, spreading pâté on a piece of house-made Melba toast. "I want Betty."

She wanted Betty.

The Betty wig was still crumpled under the sofa where I'd kicked it after the Carl hit, and I'd done my best to avoid thinking about it since then. I wished, suddenly, that I'd thrown the wig in the dumpster that night along with the gloves. I wasn't sure why I hadn't. If I had, I could truthfully claim that Betty, or at least this version of her, was gone for good.

As it was, I had to say something. Cynthia was watching me with uncharacteristic silence. Perhaps I had misunderstood or taken her too literally. "It's just Betty you want?"

"Do you have any other characters I haven't seen?" She raised her index finger, cutting me off before I had even opened my mouth. "Good ones, I mean." I shook my head slowly, and she laughed. "Well, listen, you don't need any. Betty is the perfect wacky neighbor for this kind of show. She'd be great as a terrible receptionist, a weird waitress at the local diner, or, if I wind up just playing myself, an obsessed fan. She could be anything, really."

"I can definitely write that type of character," I said carefully. "Something like Betty."

Cynthia frowned. "I guess the name could change. As long as she still had the wig, the attitude, the violence — probably not the profanity, depending on the network —"

"What about something fresh?" I said. "If I were, you know, kind of done with Betty. If I were thinking of retiring her, I could try something else out?"

"Of course you could." She finished crunching up another cornichon and swallowed it, reaching for a thin slice of radish. "On another show."

I took a bite of something pickled, not noticing what, and chewed mechanically during the endless seconds of silence that followed.

Then Cynthia's eyes lit up.

"Irina! Irina, over here!" She refocused on me for a moment. "Just one minute, Dana, sit tight. I'm just going to go *say hi to my very best friend, Iriiiina!*" Midsentence, she rose, her voice changing from a half-hearted apology to a squeal of excitement directed at a woman who was rapidly approaching. Cynthia edged out from behind the table and gave Irina a hug. Then the two stood next to my chair, talking at a rapid clip about some project whose name I couldn't quite catch, for almost half an hour.

It took me twenty minutes, taking tiny bites and chewing as slowly as I could, to finish all the pickles and pâté on the table. Another five to crunch up every piece of ice in my water glass and drain the last drops. Another five to twist my napkin into an unusable paper turd. I became aware that I had to go to the bathroom.

Just as I was shifting in my chair, deciding whether to go or not, Cynthia said, still talking into the air above my head: "Oh, shoot. Look at the time."

"I'd better be going too," said the woman named Irina.

Cynthia looked down at me as if rediscovering my presence by her elbow.

"Oh my gosh, Dana, I am so sorry. How rude. I can't believe this but I have to rush off to another meeting. I might actually be late already. I feel really good about this, though, don't you? I feel like there's a partnership here waiting to happen." She looked me straight in the eye, and I felt the enveloping warmth of her gaze. "You are ready for this, Dana. I know you don't feel it yet, but you are *so ready*."

Acutely conscious of the napkin turd on the table next to the crumbs of the lunch I'd eaten almost entirely by myself, I stood to better meet her gaze, but she still towered over me. "Thank you so much for your time," I said. It came out a little weak.

"Irina, wait a minute, I'll walk you out," she sang. Then she turned back to me, put her hand on my shoulder, and gave me a little pat, wearing a sympathetic smile. "You had me all to yourself for fifteen minutes. That's really good for your first L.A. lunch!" I felt two air kisses, one on either cheek, and she was gone.

Still standing awkwardly in front of the table, I pulled out my cell phone and turned it on. It vibrated in my hand immediately as messages from Amanda began filling up the screen. I called Jason. "Hey, are you heading into work any time soon?" His current day job was a bartending gig at a seafood restaurant.

"I'm supposed to go in at five." He paused, as if registering the tone in my voice. "But I was thinking of calling in sick today, if you want to hang out."

I made a point of forcing myself to go by the Days Inn where I had a reservation and check in first. I didn't want to take anything for granted. I printed out the agent contract in the motel's business center, which consisted of a storage closet with an antiquated desktop computer and an Epson, and used my phone to scan and send the signed document. All the way to Jason's house, I kept replaying Cynthia's last line. It wasn't my first L.A. lunch, not by a long shot. But I had to admit, it wasn't my worst either.

14

When I walked in the door, Jason was waiting with a big grin on his face. "It's happy-hour o'clock."

"Where are we going?"

"It's a surprise."

I looked down at my audition outfit. "Is this okay to wear?"

"Yeah, sure."

"Hang on, I brought one dress." I ran to the room where I'd slept the night before, rifled through my gym bag, and pulled out a strappy black dress I'd packed, though I couldn't have said why.

Jason smiled when he saw me in it. "That's perfect." He was so keyed up that I let him put me in his car and drive us downtown without pressing him further regarding our destination. He hadn't yet asked me about the meeting with Cynthia, and I was relieved. He didn't have to ask. He knew I didn't want to talk about it, and he was happy to create a diversion so I wouldn't have to. This was Jason and I at our best, communicating wordlessly, distracting each other from disaster. We pulled into a valet lot, and Jason handed the keys to one of those preternaturally attractive service workers you see everywhere in Los Angeles while another one opened my door and helped me out.

I cocked an eyebrow at Jason. "Fancy."

"Shut up, you like it." He herded me through glass doors and into a hotel lobby. "Look up."

I looked up and gasped. The lobby was illuminated by hundreds of vintage lamps strung upside down at different heights from a mirrored ceiling.

"We're taking the escalator to the second floor," Jason said. "There's a special elevator to the roof on the mezzanine."

"Of course there is." But it was working; I was starting to thrill to the fun of it, no longer focused on my lingering feelings of humiliation about the Cynthia lunch. As we ascended, the escalator moving diagonally through a flock of taxidermied birds in flight, I began to see the meeting with Cynthia for what it had been: a massive success. Cynthia had offered me a place in her writers' room. She had told me she wanted me on her show. It would be nearly impossible to explain to Jason how this was anything but a win. If he had heard me on that podcast, he knew about Betty, but he wouldn't have any idea why I wanted to retire her. No one who'd been following my career would —with the exception of one person, of course, the one whose dozens of phone messages I didn't intend to listen to. And now that I didn't need to keep my phone on to stay in touch with Cynthia or Jason, I didn't have to think about her either.

We waited for a few minutes by a special elevator guarded by a hotel clerk who sent only a few people up at a time. I rolled my eyes at Jason behind the clerk's back, enjoying every minute of it.

"Trust me," Jason said.

"Always."

Waved in by the attendant, we stepped into the carpeted elevator, me carefully avoiding getting my spindly heels caught in the trench between the carriage and shaft. Four tall, thin girls in various shades of tan got in after us, strapped into outfits nearly indistinguishable, by length and coverage, from bathing suits.

"I hope we get one of the waterbed sofas," Jason said.

"I hope they're heated." A rooftop in Los Angeles could get cold, even in the summer.

"Wuss." Jason elbowed me, then gestured toward the scantily clad model types in front of us.

"I don't see you wearing a halter top."

"I'm saving it for a special occasion."

As the elevator rose, a thumping beat, at first only faintly audible, grew louder. We stopped and the doors slid open on an electronic dance mix with a jaw-rattling bass, oddly incongruous in the still-glaring daylight. The serpentine girls in front of us decanted onto a strip of crimson carpet, and I saw a row of topiary animals looming against a skyline suffused with the tender, rosy glow of an early sunset. It was smog, not sunset, and the topiary animals were fake, but it still looked like something out of a movie. I stepped out of the elevator.

"Impressive," I yelled into his ear over the music.

"I'm just trying to lure you out here again," he yelled back. "Me alone in L.A. is a disaster."

We moved through the seating area, which seethed with young, attractive people perched on the edges of white cubes and shout-chatting over the music, and toward the bar. Amid the happy-hour hustlers were people in actual bathing suits, and Jason pointed to a pool at one end of the rooftop. I noticed yellow tape cordoning off one seating area and gave him a questioning look.

"No waterbed sofas tonight," he said. "They get punctured a lot, I guess by all the—" I lost the last part of the sentence, and Jason repeated it, leaning in and putting one hand on my shoulder for balance as he indicated his lifted foot.

The music surged. Instead of hearing the words, I only felt his touch on my bare skin. "The *what?*"

"*High heels.*"

I laughed nervously, and Jason used the hand on my shoulder to steer me toward a bar thronged with humanity. Observing the brutal coolness competition at the bar, I could see that the process of ordering a pair of twenty-dollar cocktails was going to take a while. "Maybe I should find us somewhere to sit," I shouted into Jason's ear, standing on tiptoe. He nodded.

I made my way toward a few seats near a giant white brick fireplace, but before I could get there, a couple of guys appeared out of nowhere, drinks in hand, and settled into them. I made the rounds, trying to look casual as I strolled the topiary aisles and passed a suite of Ping-Pong tables, where I narrowly avoided being hit by a whizzing white ball. The sun began to set; the angle of the glow became more acute, the glare off the nearby buildings dazzling. Having explored nearly the whole rooftop without spotting any empty seats, I wandered around a corner that seemed quieter and leaned against a sun-warmed wall to catch my breath. I'd been there only a moment, when, without warning, a speaker near my head started blaring a clashing electronic beat complete with high-pitched shrieks; another DJ had arrived and started his set, undaunted by the already loud ambient music. The sonic chaos drove me back toward the bar, where Jason was still waiting, empty-handed. He saw my expression and his face fell.

"This is miserable, isn't it?"

I shrugged noncommittally, not wanting to hurt his feelings and too tired to raise my voice again.

"Let's just go."

I nodded, relieved, and we stumbled back to the elevator, which was disgorging fresh heaps of the young and beautiful. On the way down we were alone in the elevator, but after the mayhem above, the silence was too peaceful to break. I had time to wonder what, in the past year, Jason had grown used to while I was trying out material in Austin coffee shops. Had he been hanging out on rooftops with Aaron Neely, hobnobbing with the kind of person who brings a bikini to a midday meeting and takes a dip afterward?

Just before the elevator doors opened, I tried it out. "So, you come here a lot, then?"

"This was my first time." He looked sheepish. "I just wanted to impress you." I snorted, and he started laughing too. "Since you're such a big shot now."

I stopped to glare at him, then broke up laughing again.

"It's pretty awful, though, isn't it?" He pointed to the ceiling with its forest of vintage lamps as we walked out of the hotel.

"I think the word you're looking for is *basic,*" I said. "But what a view."

"I hear they have a great happy hour at R & R."

We walked through the well-shaded grounds of the Central Library on the way back to the car, pausing to linger under the fantastical foliage. Jason put an arm around me, casually, as if it were no big deal.

"So—you're staying another night?"

This time Jason had ordered an omelet with hash browns. As I ate my burger, I thought, *Jason will always be the kind of guy who orders breakfast for dinner.* Maybe I knew him too well at this point. "A few more days, at least."

"Are you apartment hunting?" He thwacked the ketchup bottle over his hash browns a couple of times.

"I don't think I'm ready for that yet. Anyway, it's not like I have tons of money lying around. I'd have to nail something definite down before I—"

"That's exactly what I wanted to talk to you about." A glob of ketchup landed on his plate, but he didn't seem to notice. "I was only kind of joking last night about splitting the rent. I haven't had much luck in the roommate department since you left, and I can't afford to live alone much longer. So if you did need a place . . ." He trailed off, placed the ketchup bottle on the table, and poked at the mess on his plate.

I couldn't believe it. He was asking me to move in with him. Without so much as a word about what had been going on between us —the touching, the handholding, the date spot—he was asking me to reappear in his life as if I'd never left it. With no idea what, if anything, we were to each other.

"What exactly are you saying, Jason?" I knew, but I needed him to say it. To admit, at least, that he needed me.

But he began backpedaling immediately. "Or not. If you're not into the idea."

I continued eating my burger and kept my mouth full for the rest of the meal so I'd only have to nod yes or shake my head no.

When we got back to Jason's place, he put on a comedy special we'd both heard about, and I relaxed a little into our old, familiar rapport, chuckling intermittently, picking apart the jokes, pointing out what worked and what didn't.

And then, half an hour into it, he was leaning on me again.

"Don't do that," I said, throwing his arm off the back of the sofa.

"What, this?" He ruffled my hair.

"I'm serious. Stop." I jerked away. "Jason, what is this? What are we doing here? I need to know what's going on."

He took a deep breath and smoothed his hair back off his forehead in the old gesture of frustration. "Dana, when I said I'd had bad luck with roommates, I meant—well, my last roommate was actually a girlfriend. Ex, now." He shook his head, his hands on his knees. "It turned out she was just using me for my industry contacts. It totally destroyed my sense of trust."

I sat, stony-faced, and waited for him to finish.

He gave me a look of earnest appeal. "I know I'm sending mixed signals here. But I'm just not ready to make any new commitments yet. Do you know what I mean?"

I stood up. "I'd better go."

He looked surprised.

As I spoke, I hunted around for my heels. "If you're expecting me to sit here and listen to you talk about your girl problems yet again —I just can't do it anymore." I laughed. "God, how many times have I listened to you bitching about some skinny blonde who didn't treat you right? Poor Jason. Poor, poor Jason." The blood was rising to my face. Where had I kicked them off? "And to think, I was worried that maybe you only wanted me to move in because I'm an asset. Now that I'm more successful than you and all."

His expression changed into one of angry protest, but I stopped him before he could get a word out.

"But no, it's not even that crass. I was flattering myself. You're just on the rebound. Again. And you want someone to listen to you and pet your head and pick up your mess. Well, I don't care if this bitch used you or cheated on you or what." Thinking of what my mom had said about Jason, I threw my shoulders back. "I don't pick up other people's messes anymore."

"Dana—" He put a hand out toward me and I flinched away.

"Destroyed your sense of trust," I sneered. "That, by the way, is bullshit. If you don't trust me by now, you're never going to."

"Hang on a minute. Who doesn't trust who?" He stood up too, and I moved around so that the sofa was between us. "You haven't even told me why you're here. You're obviously sitting on something huge. You've been carrying it around like it's a state secret or something. Your phone is blowing up—it can't all be agent calls and Cynthia Omari or you'd be returning them. You're pretty keen to hide who it is, aren't you?" I looked away. "So what are you doing here? Showing up out of the blue, without even returning my text—holding hands, cozying up, crashing in my spare room." His indignation was swelling. "For all I know, that's your boyfriend trying to get hold of you."

"I don't have a boyfriend," I snapped, finally spotting my shoes under the kitchen table and leaning down to grab them.

"An ex, then?" He stepped in front of the door, perhaps unconsciously. "Or someone else you're not going to tell me about?"

"Maybe it's none of your business." Since he was blocking the door, I wheeled and stormed down the hall to my old room. My gym bag was lying open on the mattress, and I grabbed my jeans off the floor, where I'd dropped them when I'd changed hastily earlier in the evening, and threw them into it.

"This is exactly what I mean," he said, following me. "This. All this time we've known each other, you've never opened up to me." He took a few steps toward me, and I stood up, shouldering the gym bag. "Am I supposed to leap into a relationship with someone who won't ever talk to me about what's eating her?"

"What's eating me—" I pushed past him and headed down the hall, Jason right on my heels.

"Let's start with that meeting today. It didn't go well. Will I ever know what happened?"

"You could start by asking."

"And have you walk out, like you're about to do right now."

"Damn straight I am," I said, marching toward the door, grabbing my purse on the way. I stopped and turned around with my hand on the doorknob. "Since we're telling the truth here," I said, "don't pretend you've ever wanted to know how I feel, Jason. You've done your best to avoid it the whole time we've known each other. If you ever asked—and I told you—then you'd have to admit—"

I choked, thinking of all those afternoons hanging out with Jason, how I'd tried to shove my feelings down, pretend them away. The clueless, clumsy teenager I'd been, spending the night over at a boy's house, hoping one day he'd see me as more than a friend. And instead of the teen-movie ending I'd been waiting for, the kiss and the corsage and the cool soundtrack, I'd been violated so deeply that I couldn't have put it into words for anyone, even if I'd wanted to. *That.* That was what having your trust in the world destroyed looked like.

But he was still standing there, playing dumb. He was going to make me say it.

"You knew how I felt," I said. "And you used me anyway, all those years. You used me for an ego boost whenever your ass got dumped. And you used me for my talent when you couldn't get anywhere on your own." He looked as if I'd slapped his face, but I kept talking. "I'm not going to play this game anymore. It's an insult to us both. I'm done with it."

I let the door slam behind me.

The phone inside my gym bag in the passenger seat buzzed nonstop the whole drive to Days Inn. I wished like hell it was Jason calling to apologize and beg me to come back, but I knew without looking who it was. As soon as I got to my room, I threw the bag on the bed, and the phone tumbled out onto the paisley bedspread, quivering and flashing the word *Unknown.*

Something in me snapped. I picked it up, pushed the talk icon, and screamed, "Leave me alone!" at the top of my lungs. Then I powered the phone off and threw it across the room. It bounced on the baseboard and disappeared under the bed.

I went into the bathroom to get ready for bed, exhausted. Thank

God for motels, with their miniature plastic-wrapped toiletries, anonymous and disposable. I unwrapped a bar of soap the size of a Saltine, massaged it to a lackluster lather, and smoothed the suds over my skin. Splashing cold water on my face with one hand, I groped blindly for a towel with the other. Just as I found it and buried my face in it, a burst of noise started up in the bedroom, a high-pitched electronic gargling that made me drop the hand towel into the wet sink.

The motel phone was ringing.

As I came out of the bathroom, the first ring ended. After an abnormally long pause, the next shrill scream came, accompanied by a blinking red light on the phone base. I walked slowly toward the nightstand, hoping against hope it would stop its shrieking by the time I got there. I sat on the side of the bed and listened to it ring three more times before putting out my hand and lifting the cheap plastic receiver to my ear, straining at the short and tangled cord.

"Hello?"

"Dana," said Amanda. "Just listen to me."

I slammed the phone down. I tried to unplug it, but there was a sturdy plastic casing around the connection to the phone, and the other end was unreachable under the bed. The buttons under the number pad were smooth pitted black, their icons worn off, and I jabbed them all at random, hoping one of them was a do-not-disturb button.

Instead I got the front desk. "Please don't let anyone call my room," I pleaded, almost in tears, but the hotel clerk answered me in a voice rendered nearly indecipherable by the connection, and I eventually hung up, uncertain whether he had understood me or not.

Without getting undressed, I turned out the light and lay back in bed, crying in frustration, waiting and waiting for the phone to ring again. Then I fell asleep.

15

Scratch. Scratch.

I opened my eyes. The noise was coming from the door. At the crack along the bottom, a faint bleed of light ended abruptly in shadow.

Scratch.

The bed moaned as I lurched upright, and the scratching stopped. The shadow moved to one side and paused there.

The bedside clock said 3:05. My heart hammered. I lay back down as quietly as possible.

She was here. She must have seen me check in to the motel yesterday, called my room last night to confirm the number. And now she was trying to get in.

In the silence, my breathing seemed unnaturally loud. I lay rigid, trying to keep the bedsprings from crying out again, and pictured her staring at the door from the other side, waiting. We stayed like that for an eternity. The silence lasted so long, I felt my mind drifting back toward sleep and had to fight to keep my eyes open. Time seemed to slow and swell, stretching itself into a dark elastic rope between us. Amanda would never let me go. She couldn't, because the darkness that tethered us to each other came from inside me. She would go only when it was gone. And I couldn't get rid of it without her.

There was a soft knock.

As if sleepwalking, I swung my legs over the side of the bed and then eased my feet to the floor. The shadow was still there. I slid my feet over the worn carpet, one after the other.

Another knock, this one a little louder.

"Dana? Are you awake?" The low, familiar voice ran through me like a slug of bourbon, turning everything it touched warm and tingly. I ran to cross the remaining distance, flipped the deadbolt, turned the handle, and yanked the door open to see Jason, sallow in the yellowish motel lights, fidgeting from side to side awkwardly, his face twisted into a pained grimace. I burst into tears.

"Oh God, I scared you. I'm so sorry." He looked at my face, flushed from crying, and then looked down. "I couldn't sleep. I've been thinking about what you said."

My heart was still hammering. "How did you find me?"

He held up a plastic hotel pen. "You left this in my house. I found your car in the lot and got your room number from the parking spot." In his other hand, he showed me a piece of paper ripped from a spiral notebook, a few words scribbled near the top. "I swear I was just going to leave a note on your door, but—I couldn't think of what to say." He crumpled up the note and stuffed it and the pen into his pocket. "So now that I woke you up like a complete idiot, do you think we could talk for a minute?"

I hesitated, still wiping my eyes. Then I stepped back and let him cross the threshold. "I'm not getting back to sleep any time soon anyway."

"I know. My timing sucks." He stalked over toward the bed as I closed the door behind him. I took my seat at the table by the window and watched him pace. "I wish I could be like you, Dana."

"Short, stacked, and Latina? Not going to happen."

"That's fine, keep joking. I don't have any right to ask you to be straight with me. I haven't earned it. But I'm going to be straight with you." He took a deep breath. "What I meant is—you've always held it together. You don't let stuff drag you down, make you feel—wrong inside." He frowned, searching for words. "It's intimidating. You don't *need* people like I do."

"That's such a line, Jason." I thumped my fingers impatiently on the side of my chair. "That's what you tell yourself, but it's total crap. You know it is."

He whirled to face me. "Remember after graduation? We had all these big plans. Get out of Amarillo, head to Austin. Face the world together."

"Yeah, and you went right ahead and did all that. Without me."

"Not for long." He started pacing again. "I couldn't hack it on my own. Besides, you're the one who changed the plan, Dana. You always do."

"What can I say, the glamour of the Sears returns desk was too much to resist."

"Oh, cut the pity-me crap," he snapped. "You changed on me senior year, and I never knew why. You stopped laughing at my jokes. You didn't care about college anymore. I thought you wanted space." He sighed. "I didn't know what else to think."

So he had noticed something after all. "You think I didn't *want* to go conquer the world with you? I was going through something, Jason. I needed you more than ever." Looking back on that time, I couldn't remember what I'd needed, only a hazy numbness, but I pressed on. "And you left."

"Yeah, and I was miserable on my own. Why do you think I talked you into following me?" He seemed suddenly tired. "The same reason I talked you into coming out here—and I've been trying to do it again ever since you showed up at my door." He gave me the look that killed me every time, his dark eyebrows furrowed, his hair swinging forward. "I'm no good without you, Dana."

To cover the twinge it gave me, I looked away and sighed theatrically. "That's all very touching, Jason," I said. "But from where I stand, it seems like you've been doing fine. Getting jobs, palling around with Aaron Neely, dating actresses—"

At the mention of his love life, he scowled furiously, some fight obviously left in him. "You don't get to bring that up. That relationship almost killed me. I lost who I was."

"And I suppose that's my fault too?" I stood up, suddenly enraged. "Because I wasn't there to babysit you while you dated yet another girl who *wasn't me?* I'm not your training wheels anymore, Jason. If you can't handle an adult relationship without your little—"

"Without my best friend?"

"Your security blanket," I finished. "That's all I am to you. We were never really best friends. I was in love with you. You knew that, and you used me."

"I—" He started to fire back, then stopped and abruptly sat down on the bed, as if his legs had given out. "Yeah. I knew." He glanced up, shorter than me for once. "In my defense, it's not easy to know what's going on with you. You play everything pretty close to the chest." I kept staring until he looked down again. "But, yeah, I guess I knew, deep down. I just wasn't ready to do anything about it. I guess I thought—"

"That when you were done having fun, I'd be there?" I said. "Are you all done now, Jason?"

He shook his head and opened his mouth, but nothing came out. Instead, his head kept shaking, back and forth. It took me a minute to realize he was crying, because I'd never seen him cry before. There were no actual tears, just a redness around his eyes and two red splotches on his temples, spreading.

"I don't know what to say, Dana. I just need you, that's all. I always have, but I didn't know how much until the past year. I'm sorry that's what it took." He looked up briefly. "But I don't feel done. I feel . . . ready." He leaned his head into his hands.

I walked over to the bed and put my hands in his hair, pushed it away from his forehead. He dropped his hands to his thighs, and I moved forward until I was standing between his knees, letting his head fall against my chest. His hands curled around the backs of my thighs, under the jersey dress I was still wearing, warm on my bare skin. I rested my cheek on top of his head for a moment, like he used to do to me when we watched TV together, to see how it felt. Then I straightened up, put my hands on his cheeks, and turned his face up to mine.

"I'm ready too," I said, and I leaned down toward him.

His hands tightened around the backs of my thighs as we kissed. Then one hand moved to my hip and pulled me closer while the other moved to my waist, then farther upward. The warmth enveloped me from every point of contact — his wet mouth, the bristle on his lip scratching mine, his inner thighs against my hips, his hands moving with a slow greed. He moved a thumb over my nipple and I gasped and closed my eyes. But at the center of the red, warm darkness behind my eyes there was a spot of icy cold that refused to melt away. A wave of dizziness, and I couldn't feel Jason's warm hands anymore, just the black hole opening to swallow me and a voice in my head that sounded exactly like Amanda whispering something.

I'm still here.

I opened my eyes and took a step back.

Jason opened his eyes too. "What's wrong?"

"It's okay," I said. "I'm just—it's late." To have something to do with my hands, I gestured toward the clock. It was 4:17 a.m.

"Yeah." His hands still rested lightly on my hips.

"We'll talk more tomorrow." I ran a hand through his hair. "I'm glad you came over."

He stood and was suddenly much taller than me again. Remote, but warm. "Thanks for letting me in."

"I'll be here tomorrow," I said. "I'm not really kicking you out."

"And I'm not really leaving."

He leaned over to give me a kiss by the door. Just a light peck, but it felt like a promise. Then he was gone.

16

I awoke a few hours later to morning sun streaming in under the curtains. Outside, the sounds of a motel by daylight banished the specters of the night before; engines revved in the parking lot, car doors slammed. A woman passing my door hollered back to someone to be sure and look under the bed one more time, and for a moment I remembered the last family vacation before my dad left: Big Bend National Park, when I was six. On a canyon walk I'd grabbed a deceptively fuzzy-looking cactus and cried all the way back to the motel, where, to placate me, my parents ordered *Matilda* on pay-per-view. The three of us piled onto the bed to watch the movie, them leaning side by side up against the headboard, me on my stomach with my chin in my hands. I think it was one of the last times my parents were happy together. I wish I had turned around even once and looked at their faces, so I could be sure.

After a moment of equivocation, I leaned over the side of the bed and reached until my fingertips brushed the corner of my phone.

Fumbling a little, I managed to hook the edge of the case and drag it out. I took a deep breath and turned it on.

For the first time in forty-eight hours, there were no new calls or texts from Amanda.

Could she finally be getting the message? Or, having located my motel room, was she just switching tactics? The thought was disturbing but, in the morning light, easy to brush off. I didn't know how she'd found me—through some sophisticated hacking technology, I assumed—but the important part was that, after hearing my voice on the line once, she hadn't tried again.

The superstitious part of me connected her sudden silence to Jason. The more Jason had come back into my life, the more Amanda's presence had seemed to fade. His appearance in my room last night—our fight, the kiss—seemed to have banished her altogether. In daylight, the pact Amanda and I had made no longer felt like a dark secret; it was as flimsy and insubstantial as a slumber-party dare. After all, Jason and I had grown up together, loving the same TV shows, hating the same hometown, yearning for the same escape routes. No one but my mother had known me longer—not even my dad, who hadn't sent me a birthday card since I turned twelve. Whereas Amanda had materialized out of thin air only a few short months ago with no connection to me at all. We had no mutual friends, no shared interests, nothing in common but a couple of failed stints in L.A.—and what was more common than that? Jason and I were going to share something much rarer, a magical combination of love and success.

As if on cue, a text appeared on my phone, not from Amanda but from my newly acquired agent, who'd managed to book me an audition today, on my third day in L.A.—in just a few hours, as a matter of fact.

I wanted to crow out loud. So Cynthia, who'd practically offered me a job on the spot yesterday, wasn't even my only iron in the fire. I'd been in town three days and already I was doing better than I had in the four years I'd lived here. Maybe being the second-funniest person in Austin wasn't as good as being the funniest, but it had opened doors. Or had someone seen me in the café with Cynthia and decided that my star was on the rise? In any case, if I wanted to retire the Betty character, letting all her disturbing associations fade permanently from my mind, there was no reason to think it would kill my career. I would survive, stronger than ever without her.

I took a look at the audition details. A pilot for a sitcom set in an advertising firm in the eighties, *Mad Men* by way of *WKRP*, according to the sketchy description. Which meant, I was sure, that I was being invited in to read for the nerdy brunette foil to a ditzy blond secretary. Fine. The producer was on a winning streak; I would play straight man to a dumb blonde any day of the week to be associated with his name. I rooted through my bag for my audition outfit, pulled it on, and added a pair of nonprescription glasses I carried around for just this type of occasion. Then I slipped the folder with my headshot and resumé into my purse. Ready to go.

On an impulse, I pulled out my phone and texted Jason my good news. If we were going to try to be together, I would need to get used to sharing things like this with him. It wasn't exactly baring my heart, but it was a beginning.

On my way out the door, the hotel phone by the bed caught my eye, and for a moment I thought the red message light was flashing. I forced myself to stare at it until I'd satisfied myself that it was just a trick of the light. Then I left.

The moment I walked into the waiting room, I realized this was more of a cattle call than an audition. I tried not to let the number of bodies in the room get me down. At least I was right about the casting balance of women on the show; the room was crowded with a dozen or so tall, skinny blondes that I imagined in the Loni Anderson role, some with hair teased up to suggest an eighties bouffant. The brunettes on offer were a little more varied, though not much. I was definitely the shortest and curviest of the bunch. Also the funniest, I told myself, to psych myself up, noting with relief that Jessie, the brunette junior ad exec I was auditioning to play, was no boring straight man but a comic-relief character. The waiting room might be wall-to-wall actresses, but I would lay bets I was the only comic.

The brunettes seemed to be going first. Still, by the time an assistant cradling an iPad pointed to me and waved me in, I'd read four back issues of *People* magazine and a dog-eared *Entertainment Weekly* cover to cover. I handed off my headshot and resumé to the assistant, and she passed them to the casting director, a redheaded woman with the weary, battle-glazed look of casting directors everywhere, seated at a folding table. She perked up a little when she saw my resumé. "Funny stuff, huh?" she said. "Okay, Dana, make me laugh."

I tried my best, playing Jessie as broadly as I could muster opposite the casting director's deadpan line readings. She cut me off halfway through the second page, and I tried to look attentive and pleased, as if I were about to get some invaluable notes or direction.

Never lifting her eyes from the script, as if she were reading the newspaper over breakfast, the casting director said, "I'm having trouble seeing her in the advertising department of a major firm."

Were the glasses too much? I reached up and took them off nonchalantly, just to show that they were fake.

"I mean, this is supposed to be the eighties." She looked up from her script, not at me, but at the assistant. "Get the other part?" As the assistant handed the new sides to me, the casting director finally threw a glance in my direction. "It's funnier anyway."

I glanced at the new sides, but I already knew. Office cleaner, complete with maid uniform and funny accent. The role I'd inadvertently played in Branchik's apartment, after letting Amanda persuade me that there was no other way. The role I'd sworn never to play had come so naturally and so hilariously to me that we'd both laughed until we'd cried afterward.

I read it. I always read it once I was in the room. They said if you got ten TV casting directors on your side, you were going to make it as an actor. So I never burned any bridges. I just read the part. *Even J. Lo had to play a maid.*

The casting director and assistant couldn't tell that I was phoning it in. They laughed the whole time, more than they had for my junior ad exec. Just as audiences had in the eighties, they loved seeing a Latina shriek and clutch her heart and say, "*Dios mío,* Meester Kendall!" *Note to self,* I thought, *no more nostalgia sitcoms.* I thanked them for their time and headed back into the waiting room.

The receptionist perked up when I came through the door.

"Dana Diaz?"

I nodded heavily, an old, sour thought appearing in my head. It was one that sometimes came to me after auditions like this one, but it repelled me so much I tried to forget it as quickly as possible. I was wondering whether I would have gotten the same treatment if I had kept my father's last name.

"Something came for you." She reached behind her, lifted a vase filled with sunflowers off the floor, and set it heavily on the desk.

I glanced at the card just long enough to see Jason's name in the florist's scrawling cursive, and a tiny flutter of excitement chased the bitterness off. Jason must have sent them when he saw my text. It was a little embarrassing to be singled out like this, as if it were my first audition, but then, after last night, everything felt like it was happening for the first time. The flowers were a reminder that even this audition, with its old disappointment, could become a fresh start. I could see the other women in the waiting room looking at me with a touch of envy and I grabbed the arrangement.

"Sorry I couldn't get them to you before your audition," the receptionist said. "The runner came just after you went inside."

"Yeah, no worries," I said.

I stepped out of the waiting room into the parking lot and tugged at the card as I walked toward my car, squinting at it for a closer look at the messy writing. Then the vase slipped to the ground and shattered, scattering the sunflowers, and I was left holding the card between thumb and forefinger, one heavy sunflower dangling and twisting from the string by its hairy neck.

Break a leg, Dana!
My third name is:

Jason Murphy

17

I tore the card off the twine loop, letting the garish flower with its bulging, black center like an insect eye drop to the ground, and stumbled to my car with Jason's name crushed in my palm. Once in my car, I threw the hateful thing into the glove box and steadied my hands on the steering wheel, unable to start the engine.

The runner came just after you went inside. Was it Amanda in her stolen uniform? Was she here, tailing me, as she seemed to want me to believe?

The phone calls, the texts—even tracking down my motel room—none of it compared to the violation of using Jason's name, dragging him into this shameful game she had concocted to entrap me. It was a veiled threat—obviously, she didn't expect me to do anything just because she'd written Jason's name down on a piece of card stock. Probably she wasn't in town after all, just using the Runnr algorithms to torment me by remote control, threatening me with exposure as she had threatened Neely and Branchik. Spurned, ignored, she would want to ruin whatever happiness was in store for me. The fastest way to do that would be to tell Jason about the pact.

I recognized Amanda's cold logic. I'd seen her tactics applied to others often enough. What had she said about Brenna Branchik—about getting back at women? *Women learn to live with violence early on. Getting to a woman isn't as simple as a tap on the nose. You have to find something she cares about.* She'd found it, all right.

But how? I racked my brain for a time I might have mentioned Jason around Amanda. I hadn't wanted to talk to her about him, a fact that now struck me as both notable and prescient, as if I hadn't wanted to contaminate his memory. But even if I had at some point mentioned my ex-writing partner by name and she had looked up online records from my high school, tracked him to the University of Texas and from there to Los Angeles—how many Jason Murphys must there be in L.A.? How could she possibly have hunted down *this* Jason Murphy unless she was here, following me?

I started the car. I had to get out of this parking lot. Whether she was here or not, I felt her eyes on me. As soon as I made my way out to the freeway, my phone started ringing, and I snatched it up. "What do you want from me?"

"Dana?" The woman on the other end sounded as if she had been crying. "It's Kim."

"Kim!" I adjusted my tone, my face going red. "Sorry, I thought it was someone else. What's wrong?" Judging from her voice, now didn't seem like the moment for a snarky greeting.

"It's Fash."

I blinked in confusion and tried to tear my brain away from thoughts of Amanda. I still couldn't shake the feeling that she was watching me. "Fash? What about him?"

Kim spoke in a monotone, as if struggling to keep control. "It started a couple weeks ago. He was acting really weird—not that he's ever been normal." She bit back a hysterical laugh. "But this was different. He was messaging people in the middle of the night—mostly women—begging forgiveness or else ranting at them. Making threats, even. He messaged me a couple times, and I just ignored him. I ignored him." She choked. "And then last night he showed up at my house, late, pounding on the door." She started crying again. "I wish I'd let him in."

"Kim, what happened?"

"He did it early this morning, in his apartment," she whispered.

"Did what?" I said stupidly, but I remembered his mood swings in the bar, and some part of me already knew.

"There was so much blood." She was still crying. "I found the body. Nobody knows where he got the gun."

It dawned on me slowly: Fash, the website, the wicked L-shaped handguns in a grid. Amanda's voice: *Have I ever let you down?* "Oh my God."

"He was bipolar. I guess he went off his meds a few weeks ago." Kim was pulling herself together, reciting the details mechanically, as if they kept her calm. "I think maybe he figured, after winning Funniest Person, he didn't need them anymore."

Or maybe someone else decided he didn't need them anymore. The same someone who had decided Austin didn't need Fash anymore. I coughed to keep from gagging.

"Dana, the awful thing is—I knew he needed help, I just didn't care. I've never really forgiven him for what he did to me and all those other women. He never owned up to any of it. And when he won the contest, I thought, *Now he'll never have to.* And I wished for something bad to happen to him. Just to even the score, you know?" Her flat tone chilled me more than her tears a moment before. "Dana, is it my fault? Did I make this happen?"

"No. Kim, I swear you didn't."

"There was blood everywhere."

I closed my eyes and saw red: Fash in his red robe, against red walls at Chacha's, a camera flash lighting up Kim's and my frozen smiles on either side of him.

And then something occurred to me.

"I'm so sorry, Kim, but I have to go," I said, choking on the hysterical giggles that were pushing their way up my throat like bile. It wasn't funny, but I couldn't stop. With Fash gone, I was officially the Funniest Person in Austin.

Back in the motel, I sat on my bed and stared at the closed curtains, a dark brownish-red color flecked with tiny teal flowers at six-inch intervals.

Just a few hours ago, I'd been prepared to start over. Everything had seemed possible. Los Angeles. Success. Jason once more my writing partner—but more than that, my *partner* partner.

Now, from a vision as capacious and sprawling as the city itself, my world had contracted to the size of this motel room. It had been meant as a base from which to plan my new life. Now it was a cell in which I sat waiting obediently for the warden.

The motel phone rang. I picked up on the first ring. "Amanda."

"Dana," she said pleasantly.

"Where are you? Are you here?"

She laughed. "In L.A.? No. I'm in Austin."

"I don't believe you."

"As a matter of fact, I'm in your apartment right now."

"What? Why?"

"Oh, I just stopped by to look for something," she said lightly. "Then it occurred to me, with everything going on—you've heard about Fash, haven't you?—it might be a good idea for me to lie low for a little while. In case there happens to be a crackerjack IP sleuth in the Austin Police Department."

I couldn't catch my breath. I felt as if her hands were around my throat, squeezing.

"And since we've always had each other's backs, I knew you wouldn't mind. Think of it as housesitting. I tried watering your plants but I think they're too far gone."

"What happened to—" I couldn't say Fash's name. "That has nothing to do with me."

"Oh, really? Nothing? Nothing at all?" She laughed again. "I wonder why the cops knocked on your door a few minutes ago. If what happened to Fash had nothing to do with you."

"Cops?"

"Don't worry, they went away. They're not kicking down any doors yet; they just want to question some people. Standard procedure. It seems there were some irregularities with Fash's medications." She paused. I remembered what Kim had said about Fash going off his bipolar meds and felt ill. "And then there's the gun."

"Amanda."

She continued as if she hadn't heard me. "This is quite a mess, Fash's demise. Especially so soon after he was in the local news."

"Did you do it?"

She laughed. "You mean, did I pull the trigger? Come on, Dana. Do you really think I'm capable of murder?"

"I don't know what you're capable of."

"I just told him the truth, Dana." She sighed deeply. "Some people spend their lives running from who they are. They shouldn't be allowed to get away with it. If I'm the only one willing to be honest, does that make me a criminal?"

"Did you—did you mess with his meds?"

"Medication just helps people lie to themselves. You should have heard Fash talk—well, we mostly messaged—about how his pills made him feel. Numbed out, distant from his emotions. He wanted to get off them. Most people do. But people need help." The phone made a shifting sound, as if she were wedging it casually between her cheek and shoulder. "And if those people happen to use Runnr to pick up their prescriptions . . ." She trailed off.

"That's sick."

"What's sick is how many people don't even need pills to lie to themselves," she offered cheerfully. "Isn't that right, Dana?"

I ignored the taunt. "You have to tell the police, Amanda. It's gone too far. You can see that, can't you? It was a bad idea in the first place, and now—we have to stop. It's over."

"Convenient that you get to decide when it's over," she said sharply. "I'm supposed to turn myself in? Or go into hiding?"

"That would be the right thing to do, yes."

She snorted. "Which one? The one that's best for you, right? No, I don't think so. Look. Just do your mission, and you can go back to making the world laugh."

"My mission," I spat. "How fucking dare you."

"How did that audition go, anyway? Not so well without this, I bet."

"Without what?" Then, suddenly, I knew what she was holding. I covered my eyes with my free hand.

"It's strange that you left your wig behind, seeing as how it's so important for your act. Not to mention it's got your DNA all over it. Along with Carl's, I'm pretty sure. You probably left a few strands in his place, and Branchik's."

"Amanda." I pushed my hair back off my forehead.

"It would definitely tie you to at least two crime scenes."

"Amanda, don't."

"Don't what? Drop a strand or two over at Fash's house?"

"Oh my God."

"I might not need to. You guys seemed awfully chummy at that bar after Funniest Person. I'd be willing to bet his robe picked up a few strands."

My eyes prickled with hot tears as I realized she must have been there after all. Watching me win second place. Waiting for an advantage. "What do you want from me?" I said helplessly.

"The stakes have been upped significantly over the past few days, Dana. You have my third name. I need you to act on it. You'll be glad you did. Trust me."

She hung up, and I stared at the four walls of the motel room, my new life.

Jason opened the door with a dopey smile. "I was wondering when I'd see you again," he said. "Busy lady these days."

"We have to talk." Before he could respond, I said, "Not about last night."

"Okay." He stepped back and waved me in. The living room felt womblike and stuffy behind the closed curtains. Left to himself, Jason never opened them, which had driven me nearly insane when we lived together. But now I was glad for the musty half-dark of the living room. As Jason went to the kitchen to get us fresh mugs of coffee — he'd only just woken up, I could tell — I twitched one of the curtains aside and glanced out the window. Just because she'd said she was in my apartment didn't mean she was telling the truth.

Jason came back in and handed me my coffee, which I set down without tasting. My heart was already racing. There was one question I had to ask immediately, before I talked myself out of it, no matter how crazy it made me sound. As I opened my mouth to ask it, I realized, incredulously, I didn't even know her last name.

"Do you know an Amanda? Tall, skinny, curly bleached-blond hair?" I waved my hands around my head in an invisible mane.

His forehead wrinkled. "You mean Amanda Dorn? Why, do you know her?"

The perfectly ordinary last name made her sound more human than she was in my head, and the way Jason said it—casual, completely at ease—made me realize a part of me had been expecting him to blanch in horror. If I had once thought of her as an imaginary friend, over the past few days she had become my phantom tormentor. But Jason looked only a little uncomfortable, possibly even annoyed.

"Yes. Amanda Dorn," I said, trying it out. "Could she—would she have something against you?"

"I'm pretty sure she hates my guts. Does that count?" He started to say more, then hesitated, frowning.

I took a deep breath. "Jason, it's very important that you tell me everything you know about her and what she could have against you."

He put his hand to the back of his neck and scratched under his collar. "Look, Dana, are you sure you want to know? Last night, you said you were sick of hearing about my ex-girlfriends, and now you're barging in here demanding to know everything."

"Ex-girlfriend," I repeated numbly.

"Yeah," he said. "She's the one I was trying to tell you about last night."

"You're Amanda Dorn's ex-boyfriend in L.A." Hollow-eyed, in the bar, the first night we met: *He didn't hit me, if that's what you're thinking.* My reply: *Sounds like a prince.*

"It didn't last that long." He was running his hands through his hair nervously. "I mean, give me credit, I figured out she was crazy pretty fast." He glanced at me. "She's not a—a friend of yours, is she?"

I shook my head, my eyes on the floor.

"Thank God." Jason had taken a large swig of coffee and set his mug down again. "I met her at an audition, and we started talking. I should have known better. Actress on the make. This was when I was hanging around with Aaron Neely, and a lot of people were giving me time because of it. I wish I could go back and—" He flushed. "Look, I got kind of a big head, I'll be the first to admit it. But I paid the price. Amanda Dorn was a grade-A, gold-digging, star-fucking nut job. When I figured out she was more interested in meeting Neely than in dating me—it made me feel kind of crazy for a while too."

"She wanted to meet *Neely?*"

"Oh yeah. She talked about him incessantly," he said bitterly. "I guess she'd seen what kind of arm candy he carried around and thought she might just fit the bill. I think she'd auditioned for him or something but couldn't get anywhere with him on talent alone." He wrinkled his nose. "She was a terrible actress."

Yet she had fooled me. So Amanda had a grudge against Neely too —one she'd neglected to mention. Had he harassed her too? Or had he just rejected her? Maybe she was only using me as an excuse to get back at him, just like she wanted to get back at Jason. What had she said about her evil ex-boyfriend? That he wouldn't let her talk to other men at parties? And I'd listened sympathetically, nodded along. Swallowed her side of the story right away, without any proof. Flattered by her praise and embarrassingly eager to make my first real female friend, even if it was just a random stranger in a bar. If her ex hadn't happened to be Jason, I would have gone on thinking of him as the psychopath who had done her wrong. My stomach sank as I thought first of Branchik, then of Carl. I had done those things to human beings, for someone whose last name I hadn't even known.

Was it possible that my experience with Neely—still fresh, at that point, though now it seemed impossibly far away—had warped my perceptions so completely? Or had I always been so willing to believe the worst of men, even before Neely? And if so, was it because of Mattie, or was something else wrong with me? Something even deeper?

"Are you okay?" Jason said, and I realized I had been quiet for a while. "We really don't have to talk about this. I said I wouldn't burden you with this stuff anymore, and I meant it."

"You called her crazy," I said carefully. "What kind of crazy?"

"Well, just to give you an idea—after we broke up, I found spyware on my phone. And the fights we had, the yelling and screaming—"

He kept talking, but my ear snagged on the word *spyware*. I hadn't heard it before, but it reminded me of Amanda talking about planting malware in Carl's computer. *I'm in charge of software.*

Software, malware. *Spy*ware.

I clapped one hand over my mouth and one hand over Jason's.

"What—" His voice came out muffled.

I shook my head violently, put my finger to my lips, pressed my hand over his mouth harder. Pointed to my purse with a pleading expression.

Slowly he raised his hand to my wrist and pulled my hand away.

I opened my purse and pulled my phone out between my finger and thumb, as if I were handling something that could turn around and bite me any minute. With the other hand I made a helpless gesture. *What do I do?* I mouthed.

Jason gestured to my car outside. I nodded, lifted my keys as silently as possible out of the bag.

Say something, he mouthed.

I shrugged, panicked.

"About these fights," Jason said out loud, and I almost jumped. "She and I would just, you know, go at it. Scream at each other for hours on end. It was awful. I cared about her, but she was just out for her."

"You know what?" I was catching on. "I'm starting to remember why I didn't want to hear anything about this. It sounds like you still care about her, Jason. Maybe everything she told me was right about you."

"Dana, don't leave!" Jason jumped up from the sofa and pointed frantically toward the door, jerking his head and lifting his eyebrows.

I grabbed my keys, making sure they rattled loudly. "I'm just going out to my car. I need a minute away from this crap." I opened the door and walked out. "Maybe I'll come back in after I cool down. Just give me some space." I stalked down the front walk to the car, my heart pounding, acutely conscious that I was alone with Amanda now. I unlocked the car, tossed the phone onto the front seat, and slammed the door. Then I hurried up the walk and into the house.

Once the door was closed, I leaned my back against it.

"So. You too, huh?" Jason said.

I started laughing weakly. I couldn't help it; it was nerves. "What exactly is spyware?"

"Exactly what it sounds like," he said. "It turns your phone into a tracking device. Your stalker can see who you're calling, who you're texting. Where you are."

Where you are. A motel. A film studio. Jason's house. I fought down panic. "How does it get on your phone?"

"A couple of different ways. I'm pretty sure she just installed it on my phone when I wasn't paying attention. But some people e-mail it as an attachment, like a virus. Or you could even text a link and hope they follow it."

A link. Like the one to the Aaron Neely video.

"And she could really have been listening to us this whole time?"

"The prefab spyware packages available on the internet would give her access to e-mail, texting, browser history, that type of stuff," he said. "But what she put on my phone was much more sophisticated.

The memo recorder was locked in voice-activated mode, so she could listen in on everything I did. The guy I took the phone to was pretty impressed. He said he couldn't be sure he had caught all the features. I wound up just buying a new phone." Jason looked at me. "Dana, just tell me what the hell's going on. How do you know Amanda?"

I groaned. "She lives in Austin now. She came to one of my performances. She pretended—I thought we were friends. She never mentioned you. Not by name, anyway."

"Well, she definitely knew your name."

Random stranger in a bar, indeed. It was even worse than I had thought. And I had been even stupider than I'd thought. "You told her about me?"

"Yeah, I mentioned you. I mean, of course I did. All my stories have you in them." He squeezed my hand briefly. "Once she found out my former writing partner was a woman and my best friend on top of that, she would never believe we were platonic. She was insanely jealous." He smiled slyly. "I guess she was onto something."

"This isn't cute, Jason." I pointed out the window to my car. "She knows I'm here, and she knows I'm with you. She's been sending me creepy messages. Today she sent me flowers." I shuddered, thinking of the note. I couldn't tell him what she really wanted, not without explaining the whole thing. But I could come close. "I think she wants to hurt you."

"She wouldn't be the first."

"Jason! I'm being serious." I saw Carl's face, bloodied and crying for mercy. Fash and the gun. "If she wants to harm you, she'll find a way. I know what she's capable of." And not just her. Suddenly I lost it and started crying. "This is all my fault."

"Whoa, hey, wait a minute," he said. "Slow down. Nobody's going to hurt me. Least of all that crazy bitch." I looked up at the epithet. It was the same word I had called her when Jason and I were fighting about his ex, but it sounded different now that I knew who we were talking about. More evil, more powerful.

"She called me last night," I said. "She figured out where I was staying."

"If your phone was bugged, that would be easy to do. But it's easy to fix too. We'll take your phone somewhere, get it wiped. You can stay here."

"Why? Why is she doing this?" I sobbed. "Why does she hate me so much?"

He took my hands between his. "It's me she hates. She can't stand the idea of me being happy. It's just her rotten luck that she stumbled on the person who makes me happiest and sent you straight into my arms." At this, I sniffed and hiccupped. "Nothing's going to happen to you, Dana. Not while I'm here."

But he didn't know what Amanda had on me: the wig, the evidence at three different crime scenes. "What are we going to do?"

"We turn the tables on her." I looked at him questioningly. "Let's be smart about this. She doesn't know we know about the spyware. That gives us an edge. If you scrub your phone, she'll figure out we're onto her. As long as she thinks she's in control, it'll buy us time. Plus, she won't be able to resist getting in touch as long as she still can. That gives us a way to track how crazy she's getting."

"And records for the police."

"Yes, if it comes to that."

I hoped it wouldn't. "In the meantime, we can use it as a decoy."

"Exactly. We'll pick you up a burner before we get started."

"Where do we start?" I had a feeling I knew what he was going to suggest.

18

We started with Runnr.

Jason wanted to stash my bugged phone in the glove compartment of my car, but my paranoia had swollen over the past hour like an allergic reaction to a bee sting, and I felt sure Amanda's tracking software would know the difference between the house and the street in front of it. While Jason went to Best Buy for a disposable phone, I searched the house and found some leftover insulation in the recording studio's closet. I tried to cut it up, but ordinary scissors couldn't get the job done, so instead I wrapped the whole irregular-size piece around the phone and then sealed it tightly with black electrical tape. When I was finished, I had made a giant, spongy pillow completely covered in black. I set the lumpish thing in the studio closet and closed the door to the room in relief just as Jason got back with the burner.

"It's all set up and ready to go except for your security thumbprint," he said.

"Wow," I said, checking the smartphone out. I was expecting

something more in the flip-phone vein. "I didn't even know they had that feature."

"It was a little extra, but I wanted you to feel safe," he said, blushing.

"What do I owe you?" I reached for my purse, acutely conscious that I had only a couple of twenties. This phone looked more expensive than a couple of twenties.

"Just your firstborn child," he said. "Also a kidney, if I need it."

"Jason."

"Forget it," he said firmly. "Let's make that call."

I put on my best reporter voice for the media contact at Runnr, but she seemed unimpressed with my made-up credentials and none too happy to be confronted with yet another journalist covering sexism in Silicon Valley. "Sexual harassment claims are taken very seriously by Runnr," she recited in the crisp, dry tones of rote memorization, "and handled promptly by HR in accordance with the highest standards of employee protection."

"Of course," I said. "I'm wondering if you'd be willing to discuss one particular case in detail."

"We are not legally allowed to discuss—"

"Her name is Amanda Dorn."

There was a pause.

I tried backing off. "Perhaps you could start by confirming that she was an employee?"

"I would have to check with our human resources department."

"Did Amanda Dorn file a sexual harassment claim at some point in her employment?"

"That's another matter for HR," she said. "In the meantime, please consider filling out the media-request form you'll find on our website." The line went dead.

Jason had been leaning forward, listening. "We should call HR before she does."

"Sure, good idea." I turned to his laptop and started searching for the number on the Runnr site.

"Let me try this time." He looked excited, like a kid prank-calling the neighbors.

I stared at him. It struck me that Jason had no idea of the stakes of the game we were playing. Amanda was out for blood this time, I could feel it, but to him this was just a chance to get back at an ex-girlfriend he'd never forgiven. With a slight pang I realized that he was just a little too interested in digging up dirt on Amanda. I'd known him too long to mistake the contemptuous expression on his face when he said her name for indifference. Maybe he'd been waiting for a chance to find out about her past since they'd first gotten together—in her motorcycle jacket, with her wild hair and hollowed-out eyes, she must have seemed as mysterious to him as she had to me.

I pushed the thought firmly out of my mind. Jason had no way of knowing how much danger he was in. Unless I told him about Fash, the gun, the whole awful pact, he would never believe Amanda was capable of murder. To make him understand everything would be to confess my own shameful involvement with Amanda's schemes, something I couldn't do. And that conversation had the potential to bring up all kinds of things I didn't know how to talk about with Jason—what his friend Neely had done, and even what his brother had done. I couldn't have said exactly why I wanted to protect him from that knowledge, except that it didn't seem fair to make Jason so angry about things in the past he'd had no control over. Far better that he saw what we were doing as nothing more than a petty game.

I just hoped he wouldn't find out for himself how games like that worked out.

"Fine," I said, handing the phone to him. "Knock yourself out."

Jason turned the volume all the way up so I could hear what was happening, and I leaned in close as he dialed the number.

A high-pitched female voice answered. "Runnr human resources department, this is Callie."

"Hi, Callie, I'm Jason Murphy." He sounded more confident using his real name than I had with a fake. "I'm with the website Pro-Publica. Have you heard of us?"

"Of course," Callie said. "Have you tried calling our media rep—"

"I just talked to Renée. She sent me here to confirm some details," he said with ostentatious seriousness. "I'm reporting a story about the costly epidemic of frivolous sexual harassment suits in Silicon Valley." He winked at me. "We got a tip about an Amanda Dorn who used to work there. First, can you verify that she was a Runnr employee?"

Callie's voice grew warm and deferential. "Of course. Yes, Amanda Dorn worked here. Let me pull up her information." After a brief pause, she read off the dates of Amanda's two-year employment at Runnr. "Her termination was an extremely unfortunate circumstance for everyone involved. I can't disclose the name of the employee she accused—baselessly, as an investigation into the incident revealed. But I can say that the grounds for her termination had nothing to do with that suit. In fact, a countersuit was filed against her for harassment, stalking, and illegal use of proprietary company software."

"I see," Jason said, making eye contact with me and raising his brows dramatically. "Anything more you can tell me about the countersuit?"

"Well," she said in a lower tone, as if in confidence, "Ms. Dorn unfortunately was not a good fit from the very beginning. After a brief period of productivity here as an entry-level programmer, her supervisor, whose name I'd rather not disclose"—*Branchik,* I mouthed at Jason—"gave her a poor performance review, which kicked off the initial accusation. Her evidence included private photographs from the personal device of the accused. In investigating how she came by these photos, it was discovered that Ms. Dorn had been using Runnr's proprietary code to develop her own app, an inappropriate use of company property in violation of intellectual property laws as well as the employee manual."

"So that's why she was fired?" Jason prompted.

"There was a settlement," Callie said, pronouncing the last word as if it were something sour in her mouth. "She obviously had to leave once her theft had been revealed and her access revoked, but she refused to resign until she'd extracted a fair amount of money from Runnr in return for a nondisclosure agreement. An agreement she has obviously violated," she said in a slightly chilly tone, "since I am speaking to a reporter now."

"I can't tell you how much I appreciate your taking my call. This topic is such an important one." Jason always knew how to lay it on thick.

"And we appreciate the chance to set the record straight," Callie said. "Runnr is a fair company where women are treated as equals. I should know." She went on, in a slightly warmer tone, to discuss the various benefits and accommodations she herself personally had received from Runnr during two pregnancies and a cancer scare. Next came a list of initiatives from the CEO to improve the hiring and performance of women in tech. Jason rolled his eyes and waited for her to finish.

"Thank you so much," he said when she took a breath. "You've been so helpful, and I'll be sure to follow up if I have any further questions."

Sensing he was about to hang up, I mouthed a question for Callie at him. He squinted and shook his head, confused. I grabbed an envelope on the table nearby, flipped it over, wrote down three letters, and underlined them.

"Ape?" he said out loud. "Oh, app. Sorry, my handwriting . . . what app was she working on?"

The question must have knocked Callie off her talking points, because her response came out too rushed for me to catch more than a few words. Jason let her speak without interruption, his eyes widening. "I see, I see," he said and gave me a thumbs-up sign.

When she ran out of steam, he thanked her again, hung up, and grinned at me. "That last question really set her off. Apparently, in addition to ripping off the Runnr code and database for a side hustle, Amanda bugged four computers in the C-suite and collected a bunch of confidential e-mails that she threatened to release to the public." He chuckled, shaking his head. "You have to admire her guts. Anyway, there must have been some good stuff in there, because they dropped the countersuit and settled."

"What do you mean, good stuff?" I frowned. "Like Doug Branchik's dick pics?"

He raised his eyebrows. "Our friend Callie says there were rumors about his behavior around the office. Obviously, Amanda heard the rumors, saw a weak link, and filed the harassment suit against him preemptively." I gave him a questioning look. "As a shield for the app. That way, when they found out about her theft of company code, she couldn't be fired without it looking like retaliation," he explained. "Honestly, I doubt Branchik was ever even interested in her."

I thought of Amanda's elaborate explanation for why we couldn't use Branchik's dick pics in our revenge plan. Maybe they didn't exist. "So you think there were no pictures?"

"Even if there were, we only have her word that they weren't consensual. Guys like that are pretty easy to get compromising photos out of."

Guys like that. It rang a bell, and again I heard Amanda's voice in my head. It was precisely how she had described Branchik the first time we met. Jason too. I drowned out that thought with another question. "Why do you think Callie got so mad when you asked about the app?"

"It's a touchy subject. It was highly offensive," he said with a grimace. "Not to mention derivative. Sort of like a dating app but without the dates." I looked at him quizzically. "Women record and rate every instance of so-called bad behavior from the men in their lives —bosses, classmates, friends of friends; the garbageman, I presume. The app uses GPS to share ratings of all the men in your area. Which is sick enough, right?" He leaned in. "But the creepiest thing is, instead of matching you to someone else who shares your love of sushi and *Star Trek,* it matches you to someone who qualifies for—get this —'remote retaliation.'"

"Remote retaliation." The hair on the back of my neck stood up as I repeated the words.

"Yeah. How messed up is that? Like taking out a hit on someone. The name of the app was something like You Scratch My Back . . . or, no, I'll Get Yours . . . what was it again?"

"Got Your Back?" I kept my face carefully averted.

"That was it!" He snapped his fingers. "Stupid name for an app, if you ask me. It's probably meant to be all one word, or maybe the vowels are replaced with dots or it's capitalized funny or something." I stayed silent and he went on. "Anyway, it doesn't matter. That's pretty juicy, right? And definitely illegal. An app for hiring a hit man?"

"Woman," I corrected him mechanically. "And it wouldn't be hiring. She'd want to make it some kind of trade or a point system. So you get out of it what you put in."

He gave me an odd look. "What, did she mention this revenge app to you?"

"Not specifically," I said, picking at a thread in my sleeve to avoid meeting his eyes. "But it's the kind of thing she would like. The mutual responsibility, the sense of community. Like a neighborhood watch." I was stumbling over my words.

"You two spend a lot of time talking vigilantism?" Jason said. "She must have been pretty comfortable around you."

"Yeah, we were BFFs," I snapped. "We made each other friendship bracelets and everything. Look, I'm not saying it's not crazy."

"Batshit crazy," he said emphatically. "And, more to the point, illegal. What do you want to bet she's still working on some version of that thing? If we got hold of her computer and turned it over to the FBI—"

"We don't have her computer," I pointed out. "It's in Austin with her, last time I checked. And anyway, as long as the app's not finished and she's never taken it public, she could probably claim it was just a joke."

"A real laugh riot." Jason turned his face away. "Ruining men's lives."

"Presumably, the men who got their lives ruined would have ruined some women's lives first," I couldn't help adding.

"Based on hearsay." He looked back at me in disbelief. "Don't tell me you're on her side in this."

"I'm on your side," I said quickly. "All I'm saying is—think about it, Jason. Why was it so easy for Amanda to set up Branchik?"

"Because of rumors."

"Yeah, rumors," I said. "That's what it's called when women warn each other in private."

"But most of those rumors are completely made-up," Jason said. "They're just gossip."

"Maybe a few of them," I said. "But for every woman who makes up rumors about *guys like that,* I bet there are ten who didn't even tell their closest friends what happened to them. They were embarrassed and ashamed, so they just put their heads down and kept quiet." Or flunked out, or moved away, or hid in the spotlight. Told their secrets to a microphone.

He was staring at me, speechless, his expression unreadable.

"I'm not saying I agree with her." My voice had gotten higher, and

I took a moment to think about what I did mean. "I'm just saying, I get why someone would—fantasize."

"Fantasize? About what?" He looked at me with horror bordering on revulsion. "About doing what, Dana?"

I thought of Fash. Aaron Neely. Mattie. I thought of what was on Carl's computer screen that night. About the power men fantasize about. Power over women like me, women like Amanda. For some, it was more than a fantasy. It was something they did in the dark, in basements and back seats, and even in sunny daylit offices, because they were confident that no one would care.

No one important, anyway.

"I'm on your side," I repeated helplessly.

"Forget it. I have to get to the restaurant. I'm late for work as it is." Jason grabbed his keys off the counter and started for the door. Then he turned around. "Do me a favor? If this app thing isn't really so bad, this plan of Amanda's to orchestrate a massive network of revenge crimes, then find me something worse by the time I get back. Something we can use." He left, slamming the door behind him.

It was all I could do not to laugh. He had no idea how much worse it got. It was just a matter of finding something that wouldn't drag me down too.

19

Hey, Kim, it's Dana," I said quickly, knowing my new burner would come up looking weird on her caller ID. I'd been saving the call for when Jason left, hoping she could turn up some new details for me, something to link Fash's suicide to Amanda. "Just checking in. I'm sorry about getting off the phone so fast last time. The Fash thing just hit me really hard."

"I get it," Kim said shortly, and I winced. She had, after all, been the one to find his body. "The police came around again yesterday. They keep coming back at me with more questions. Something's wrong."

"You think?" It came out sarcastic, but Kim wouldn't mind. After having to hide what had happened with Fash from Jason, just talking to someone who knew about it was a relief.

"I mean, more wrong than we thought," Kim said. "Like, maybe it wasn't suicide after all."

"Murder?" Somehow I wasn't as shocked as I should have been. Amanda had been perversely offended when I suggested she'd pulled the trigger herself, as if it were too crude an intervention for her, but what I'd seen in the Neely video hadn't been subtle. "Who would have wanted Fash dead?" *Not me. I hadn't wanted that,* I argued silently with myself.

"I have no idea," Kim said, and I rubbed at my tense neck muscles, trying to ease the ache. "But there's something strange happening in the Austin scene. There've been rumors going around about Aaron Neely too. Remember how he ghosted on the Funniest Person contest? One of the other judges staying at the same hotel saw him checking out, and they said he was limping, leaning on his assistant, wearing dark glasses to cover up bruises. He looked like he'd been hit by a truck." I had a pretty good idea of what he'd looked like, having seen the video. "It's all over the forums. One guy who's worked with him before is ready to swear it was a drug deal gone wrong."

I almost laughed, thinking of Aaron and his smoothies, his performatively clean lifestyle. "Sounds like he was hiding something, all right," I agreed in what I hoped were vague enough terms.

"The point is, that's two people directly connected with the contest put out of commission within weeks of each other."

I let my breath out with a whistle, as if the thought had never occurred to me. "So was Fash into drugs? Do they think the contest is a front for something?" I hated myself for trying to throw Kim off the scent, but by design, every act of violence committed by Amanda could more easily be traced to me than to her. I had to find out what I could without letting Kim get too close to the truth.

"It does look suspicious. I think that's why the cops keep sniffing around us."

"Us?" My neck tensed again. "You mean you and me?"

"They keep calling me, asking where you are." I stifled the desire to cut her off and ask for specifics. "We were the two runners-up in the contest. Either they're worried about our safety, or—"

"Or they're checking out possible motives," I finished. I remembered something she had said in the last conversation: *There was blood everywhere*. "Do they really think we would ice our friend for a crack at first place in some local contest?"

"'Friend' is stretching it," she said wryly, the old Kim for a minute. But the laugh that followed sounded hollow. "Anyway, I did tell you I'd kill myself if I didn't do well this year. I guess it's not that big a leap to imagine I'd kill someone else."

There was a pause as I took this in. Men like Fash drove women out of the scene all the time. All I had done was try to find a way to drive a man out for once. If I happened to benefit from it—if I was now, technically, the funniest standup in Austin—did that constitute a motive? I shook my head. I couldn't have a motive for a crime I didn't commit.

Then something occurred to me. "Kim, you found him in his apartment, right?" There was silence. "How did you get in?"

"The door was unlocked," she said. "Some of his friends were worried about his posts on the forums, and since I'd been the last to see him, I volunteered to go check on him. I knocked for a long time before I tried the door." Her voice caught, and she took a deep breath. "Last time I ever walk into somebody's house like that."

It was beginning to sound to me like a setup. Kim had been the last to see Fash and the first to find him. She had walked right into the scene of the crime. Amanda didn't need to have been at Chacha's on the final night of the contest; she could have overheard us talking about Fash in the bathroom over my bugged phone. What if she'd bugged Fash's phone too? Maybe she knew he had been pounding on Kim's door that night, had listened in as he cried and screamed at her to let him in. Maybe Amanda had taken it upon herself to punish both of them: Fash, for what he'd done to Kim, and Kim, for her silence.

It was a sickening thought. The Brenna Branchik rule: To punish a woman, you have to get in her head, get her feeling guilty enough so she'll walk right through the unlocked door into a bloody crime scene. Maybe, in the end, even implicate herself in a murder.

"Who did?" Kim asked.

"What?" I snapped back to the conversation.

"You said, 'She left the door unlocked.' Who?"

"Fash. I meant F-Fash left the door unlocked," I stammered. I had to get Kim out of harm's way. "The police haven't told you to stay in town, have they?"

"Not yet."

I breathed a sigh of relief. "Do you think you could get away for a few days?"

"Maybe. My manager at the bar took me off the schedule this week. They're good people over there." Her voice started to tremble. "In all honesty, I'd love to get away. Not from the police. From my friends, Fash's friends. Everyone knows I was the last to see him alive." She hesitated, then went on. "There's another rumor going around on the forums—that he killed himself because I wouldn't go out with him, and I told other women to steer clear." She laughed weakly. "I feel like the dudes in the scene all give me side-eye wherever I go. And the women won't say anything, even if they know better. Don't speak ill of the dead, I guess." Now she was crying. "But just because this awful thing happened to him doesn't erase what he did to me. To a lot of us."

"Of course it doesn't," I said. "I believe you. And it's not your fault he's gone."

She sniffed hard a few times, took a deep breath, and started talking in her normal voice again. "Anyway, I'm persona non grata around here. I'd love nothing better than to leave this shit behind, but I've got nowhere to go."

The solution came to me all at once. "What about Amarillo? If you could drive there, my mom would put you up in a heartbeat. And she wouldn't bug you, except to make sure you got fed." My mother always knew what not to ask. It was one of my favorite things about her. "I mean, it's no resort town, but it's quiet there."

"Thanks, Dana. It's a nice idea." She sighed. "But I doubt your mom wants some random person in her house."

"I'll let her know you might be coming, and she can leave a key under the mat for you. That way you don't even have to decide now. It can be a last-minute thing." There was silence. "Just consider it."

"Okay. I'll think about it. And thanks," she said. "I've already said this, but it means a lot to me that you'd take my side in this after all that stuff before."

"Sure. We've got to have each other's backs," I said, then winced to hear the words come out of my mouth. "I just wish I were in town to help out."

"Where are you, anyway? It doesn't sound like you're in Amarillo. That's where everyone thinks you are."

"I'm in L.A." After a beat I remembered why. I'd almost forgotten it sounded like good news to a normal person. "I got some auditions out of that podcast I did."

"Oh, man, that's great. Break a leg." She sounded relieved to be on a new topic. "Where are you staying out there?"

"In my old place," I said. "With Jason."

There was a chilly pause, and when Kim spoke again, her voice sounded stiff. "Don't worry, I won't tell anyone where you are. Even the police."

"Thanks," I said. "I appreciate that. I don't want anyone to think—"

She cut me off. "No problem. After all, we have to have each other's backs, right?" She said it with a hint of irony, I thought, but then, Kim always sounded a little sarcastic. We said our goodbyes, and I texted her my mom's address. Then I wrote an e-mail to my mom to let her know Kim might be dropping in sometime that week.

It wasn't much, but it was all I could do. I prayed Amanda hadn't planted clues in Fash's apartment to implicate Kim—though a small voice inside me that I couldn't quite silence said, *Better Kim than me.*

Alone in the house, I started looking around. With Jason gone, the fact that Amanda had lived here, if only for a short while, impressed itself on me fully for the first time. Amanda had been exorcised, the bugged phone swaddled in sound-muffling foam and banished to the studio, but this had once been her home. I tried to imagine her sitting on the sofa with Jason, pouring a glass of wine at the kitchen counter, curling up in his bed. As disturbing as it was, it was a place to start. Slowly, to preserve my vision of her, I got up and began walking through the house, keeping my footfalls soft so as not to frighten her ghost. I thought of Henry's objects and the stories they told about themselves. Maybe, just maybe, Amanda had left something behind that told a story about her.

I studied every room, but nothing I saw looked like Amanda; everything reflected either Jason's benign neglect or my long-ago contributions. There were the rugs I'd picked out from Ikea to cover the tile floors that had been bare when I'd moved out here to join Jason. The curtains, too, were mine, cheap panels from Target, now faded in the middle and dirty at the hems. The pair of mismatched Goodwill armchairs, and the wall art, portraits on black velvet and badly painted landscapes. I walked down the hall, past a big-eyed cat in nursery pastels that always freaked Jason out, and forced myself to take a long look at his bedroom. There by the unmade bed was the nightstand I'd found for him at the Salvation Army to replace the cardboard box he'd been using when I moved in, its wood surface now scummed over with a year's worth of sticky coffee-cup circles. The closet bristled with empty hangers and a few plaid shirts like crooked flags; most of his clothes were wadded up on the floor.

If Amanda's ghost was here, it was being very quiet.

I opened the door to the studio. This had once been my bedroom, I thought with a pang, but you would never know it. I had been expunged as thoroughly as Amanda had. There was even some scarring on the outside of the door around eye level, as if someone had chipped away at the paint, perhaps preparing to strip the wood. I checked the perimeter of the room, moving mic stands, music stands, and a mixing board carefully away from the walls to make sure I wasn't missing anything. I opened the closet and tried not to flinch at the sight of the shiny black pillow that held my bugged phone. A banker's box in the closet turned out to hold more cables and a smaller mixing board. I continued to move around the house, opening all the cabinets and closet doors, looking for some trace of Amanda.

Standing in the hallway, I spotted the attic door, a rectangle in the ceiling with a short piece of cord dangling from it. After hunting fruitlessly for a stepladder, I dragged an armchair from the living room into the hallway and stepped up onto the seat. My fingers barely reached the end of the braided cord, and it took several excruciating minutes of hopping up and down on the chair before I got a tight enough grip. The attic door let out a grating screech as it opened, and a shower of silt fell on my upturned face. I lost a few minutes coughing and crying the sharp granules out of my eyes before unfolding the ladder and climbing up, the ladder protesting my every step with a metallic groan. My head and shoulders in the dusty attic at last, I looked around.

Ribbed ducts, a stack of two-by-fours, and pink fiberglass insulation under a thick coating of dust and cobwebs. That was all. Not a box in sight.

I climbed down the ladder and folded it up again with some difficulty, shoving the door shut with a vindictive slam. Then I dragged the chair back to its place in the living room and flopped down on it, sweating with exertion and covered in attic filth from the waist up. Rubbing a streak of dust off my shirt, I thought about how different this place was from Amanda's apartment in Austin—all clean lines and vibrant, unsullied colors, impersonal and ascetic and sparkling clean. There was no evidence that a person who liked those things had ever lived here. I began to despair.

A shadow behind the living-room curtains, followed by a clatter, made me jump. It was only the mailman, I realized, my heart still pounding. Jason and I used to say we lived in a Bermuda Triangle for the US Postal Service because the mail always came to our street last, and when it came, half of it was misaddressed or misdelivered. For old times' sake, I opened the door and flipped the lid on the mailbox. Not much had changed; with the single exception of a postcard chastising Jason for an overdue dental appointment, the small pile of envelopes consisted entirely of mail for former tenants. I flipped through them idly as I pushed the door closed with my foot: Julie Moore, Rebeccah Farrell, Keith Ho, Mr. J. Soriano . . .

Former tenants.

Before I moved in, Jason had always thrown mail to former tenants away, but I had insisted we stow it in a kitchen drawer instead, fully intending to forward it when I had time. That never happened, of course, and eventually we started calling the drawer "the sinkhole." When I lived here, I'd emptied it into the trash can every couple of months, but I was pretty sure Jason had never cleaned it out on his own.

I went to the kitchen, the mail still in my hands, and knelt to open the bottom drawer. It was stuffed so full of envelopes I could hardly wrench it open; I had to reach my hand to the back of the drawer to clear the logjam. When the drawer finally jerked open, a bank statement popped out, fluttered through the air, and landed on the tile floor by my knee. It was addressed to Ms. Dana Diaz.

"Thanks a lot, Jason," I muttered.

I sat on the floor and started digging through the top layer of mail. When I saw the peak of a capital *A* poking out from behind a Free People catalog, my heart skipped a beat. It was only a special offer from Sephora, but it was addressed to Amanda Dorn. I'd found a trace of her at last.

I started scooping out thick handfuls of red-stamped bills, credit card offers, catalogs, circulars for special elections and ballot initiatives, expired sandwich-shop coupons, wedding invitations, Christmas cards, and plain white envelopes with and without plastic windows, dumping them all on the floor in front of me. I forced myself to check the name on each piece of mail, no matter how trivial it seemed, before throwing it away. Every item addressed to Ms. Amanda Dorn gave me a little jolt of adrenaline, followed by a tiny crash of disappointment when it turned out to be junk mail. Still, I opened each and every one, just in case I was missing something more important than a special offer on a year's subscription to *Bon Appétit* magazine.

By the time I finished going through everything in the drawer, I had opened some fifteen pieces of Amanda's mail, all of it useless. Not so much as an alumni magazine to give me a hint about her pre-Runnr past, much less the letter from home I had allowed myself to hope might be hiding in one of those plain white envelopes, entreating her to visit an ailing mother, forgive an abusive father. I sat, defeated, cross-legged on the kitchen floor under a pile of mail.

A moth struck the windowpane near the kitchen-sink light, and I jumped. It was dark outside, the window a black square.

It was late. I lifted myself up onto my knees, ignoring the prickles as circulation returned to my feet, and peered over the counter at the microwave clock. I had been doing this for two hours. Jason would be home soon. I sighed and opened the drawer again, this time yanking it so hard it jumped the tracks and came all the way out.

There, at the bottom of the cabinet, was a pile of envelopes that had overflowed the drawer and slid back behind it. The one on top was for Amanda.

I ripped it open. The letter inside was dated March 30:

Dear AMANDA DORN,

Thank you for being a valued customer of Saf-Stor, AMANDA! In order for Saf-Stor to continue to offer you the best storage experience possible, your discounted rental rate for UNIT NO. 302 will be adjusted effective MAY 1, 2017, to the current rate of $145. This letter is your 30-day notice . . .

I lowered the form letter in disbelief. Amanda's stuff wasn't in Jason's house, but it wasn't in her new place in Austin either. I thought back again to the apartment where we'd spent so much time conspiring together. The clean, bright, sparkling-new furniture, the perfectly straight row of Blu-rays — *Jaws, Die Hard, When Harry Met Sally, Clueless* — movies to please the broadest swath of humanity possible. I remembered Amanda rummaging through nearly empty cabinets, looking for a corkscrew; pulling bottle after bottle down from the wine rack on top of the refrigerator, checking the labels, putting them back. Amanda didn't have perfect taste in furniture and boring taste in movies and the ability to keep everything looking brand-new. She was renting an Airbnb. She had put her stuff in storage when she moved in with Jason, and it was still there. In — I scanned the letterhead — Glendale.

I raced to Jason's laptop to look up the hours, but the facility had already closed for the night. It would reopen in the morning at six thirty. Jason and I would be there.

20

Jason returned from work shamefaced over our fight and his angry exit. Amanda's letter brightened his mood considerably.

"Nicely done! There's no telling what's in that storage unit." He tried to chuck me under the chin playfully, and I jerked my head away. "You were always the smart one, Dana."

"And you were the negligent, non-mail-forwarding one." I held up an expired coupon for a mall nail salon. "Good thing I remembered the sinkhole."

"Ahhh, sorry. I promise I would have forwarded anything that looked important." As I nodded skeptically, he said, "I'm assuming you want to get there first thing in the morning? So let's get to sleep now, unless . . ." He trailed off.

"Yeah," I said. "Sleep is good."

The subject of where I would sleep had become an awkward one. On the one hand, it felt silly to go all the way back to my motel every night, and I didn't like the idea of sleeping alone in a place where I was at the mercy of the desk clerk to shield me from Amanda's calls. At the same time, my relationship with Jason was still somewhat ambiguous, and sleeping in his bedroom didn't feel right either. With the exception of one four a.m. kiss, our physical intimacy with each other had always been on the order of shoulder-punching. We had fallen asleep side by side countless times, sometimes leaning on each other, but never in bed. I could tell Jason was ready for more, but, in a role reversal that struck me as ironic, I wasn't ready, not yet.

I told myself it had to do with the dire situation we were in and the fact that I was still shielding Jason from it. Of course our amateur sleuthing seemed fun to him, even a turn-on. But the work of pretending that fun was all it was left no room in my emotional landscape for romance. I told myself that after we were through with Amanda, everything would feel right again. Regardless, his body language had become one of subtle overtures, and he hadn't failed to notice that mine had become one of rejecting them. The mattress in the recording studio solved the problem temporarily, though it was hell on my back.

To stall, I asked a question that had been on my mind since I'd found the letter. "Got any ideas for getting into Amanda's storage unit?"

"As a matter of fact, I do," Jason said. "We'll talk about it tomorrow. Until then, don't worry your pretty little head about it."

A chill went through me. His flippant attitude during our investigation reminded me of the way he'd been about Mattie's truck. Maybe that was why I had trouble feeling romantic toward him. Anything that reminded me of Mattie gave me a swell of nausea that was hard to dispel.

I suppressed the feeling as best I could and tried to join in the banter, moving down the hallway toward the studio. "Just a second ago, I was the smart one. Now I'm the pretty one?" I reached the door and turned around to find he'd been following close behind me.

"You're both," he said, and he leaned in for a kiss, which I accepted mutely. After he drew back, he studied me for a moment.

Without meaning to, I held my breath.

"Okay," he said finally. "I'll see you in the morning."

"Good night, Jason," I said. And closed the door behind me.

"So that's when we decided it was time to move in together."

Jason had been holding my hand during the conversation with the Saf-Stor employee, whose name, according to his badge, was Delrick. Now Jason drew my hand all the way onto his lap and gave it a squeeze and said, "Right, honey?"

I smiled apologetically at Delrick, who was clearly struggling to appear more interested in his first customers of the day than in the cup of coffee sitting half finished on his desk.

Jason's plan was to rent a unit on the same floor as Amanda's, then cut her lock and replace it with a new one. He'd read about a rash of similar crimes in the L.A. area; not only was it easy to do, but if the staff discovered the break-in, they would think it was just petty theft and not investigate further. The hardware store opened even earlier than the storage facility, and we'd loaded up my purse with a lock, bolt cutters, and X-Acto knives for opening the boxes once we got in. But the plan had been too simple for Jason's taste, and he had spiced it up by concocting an elaborate story about why we needed the storage, one involving absentee roommates and rising rent and, of course, our romance, which was always meant to be.

I let him finish his spiel. Then, to nudge the clerk awake and feed him his next line, I added: "To be honest, the one-dollar move-in special is what convinced us."

Jason glared at me, but the clerk nodded.

"It's a great deal," he said, moving into the rapid-fire patter of the salesperson who works on commission. "Let me just explain to you the terms and conditions —"

The terms and conditions included the final month's rent, but I was too impatient to complain. Twenty minutes and a hundred and twenty dollars later, the clerk rode the freight elevator up with us to the third floor and showed us to our unit. We walked together down a long, white corridor full of gray, numbered doors.

"This is very *Alice in Wonderland*," Jason said.

"I was thinking more *Tales from the Crypt*. 'Behind one of these doors is a million dollars. Behind one of them is a flesh-eating ghoul.'"

"What's the one set in an insane asylum?" We were both a little punchy, as if we were approaching the finish line of a scavenger hunt. The clerk walked ahead, trying his best to ignore us, and Jason dug his elbow into my side as we passed door number 302.

"Just a few more . . . here it is," the clerk said, stopping in front of our unit and turning the handle. The light flickered on inside automatically as the door opened, revealing a dingy white interior. "Want to take a look?"

"Absolutely," Jason said with fake enthusiasm. He stepped into the box and pretended to admire the scuffed white walls. "Honey, come check this out. Roomy."

"You're free to start moving things in right away."

"We absolutely will," I said, joining Jason and putting an arm around his waist as he threw his around my shoulder.

"Great." The clerk looked relieved to be rid of us. "Let me show you how to set up the keypad, and I'll leave you to it."

"Keypad?" Jason released my shoulder, his tone suddenly deadly serious.

"Each unit is locked with a motion-sensor alarm, controlled by the keypad on the handle, with a code that only you have access to," the clerk said proudly just as I realized I hadn't seen a single padlock on any of the doors. "We take your security very seriously. Those other self-storage places, where you bring your own lock, they get broken into all the time. People just cut the locks with bolt cutters."

Suddenly, the fourteen inches of steel in my purse felt very, very heavy.

Jason watched politely as the clerk showed him how to set his code, only once throwing a glance back toward me with something like panic.

"How are we going to get in?" I whispered when the clerk had gone down the elevator.

"Just give me a second to think," he said, rubbing his closed eyes with his fingers.

"Come back inside, there are cameras out there."

Jason followed me into the unit. Then his head snapped up. "Cameras! Do you think we could get our hands on security footage of her keying in the code?"

"Even if they keep the security tapes long enough, we'd have no idea how to find the right one," I pointed out.

He frowned. "Well, there must be a master code. The building manager has to be able to get in, right?"

"Right. So how would we get the master code?"

"Maybe you can go flirt with Delrick," Jason suggested. "Distract him while I snoop around his desk."

"Or maybe he's gay, and *you* can go flirt with him," I snapped. "Anyway, after your hardcore lovey-dovey routine, that's going to be a tough sell for either of us."

"Okay, okay, I'm just thinking out loud here." He looked at the bank of doors. "Our unit is on the same side of the hall as hers. What about cutting through the walls?"

"You really want to tunnel through seventeen storage units between ours and hers?" Jason was getting frustrated, but I went on. "Besides, he said the alarm was hooked up to a motion sensor. That means any movement inside will set it off, not just the door opening."

"Well, maybe we should just give up, then!" Jason exploded. "Unless you have a brilliant idea."

"I might," I said. "Hang on a second." I opened my purse, handed him the bolt cutters, which were getting in the way, and dug out my black makeup bag. "Let's go take a look."

We walked down the silent white hallway to the door marked 302 and squinted at the keypad. Jason reached out a hand to touch the buttons.

"No!" I yelped and slapped his hand away. "Stay back there." I unzipped my makeup bag and pulled out a blush palette that had shattered a long time ago when I dropped it on a bathroom floor. It was an expensive brand, and I had carefully hoarded the glittery pink powder in its black compact, carrying an extra-soft brush with me that wouldn't pick up too much at once. I dipped the brush carefully in the compact, shook off the excess powder, then applied it lightly to the keypad. Leaning over, I blew gently.

"Look." Most of the blush had scattered, leaving a granule here and there. Only three buttons looked different: 2, 6, and 8 were frosted with dark pink powder where fingers had pressed them repeatedly, leaving layers of prints, the whorls of which were faintly discernible around the edges.

"Okay, cool," Jason said. "But there's one problem. It's a four-number code."

"So she repeated a number."

"Which one?"

I squinted and looked closer. One of the prints was much darker than the other two. "I'd say it's the eight, by the look of it."

"Two-six-eight-eight."

"Or two-eight-six-eight," I said. "Or eight-two-six-eight, or . . ."

"So how do we know which one it is? We can't just start trying them out. The alarm'll go off. And who knows how many combinations you can make out of those four—"

"Twelve," I said. I'd been scribbling on the back of a receipt I'd found in my purse.

"What is that, a factorial?" Jason squinted over my shoulder. "That's ninth-grade math. You remember Mrs. Farber's class?"

"No, dummy. I just listed them all out." I looked at the four-digit combinations and thought. It reminded me of looking at Carl's Runnr data with Amanda, searching for the pattern and coming up with *Game of Thrones*. What was the pattern here? Which one of these would Amanda have picked, and why? "I bet it's a word."

"Or it's totally random, filed away in a password-protection app," Jason said.

I remembered writing my number on a napkin for her the night we met. "You know Amanda. She doesn't even use social media. She wouldn't trust a program like that. I bet she'd come up with a word she could remember instead."

"So the numbers would correspond to letters?" Jason frowned and looked at the ceiling. "If two is B . . . and six is F . . . and eight is H? B, F, H, H? What can you spell with B, F, H, H?"

"Nothing," I said. "Get out your phone."

He pulled out his phone, and I pulled up the keypad screen and pointed to the tiny letters below each number.

"The phone keypad? That'll take forever," he protested. "With twelve number combinations, and then each number could stand for one of three letters . . . how many possible combinations is that?"

I shrugged. "I don't remember enough from Mrs. Farber's class to even take a guess. So we should get started."

We went back to our unit, and I found a scrap of paper for Jason to write on, thinking that sometimes it pays to be a little woman with a big, messy purse. I split the list of twelve numbers in half, gave six to Jason and kept six for myself.

"This is going to take forever," Jason complained.

Handing him a pen and uncapping an eyeliner pencil for me to write with, I said, "The good news is, there aren't going to be that many letter combinations that make actual words."

There were even fewer than I'd thought there would be, but Jason was right, it was slow going. At the end of an hour, we had the following words:

AUNT, BUNT, AUTO, TUNA, BOUT, CUNT

"Obviously, you know which one I think it should be," Jason said. "Ha-ha."

"Well, what else? Does she have nieces and nephews? Is she really into tuna?" He rubbed the bridge of his nose. "Wait a minute, does she have a boat?"

"It can't be B-O-A-T, B and A are both on the two and there's only one of those." I looked over the list, feeling sure we had missed some letter combinations. I stared at the phone keys. "B-O-T-T? Is that a word? How about N-A-T-T?"

"No and no."

I looked again and blinked. A cold feeling started up in the pit of my stomach. It couldn't be, but suddenly I knew the answer. "Try six-two-eight-eight."

"What's the word?"

"I just have a hunch. Key it in."

"Tell me the word first."

"Look, either it's right or it isn't. But there's nothing on that list that makes any sense," I said. "Just key it in. Otherwise we'll be here all day."

"You key it in."

I took a deep breath, approached the keypad, and hovered my fingers for a moment over the three smudgy numbers, waiting to feel some special warmth from them, some confirmation that I was right. Then I punched them in quickly and stood back.

The red light by the handle turned green and there was a quiet but satisfying click. I turned the handle and the light inside Amanda's storage unit came on.

Jason and I stood staring into the unit for a second. Then we both started yelling and jumping up and down. He leaned over and gave me a bear hug, picking me up and setting me back down again. "What's the password?"

"It's Matt," I said, suddenly sober. "That's why I didn't want to tell you."

"What, because of my brother?" He frowned momentarily, then recovered. "There are a lot of Matts in the world, Dana."

It was true. There were a lot of Matts in the world. But only one of them was my third name, the shadow hanging over my relationship with Jason, and the key to whatever bond I'd once shared with Amanda. I shook off the coincidence. "Maybe we'll find out more about Amanda's Matt inside. Let's see what's in there."

We walked in, squeezing into the path between two banks of boxes, and shut the door behind us. The latch clicked. The light went out. It was pitch-dark.

21

H ang on."

A dim blue light illuminated the underside of Jason's face and his hand, his index finger tracing a pattern on the surface of his phone. Then he found the flashlight button, and the light blossomed outward into a fat white cone that made the square of the ceiling glow and threw violent shadows on the walls behind towers of boxes. As Jason moved, the shadows swung crazily, and every time I blinked, I saw the afterimage of the phone's bright rectangle burned on my retinas.

The storage unit was the same size as ours, but Amanda's possessions had the odd effect of making it seem bigger. The boxes were stacked almost to the ceiling, and a few large pieces of furniture caught the light — I made out the nubby texture of an upended sofa, the pressboard back of a dresser. A couple of narrow, crooked aisles penetrated the wall of stuff to allow access to the boxes at the back. Maybe it was the shadows leaping on the walls, but it was easy to imagine the lumpish shapes extending indefinitely in either direction, the twisted aisles snaking through them like a labyrinth. A place to get lost in. My chest tightened suddenly, and I felt short of breath.

"Does the door—"

"The inner handle doesn't lock," Jason said impatiently. "Otherwise people would get stuck in here all the time."

The thought wasn't as comforting as it should have been, but I forced myself not to dwell on it. "Right. Where do we start?"

"Just look for the box marked 'Amanda's Darkest Secrets.' Shouldn't be too hard to find." Jason's tone was sarcastic, but I knew him well enough to detect that he, too, was unnerved. In the artificial midnight of the storage unit, it was easy to forget that it was eight o'clock in the morning outside. Somehow the bright and antiseptic hall made it feel even darker and lonelier in the unit, like the inside of a mouth.

"Let's just start opening boxes," I said. "We'll start with the ones up here and work our way back." I pulled out the X-Acto knives and handed one to Jason.

"Cheers." He took it and knelt down by a large box, and I did the same, using the display light from my phone to illuminate corners Jason's flashlight left in shadow.

My first box was labeled KITCHEN in black Sharpie, and, sure enough, the nest of crumpled-up newspapers inside seemed to hold only pots and pans. As a gesture toward thoroughness I unlidded a few pots and was rewarded with more newspapers. "What have you got?"

"Dishes. And a salad spinner."

Curious, I held my phone close to one of the newspaper scraps. "January second, over a year ago. When did you say you met Amanda?"

"Pilot season," he said shortly. "March of last year, maybe? And she was fired from Runnr in December."

"Huh. So she moved to L.A. and put her stuff in storage right away. What was she doing between January and March?"

"Apparently eating gritty, unspun salads," Jason said, tossing the plastic bowl back in a box. "Come on, we have to move faster."

We worked silently after that. After a few more kitchen boxes I gave up on looking through the whole box and started trusting the labels. Amanda was nothing if not organized; she might have moved quickly after her exile from Runnr, but she hadn't thrown her stuff into boxes any which way. Still, I couldn't suppress a mild disappointment at seeing her possessions collected in such a prosaic and orderly fashion. It wasn't just that a boxful of kitchen appliances doesn't tell you much about a person's deepest motives for stalking you and your new boyfriend; it was that the appliances themselves were on the dull side. Amanda must have made good money, and the settlement from the suit must have been substantial as well. Drawing my finger back in pain from an inadequately wrapped blade that turned out to belong to a Cuisinart food processor, I admitted to myself that I'd been hoping for something more glamorous. I mean, *I* had a Cuisinart.

I had been imagining some kind of fall from glory for Amanda —a fabulously rich Silicon Valley lifestyle snatched from her during the Runnr debacle and then her ensuing wrath. But by the time I unearthed three pairs of nearly identical worn black boots in a box marked CLOSET, I'd begun to realize that the story Amanda's objects were telling was not one of a person who cared about expensive things. Her taste was subdued; the motorcycle jacket she wore even in muggy Austin weather was probably her nicest possession.

Where were the yearbooks, the photographs, the old diaries? Where was the stuff that made her human? We were here to get revenge on Amanda, and she herself had told me how to do it: *Find something she cares about.* What did Amanda care about?

Jason was having no luck either. "This is bullshit," he said. "There's nothing here. I just looked through three hall-closet boxes. Unless she strangles her victims with extension cords and then melts them with the acid from triple-A batteries, I'm not sure we've got anything here."

"Just keep going," I said. "There's no other way to get through all this stuff."

"Fine." He stood up and groaned as his knees popped audibly. "But I'm starting over from the back end." He dusted off his hands on his jeans. "I bet that's where all the good stuff is. At the very least, a vibrator."

"Wait!" I said, but he had already picked up his phone and was making his way back through one of the narrow aisles. The shadows in my half of the unit leaped all the way up the wall, and then everything vanished as Jason went behind the tallest stack.

"I'll meet you in the middle," he called.

"Thanks a lot," I muttered as I waited for my eyes to adjust to my disposable phone's puny glow.

For a few minutes the only sounds were the scuffing of cardboard boxes as Jason brushed against them, punctuated by an occasional yelp of frustration as he banged his knee. "There's so much stuff piled up, I'm not even sure I can get to the back," he said, and then: "Ohhh. Oh my God."

"What?"

"Dana, come here. You have to see this."

I got to my knees with some difficulty and used my feeble phone light to pick my way in between the boxes. I saw what he meant about the piles getting higher and denser; at one point the path bottle-necked and I couldn't figure out how to get any farther back, but then I noticed a tiny throughway to my left. I could see Jason's phone light in the triangle formed by a rolled-up rug leaning against the stack of boxes, and as I stooped to avoid hitting my head, I saw that the rug formed a kind of doorway, on the other side of which Jason was standing, holding his phone aloft.

We stood together in a clearing about four feet deep and running the length of the back of the unit. By the light of his phone, I could see a futon against the wall, neatly made up with a pillow and coverlet and an extra blanket; a small desk and chair were pushed up against the opposite wall. Four high-powered flashlights were lined up on the floor near our feet, where they could be accessed quickly and rotated out easily. A small, battery-operated minifridge by the futon doubled as a nightstand. The scene was unbelievably creepy, like stumbling on the abandoned nest of some predator in the woods. If it had been messy or squalid, it might have simply looked pathetic. But something about the excruciating neatness of the little lair made it seem like a perfectly executed step in some elaborate plan.

"She was living in a storage unit," I said, too dumbfounded to keep from stating the obvious. "Why on earth . . ." I touched the bed gingerly and then withdrew my fingers with a shudder. "I mean, she must have had plenty of money after her settlement." What did Amanda care about? Cross comfort and basic hygiene off the list.

But Jason had moved closer to the bed, still holding his phone aloft, and now he made a strangled noise in his throat. There was a row of pictures arranged neatly on the wall above the bed in a Scotch-taped grid: photographs of women, most of them selfies printed out from social media sites. Jason stared at them.

"Exes," he said, looking like he was about to throw up. "Mine. Jesus, she's obsessed. This goes back all the way to high school. Remember Lizzie Reynolds? She's the one who dumped me right before prom." He looked at me. "This is, like, serial-killer behavior, Dana."

"Well, it's a lot worse than the app." At least we had the answer to what she cared about. I leaned in for a closer look and gasped. "Oh my God, Kim." Somehow seeing a familiar face in the rows of pictures brought home how disturbing our discovery really was.

"Rinski? Yeah, we went out for a while," Jason said stiffly. "A long time ago."

"She told me. We've been hanging out lately." Amanda had obviously been targeting her too. I hoped she had taken my advice and gone to my mother's house in Amarillo. I vowed to call and urge her to do so as soon as we left the storage facility.

While Jason continued to look, I dragged a banker's box of binders out from under the bed and started flipping through them. Most of them were full of code, indecipherable to me, but one was dedicated to printed-out spreadsheets similar to the one she had shown me listing her online harassers. But these were all women's names. I poked Jason. "Do these look familiar?" Names, birth dates, and current and past residences were listed neatly alongside phone numbers, names of relatives, current and past jobs.

He nodded up at the wall. "These are like dossiers. How long has she been stalking me?" There was real fear in his eyes.

But I was puzzling over the paper trail. Why hard copies? "She likes them for her own secrets," I said slowly to myself. "She only stores things online when she wants other people to find them."

"Great. Let's get some pictures and get the hell out of here."

He began snapping pictures while I examined the wall, searching.

Jason saw what I was doing. "Don't bother," he said. "She was hunting down girlfriends. Which you weren't, at the time."

We both went silent. It was absurd to feel hurt that I didn't merit inclusion in some sicko's photo gallery, but it served as a reminder of how much more Jason had always meant to me than I'd meant to him. I'd always known Jason had a thing for skinny blondes, but with all their photos taped up here, it was impossible not to notice their striking similarities. No wonder Amanda had looked vaguely familiar to me when I first met her; I was staring at a physical type I knew all too well. Now that we were together at last, the thought of all these women he had dated briefly and then broken up with made me feel a little nauseated. I wasn't an ex-girlfriend. But would I be someday?

"Well, this looks batshit crazy," I managed weakly. "And it's hard evidence. I bet there's more in that box too." I thought nervously of Kim, hoping she was out of Austin. "Do you think she's contacted all these women?"

"Maybe. If someone went looking for people who hate me, the pictures in this storage unit would be a pretty good place to start."

"You're one of those bridge-burners, I guess." Still stung by the comment about my missing photo, I couldn't help myself. I'd never spent much time thinking about why Jason's girlfriends never hung around. I was too busy being delighted at how quickly they vanished in the rearview mirror to wonder where they'd gone. "Leave a trail of angry women in your wake."

"This one's the angriest," he said. "At least, I hope so." He went back to taking pictures, and I continued looking through the binder, keeping my thoughts to myself.

Jason broke the silence. "Did Kim say anything about me?" he said in an odd tone. "We didn't part on good terms."

"We avoided the topic, to be honest." I couldn't have said why my next statement had the sound, even to my ears, of a warning. "I really like Kim. We're friends."

He started to say something, then swallowed it.

I threw the binder back into the box with disgust. As I did so, something white and rectangular slipped askew and poked out of the side of the binder. I plucked it out and looked at it quickly, then stuck it in my purse, the blood rushing to my face.

The thick white envelope was addressed to me at Jason's house.

It had already been opened, and the return address was mostly torn away. But what was left clearly indicated it was from Clements Unit.

I was in the binder after all. Along with Mattie.

Jason was quieter than usual on the way home and seemed chastened. Though we had found exactly what we were looking for, it didn't cheer him up; his spy-movie antics had faded away the moment we found the photos. Maybe he was frightened for the first time. Or maybe, I thought, he just didn't like the version of himself he saw reflected in the eyes of past romantic partners.

But then, who likes to be reminded of failure? The sheer quantity of women in his past was sobering. His darkened mood would ordinarily have worried me, and I would have spent the ride home commiserating with him over Amanda's sick obsession and finding subtle ways to reassure him that the contents of the binder didn't make me think any less of him. Instead, the silence in the car was something of a relief.

Or at least, it would have been if I hadn't had the letter in my purse. I held the purse on my lap and stared resolutely out the window, watching the L.A. sprawl inch past and counting the minutes until I could be alone to read it. To distract myself, I dialed into my voicemail remotely and was relieved that there was nothing from Amanda. The only message was from my mom, informing me that my nice, funny friend from Austin had arrived safely last night and gone to bed after a late dinner. I breathed a sigh of relief for Kim's sake, then cast a sidelong glance at Jason, but he was deep in his own thoughts.

By the time we got home, Jason had finally come out of his bubble enough to notice my distracted state, but of course he assumed he knew the reason for it. As soon as the door closed behind us, he moved to embrace me. I felt his arms pressing my purse into my side, and the letter in it seemed to burn through to my skin. I let him hold me for a moment, forcing myself not to break off the hug.

"Hey," he said, drawing back to look down at me, his arms still around me. "I hope you know—all those girls in my past—now I know how dumb I was. Too busy chasing after what I thought I wanted to see what was right in front of my eyes."

I smiled up at him, not trusting myself to speak.

"I don't want you to think that's what I want, not anymore. That was a wall of my mistakes. And she was the last one, thank God."

I didn't need to ask who. "I'm not hurt," I said. "Honestly, I'm not."

It was Jason who seemed hurt. He needed more than absolution from me; he needed comfort. Under the pretense of reassuring me, he kept finding excuses to touch me, drumming his fingers on my knee as we sat next to each other at the table, squeezing the back of my neck when I said I was tired. Finally, in desperation, I waited until he was looking the other way, then slipped the letter into my waistband so I could sneak it into the bathroom.

Alone in the bathroom, I turned on the tap water to cover up the rattling of paper. My hands shook uncontrollably as I pulled the letter from the envelope. I took a deep breath to compose myself and unfolded it.

It was handwritten with a ballpoint pen in surprisingly neat lettering. Laurel used to say that in our age of electronic communication, a glimpse of someone's handwriting is more intimate than a glimpse of his underwear drawer. I tried to imagine Mattie hunched over a tiny desk in his dreary cell, lank black hair falling over his bulging forehead, shaping each word carefully, starting over with a fresh sheet whenever he made a mistake. Before I could begin to feel sorry for him, I had a sense memory of the TV room, the dull pressure pushing my spine against the sofa springs. After all, what did it cost Mattie to rewrite a letter once or twice? Where he was, he had all the time in the world.

Dear Dana,

Please don't throw this letter out without reading it. I started going to group in here because the laws like it, but now it's got me thinking about the past, mulling over my mistakes. I'm writing to say: I'm sorry about what happened that night you spent at our house. For years I tried to forget about it, or at least pretend it wasn't my fault. It's only now that I've heard a lot of guys talking about it in group that I really get what rape does to a person. And that's what it was. It was rape.

I fumed. Of course it wasn't Mattie's fault he'd raped me. Just like it wasn't Neely's fault he'd exposed himself to me in the back of an SUV. It was never their fault. It was mine, for being in the wrong place at the wrong time, wearing the wrong dress, looking the wrong way. I didn't feel much like reading the rest, and the only reason I didn't crumple the letter up right then was that I needed to know what Amanda had found out about me from it.

I always felt mean when you came over. You'd hang on Jase's words, looking at him with these wide eyes, like he was some kind of prize. No one ever looked at me like that. In our family, Jason was the smart, funny one, and I was the ugly, stupid fuckup. And believe me, he made sure I knew it.

I kept him in line most of the time. Dad used to beat me up, especially after he didn't have Mom to push around anymore. Jase never got any of that. He was so little when Mom left, he didn't really get how bad it was. I felt like it was only fair if I gave him a hard time. To even the score, sort of.

He was too scared of getting whaled on to say anything to my face, but he used to pull these dumb tricks to remind me how he could get away with anything. He did it even when we were little. My mom had this jar shaped like an owl where she kept the cookies for our lunches. After she left, Jase and I used to sneak Oreos when my dad was at work. Well, one day I got caught and spanked, and the jar got moved to the top of the refrigerator. A few days later there was a big crash, and my dad found Jason on the floor, surrounded by Oreos and blood and broken pieces of jar. He'd climbed up there to sneak some cookies. This time I got pounded within an inch of my life, because, see, it was *my* fault the jar got moved in the first place and Jason fell.

Jason could do no wrong. He hated our dad too, but he could manipulate him. When he did get in trouble, he could always get out of it, crack a joke and get a laugh. And it didn't stop when we got bigger. Jason narc'd on me when I was selling pot in high school so I'd get kicked out and he could have his own private TV room. And I'm pretty sure he let my dog Kenny out that time, maybe even drove him somewhere and dropped him off in a field. Or worse. Of course I got blamed for leaving the gate open, but Kenny never ran off like that before.

I couldn't believe what I was reading. No wonder the letter was so long; Mattie's childhood traumas, no doubt, could fill a library. I guessed this had all come up in "group." So it was his father's fault that he had raped me, or Jason's fault, or possibly their mother's, since she'd left her boys to be raised by an abusive man. Well, it didn't scan. Mattie was the one who had been avoiding responsibility all these years, not Jason. And here he was, still trying to get out of it, spending more of his supposed apology letter wallowing in self-pity than actually apologizing. Moreover, his accusations toward Jason sounded delusional. As if Jason would risk wrestling that mountain of bristling fur into a car alone. Either Mattie was truly paranoid or he was just very, very into blaming Jason for the bad things that had happened to him. I suspected the latter.

Anyway, all of this was beside the point. So Mattie had had a rough childhood. Jason had too, and so had I. Not everyone with a rough childhood grew up to be a rapist or an abuser or an internet troll. We all had choices.

I thought uncomfortably of Carl's face, bloody and bawling, and glanced quickly back at the letter.

That night—you know the night I'm talking about—I was drinking before I came home. Then I saw you and Jase laughing it up together in front of the TV, and the mean feeling started. I don't know what made that night so much worse than any other —maybe it was a tough day at work, I don't even know. I just know I felt alone. And angry.

After you fell asleep, Jason and I got in a fight. I wanted to make him feel as small as I felt. It pissed me off, how he always had this adoring fan. I started giving him shit about you, calling him a fag for not sealing the deal, that kind of stuff. Told him he'd never be a real man. We were drinking, and stuff started coming out. He said I was just like Dad, and Mom left to get away from me. That made me go kind of crazy, I guess. I just wanted to get back at him, hurt him, I didn't care how. We fought some more, and he stormed off. And then . . . well, you know what happened next.

I knew. I remembered all too well his tequila breath in my mouth, his forearm pushing down on my collarbone while his other hand yanked at my jeans. And all he'd wanted was to get back at Jason. I wasn't even a person to him — just something he could take away from his brother to prove who was the bigger man. I felt too disgusted for tears. For the first time, I regretted that I hadn't given Amanda his name. Even if he was already in Clements by that time, I trusted Amanda could find a way to make anyone's life hell.

Suddenly I realized: Amanda had read this letter long before she met me. She'd known about Mattie the whole time — before I told her about Neely, even. She had sent me into the Carl hit knowing I had been raped; knowing, perhaps, I'd be triggered. When I came back with blood on my hands, she'd guessed right away what had happened. "You have one more, don't you?" she'd said. All that hounding me for the name was just a charade. She knew very well who my third name was — and *where* he was.

Afterward, I waited for you to tell someone about the rape, but you didn't. So I didn't either. You kept coming over to hang out with Jason, like nothing happened. I let myself think it couldn't be that big a deal. Maybe I was mad at you, that you liked Jason so much you'd still come over even after that. I pushed it down, told myself it had nothing to do with me. Now I know that's bullshit. I'm not the only one to blame, but I'm still sorry for my part in the whole thing. Most of all I'm sorry that I didn't understand how much you were hurt that night. I was so focused on Jason, I hardly saw you as a person at all.

I guess maybe I owe Jason an apology, too, for some stuff. He's my brother and in group they say I must love him deep down. I don't know about that. All those years beating up on him probably made him worse, and some days I wish I could take it back. Other days I'm still so mad, I feel like I could kill him. The prison shrink says it's my father I really hate, but what the hell. Someone has to hate Jason. It might as well be me.

Matthew Murphy

I read the letter over three times.

The first time, I could barely make it to the end, my stomach heaving.

The second time, I read it slowly and thoroughly, without stopping, angry tears burning my face. *I'm not the only one to blame.* What a coward.

The third time, I skimmed, trying to imagine Amanda's thoughts when she'd read it. The letter was in a prison-issue envelope with Mattie's return address at Clements clearly marked on the outside. Amanda must have snagged it before Jason got a chance to see it. Which meant that even while they were still living together, she was already sneaking around, looking for ways to ruin Jason's life. She must have been burning with hatred when she read Mattie's words —*I'm still so mad, I feel like I could kill him . . . Someone has to hate Jason. It might as well be me.* In Mattie, she'd found her strongest ally yet; she'd even made his name her new password. How could I find out whether they were in contact and, if so, what they'd said? It was someone's job at the prison to read all the prisoners' mail, incoming and outgoing. If I just had someone on the ground—

Kim. Kim was in Amarillo visiting my mom. She was gutsy enough to do a little undercover work, and she was in need of distraction. She could start by visiting Mattie at Clements. With her improv experience, she could even pose as Amanda—she was tall and blond and could pass for her if he'd only seen photographs. I'd have to call her as soon as I could, on my mom's landline. With Kim on that photo wall, I wasn't convinced her phone would be safe.

I flushed the toilet and turned on the tap to conceal the sound of me folding the letter back up and stashing it in my waistband again. When I came out, Jason was sitting on the sofa holding my old phone —the bugged one. The duct-taped packet of insulation lay beside him, slit up one side. He immediately held the phone out to me.

"You have some new messages," he said with a wink to show he was speaking for the benefit of our eavesdropper. "It looks like your mom called."

Confused, I took the phone and played along. "Oh yeah? I've been meaning to call her. Thanks."

He grabbed a pencil and paper and scribbled, *You shouldn't let your phone die or she'll figure out that you're not using it. I got it out to charge it.*

I nodded, found my charger in my purse, and plugged it in. He was right. Besides, the presence of the bugged phone gave me an excuse to take my burner outside to call my mom's house, where I was hoping to find Kim. It was true I wanted to keep my conversation with Kim safe from Amanda, but I didn't want Jason to hear it either.

My mom's phone rang longer than usual, and for a moment I worried she was out, even though it was a weekend. When she picked up, she sounded a little distant.

"Hi, Mama, it's me."

"Mija!" Her voice changed instantly. "I thought it was somebody selling something. The number on the caller ID looks funny."

"It's a new phone."

"Please take some more coffee, dear, it's just going to go to waste," she said, her mouth away from the receiver. Before I could ask her to put Kim on, she started talking to me again. *"Mija,* I don't want to worry you," she said, in a tone indicating she was clearly worried herself. "But I got a call yesterday from the police."

I froze. "The Austin police? About what?" It had to be Fash. I cursed myself for telling Laurel I was staying with my mom in Amarillo.

"They wouldn't tell me, *mija*. It's you they want to talk to. They said you weren't answering your phone. I told them you were off running errands and I didn't know when you'd be back."

I let out my breath with a sigh. Trust my mom to be cagey with the police. As a Mexican-American immigrant in Texas, where ICE crackdowns could make anyone with an accent a target for harassment, she distrusted officers of the law, though she was unfailingly polite to them. "Thanks, Mama. You told them right. And I'll be back soon, when I'm done with what I need to do out here." *You won't have been lying for me,* I promised silently.

"Okay, *mija,* but you should probably call them back before that. I said I would give you the message. I'm sure you haven't done anything wrong."

"I haven't." I reminded myself there was no reason I would be a suspect in Fash's killing—Fash had never hurt me directly, and I hadn't been near him on the night of his death. It was a mark of my mounting paranoia that I felt that even my mom, who knew nothing about any of it, could harbor suspicions about me.

Suddenly I felt desperate to convince her that I was doing something legitimate. "I might be moving back out here to L.A., Mom. I had an audition yesterday. I have an agent now and everything." There was no need to mention the offer from Cynthia Omari, since it might fall through. Anyway, my mom had only the haziest idea of what a podcast was.

"That's so wonderful, *mija*. Your friend was telling me all about that contest you won in Austin. Why didn't you say anything when you were here?"

"Well, it was only second place," I corrected her, thanking Kim silently for having blurred the details to make me sound better. "Would you mind putting her on for me? I have something to ask her."

"Oh, *mija,* she's just leaving! Let me catch her. I'll have to put the phone down for a minute." I heard the scratchy sound of a telephone receiver being set down on a soft surface.

Why would Kim be leaving after just one night? I wondered if something had happened to scare her and cursed myself for not getting in touch earlier. It was a tall order to ask her to visit Clements now, but she was the only person I could trust for the job. I was starting to think she was the only person I trusted, period, at least when it came to this Amanda business. I remembered my impulse to tell her about Aaron Neely, back before the Funniest Person semifinals, and wondered what had kept me from doing so. If only I had told her, maybe things would be different now. Kim would have believed me, and she wouldn't have laughed; she knew just how dark men like Neely and Fash could make our lives. At the same time, I knew instinctively that she would have had no patience for the likes of Amanda, with her bruised-looking eyes and her delusions of grandeur. Kim wouldn't have listened to Amanda for even a minute, and I hoped that was what she was about to tell me. The telephone made a few more rustling sounds, and I crossed my fingers.

"Hi, Dana. New phone number?"

My heart stopped. My blood thrummed in my ears. And yet even so, it was a split second before my brain caught up to what my body already knew.

In the meantime, Amanda went on. "Thanks so much for giving me directions to your mom's house. She's so nice! We were up late last night, chatting over a cup of tea. Talking about you, mostly."

I caught my breath at last, tears prickling in my eyes. "Get out of my mom's house, Amanda. Right now."

She laughed. "All good things, I promise. No embarrassing childhood photos were shared."

"Get out of that house before I call the police."

"Oh, you really should," she said, affecting a serious tone of voice.

"Your mom told you they were looking for you, right? The sooner you call back, the less chance there'll be any misunderstanding. What do you think they were calling about, Dana?"

I was speechless.

"Anyway, she was telling me what a loyal friend you are. Like with your friend Jason from high school. That's him in your prom picture, isn't it? And I was telling *her* that I know I can always rely on you when I need something. Especially when *you owe me one.*"

"I don't owe you anything."

"Oh, yes, you do," she said teasingly. "And I think it should be at least as good as what I did for you, don't you?"

So that was it. She didn't want me just to hurt Jason; she wanted me to kill him. An eye for an eye, a tooth for a tooth. A death for a death. She was homicidal. Thinking of her standing just a few feet away from my mother sent tears streaming down my cheeks. "Please, please, leave my mom alone. Don't hurt her."

"That would only ever happen to one person," she said brightly. "And he would deserve it, don't you think?"

"I'm not going to hurt Jason. I'm not going to hurt anyone." And yet I had before. Someone had once begged me, on his knees: *Please don't hurt me.*

"Yes, you will," she said, as if reading my thoughts. "But just to make sure everything goes smoothly, I'm heading out to see you."

A chill went through me, followed by an electric surge of rage. "If you're planning on cleaning out your creepy little rat hole, don't bother," I said. "We took pictures of what we found there. All the proof we need that you're a psychopath."

She was totally unruffled by the news. "Thanks for checking on my stuff. Now maybe you understand why you're the best person for the job. Though, honestly, I think you already knew."

"Shut up, shut up, you lying *bitch!*"

"Dana, if there's one thing you know about me, it's that I'm honest," she chided. "*Brutally* honest."

"I'll kill you," I whispered. "If you come near me or Jason, I will kill you."

She laughed again. "Is that a promise? I have a promise for you too: I will never, ever lie to you, Dana. Remember that. What's that, Mrs. Diaz?" I squeezed my eyes shut to block out the mental image of Amanda faking pleasantries with my mom. When that didn't work, I imagined bashing in Amanda's skull, but her face morphed into a man's face and began begging for mercy. *Please don't hurt me.*

"Listen, I have to get on the road, you know the drive to L.A. is a killer . . . Oh, and I'm bringing you that wig you left in your apartment, in case you need help getting into character. You're welcome. Okay, your mom wants to talk to you again, I'm handing her the phone . . ." There was another shuffle of the receiver, and I heard, distantly, the words "Bye, Mrs. Diaz!"

"Mama? Mama? Is she gone?" I fought to keep my voice from betraying my tears.

"Yes, darling, she just walked out the door. Did you need her again?"

"Are you okay?"

"I'm fine, *mija*! I wish you wouldn't worry so much."

I held the phone away from my face for a second and sobbed as quietly as I could. Now that the danger had passed, there was no need to scare her. The game was up; Amanda knew I had a new phone, which meant she knew Jason and I were onto her. And she was on her way.

"*Mija*? You still there?"

I pulled myself together. "Mom. I need you to tell me everything you and Amanda talked about yesterday. It's important."

"Oh, sweetie, I don't know. She's very easy to talk to. She told me more about what's going on with you than you ever do."

I swallowed hard, at the thought of her in my bedroom, looking at my high-school yearbooks. "She said you talked about Jason. What did she say?"

"You didn't tell me they knew each other. His brother too."

"She talked about Mattie?"

"She's his pen pal. What a nice girl, cheering up an inmate. I guess everybody needs a friend."

I almost laughed but choked it down. "I love you, Mama. Please take care."

"You too, *mija*."

I hung up. There was no more time to waste. It was time to tell Jason.

The question was, what?

22

Jason's face darkened at the mention of Mattie. "My brother? What does he have to do with any of this?"

We were sitting in the booth at the R & R. I didn't want to talk in the house, or in my car, or near either of our phones. Anywhere might be bugged. I'd insisted we sit on the same side of the booth so that we could talk in lowered voices — though now I felt worried there could be someone behind us, listening in behind the high partition. It was as likely as anything else that had happened.

I took a deep breath. "Amanda went to Amarillo to visit Mattie in prison. I think she's been writing to him for a while."

"So you were right about the password. She must have been writing him before we broke up." Jason pushed his coffee mug away and put his head in his hands. "You know Mattie's always hated me. Who knows what lies he told her? No wonder she stopped trusting me."

"Why does Mattie hate you so much?" I said, trying not to betray the fact that I'd already read one explanation.

"Oh, I don't know. Sibling rivalry stuff, I guess. I got good grades and Mattie got Fs, so Dad always rode him harder than me. He probably thinks it's all my fault he's in prison. He likes to blame other people for his problems." He looked up. "And he used to creep on my girlfriends too. Any girl liked me better than him, it drove him crazy. Even you."

It was so close to what was in the letter, it was a little eerie. Hearing Mattie's words corroborated gave me a strange feeling, just like hearing Amanda's Runnr story had. The same story, or at least a story with more or less the same details, could sound so different, depending on who you trusted. And I trusted Jason. But then again, I had once trusted Amanda. Only what I knew about Mattie kept me anchored to the version of reality that came out of Jason's mouth. I could never trust anyone who would do what Mattie had done to me.

But while I was considering this, Jason's face had started flushing, and now it was a dark, angry red. He stared into his coffee.

"What is it?"

"It's just—I knew it. I knew there was someone else. I thought maybe she was seeing Neely behind my back." He chuckled grimly. "How could I be so blind? My own goddamn brother."

I felt us veering into dangerous territory. "What could he do? From prison, I mean."

"Besides seduce my girlfriend by snail mail?" He laughed bitterly. "Tell a bunch of lies about me, give her a reason to hate me even more. He probably helped her find a bunch of my exes to tell her even more lies."

"Could he—would he want to have you killed?"

Jason paused, sobered by the question. "I always knew he wanted my life," he said. "I didn't think he would ever try to take it from me. But maybe I was always just a little bit naive about how far he would go."

Mattie's weight. The smell of tequila in the dark.

"Jason, Amanda is headed here, right now. She's on the road. She's about"—I reached for my phone to check the time, but I'd left it in the car—"about twelve hours away is my best guess." I took a deep breath. "I think she's out to kill you."

He looked at me for a long moment, frowning, as if he hadn't heard. "How do you know all this shit about my brother? Have you been talking to Mattie too?"

"No!" I thought of the letter in my purse and wondered what he would do if he found it. "Did you hear me, Jason? Whether or not Mattie's behind it, Amanda is coming here to kill you."

"I'm not afraid of that skinny bitch," he snarled. "She wouldn't have the guts."

"Jason, she's violent. She may even have killed before. Just trust me."

"Then we'll call the police."

"We can't," I said miserably.

"To hell with that," he said. "It's past time for a restraining order. We have enough evidence for that, if nothing else."

"Let's go." I couldn't tell him here, not in the restaurant.

Jason waved the waitress over, and she pulled the check out of her apron pocket and handed it to him with a knowing smile. "I had it on me just in case," she said. While Jason dug through his wallet for a credit card, she said, "How long have you two been together?"

"Not long," I said just as Jason looked up from his wallet and said, "Four days."

"I knew it," the waitress said. "Same side of the booth. That's either less than a week, or it's twenty years. And you two don't look old enough to have known each other that long."

"You'd be surprised," Jason said with a smile.

I pulled two twenties out of my pocket and threw them down. "Keep the change," I said, and her eyes widened gratefully. She'd go to her grave thinking her tableside patter had done the trick, and in a way it had. I would have tipped a lot more than 40 percent to get the hell away from that diner and its memories.

Back at the house, I didn't tell him everything. I left out Aaron Neely and Doug Branchik and Carl M. I let him think it had all started with Fash groping me, with what he'd done to Kim and other women in the scene. I let him think the pact was completely hypothetical—just two women talking in a bar, the way women do when men aren't around. An inside joke. I told him I'd never taken it seriously, never planned to do it, and had no idea Amanda would go so far.

In other words, I told him almost nothing.

But it was enough. He looked at me like I was a complete stranger. "Jesus, Dana. What the hell were you thinking?"

"I know it sounds crazy," I said. "But—"

"Try criminally insane." He shook his head. "You told Amanda to go rough some guy up, and now he's dead. And you're telling me she wants you to do the same thing to me?"

"Which, obviously, I would never do!"

"Well, thanks a lot," he said sarcastically. "I appreciate that you're not going to kill me."

"I didn't even know you knew each other. Or I would never have—"

"Pledged to kill a total stranger?" He looked at me with disgust.

"Not kill," I protested guiltily. "Anyway, it was just a joke."

"Yeah. Not one of your best." He slapped his hands down on his knees and stood up.

"Okay, you're right. It was stupid and juvenile," I said in desperation. "But I never meant—"

"Then maybe you shouldn't have listened to that crazy bitch in the first place."

"I told you, I didn't know she was serious. How could I?"

"I'm not talking about Amanda."

I stared at him.

"Kim starts talking smack about what some guy may or may not have done, like, years ago, and you decide to pass his name to a total stranger? For her *hit* list?"

"I can't believe you would talk about Kim that way. In case you haven't noticed, she's my friend."

"Yeah, I know," he said. "Weird, right? It almost seems like you're the one hunting down my exes to become best friends with them."

"I didn't say she's my best friend," I snapped. "*You're* my best friend. But I happen to like Kim. And what's more, I believe her. Don't forget, Fash did something to me too."

"He groped you, horror of horrors." I stared at him in disbelief. "Look, I'm not saying it's nice, but—he was drunk, right? Maybe his hand slipped."

"It wasn't an accident, Jason. He grabbed my breast and rubbed his hand up and down, and—I can't believe you're giving me the third degree on this. What's next? Do you want to hear what I was wearing that night so you can decide if I was asking for it?"

"Forgive me for questioning your story just a tad more carefully than you questioned Kim and Psycho Revenge Lady before you bought their stories hook, line, and sinker."

"You know what?" I had stopped feeling guilty and was getting angry. "This is exactly why we don't talk about this stuff when men are around. Because you bend over backward to defend the guy, even if you've never met him and you've known the woman for years."

But he hardly heard me, he was so angry. "You knew Amanda for all of five minutes. And you believed her, despite the fact that she happened to be a psycho with advanced cyberstalking skills and a background in blackmail."

"She must have left that off her resumé," I said. "I guess I should have done that second round of interviews in my friend-making process after all."

"You should have done something, Dana." He dropped the sarcastic tone. "All I'm saying is, she probably has all kinds of recorded evidence against you. Conversations on your phone, texts, e-mails—"

I sucked in my breath sharply. I'd been so focused on the fact that Amanda was stalking me that I hadn't thought of incriminating evidence, but of course she could have saved all our interactions. Screenshots of every text, recordings of every phone call. For a moment I thought frantically back over our conversations, trying to remember exactly what words we had used and wondering how they could be interpreted. It was so awful, I clamped my mind shut on the memories. "We were careful."

"Think, though—you said something on the phone sometime, right? Whatever your joke was? You talked about a hit?"

There was a long pause. Finally, I said, "A strike."

He just shook his head. I put my hand on his elbow, and he threw it off. And stalked out of the door.

I followed and caught up to him striding down the uneven sidewalk, letting the overgrown bushes and trees bend against him. As I scrambled to keep up with him, they flew back and thwacked me in the chest, the shoulders, the face. I threw a hand up to shield my eyes and pressed on. "I know it doesn't make any sense. I know that. I just —if you only knew."

He kept walking. My legs were so much shorter than his, I almost had to break into a run to keep up.

"Sometimes it feels so dark, just waking up every day as a woman, in a woman's body. What we go through. What we have to live with. Groped, harassed, stalked, followed down dark alleys. It makes you paranoid." He snorted. "Except you're not really paranoid, because there really are people out to get you. Men. A lot of them." Jason's pace didn't slacken and I was running out of breath, but I couldn't stop talking. I thought of Amanda, Kim, Ruby, Becca. "Every woman I know has gone through something. Raped, assaulted, harassed, forced out of jobs. Trapped in abusive relationships. We talk about it with each other when the guys aren't around. And since most of us aren't out there making revenge pacts, I don't know what the incentive would be to lie."

"I don't know. Ruining someone's reputation?"

"More like warning someone. So that when it happens to her—which it always will—at least she'll know she's not alone, she's not crazy, it wasn't her fault."

I had been walking faster and faster in Jason's wake, shouting the words louder and louder, trying to reach him with my voice if I couldn't with my body. On the last word, a particularly large branch swung back from Jason's shoulder toward my face, and just as my hands flailed up to swat it away from my eyes, I felt the tip of my shoe wedge in a crack. With sickening speed, the sidewalk lurched up to meet my face, and my hands couldn't get there in time to stop it. My nose smashed into the concrete, sending jolts of red lightning deep into my skull and filling my mouth with a nauseating smell like dead birthday balloons. The world went black.

And then Jason was kneeling over me, tears in his eyes.

"Dana, Dana. Thank God you're awake. Are you okay?"

I nodded weakly. "Was I unconscious?"

"I'm not sure. Your eyes were only closed for a few seconds. But don't go to sleep, okay?"

I wheezed out a laugh, but when my head began throbbing in rhythm, it turned into a groan. "Not looking for a nap, under the circumstances."

"We need to get you to a clinic. You might have a concussion."

I struggled to prop myself up on my elbows, and the change in elevation lit up acidic patches of raw flesh along the right side of my face, where the concrete had bitten deeply into my cheekbone and brow. "There's no time. I'm fine." Something felt different, but I couldn't have said what it was. If pressed, I might have said the day had changed colors. That was all.

He gave me his large, warm, rough hands — their size and warmth and texture all radiating something like a different color than they had before — and helped me to my feet. We began hobbling back toward the house, his arms around me, partly supporting my weight. I leaned hard, forcing my feet to walk forward even when I lost my vision in black clouds for a moment. *No blood in the water* was all I had, and I clung to it.

Once Jason had helped me back into the house and onto the sofa, he disappeared into the kitchen for a few seconds. He came back with a brick of frozen broccoli in one hand and a package of rock-solid-frozen chicken breasts in the other. "Sorry, the icemaker's broken," he said. "Hold these to your face to keep the swelling down. I'll go get you some Advil for the pain. Here, try wrapping them in towels."

I had gingerly touched the icy blocks to my nose and cheek and immediately winced away. The kitchen towels Jason brought softened the sting for a moment, but soon the cold gnawed its way through the cloth, stiffening the pile until the loops of thread felt like tiny daggers digging into my skin. I swallowed four Advil gratefully and inhaled the stale balloon smell and waited for the pain to ebb.

Jason watched me.

"Can I ask you a question?" He paused for what seemed like a long time, and when I didn't answer, he went on. "You said *we*."

"We," I repeated, dumb head aching.

"What *we* go through."

A connection throbbed back to life in my brain, a different kind of pain. I shook my head. "I can't fight about this right now."

"I don't want to fight. I just want to know—all those things you said. Have they ever happened to you? I mean, the serious ones?"

I could have asked him which ones *he* thought were the serious ones. I could have told him that asking if anything serious has ever happened to a woman—it's like asking a comic if any of his jokes are funny. By asking the question, you've made it clear who's in charge of the answer.

But I didn't. I just nodded and braced myself for his next question.

"Did—something happen to you in high school?"

My eyes flooded with tears. It wasn't what I had expected. All these years, and he'd never once asked. Just like he'd never asked what happened with Neely. I'd grown out of the hope that he eventually would, someday. And now, I didn't even have to nod to make myself understood. His face registered the impact of my expression as if it were a blow. He broke eye contact, looked down at his hands. All the things men do instead of crying.

"I always wondered," he said. "But I was just a stupid teenage boy. I didn't know how to talk about anything important with anyone, much less ask what was wrong . . . I'm still pretty bad at it, I guess."

I whispered: "Not your fault."

"No, I knew something was up. I knew you were hurting. But you didn't say anything, so I didn't either. I figured whatever was eating you, it couldn't have been that big a deal."

The words echoed curiously in my throbbing skull. They were the same words, almost, Mattie had written. The memory put a sudden fire in me. "It was a big deal. It was rape. I didn't say anything because of who did it."

He caught my tone and looked up sharply. A treble thread of anxiety made its way into his voice as he asked, "Who?"

I nodded, as if he had spoken the name and I was only agreeing with him. Even as the tears tipped out of my eyes and down my cheeks, blazing hot new paths over my numbed-up wounds, I hardened my voice to say what we both knew I was going to: "It was Mattie."

I thought I saw a moment of relief, and then his eyes went bright with fury. "God, that bastard. That fucking bastard."

My chin began to shake, completely out of my control, as if the name had broken something on its way out. Fresh spasms of pain rippled through my face and I discovered my hands were shuddering, too, and the frozen blocks shuddering with them. My chest quaked, and I surrendered to the involuntary motion, the force of release buffeting me back and forth between larger and larger parentheses of movement.

I'm scared, I said, only it came out a silent chattering.

Jason released his tight jaw, his eyes widening with alarm. He had been sitting on the sofa facing me, our knees almost touching. Now he crushed me in his arms and leaned into my shaking body, which shook all the harder as his grip pressed new pain out of me.

"Dana, I'm so sorry," he said, many, many times.

Then: "Dana, don't be scared."

Then: "No one's going to hurt you. I'll kill them if they try."

But it wasn't Amanda or even Mattie I feared the most. It was Jason's fury, and mine.

23

When my shaking subsided, Jason drew back, but it was too late. Every breath hurt.

"When can I have more Advil?" I said, moving my face as little as possible around the words.

"I think they're every four hours. Let's see, you took a dose around four o'clock . . . What time is it now?"

But I had already pulled out my phone and gasped so hard, I had to press my hand to my jaw to get the words out: "You've got to be kidding." I showed Jason the phone in anguish. "It's six, Jason. She could be here in ten hours." And we had wasted the whole afternoon in arguments and tears. I felt the panic start to rise but fought it, knowing I would only hurt myself more. "We have to make a plan."

"I know, I know," Jason said, pressing his middle finger to the bridge of his nose and closing his eyes. Then he opened them again, looked at me, and stood up decisively. "But first, let me get you something for the pain. You can't plan anything in this state. You can barely even talk."

I nodded mutely. He disappeared into the bathroom and I heard the water running. He came back with a pill and a glass of water.

"What is it?"

"Tylenol with codeine, left over from dental work. It's fine to alternate with Advil." He smiled. "You may feel a little woozy. "

"Better than feeling like a cracked bowling ball." I took the pill and swallowed it down. "Jason, what are we going to do? She's on her way, and she wants you dead."

"She's none too fond of you right now either, I take it."

"In her mind, I broke my promise." I put my hand to my head experimentally, looking for a place that didn't hurt. "What I don't get is, how does she think she can get me to do it? It doesn't make any sense. She's delusional."

"If I had to guess, I'd say that's exactly what she wants you to think."

I looked at him, puzzled.

"The stuff she's been doing—finding out your motel-room number, sending you flowers, threatening your mom. Calling you from *inside your house*. It's all just scare tactics, like something from a movie. She's trying to scare you."

"It's working." The medicine was working, too, taking effect much faster than a regular Tylenol, and I enjoyed a lightening sensation as the pressure at the bridge of my nose eased slightly.

"But think about it—she never actually does anything, does she?" I started to say something, but he cut me off. "When it comes right down to it, we don't really know she hurt Fash, do we? I mean, officially it was a suicide. You said yourself the guy was messed up. People go off their meds all the time. It's sad, but it's not murder. What if that's really all that happened, and Amanda saw her opening and took the credit for it? The way terrorist groups claim responsibility for crimes they had nothing to do with."

It was such a persuasive argument that for one beautiful moment,

I almost let myself believe it. Then I remembered the Neely tape and shook my head. "You don't know what she's capable of, Jason."

"Well, that's the point, isn't it? To keep you guessing, throw you off. That thing with your mom was the last straw. Anyone who knows you at all knows you care more about protecting your mom than protecting yourself." I looked at him in surprise—maybe he paid more attention to my feelings than I'd given him credit for. But he went on. "So she gets closer and closer, and you get more and more scared. And meanwhile, she's also turning us against each other, isolating you, making you paranoid."

Maybe there really was something to what he was saying. I had been so shaken after our argument that I had almost begun to think of Jason as the enemy. The thought made me a little dizzy. "Psychological torture."

"I'm telling you, she knows how to get under people's skin. You should have seen me after she was done with me." He was buzzing with the thrill of putting the pieces together, the same way he'd been after the Runnr call. "Given enough time, she thinks she can break you. And the Fash thing—it just buys her time. It's something to hold over your head so you can't go to the police. So you have to sit here for hours and hours and think about all the ways she could hurt you and the people you love."

"But the Fash thing doesn't have to be true to hurt me," I pointed out, struggling to make sure I located the right words. My head ached less, but Jason's rapid pacing was making it spin. "Assuming she has me on tape with a motive, it doesn't matter how much she was actually involved. She can just plant the evidence that makes me look guilty. Maybe she already has. The police want to talk to me."

"They would anyway, because of the contest," Jason argued. "You and Kim."

I felt exasperated and lightheaded. The fear that Amanda was going to manipulate me into killing Jason somehow, so absurd a moment ago, had been stealing into my mind over the course of the conversation, like an invisible gas slowly filling the room. I shook my head to clear it. "Okay, fine. Let's say there's no real danger from Amanda. She's still headed here, and she's still making threats that would worry any sane person. So what do you propose we do? Nothing?"

"What else can we do? You're not going to carry out her revenge hit on me, I take it. She's trying her best to convince you something terrible will happen if you don't. Fine. I say we call her bluff. Let's find out what the terrible something is. We have as much dirt on her as she has on you."

But somehow, I felt sure the terrible something wasn't calling the police. "She'll try to kill you herself," I said. "Or me. Or both of us."

"I'm not letting you out of my sight. So if she's not bluffing—and I know she is—"

I looked at him. "But if she's not?"

"Whichever one of us she's after, she'll have to get through me first," he said grimly.

Eight o'clock. We lay on Jason's bed together, side by side, holding hands, the sky darkening outside the curtains. I felt myself sinking into the bed. I couldn't remember how I'd gotten there, though I knew it had something to do with utter exhaustion, and with fear.

"We could leave," I said. "Just drive away."

"Give up our lives," Jason said from somewhere far off. "Then she goes to the police. You get arrested."

"Maybe she just wants money."

"We don't have any money."

There was a pause.

"She doesn't want money," I said. I didn't tell him how I knew.

• • •

"Don't go to sleep," Jason said.

I jerked awake.

"I don't think it's a concussion," I tried to say, but it came out thick. "Anyway, that's a myth, about not letting people go to sleep."

"No, it's not."

"Yes, it is. You just have to wake them up every couple of hours."

"Go to sleep, then. I'll wake you up every couple of hours."

"Just wake me up if I die," I said, already drifting off.

Sometime later, Jason and I made love in the darkened room. He curled protectively over my body, and I bobbed and floated in the darkness, straining upward and sinking down into the bed at the same time, trying to forget something. I almost succeeded. At the point where Jason's glance went hard, that glazed look men get when they vanish in an orgasm — a light was extinguished. Something in me vanished too.

When I woke up again there was a stranger in the room, watching us sleep.

I sat straight up in bed, clutching the sheets around my torso and blinking against the light. It took me a few moments to realize it was Jason silhouetted in the doorway. The lump on the bed I'd thought was him was only a pile of pillows.

"What time is it?" I blinked, groaning as I felt the next wave of soreness hit me. It was all the way through my neck and shoulders now. I felt like I'd been dropped from a tall building.

"It's seven o'clock in the morning," Jason said, setting a mug of coffee on the nightstand. "She didn't come."

"I dreamed she was here," I said. "Standing at the foot of the bed with a knife, waiting for us to wake up. In one dream she was cutting the bed in two. My half of the bed fell into the ocean." I shuddered. "And then the whole thing would start over again."

"Well, she's not here. I've already checked your phone—nobody called or texted." He beamed. "I told you she was trying to scare us."

"She's just been delayed."

"Maybe the police are looking for her by now. If they are, it would be suicide for her to show up here."

"Or maybe—" I didn't want to say it out loud, but my mouth felt like it was moving on its own. "Maybe she really was here during the night."

"Dana." He sat down on the bed and put his hand on my thigh.

"Maybe I really did see her standing at the foot of the bed. Maybe she's watching the house now or waiting for me back at my motel." My voice was getting higher, hysterical, but I couldn't stop it. "She wants to kill us, Jason!"

"Dana, don't be like this."

"She was here," I said, like a child. "I know she was. I saw her. It was real!"

In a movie, he would have slapped me out of it. What I wanted was for something shocking to happen, and a slap probably would have worked. But Jason didn't slap me or shake my shoulders. Instead, he sat quietly beside me on the bed, looking at the ground between his knees and rubbing my back silently as I heaved and wheezed my way through the panic attack. After I'd taken in too much air and made myself dizzy, the tears came and I leaned on his shoulder and allowed myself to go limp and sob it out.

When I'd quieted down, I stretched out my hand. "I think I'll take that coffee now," I said.

"Better have some water first," Jason said. "Hang on." He got up, and although I wanted the coffee and it was just sitting there a few feet away from me on the nightstand, I felt as if it were too far to reach. The tension of waiting had infected the world around me, and the air seemed thick and alive, a seething, malicious medium that pinned me on all sides. Under the circumstances, moving a few feet, or even inches, felt as impossible as getting out of bed and running a marathon.

In the kitchen on the other side of the wall, I heard Jason getting me a glass of water from the tap. It reminded me of something in my dream, but I wasn't sure what.

When he came back and offered me the water, I took it and looked into it for a long time. Then I said, "Jason."

"Hmm?"

"Why didn't you want Amanda to meet Aaron Neely?"

"What?"

"Why didn't you introduce them?"

"Why, should I have?"

"You introduced me," I said. "You introduced me to Aaron Neely."

There was a strange pause as he looked at me. I could see his image in the glass, reflected upside down, flattened to a sliver.

"Yeah," he said shortly. "And look how that worked out."

"It seems like it worked out pretty well. For you, anyway."

"What is that supposed to mean?" I stayed silent, and he jerked the glass out of my hand, spilling a little water on the sheets. "What is that supposed to mean?" he said again, louder.

I reached a finger through the thick, seething air and touched the dark spot where the drops of water had been absorbed into the sheet.

"I don't know," I said. "I don't know what I mean."

"Look, I'm not the reason you lost Neely's respect." I stared. "You came home with your hair all messed up, dress all crooked, holding your high heels in one hand. Frankly, you lost some of my respect too. You can't blame me for not wanting it to happen with my girlfriend."

"Because Amanda was Neely's type."

"Yes. I'm sorry to be crass, but look at the tabloids. Yes, Amanda is Neely's type."

"And I'm not."

"Not for—" He broke off.

"Go on." I looked up for the first time and saw that Jason was staring down at his feet, ashamed.

"Oh, forget it."

"No, I won't be mad. Just say it."

He stayed silent.

"Not for public appearances," I finished for him. "Just for fucking."

Jason scowled. "Isn't that what happened?" he asked.

"As best I can remember," I said, "he only jacked off on my dress. But keep in mind, he drugged me first, so I might have missed something."

"Oh, come off it."

"He did."

"Neely doesn't need to drug women to get laid. Believe me, I hung out with him at parties. Besides, those rumors have been flying around for years."

I gasped. "You *knew?*"

"Everybody knows," he snapped dismissively. "And yet somehow, none of these claims are ever made in public or brought to a court of law. Because they're just baseless, malicious rumors. Not a single case has gone to trial."

I thought of Amanda's settlement with Runnr, the nondisclosure agreement she had violated by telling me about it.

"You knew about the rumors, and you sent me to meet him alone."

"I was supposed to be there, Dana, remember? And besides, like I said—I didn't believe it."

"Like you don't believe me now."

"This is absurd. You were dazzled by the guy. I get it; he's dazzling.

So you drank too much, and you went too far, and then you woke up with regrets in the morning. I think we've all been there. It's called a mistake."

"I came home the same afternoon," I said slowly. "And I didn't drink. I had a smoothie. A kale, beet, and roofie smoothie." He looked skeptical. "Are you saying I just came down with something at random?"

"Maybe."

"Like what you had?"

He opened his mouth, then closed it. "Sure," he said.

"You weren't sick, Jason," I said. I was shaking, but the air had cleared of squiggly worms and I could move through it again. I stood up and started grabbing my clothes off the floor. "You played sick so you could set me up with Aaron Neely."

"You went," he said. "You went without me."

"Yeah, I did," I said. "That's how Aaron wanted it. So he could drug me and jerk off in front of me like he did with all those other women you don't believe."

"Dana," he said, crumbling. "I didn't know. I mean, yeah, I thought maybe he'd make a pass at you. What did I care, we weren't dating. It never worked with us."

"Because I wasn't your type?"

"Why do you make me say everything out loud?" he yelled. "Why do you have to drag everything out and beat it to death? No, you weren't my type! So what? I can't date a hot actress, a model, if I feel like it? What's the big deal?" He looked desperately sad. "I swear I didn't know. I thought—look, I thought you'd come home after flirting with Neely for an hour and we'd be writing our show together, just like we always wanted, and it wouldn't make a difference."

"You should have told me," I said.

"Maybe I just wanted to see what you'd do."

"A loyalty test? To see if I was still your faithful servant? You wanted to see *what I would do?*" I found my purse with my keys in it. "Well, now we know—what I did was get sexually assaulted for the second time in my life, that's what. Thanks a lot."

On the way out of the bedroom, I slipped on something soft on the floor. With an excruciating effort, I kept myself from falling a second time in twenty-four hours, putting out my hands to catch myself on the bed.

I looked down to see what had tripped me and recoiled. It was the Betty wig. Amanda had been there in the night after all.

24

I stood looking down at the wig in my hand. Its white-gold sheen had dulled; the plasticky waves were now snarled and puffed into an ashen rat's nest. For all I knew, Carl's DNA clung to its tangled strands.

Somewhere in the background, I heard Jason saying over and over again, "She watched us sleep. She watched us together. She watched us."

Strangely, I felt no inclination to panic. The panic had arisen only when Jason insisted there was no need to worry. Now, the ghost haunting the house had become a concrete piece of evidence, a signpost, a curiously intimate message. It was the serial killer's calling card, the bloody horse head in my bed. We understood each other now, Amanda and I. The message was loud and clear. Equally clear was the message I had to send back.

There was a fire pit in the back yard, where Jason and I had invited friends over, back when we still had mutual friends. Had they really been friends? Or had one of them put a hand on my knee once as we sat partially illuminated around the fire pit and implied he might consider introducing me to his agent if I slept with him? I honestly couldn't remember. Before Neely, that stuff happened to me all the time, and I barely even noticed. Like the hecklers, I brushed them off. But the rage had been building secretly, all the same, like the smoldering cigarette butts we'd bury in kindling to start the flames. That's what Amanda had been drawn to. The smoke coming off me must have been like a bonfire.

It was time to rage.

With my free hand, I grabbed a pack of cigarettes and a lighter off the counter and opened the back door, ignoring Jason's frantic questions. Standing in front of the pit, I tossed the Betty wig onto the charred remains of someone else's fun time. It sprawled pale and serpentine on the black, a stranded sea creature baking in the sun. Then I pulled out a cigarette, lit up, and smoked a third of it before dropping it onto the wig. Where the butt landed, the white-blond strands caught, curled, and writhed black, sending a toxic exhalation into the smoggy L.A. morning, an odor as nerve-shattering as a scream.

"Smell that?" I muttered vindictively. Then, just in case she really was close by, hiding, watching, breathing in the burned-plastic reek, I said a little louder, "That's what I think of your pact."

For good measure, I lit up and then dropped five more cigarettes onto the pile, finishing the pack. I watched until every last piece of what I'd done, what Amanda had wanted me to become, had twisted up and melted away.

I was done with pacts and alliances, partners and friends. What I needed was a plan.

When I got back inside, Jason had calmed down. He was sitting on the sofa, looking shell-shocked. He held up his phone and showed me an image attached to a text. I already knew what it depicted. It was excessive, unnecessary. Just another slasher-movie flourish.

"Great depth of focus," I said drily. "Like an Ozu film."

But Jason hadn't heard me. He was shaking his head in disbelief. "There weren't any extra keys," he said helplessly. "She must have made a copy. She played me every step of the way."

I threw the empty pack of American Spirits onto the sofa next to him. "You want to go to the corner store and pick up some more of these?"

He looked up at me like I had lost my mind.

"I know, I know, you only smoke when you're drinking. You've told me a million times. Don't worry, I'm done badgering you to quit."

"I'm not leaving you alone, Dana." His eyes were wide.

"It's just the corner store. It's five minutes away." We'd walked there and back a million times. "I'll be fine."

"She's here," he said firmly. "Maybe still close by. I'm not going anywhere."

"Listen to me," I said. "We need to split up. It's you she wants. As long as we're together, you're putting me in danger. I need you to create a diversion, draw her off long enough for me to leave."

"The motel again? Dana—"

"Not the motel. I'm going home."

"Home?" He looked around the house, confused, as if he'd already forgotten I'd ever lived anywhere else.

Time was running out. I had to get him out of the house. "This isn't working, Jason. All we do is fight. If we're ever going to be friends again, I need to get out of L.A., back to a place where things make sense. I don't know, maybe I'll stay with my mom in Amarillo for a while. Get a job. No, don't look around for the bug—I left it in the other room, and anyway, this isn't for Amanda's benefit. It's for mine. If she can hear me, she'll be thrilled that I'm giving you up."

"Wait. Just wait." Jason stepped toward me, his hands reaching out blindly to grab me. "Don't go. I'll leave if you want. I'll draw her away.

I don't want to put you in danger. But—please don't go just yet. Don't let her get between us. We'll talk this out when I get back."

"Fine. I'll wait. But you have to go somewhere far. Let her follow you somewhere isolated, somewhere she'll think she has a chance of getting to you."

"She can get in here," he said, almost in tears. "What if she hurts you to get to me?"

"That's not her MO," I explained patiently, as if speaking to a child. "That's how she would punish a woman, not a man. She's punishing me by going after what I care about, which is you. That means, if anything, she wants to kill you twice over—once for her, and once for me." I could tell he was struggling, and I had an idea. "Look. Look. I'll put an order in for a locksmith to come change the locks. I'll get someone over here fast. I'll even do it on the old phone, so if she's monitoring that, she knows not to try it again." I went into the other room and pulled my old phone off the charger cable.

"I'll wait for him to show up."

"Jason, leave now," I said, opening the app and typing in my request. A beautiful interface, really. So easy to use, I didn't even have to enter Jason's address. It knew where I was at all times. "Or else I'm leaving. I can't be around you anymore."

"Show me," he said. "I want to see proof."

I flashed him the phone, where a map screen showed a red dot moving toward a blue dot. "Look, there's already somebody on the way. Daniel R. That's a nice, locksmith-y name."

"I just want to know you're going to be okay while I'm gone."

"He's almost here. He's a few blocks away. If you leave now, she'll follow you. Go."

Jason left. I stayed behind to wait, my hand inside the purse in my lap.

Only a few minutes went by before there was a polite knock at the door. I took the object out of my purse and held it in one hand as I opened the door.

"I'm Amanda, your runner," she said, her eyes on my stun gun. "I understand you need your locks replaced?"

25

Don't call anyone," Amanda said. "Remember what we've done together."

"You'd be in worse trouble than I would."

She shrugged. "Only one way to find out."

I backed slowly away from the door, keeping the stun gun poised in front of me. "Come in. We need to talk."

"Of course. That's what friends do." She stepped across the threshold and closed the door politely behind her. "You look terrible. Did he do that to your face?"

"You know he didn't," I said. "You've been listening in the whole time. You have the house bugged too, right?"

"Now, that's just paranoid," she chided. "You're the one who put out the Bat-Signal for me, remember?" She pulled her phone out of her jacket and pointed at the Runnr notification on her screen, the balloons and confetti showering from the sky.

"That's because I knew you would come the minute he left me here alone. What's the matter, are you scared of him?"

"Are you?"

"I don't need to be. I'm not a psycho who's breaking into the house and watching him while he sleeps with his girlfriend."

She let out a long-suffering sigh. "Dana, I've done everything in my power to open your eyes. Some people just can't look the truth in the face."

"People like Fash?" I said.

"You're still blaming me for that?" She sighed again. "You have a serious lack of imagination, Dana. It's probably your biggest liability as a comic." She considered. "Well, second biggest. You know you're only funny when you're mean, right?"

"I don't need you to tell me what's funny, thanks," I snapped. "What's funny, in my opinion, is how the people whose eyes you want to open always seem to end up dead. You're sick, Amanda."

"Am I?" she asked. She walked around the front of the couch, and I circled quickly around behind it as she took a seat on the sofa facing away from me, put her arms out, and kicked her long legs up onto the coffee table. Her hair was darker and wavier in the back, crowned around the edges with frizzy blond curls. The stun gun shook in my hand. Without her dark-shadowed eyes staring at me, I could end this right now. Shoot fifty thousand volts of electricity through her, knock her out, and then call the police. But as I stared at the back of her head, I wished I had something heavier than a stun gun in my hand. Something that would silence her permanently and end this for good. I took a step closer to her, hardly noticing my feet moving forward.

Her curls bobbed as she spoke. "At least when I hurt someone, I know exactly what I'm doing and why I'm doing it." Lazily, she half turned her head toward me, so I could barely see her profile. "Can you say the same?"

"I am so sick of this shit, Amanda. Just tell me what you want."

"You know what I want."

"I think you want an excuse to kill me," I said. "Get rid of me, the way you had me get rid of your enemies—Branchik, Carl. That way you'll never be implicated."

"Why should I be? I didn't do anything."

"Except plan the whole thing," I said. "Using stolen data from your old job."

She twisted at the waist, put her hand on the back of the sofa, and drew herself up to look me full in the face. I could see something I'd said had touched her at last; her brows were drawn violently together, her giant eyes dark. "You can't steal what you built from the ground up," she said, "and if that's not the law, then it should be. They're the ones who stole from me, years of my hard work. And then Branchik got rid of me the way they get rid of any woman who might start asking for more. What do you think happened to the other women who brought allegations against him? They got demoted or 'moved horizontally'"—she put air quotes around the words—"to teams where they'd never have the chance to rise through the ranks. Or they quit and went somewhere else, where it probably happened all over again."

"Or they revenged themselves on a few of their coworkers," I said. "Not to mention customers."

"Only the ones who deserved it," she said. "You know this is how they destroy us, Dana. Don't pretend you don't."

"Nobody's destroying me," I said. "I'm doing fine. Except for you."

"You're doing fine *because* of me!" She stood. "Why can't you see that? I freed you from the fiction that everything was okay. I gave you permission to see the obvious. I set the real you free."

"The real me? You mean the me who's twisted and angry and paranoid, like you?"

"Just because you're paranoid doesn't mean they're not out to get you, Dana," she said with a smile, but it was weaker than the ones before. "Don't you know that yet?"

"And now you want to take credit for my success," I continued. "Why, because of Betty? I burned the wig, Amanda. I don't need her anymore. And I don't need you either."

"That's just what I've been trying to tell you." She stepped around the sofa, and I took a half step back into the hallway before I realized I'd just put her between me and the only exits. "Let the masks go. Get rid of them. You don't need the lie. You can admit it now." Her voice took on a wheedling tone, and she started slowly walking toward me, as if coaxing a frightened animal to her. "I didn't go to that open-mic looking for you that night. I went looking for Kim. But as soon as I saw you deal with that heckler, I knew it was you I wanted. I chose you, Dana. I chose you."

"Don't come any closer." I held the stun gun up in front of me.

"Or what? You'll shoot?" She casually pulled something out of her jacket pocket.

I gasped, and my eyes widened to take in the handgun. Suddenly it all made sense. "That's it. You're going to kill me, and you're going to pin it on Jason. Oh my God."

But she turned the gun around and held it out to me.

"It's for you, Dana. Take it."

We were both in the narrow hallway now, Amanda leaning forward with the gun outstretched toward me, me shying away from it with one hand on the stun gun, the other leaning against the wall, which seemed to be tilting somehow. I wondered why the pictures, the kitschy portraits Jason and I had bought at Goodwill for a joke, weren't tilting too. I saw the painting of the big-eyed cat out of the corner of my eye and almost jerked to the side, it reminded me of Amanda so much. She was pushing me toward Jason's bedroom, still offering the gun.

"How do you know I won't use it on you?" I said. But I didn't grab it.

"All the things he used to say to me," she said. "He told me I was garbage, Dana, and I believed it. I felt like garbage. You saw where I was living after Runnr. My whole life had imploded. The only thing I cared about was finishing the app so it wouldn't happen to anyone else. But he got to me first." She advanced toward me like a zombie, dead-eyed, but her words came faster and faster. "We had sex where he treated me like a thing. He wanted to pretend I belonged to him. I didn't have friends, much less contacts in the industry. All I had was money from my settlement, and he wanted it. I paid the rent, and I paid the bills, but I let him pay for me in public, buy me drinks, buy me dinner, sometimes with my money, so he could feel like a big man. He watched me like a hawk. He texted me constantly. If I had an audition, he blew up my phone until I came home. He put software on my phone—yeah, the same stuff I put on yours. Only mine is a more sophisticated version, because I'm smarter than him. Way, way smarter." She shrugged. "That doesn't help when someone is abusing you, to know that. But I know it now."

"You're lying." I felt Jason's bedroom door yawning at my back.

"I've never lied to you, Dana. Never." She cracked a sick grin. "You lie to yourself."

"I don't know what you're talking about."

"It started with him checking the messages on my phone," she said with a lilt in her voice. "Has he ever done that to you, Dana? Have you found him with your phone in his hand?"

I shook my head, a vision of Jason holding my cell phone when I got out of the bathroom flashing through my mind. "No."

"Now you're the one who's lying," she said with her short laugh like a fox's bark. "Ask Kim, she'll tell you. It starts with a little harmless snooping, and it ends with you locked in a soundproof room, throat too bruised to scream even if anyone could hear you." She reached her left hand up to her neck with a shudder, closing her eyes momentarily.

I saw my opportunity and lunged for the gun, but she opened her eyes and yanked it back. "Ah, ah, ah, not unless you're going to use it on him," she said. "And if you aren't, which I'm starting to think you aren't, then you're going to have to let me use it." She reversed the grip so that it was pointing toward me.

I went rigid in Jason's doorway, pinned between the gun in her hand and the gaping hole that was the door to his bedroom.

"The problem is, that wouldn't be right. I can't do this one for you." She sounded almost childlike, explaining the rules of her game. She was starting to unravel. "You have to do it for me. Or, better yet, for yourself."

There was something in Jason's bedroom, in the open space behind me, I didn't want to think about. Something about last night. "Why should I believe you over him?"

"You don't have to," she said. "That's the beauty of it. You have your own reasons. Mattie told me everything."

At the mention of Mattie, I threw the stun gun at her eyes, hard, and when her hands flew up to shield her face, I skirted to her left, trying to get around her. But I made it only halfway, and then she had the gun up again. I ducked into the studio that had once been my room. Swathed in black corrugated soundproofing, with thick black curtains over the windows, it was a black hole, and as I stumbled backward into it, my eyes took a moment to adjust. I crouched behind the door and waited.

"Dana? Dana, I don't want to hurt you." As she stepped into the room, her right hand feeling around for the light switch, I heard her kick something, and the stun gun that I had thrown at her a moment ago skittered forward.

I lunged for the stun gun, grabbed it, pulled the trigger, and held it to her hand. She let out an unearthly yowl, and the door jerked forward and hit my nose. The pain was blinding, but I heard her gun clatter to the floor. I dropped to my knees and searched for it with my left hand. Amanda's foot smashed into my cheekbone and new fire shot through my skull, igniting yesterday's fireworks all over again. I dropped the stun gun and heard one of us kick it away.

But just then, my fingers closed on the handgun.

I scrambled backward, still on the floor, with the gun in my hand. Standing over me, Amanda paused for only a moment. Then she kept moving forward, her eyes a curious blank, glittering out of the darkness like a cat's.

"How could you let him touch you again after what he did?"

"You really did watch us."

She frowned. "Did I? Are you sure?"

"The picture."

"Maybe I have cameras in Jason's house. I was there long enough to do just about anything in there."

"But Betty—you left the wig." The panic had risen sharply in my chest at the thought of the house being bugged, and I worked hard to fight it back down.

"Okay, maybe I really was there," she agreed.

"I thought you never lied."

"It was a joke," she said. "You of all people should know the difference."

Just then, there was a thud, and Amanda crumpled to the ground. Behind her, Jason stood with a baseball bat in his hands.

I lowered the gun slowly.

"The locks are still the same," he said. I started crying as I scrambled to my feet. Then a head rush turned on all the lights at once, lights I didn't know were even in the darkened room, exploding in front of and behind my eyelids. I lost a few moments leaning against the soundproofed walls and then fell through them, to the other side of darkness.

. . .

When I opened my eyes, I was sitting on the floor. A few feet away, Jason crouched over Amanda, the butt of the gun jutting out of his back pocket.

"Oh, good, you're awake," he said. "I was about to come check on you but I had to finish this first. Don't worry, she's not going anywhere."

Amanda lay on the floor, still in her jacket, wrists bound with bungee cords. Electrical tape covered her mouth, the same thick black vinyl Jason had used all over the room. He wore the rest of the roll on his wrist like a bracelet. Amanda rocked a little, moaned, and went limp again. I looked back at Jason. He was standing in the center of the room, right under the ceiling fan, shifting his bulk from side to side. The top of his head almost brushed the light fixture. I'd never noticed just how tall he was before, and how big in the shoulders.

"I don't know how we're going to do this," he said.

"Do what?"

He looked down at Amanda's limp body grimly.

"Jason. You don't really mean—" I couldn't finish the sentence. My head was splitting anew, my body stiff and sore.

"There's no other way, Dana. We called her bluff, and she came here with a gun." He pulled it out of his back pocket as if to show me, weighing its heft in his hand. Then he lowered the gun to a forty-five-degree angle and straightened his arm, almost tentatively.

"Jason!"

"Relax, we're not going to do it in the house," he said. He frowned, rubbing the bridge of his nose the way he had in the storage facility. "Or maybe . . ." A flicker of excitement passed over his face.

I started to panic. My head felt too heavy to let me stand up, but I got to my hands and knees. "Jason, let's think this through."

"I am thinking. We can cut the panels up afterward, that part is easy. The problem is coming up with a place to dump them. But the beauty is, they're black, so as long as no one brings a black light in, we have some time." He walked to the closet and started rummaging around. "I know I put the leftover plastic sheeting in here. We'd have to cover the floor too."

"You keep saying *we*—" Still on hands and knees, I interrupted myself with a cough that made the place behind my eyes throb. "Why do you keep saying *we*?"

A huge, shiny piece of black plastic emerged from the closet. Jason's limbs came into view a moment afterward, and he dumped the tarp on the ground.

"We're in this together, Dana. She's after us both, not just me. And she's just going to keep coming until she's . . . taken care of." I was trying to rise, but at this I went lightheaded again and retched. He looked concerned but didn't stop smoothing the plastic over the floor next to Amanda's slightly stirring body. "Besides, you're the reason we can't go to the police."

"We can," I said, gasping. "We can go. I'll go."

"No, we're past that now." Almost level with Amanda on his hands and knees as he worked, he looked down at her face with disgust. "She destroyed my life with her lies, and now she's destroyed yours too. She has to be stopped, and I can't do it alone." He rolled Amanda onto the plastic as she protested feebly, half awake.

I can't do it alone. Just like Mattie's truck. That gave me an idea. "But you'll have to. I won't help you, Jason." *Chicken out,* I thought silently in his direction. *You can't cross this line without me.*

A look of desperation crossed his face for a moment, but then he went back to the business of spreading the sheeting out as far as it would go. "Then I'll do it alone. I'll figure it out." He perked up. "This room is actually the perfect place to do it. Like a giant silencer." He looked around at the soundproofing panels, and I got another flash of the day Amanda and I met. *He didn't hit me. He did other things.*

"This was it, wasn't it?"

For the first time, he looked up sharply from what he was doing. "What do you mean?"

"The soundproof room. So no one could hear her scream."

He stared at me. "You don't believe that stuff about me locking her in?" He got to his feet indignantly. "That's another of her ridiculous lies." I stayed silent, and he took a step toward me, desperation on his face. "Dana? Come on, you have to believe me. She's lying. I mean, sure, we had fights. But that's just her being a drama queen." He watched my face, and suddenly the desperation was gone, replaced by irritation. "You don't believe me? Check the whole house, there's not a single door that even locks."

"There wasn't when I lived here," I said. "But I did notice some scarring on the door when I was searching the house. What was there, Jason? A sliding bolt? Why would you need a bolt on the outside of the door?"

He was silent.

"Anyway, how do you know what she told me about you?" I said slowly. Then I pulled my disposable phone out of my pocket. The one he'd bought at Best Buy and brought home for me. The one he'd activated and set up when I wasn't in the same room. I looked at it in horror for a moment before hurling it across the room as hard as I could. It bounced off the soundproofing. "It's bugged."

"Dana," he said. "We have to trust each other."

"But we don't, Jason. And I think I know why."

"Listen. Listen, Dana!" He took a deep breath, composing himself, then looked down at the gun in his hands, then at Amanda. "I'm not the world's greatest person. I'm trying, but we both know I fall pretty short. And honestly—" He seemed to be avoiding the sight of Amanda, but his gaze was drawn back to her again and again. "I have some intimacy problems, okay? Because of Mattie, because of my dad. Because my mom ran out on all of us and left us there to rot."

"Yeah, I know." It was something Jason and I had in common but never talked about. The sense of abandonment—his mother, my father. The hole in each of us, the embarrassing hole we had both learned to cope with by joking about it. We gravitated toward each other because we knew we would never ask each other what was beneath the jokes. Never take the joke seriously, even when it spoke the truth out loud. Even when we were hiding in plain sight. Despite myself, my eyes began to well up.

Jason was near tears too. "Face it, Dana. I'm a mess. We both are, but you've always been stronger than me. I'm an easy target. That's why I attract messed-up, manipulative women like her again and again. Women who know how to push my buttons, make me do things I don't want to do."

"Make you?"

"I know I shouldn't let it get out of hand. That's why all my relationships end so fast. Because I recognize what's happening, and I try to do the responsible thing and end it. Why do you think I left Austin for L.A. in the first place? It was Kim. Things were getting bad between us, and she started spreading rumors. I had to leave before she poisoned the whole scene against me. I know you don't want to hear this, but she's one of *them*."

I'd never spent much time on the Austin comedy forums. I'd actively avoided them, in fact. What had I been afraid of finding out, and why?

"I didn't want you to be one of them. I always knew you were better than those women I dated. That's why I didn't date you, *because* you were better. I didn't want to—to sully what we had."

"I don't think a relationship sullies things, Jason," I said, finally making it to my feet. "Not a normal one."

"This time is different, though." His eyes lit up. "I've finally recognized my pattern, and I'm trying to change." He seemed to have forgotten the gun in his hand, and he was waving it around alarmingly. "When I agreed to give us one more chance—"

"What do you mean, one more chance?" I said. "Why do you always talk like we've tried this before?"

And then Jason got a huge, stupid smile on his face, and the gun dropped to the floor.

I started to repeat my question louder, a horrible thought dawning on me. I remembered his anxious face, waiting for me to tell him who had done *that* to me, and his relief when I'd said "Mattie." What had he been worried I would say? "What do you mean, one more—"

But Jason was grinning maniacally, his face stretched in a ghoulish laugh. Then his head jerked backward and his body went rigid. He slumped to the floor with a heavy thud. Next to him, I saw Amanda crouched on the plastic sheeting, holding the forgotten stun gun, the bungee cord she must have been working to loosen this whole time still wreathed around one wrist. Now she was reaching for the real gun, the one that had fallen out of Jason's hand.

Time slowed as Amanda touched the gun lightly, spinning it on its axis, then hooked a finger around the trigger loop and began tugging the gun closer, sliding it along the floor. In a moment she would have it in her palm. Her face looked eerily calm, determined but relaxed, as if she knew who she wanted to hurt, and why. The bruise-colored rings around her eyes were like a special kind of darkness radiating from within, tinted with sickly yellowish green and purplish blue from the blood vessels beneath her thin skin. Hypnotized by that darkness in which everything was mysteriously visible, I couldn't move.

I couldn't move.

It was dark in the TV room except for the screen. I was asleep. I woke up with someone on top of me. I couldn't see him. I only felt him, smelled him, tasted the blood when my teeth cut my lip. I'd known with every fiber of my being who it was, but I couldn't see him. So I'd let myself think—know, even—otherwise. And that certainty had colored everything ever since. My relationship with Jason. My response to Amanda. Even how I'd interpreted Mattie's letter; I'd been infuriated that he'd described what happened to me that night as being someone else's fault.

"You," I said.

Jason was already moving again, rolling over to one side to get up, but Amanda was now holding the gun in both hands, aiming the muzzle at his head. Both still lying on the floor, each rolled onto one shoulder, they looked, for a moment, like a flattened-out parody of a shooting at point-blank range. Or like lovers lying in bed together, one of them reaching out to stroke the other's hair. Jason screamed for help.

Unstuck in time, I thrust out my hand and felt it bump into something cold and heavy, a metal rod that yielded to my touch. Before the mic stand could tip all the way over, my fingers closed around the shaft, and I hefted the heavy base up over my shoulder.

Amanda never saw it coming.

Finding the strength somewhere, I swung the mic stand again and again and again, until everything was still.

Puddled on the black tarp, the blood looked like standing water after a storm. When I looked down into Jason's black eyes, the tears in them making them blacker still, I couldn't help it. My eyes started tearing up too.

"We *tried* it?" I said to him. "You wanted to believe that's what happened. But deep down, you knew what it really was. After I told you what Mattie did—what I *thought* he did—you finally felt in the clear. But you were the one who had something to prove that night, weren't you?" He said nothing. "You didn't ask. You didn't even wake me up. You just started. And once you started, you wouldn't stop."

He stared up at me, uncomprehending.

"It was you, not Mattie. You raped me."

A trickle of blood overspilled his eyebrows and ran down his eye socket, hugging the side of his nose. The black eyes turned slowly red, then began to weep. A single, bloody tear.

I was over Jason at last.

Amanda was screaming.

She looked up, saw me standing over Jason's body holding the mic stand, and scrambled backward in terror, slipping in the blood. I waited patiently for her to find her footing on dry ground.

"Here," I said. "Hold this for a minute."

Dazed, Amanda took the mic stand from my hands and clutched it to her chest, watching me in terror, her eyes darting once in a while to Jason, as if he might get up and try something. I kicked the handgun to the opposite side of the room, then located the stun gun, which was half covered by the tarp, and kicked that across the room too. Then I walked over to the disposable phone lying by the wall and pocketed it.

"You saved my life," Amanda said, still hugging the mic stand, letting it support her weight like a crutch. "He was going to kill me, Dana. He had me tied up and—" She shuddered. "He was going to kill me this time."

I stared down at his body and wondered if he would really have done it. I thought of the truck he was too scared to steal by himself; the way he'd offered me to Neely to win his favor; the rape he'd been so happy to believe his brother was guilty of so he could go on believing what we'd had was just bad sex. The things he'd done to Amanda because he thought she deserved them. Ultimately, the only crimes Jason ever committed were the ones he couldn't admit to himself were real. And even those, he'd relied on me to corroborate.

But all that was over.

"I'm going to call the police." I dialed 911 on the burner, leaving bloody prints on the buttons, and held it to my ear.

"He had me tied up," she repeated, rubbing her wrists as she stared down at his crumpled body. "But this time I got away. I got away."

"You can try claiming self-defense." The phone started ringing. "Although it's going to be your word against mine."

"What?" She was still groggy, moving slowly, like a person underwater.

"You didn't kill Fash, did you?"

Dazed, she shook her head no.

"Right. You never said you did. You just let me believe it so I'd have to take your third name," I said. With my free hand, I gestured to Jason. "Well, I did. And now it looks an awful lot like you owe me one." She stared at me. "He was my third name too, as it turns out. I guess you knew that, if you talked to Mattie." I closed my eyes for a moment, then opened them. "But don't worry, Amanda. You can still do your part." I smiled and looked pointedly at the mic stand. "You can still get my back."

"Dana. What are you—" She looked down at the mic stand too and then suddenly dropped it as if it had burned her. It clattered to the floor, the base rolling, describing a wide arc that came to rest against Jason's solid body. "Wait a minute."

"He was your kill, Amanda," I said. "This one's on you. And you did most of it anyway. Everything but pulling the trigger." She started to come toward me. "Speaking of feeling triggered." My eyes on hers, I started to sob hysterically into the phone.

"Dana—"

"Nine-one-one, what is your emergency?"

As I gulped and hiccupped into the receiver, Amanda looked again at Jason, then at me, as if doing some difficult math problem in her head. Then she seemed to give up. She looked down at him once more and said, "I'm glad he's dead."

The dispatcher begged me to be calm, and I managed to choke the words out through my hysteria: "She killed him. My boyfriend's ex. She's been stalking us. She's still in the house." I rattled off our address. "Please come quick. She's—oh my God!" I screamed once and let the phone drop to the floor with a clatter. Then I scooted it past the door frame and kicked it as hard as I could down the hall. "They'll be here soon. We live right around the corner from a police station." I looked down at Jason. "Lived." I gestured at my two black eyes, my bloody nose. "Wait until they see what you did to my face."

Amanda was still swaying uncertainly, eyeballing the gun and the stun gun where they lay on the floor across the room.

"I wouldn't," I said. "I could get there a lot faster than you. For what it's worth, I believe you. I think I always did. You've told the truth about everything, haven't you? Branchik and Carl M. And Jason."

She nodded, eyes wide.

"Truth after truth, and where has it gotten you? Nobody wants to believe the world is what it is. I don't blame them. Look at what the truth has done to you, Amanda. Look what you've become."

But it was me she looked at, her eyes narrow. "I have everything on you, Dana. Every word you said while you were beating a man half to death. His every scream, auto-recorded and filed away on a little flash drive about this big." She held her thumb and forefinger an inch apart. "And only I know where it is."

I panicked for a moment, then shook the image from my mind.

"You're bluffing," I said. "If that drive exists, you'll never turn it over to the police. You'd go down too."

She wheeled and started for the door, and I was tempted momentarily by the mic stand. But the police sirens were already wailing in the background and putting my fingerprints over hers would ruin valuable evidence. Besides, I needed her alive. I needed her to tell the truth once more in court, where a dead woman is easier to believe than a live one, every time.

ONE YEAR LATER

26

So, a moth walks into a psychiatrist's office and lies down on the couch."

The important thing about telling a dumb joke onstage is the irony. I have mastered it, along with the voices, the flat affect, all the slightly distancing techniques that come with the more absurd, less autobiographical standup I do now. No more bits about my mom, my hometown, my weight. It's too easy to slip into the kind of confessional standup that so many women do onstage, throwing yourself under the bus, showing your belly. I wouldn't say what I do now is less personal; in a way, it's more intimate than ever, because it leaves me room to bleed. If there's anything I've learned about comedy, about life, it's that the blood is *always* in the water. The trick is developing a taste for it.

"The psychiatrist says, 'Tell me a little about yourself. What do you do?' The moth says, 'I'm a family man. I have a wife, kids. A two-car garage. I guess you could say I have it all.'"

Nervous titters. The hometown crowd packing the North Door

for the taping of my comedy special tonight definitely have the right look. They shift eagerly from side to side, giggling nervously through the setup, conscious of the cameras trained on them and loosened by the drink coupons we handed out liberally at the door. The North Door, known affectionately as the ND, is an awkward space, cavernous and mouth-shaped, but uniquely photogenic when filled to capacity, its staircases and randomly placed balconies lined with audience members craning their necks for a better view. There's a rumor going around that the ND is in danger of closing its doors, like so many of Austin's beloved downtown venues; its position just east of the freeway has protected it thus far, but the east side is no longer safe from gentrification. Laurel's Paper and Gifts is the latest casualty, I noticed when Ubering past my old workplace on the way here. It looks like the new owner kept part of the old name, probably to save money on signage. The sign now reads LAUREL + HENRY.

"The psychiatrist asks"—on this line, I lean forward, my lips so close to the mic I'm practically making out with it—"'And how does that make you feel?'"

If the rumors are true, this comedy special might be among the last shows performed here. It's sad, of course, but I'd be lying if I said it hadn't influenced my decision to record here, in a homely venue that still projects something of a "weird" Austin vibe, even if the clubs that graced the city in the *Slacker* era of weirdness are all long gone. If the ND does shut down, we might see a nostalgia boost in the streaming revenue. Cynthia would like that, and keeping Cynthia happy is as important as keeping the audience laughing.

It was Cynthia's idea to tape in Austin in the first place. A hometown hero always gets a warm welcome, and my reputation in L.A. is still tinged with scandal. Here, the reverberations of Amanda Dorn's celebrity-adjacent murder trial are faint, dimly associated with typical West Coast excesses, and ultimately outweighed by my status as a local girl. Cynthia had her own reasons for wanting to film here, of course, as she does for everything. She liked what she saw when she judged the Bat City contest; she thinks Austin is the new Portland and wants to set the show we're developing here. She'll be spending a few extra days in Austin after the shoot, scoping out locations. I hooked her up with Kim Rinski as a tour guide — it was the least I could do. Although I will never know exactly what Jason did to Kim when they were dating, I understand now why she stopped talking to me and declined my invitation to Amarillo when she found out Jason and I were together. I'm not sure how much she's guessed about Jason's demise, but if she has intuited the truth somehow, it hasn't endeared me to her further. Maybe a role in one of Cynthia's projects, or even a guest spot on *The Bestie Cast,* will soften her toward me again.

As for me, the minute we wrap, I plan to hop the first flight back to L.A.

Onstage, the moth is giving the psychiatrist his usual line: "I'm fine, I guess. I haven't really thought about it." The shrink replies, "Are you sure you don't have a guilt complex?" And the moth says, "Not really. I'm pretty happy with my life." "Perhaps you're having a midlife crisis?" "No, no," says the moth.

Whether a joke kills or bombs depends more on how you feel telling it than on the joke itself, and the moth joke is proof of that. It's inane, yet it gets bigger laughs on every line. I've stopped trying to figure out why, which Cynthia says is the key to success. Let your id take over, she told me once. The audience can feel the truth coming through the gag, even if they don't recognize what they're getting, and it's a shock to the system. As someone intimately familiar with what a person getting shocked actually looks like, I can assure you that this is a lousy metaphor, but I nodded when Cynthia said it. My long years as Jason's sidekick made me into a fantastic listener.

Finally, after a few more shaggy-dog lines, I get to the punch line: "'The light was'—*squish*."

I mime the psychiatrist nonchalantly grinding the toe of his shoe on the stage. The audience erupts. In my normal voice, I say, "I'm sorry, did I not mention he's a moth?" The laughs are going strong, so I throw in my tags. "His insurance doesn't cover mental health. Also, he's, like, this big." I hold my finger and thumb an inch apart. "Never forget, y'all. Size matters. Take it from a double D."

And so forth.

The trial went like clockwork.

In the first of several windfalls for the prosecution's case against Amanda Dorn, Amanda did not hire her own attorney, taking the court-assigned public defender instead. At first I assumed this was a deliberate move on her part; after all, with the remainder of her settlement money, she could have afforded someone expensive. I racked my brain trying to figure out her angle, but the answer turned out to be simple. In addition to the criminal charges, Amanda was facing a civil suit from Runnr for breaching her nondisclosure agreement. Beyond her illegal use of trade secrets, the crimes she'd committed dressed as a Runnr employee had damaged the company's reputation, they claimed, forcing them to state publicly, with contrition, that they were overhauling their hiring process and instituting background checks for their customers' safety. In the meantime, they had filed a vindictive injunction to freeze Amanda's bank accounts until after the criminal claims were settled.

To give Amanda's harried-looking public defender credit, I'm sure she tried to keep Amanda far away from the stand. But Amanda has always been her own worst enemy. The only defense she would consider was the truth—that her lesser crimes were committed on behalf of the comedian Dana Diaz, with whom she had entered into a revenge pact and who had committed similar crimes for Amanda, including the killing of Jason Murphy. It was the truth, but it sounded like something I had dreamed up for a Betty monologue. The prosecution's case was that Amanda was a deranged fan who, after obsessively stalking an ex-boyfriend, had transferred her fixation to me. I felt for Amanda's attorney.

On the stand, Amanda burned with a phoenix-like radiance that must have struck the jury as something akin to lunacy. I recognized it as unrepentant zeal for her mission, and although it frightened me, I couldn't help but find it scorchingly beautiful as well. Gaunter than ever after her time in custody awaiting trial, she spoke of the app she'd been creating in the tender tones of a mother talking about her only child. Of Jason, she spoke as little as possible and always with contempt, repeating her eyewitness account of his murder with very little embroidery. Her comments about his past abusive behavior raised objection after objection from the prosecutor, all along the lines of "The deceased is not on trial!" The defense sat back and let Amanda's testimony about Jason's abuse get struck from the record, since it only provided the prosecution with a motive.

She spoke of me frankly and fervently as a friend with whom she'd had differences, and this, along with her fiery description of the injustices inflicted on me by the men she'd targeted, did 90 percent of the prosecutor's job for him. Ruby did her part, too, recalling, with a thrill in her voice, how I'd told her about meeting Amanda the morning after it happened and how she'd warned me to watch out for my new "number-one fan."

"A real boundary pusher, is what I said," Ruby said, wearing a sober navy suit from the forties. "But Dana is just so trusting."

By the time I took the stand, the groundwork had been laid for my strongest performance to date. After all, I do my best work in front of a microphone, where the truest truth comes out sounding

like hilarious exaggeration and where a lie, if guilelessly told, can become historical fact. Besides, it was all so nearly true. The story of
how Amanda and I met at one of my standup gigs. How at first I
thought her talk of revenge was a joke and how troubled I was when
I started to suspect she was serious. My attempts to distance myself after that, corroborated by the phone company records showing
Amanda's increasingly frequent calls. And then, so few people had
ever actually seen me with Amanda—we had been as careful as secret
lovers. I was even able to point to the timing of my well-known stage
creation Betty and confess, with the embarrassment of someone revealing tricks of the trade, that Betty had been partially inspired by
the real-life character I'd met in the bar that night. This, too, was
close to the truth.

"I was exaggerating for comic effect," I explained, and then shook
my head. "I never imagined Amanda was really dangerous."

What the police had discovered in Amanda's storage locker had
done the rest.

Thank God, the flash drive full of spyware recordings—if it even
existed—was inadmissible, since California requires two-party con-
sent for all recordings. Given the lack of any evidence, the truth was
an outlandish defense. But perhaps Amanda knew the video of her
beating Neely with the steering-wheel lock would surface eventually.
And once it did—edited selectively to ensure Neely's cooperation
and corroborated by security-camera footage of Amanda in the hotel lobby—there was simply no point in denying she had committed
assault and battery under circumstances remarkably similar to those
of Jason's murder. When Neely himself took the stand after months
of seclusion to testify that he was the man in the video and identify
Amanda as his attacker, you could practically feel the stampede of ce-
lebrity-trial junkies coming from miles away to join the mob of journalists already reporting on the trial of the so-called Runnr Revengr.

"She destroyed my health, both physical and mental," Neely said, and I believed him; he looked much thinner and sallower than when I had seen him last, with puffy bags sagging under his eyes. I couldn't believe I had ever been afraid of him. "My career will never be the same. *I* will never be the same."

Questioned about the attack, Amanda refused to be cowed. "I came back in the room and the man had his Willy Wonka out. What would you do?" she snapped.

The judge pounded his gavel and the prosecutor loudly announced that Aaron Neely was not on trial either, but the damage had been done. Amanda's flippant allusion to rumors that had been circulating on the internet for years seemed to mark a turning point for the trial. For the first time, she had gained the sympathy of her audience. Within hours, T-shirt vendors popped up like mushrooms on the sidewalk outside the courthouse selling images of Neely Photoshopped into a purple Wonka tailcoat and top hat. Overnight, a handful of think-pieces sprouted up with titles like "Amanda Dorn, Feminist Hero?" and "I Wish I Had Done What Amanda Did." For a moment it seemed that public opinion had swayed in Amanda's direction. At the peak of the frenzy, a sextet of radical feminist protesters were dragged from the courtroom after they all stood up simultaneously in the gallery, mouths duct-shaped shut, and unzipped their orange jumpsuits to reveal the words FREE AMANDA Sharpied on their bare breasts.

That was the beginning of the end, however. After just a few days, the men's rights activists who'd been loudly protesting Amanda's deification were joined by second-wave feminists in the *Atlantic* and the *New York Times* worrying about the slippery slope and Twitter personalities lambasting Amanda for trying to pull a woman of color (me) down with her. And then, just as the tide was turning, something much worse came out. A leak in the Austin Police Department revealed transcripts of Facebook chats between Amanda and Fash Banner, the tragic young comic who had killed himself after going off his psychiatric medications. While there was nothing technically incriminating in the leaked conversations, it certainly sounded like Amanda was encouraging him. "They want you to be numb," one chat transcript read. "I've been there. But I went off mine in January, and I'm free now. You can be too."

The next day in court, Amanda's lawyer said that, in light of recent revelations about her client's mental state, she wanted a psychiatric evaluation to determine whether the defendant was competent to stand trial. Amanda promptly fired her counsel and announced that she was representing herself. No mistrial was declared; on the contrary, the judge appeared to relish this new turn of events. Apparently, he did not appreciate the media circus Amanda had brought into his courtroom, and he seemed delighted as the odds mounted against her.

But the final blow to the Free Amanda movement came in the form of a surprise witness for the prosecution, a scruffy programmer from Austin who'd been attacked under similar circumstances as Neely and Jason during the same six-week period. When the prosecutor called to the stand Carl Montgomery, who looked the same as the last time I'd seen him except for a rusty beard covering half his face, my heart nearly stopped.

"That's her," he said, and I pinched the skin of my thigh as hard as I could to keep from bolting from the courtroom.

But he wasn't pointing at me.

Never have I been so grateful for a man's inability to rip his gaze away from a television screen full of naked women long enough to pay attention to the real woman standing in front of him—at least, not until he was being pummeled too hard to know the difference between tall and short, real blond and fake. To be fair, I guess we all look alike when you're getting kicked in the groin.

Amanda had no alibi for the Carl attack. I remember the exact moment when her shoulders slumped at the defense table and she seemed to accept her fate. It was when Carl, who'd been absent-mindedly rooting around in his beard during his testimony, scratching his fingers back and forth hypnotically, suddenly pulled the hairs aside. The scar was the thickness of a pencil in the middle and straggled a good six inches across his face, from one ear all the way down to the jaw, where it was joined by another one across his chin. There was an audible gasp in the courtroom.

Amanda never admitted to either the Carl strike or Jason's murder. But as the story shaped itself around her, even she must have been able to tell that her denials sounded increasingly hollow. Even her staunchest defenders, the ones who still maintained she was justified in what she'd done, didn't believe her. The guilty verdict was returned with dizzying swiftness, the sentence of life without parole unusually harsh for a woman. The judge stressed in the sentencing that Amanda was being made to answer not just for the life she had taken, but for her specious justifications, which diverted attention from the real victims of rape and abuse.

As officers of the court led Amanda away in handcuffs, the adrenaline that had sustained me during the months after Amanda was taken into custody at Jason's front door in her Runnr uniform drained away. She looked over her shoulder at me once, the only time she had actively sought my gaze since the trial started. When I saw her with all the radiance gone out of her, everything she had done—the stalking and spying and harassing and threats—faded, and I remembered only the first time I had seen her friendly face in the crowd at Nomad, how grateful I'd been that night for her unrestrained laughter. By the time her blond hair vanished around the corner, my head was spinning with a sensation far more disorienting and nauseating than any metaphorical prison I had been locked in before. A therapist might call it survivor's guilt, but it was only freedom—Amanda's last, poisoned gift to me.

If I have not included my feelings about Jason in my account of the trial, it's because I kept him firmly out of mind for its duration. I had spent so much time missing him already, maybe I was all tapped out of that particular emotion. Besides, the Jason I'd pined for since the eighth grade, the Jason I had missed when we were apart and trembled for when we were together, was a figment of my imagination. If I still felt a pang now and then, it was only for the remembered warmth of him leaning up against me in that beanbag chair in front of the TV so long ago. Whenever I did try to think about him, and thus about what I'd done, I encountered only a ragged hole, like a prom picture with someone's face cut out of it.

The face that haunted me was Amanda's. I remembered her stumbling off in handcuffs, her zealot's certainty cracked and dribbling down the drain along with her vision, however twisted, of justice by and for women. More than the app itself, that vision had given her power and purpose, made her nearly invincible. I'd found the thing she cared about at last, and I'd taken it away forever.

There was nowhere to go with that realization but home. Letting my apartment in Austin go, too apathetic even to keep my crappy possessions from being thrown into the alley, I slept all day in my mom's house and stared at the ceiling all night. She cooked for me and made sure I had clean sheets and clothes to wear, but she asked no questions. When journalists inevitably found Amarillo on the map and appeared on our doorstep, she maintained her air of gentle bewilderment, pretending not to understand their questions as she made the short walk between house and car when she went to work every morning and came home at night. Her English comprehension has always been selective.

Cynthia Omari was the one who pulled me out of the black hole I'd fallen into after the trial. I'd been ignoring Cynthia's phone calls along with everyone else's, deleting her messages without listening to them, but, no more easily deterred than the reporters, she'd eventually tracked me down and beaten a path to my mother's door, where she was waiting when my mom came home from work one day. With her unerring instinct for such things, my mother waved her in, calling out two words before disappearing: "*Mija,* visitor." It was benevolent self-interest on Cynthia's part; she was convinced that the notoriety of having sent the Runnr Revengr to prison would, after it had faded a little, ultimately help my career. She was right. Cynthia is usually right about such things.

Since she coaxed me back to L.A., Cynthia has been my unofficial mentor. There were countless fifteen-minute lunches in which I learned not to be offended when she left before the food arrived; then slightly longer lunches with e-mail follow-ups afterward; and finally, I began to be invited to her gloriously spacious apartment for parties and then alone, just to have a glass of wine and brainstorm about the series we were cooking up together. I won't say we're besties, but perhaps we're as close as two people like us can be. And, it must be said, under her tutelage, I have not had to audition for a single maid role.

These days, I have taken to sending Amanda little gifts in prison, anonymously. A box of tampons. A carton of cigarettes. A bottle of fancy face wash. I imagine her bartering these things with the other inmates for what she really wants, and I wonder what that is, now that her dream is gone. Last month I sent her a ream of stationery and a box of pens in case she wanted to write to me, the way Mattie did, from her prison cell. I couldn't risk a note—not with prison administrators monitoring her mail—but I hoped, against all odds, that she would understand what I meant. *I am sorry for silencing you,* I willed her to hear when she looked at the paper and pens. *I want to hear your voice again. Tell me how to make it right.*

After a few weeks, an envelope appeared in the mailbox, late in the afternoon as always. I recognized the cream-colored stationery, and my heart skipped a beat. I sat at my writing desk with the envelope in front of me for a long time, staring at my name and address in Amanda's handwriting and the red prison stamp under the return address: SENT FROM A STATE CORRECTIONAL FACILITY. Finally, I tore off a tiny corner, not wanting to damage the letter, wriggled my thumb into the hole, and ripped the envelope open. Inside was a single sheet of paper, folded in thirds. I unfolded it.

It was blank.

The stage lights go off with a sound like a puncture wound, and the audience's applause turns to drunken yelling as soon as the house lights are up for intermission.

Cynthia waits for me backstage in the greenroom. We call it the greenroom for the duration of shooting, but in the manner of such venues, it's little more than a repurposed storage room outfitted with a couple of mismatched sofas in varying states of decomposition and a ring of broken-down vanities, one of them holding the replacement Betty wig, perched on a Styrofoam head and ready for her close-up. Craft services is a rolling cart holding H-E-B sandwich and fruit trays under plastic domes and a case of room-temperature Lone Star propped on its side in the corner behind the door. This is definitely not L.A.

In this environment, Cynthia looks somehow both resplendently out of place and perfectly at home — she elevates her surroundings until their shabbiness seems a kind of quaint homage. She snuggles into a sofa the color of day-old guacamole, typing something on her phone that she dispatches with a single tap when I walk in. A tweet, I assume.

She puts the phone away and, without getting up, opens her arms luxuriously toward me. "Darling, you are on an absolute killing spree out there. Slaying. Mass murder."

Her choice of words always leaves me a little breathless. "Thanks, Cyndi," I say, leaning over to submit to a seated half hug. As I flop onto the brown plaid sofa opposite, I say, "But they're half dead at best. Getting better all the time."

"Close enough," she says with a catlike smile. "Here's a little secret about standup specials. They're never anyone's best performance. We give what we can onstage, then fix the rest in post."

"Ah. The appearance of funny."

"Much more important than the real thing." She raises an eyebrow. "Of course, the greats have both."

It's just like Cynthia not to say the obvious next thing. I don't care. I'm used to it by now. And I know her exaggerated poise is an act. I've seen her drunk many times, after yet another normie boyfriend went running, intimidated by her public presence and long list of accomplishments before the age of forty. The last one to go, Davis Q. Brown or some such nonsense, broke up with her on network TV, appearing on a talk show the morning after *New York* magazine published Cynthia's relationship status as "happily committed" to dish dirt on everything from her clinginess to her support garments. The Cynthia that I encountered when she called me to her apartment in the middle of the night had neither the appearance of poise nor the real thing. And she was funny only in the unintentional way everyone with a broken heart is funny: snot running into her mouth, sobs that turned to squeaks halfway through, wine stains on the sofa that I happen to know cost eleven thousand dollars. I cradled her in my arms and thought, *Thanks to Jason, thanks to Amanda, I will never cry this way again.*

Since then, Cynthia hasn't dated any more normies, only other semifamous people, and if they break her heart, she doesn't confide in me about it. But she doesn't look at her phone during our meetings anymore either.

"Are we still on for Wednesday-morning punch-up?" I ask.

She nods, and I wonder if she's thinking about the same night. "I loved the last round of pages you sent me."

"You didn't think the Marvel figurine as murder weapon was too much?"

"Death by boobs-and-butt? No, I think it's perfect. Hit him with his own sexual fantasy, right?" She mimes swinging something heavy out in front of her. "Pow! Right in the kisser."

"Right in the kisser." I smile back.

"I just want to tell you again how thrilled I am to have dropped that dentist sitcom. Irina is very talented, don't get me wrong. She's still my bestie, you know? But the idea just didn't have legs. It's been done. A successful career woman with a sad-sack dating life, B-plots with the hygienist . . . it has Mindy Kaling's sloppy seconds written all over it. Workplace comedy is so Obama era, you know?"

I nod, always the listener.

"Revenge swap, though. Dark comedy. It's so right for how everybody is feeling right now. They go low, we get 'em in the groin, right? It's *Killing Eve* meets *Jane the Virgin*." Cynthia has the courtesy never to refer directly to the source of my ideas; to her, no matter how obviously a script alludes to the creator's life, it is pure philistinism to suggest a connection. Besides, I suspect that she considers anything that reminds people of the trial good press for the show. "I love that we have the whole will-they-or-won't-they vibe, but instead of some douchey, Cro-Magnon detective and his stern female partner"—she wiggles her shoulders suggestively—"it's *two gorgeous women of color,* locked in a deadly game of cat and mouse."

"I'd settle for one gorgeous woman of color and one half-Mexican gnome," I say, knowing she'll shrug again rather than contradict me. As a matter of fact, I like the way I look these days, but I know where my bread is buttered. What I'd really like to say is *Which of us is the cat and which is the mouse?* "But thanks. Have you thought any more about the title?"

She shrugs. "It's out of our hands. Last I heard, the network is focus-grouping some ideas that come earlier in the alphabet than *G*. That bumps the streaming audience by thirty percent."

"It was only a working title anyway," I say, relieved. "What about *Comeuppance?* It starts with a *C*."

"The *e* next to the *u* looks weird," she says, frowning. "Plus it's too long. Long words get cut off in streaming menus. You can lose up to fifteen percent on some platforms."

"Well, it sounds better than *Got Your Back,* you have to admit."

She gives me the Cynthia Omari special: half-lowered lids with a stripe of green eyeshadow on each. *You're protesting too much,* the look says. *We both know why that title has to go. Don't push it.*

I'm saved from my desire to push it by the sound of the door creaking open a few inches.

"Knock-knock? Dana?" The male voice sounds vaguely familiar, but from my angle I can't see his face.

"This is a private greenroom, for performers only," Cynthia states immediately, with her uncanny knack for knowing at a glance who belongs and who doesn't.

"I'm an old friend of Dana's." The voice clicks into place in my memory just as he adds, "Or, should I say, of Betty's?"

Cynthia opens her mouth to object, but for once, I interrupt her.

"It's okay. Let him come in. And Cyndi, I hate to ask, but—" I wrinkle my nose apologetically. "He's an old friend. I'd love to catch up?"

Always the graceful one, she rises off the couch. "Of course." On her way out, she flashes my guest a dazzling smile. Then she's gone, to wherever semifamous people go when they leave their protégés. Agent lunch? Helicopter pad? With any luck, I'll find out soon enough.

Carl Montgomery looks much the same as he did at trial, except the scrofulous beard is taking over even more of his face, creeping down his neck to swallow his Adam's apple and leaving rusty high-water marks just under his cheekbones. I gesture toward the sofa Cynthia has just vacated. In Carl's presence, its color turns from day-old guacamole to month-old. I can practically see the fuzz growing on it.

"Dana. Dana *Diaz!* Dana, Dana, Dana." He keeps his mouth open half an inch on the last three words so I can see his tongue wiggling back and forth.

"Carl, is it?" I say politely. "This is a pleasant surprise."

"Is it?" he says waggishly. "We didn't get a lot of time to chitchat during the trial." His eyes rest momentarily on the Betty wig but return to me almost immediately.

Under cover of a rueful sigh, I release my held breath. "That was a stressful time for everyone involved."

"Thank goodness justice was served," he says with an expression I can't quite see under all that beard.

"Thank goodness," I repeat carefully. "How's life treating you post-trial? Any book deals yet?" I'd turned one down, over Cynthia's objections, almost the only time I've ignored her advice. I don't want my first book to be about that.

"Oh, I could never write a book," Carl says modestly. "Just little sketches here and there. Monologues, like you." He puts a hand up to stroke his beard in a villainous gesture that strikes me as rather overdone. "That's right, I'm a standup now," he says. "Can you believe it?"

The truth is not diplomatic, so instead I just say, "Wow."

"Yes, I know." He pauses and stares off into the distance, a strange look on his face. "You know, it's funny, in a way I owe it all to that brutal attack I suffered last spring. Because I lost everything. Not just my job—I hated that anyway—but my online world, which was where my real life was. I didn't mention this at trial, but my hard drive was stolen during the attack." As he says the words *hard drive* he glances sideways at me.

"Huh," I manage.

"Right? That Runnr bitch got her hands on the passwords to all my accounts. My life was a living hell for six months. I had to scrub all my social media accounts, flee Reddit, retire RadioMacktive completely." He sighs deeply and looks me straight in the eye. "Those were my safe spaces, Dana. Isn't that what they're called? And now they were unsafe. I felt quite—what's the word?—*triggered*."

Good, I think, the disgusting GIFs that were his specialty running on repeat in my mind's eye.

As if he can see what I'm thinking, he nods with a faux-pious smile. "As my mother always used to say, the Lord works in mysterious ways."

I nod too. I wait for him to go on, but instead, there is a long, uncomfortable pause in which he looks away again, tugging his beard.

"Except it wasn't the Lord, was it?" he says, gaze still averted. "It was you."

I shift on the plaid couch, forcing myself not to search for my reflection in the mirrored wall to make sure I look calm. That's the kind of thing a not-calm person would do.

"No idea what you're talking about, Carl," I say, relaxing my diaphragm to keep my voice perfectly level, the way all performers learn to do in drama class. "But if I did, and to make it clear, I don't"—it always occurs to me, these days, that someone could be recording me—"I would say you probably deserved what you got. Don't you think?"

"That's as may be," he says, matching my easy tone. "Like I said, we didn't get much face time during the trial, but since your career blew up afterward, I decided to look you up, just to see what all the fuss was about. Someone was benefiting from my pain, and I wanted to know who it was." He smiles. "Along the way, digging around in the suggested videos on YouTube, I got pretty interested in comedy. I kept seeing all these losers doing open-mics and I thought, *I can do that*. There's not much difference between a troll and a heckler. And what is a comic, anyway? Just a heckler with a microphone."

I open my mouth to respond to this gem of an observation, but he keeps talking.

"But I digress. The point is, I found Betty. And after a little soul-searching, I've ascertained that it was Betty, not Amanda, who paid me a visit that night."

"You said it was Amanda under oath," I point out, thinking fast.

"Anyone can make a mistake," he says. "Eyewitness accounts are notoriously unreliable. Anyway, I have other evidence, so don't bother denying it."

Evidence. My mind goes instantly, as it often does in the middle of the night, to the recordings from Amanda's spyware, inadmissible at trial but still out there, backed up on a flash drive somewhere. Perhaps buried in one of the boxes that was auctioned off to pay back rent on Amanda's storage locker. KITCHEN. HALL CLOSET. BLACK-MAIL. Or did she send it to him from prison somehow? I saw her, thumb and forefinger held apart, saying, *And only I know where it is.* More likely she planted it somewhere safe beforehand and sent Carl the instructions to find it. My face is growing hot, and I try to force my breathing to stay slow and steady.

"Well, Carl, I'm so glad you've found your true calling at last," I say, preparing to stand up. "Now, if you'll excuse me, my break is almost over."

"I won't excuse you, Betty," he says, narrowing his eyes and leaning forward so quickly that my feet slip out from under me and I'm thrown back onto the sunken sofa cushion. "I'll never excuse you for what you did, or forgive you, or put it behind me. Isn't that what you wanted? For me never to forget?"

I shrink instinctively away from him, anticipating some violent move, flashing back to Jason's house, to Aaron Neely's back seat. I clock the closed door behind him and curse myself for having let him get between me and the exit. If I scream, will anyone hear me over the noise outside? The phone is still in my hand. Will I have time to call someone? Who can I call? Cynthia? Will she abandon her tweeting to pick up or will she let it roll to voicemail?

My eyes dart around the room, looking for an escape route I know isn't there. Instead I see Carl's head reflected endlessly between the rows of facing mirrors, countless bearded Carls stretching to infinity in either direction. As the reflections multiply into the hazy distance, the faces blur and lose their definition, while their menacing mediocrity only grows.

"What do you want, Carl?" I say simply.

He relaxes back into the sofa, relieved not to have to do whatever he was thinking of doing. "I want a piece of the spotlight," he says, made suddenly friendly by his relief. "You've got it. I want it. We can start by putting me on *The Bestie Cast*. I know you're tight with Omari." He gestures toward the door.

I take a breath. "I can't get you on *The Bestie Cast*. Cynthia is very choosy about her guest roster. Besides, it's not the best place to start you." I act as though I'm thinking, and he taps his foot impatiently until I suddenly hit on the answer. It's perfect. Right in the kisser. "TV, though. I could get you on TV. Isn't that even better?"

He narrows his eyes in suspicion. "What show?"

"Omari's new show," I say. "The one she and I are working on together. It's so new it doesn't have a name yet, but it's going to be very hot. If I tell her about you, I'm sure you'll get cast." I put a finger up in warning. Trust me, this is the role you were born to play." I imagine his face when he sees the script. The provocatively posed Black Widow statuette with which my character will beat his character— not half to death but all the way this time. He'll learn what *triggered* means. "It's a dark comedy."

He nods eagerly, his greedy, stupid face reminding me of the greedy, stupid dreams I once spilled to Amanda on our first meeting, back when my highest aspiration was to be the Funniest Person in Austin.

Keeping eye contact with him, I dial Cynthia's number and show him the phone. The fact that she actually answers lifts my spirits considerably. That was a bit of a gamble, but it was worth it to show that my capital is not spent. Not by a long shot. I have more than enough to work with.

"Listen, Cynthia? I have someone here who'd be absolutely perfect for the guy in the scene we're punching up Wednesday morning. He's a very funny guy, real up-and-comer. What do you think? As a favor to me?"

Cynthia's voice sounds only slightly put out, which I know means she wants me to repeat all this to her assistant so she won't have to remember it herself. "Sure, if he reads okay."

"Thanks so much," I say, smiling at Carl encouragingly to let him know it's going well. His face is flushed red with nervous excitement. No doubt he thought this would be harder. "Later, Cyndi." I hang up and we stand looking at each other for a moment.

"Knock-knock." Nisha, one of the crew members, opens the door and pokes her head in. "Dana, they're looking for you. You're on in five. You ready?"

I nod, trying not to look flustered. "I'll be right out."

"It's all right. I think we're done here," Carl says with an ingratiating smile for Nisha. As she ducks out again, he stands up and holds his hand out.

I rise from the couch, knocking my purse over in my haste. I need him *gone*. "We'll be in touch," I say brusquely, the taste of bile in my throat.

When the door has fully closed behind Carl, I stoop to gather the contents of my purse, blinking back the tears so as not to ruin my mascara. Even as I fumble around in the mess disgorged from my purse, I'm already thinking of a bit. *I wonder how many people die from mascara blindness every year? They should make this stuff illegal.*

My hand grabs something and I realize it's Amanda's non-letter, still in the envelope. I couldn't bring myself to throw it away. The letter is askew, and as I'm stuffing it back in my purse, it falls out and flutters to the floor. I almost stoop to pick it up, then laugh at myself for saving a blank piece of paper. I give it a savage kick that sends it sliding under the sofa, but I hold the envelope for just a moment longer, looking at the handwritten address on it, undecided.

And then I notice something. In front of the bright dressing-room-mirror lights, the envelope is semitransparent. And I can see—marks. I peer into the envelope. Four little horizontal lines, a few millimeters long, at random intervals on the inside back of the envelope, near the top:

—   -

—   —

I stare and stare at them. Then I smush the envelope flat again and hold it up to the light, staring at the return address. Faintly, through the thin, fancy stationery, I see the marks anew:

Amanda Do͟rn
Central California Women's Facility
P. O. Box 1501
Chowchi͟lla , CA 9361͟o

Ama-r-ill-o. Amarillo.

Farther down, toward the middle of the envelope, there's one more mark, this one longer than all the rest. It lines up with just one word in my address:

Dana Diaz
2990 Coburn Drive
Los Angeles, CA 90239

Drive.

Amarillo. Drive.

So Amanda has one last message for me after all. Is it a warning? A threat? Or is she just telling me to go back home? After all, I willed her to tell me what to do. I think of her smiling at my mother, looking at the prom pictures in my bedroom, and shudder. It has to be a threat or she wouldn't have gone to the trouble to encrypt it.

Amarillo. Drive. *Go home, Dana. You don't belong here, and you certainly don't belong in L.A.* But I knew that already. Drive home? Maybe I will. But for now I have a show to finish.

I crumple up the envelope and throw it in the trash can by the door on my way out.

Outside the greenroom, I spot Cynthia talking to the director in the wings and head over. "You're still here?" I ask her.

"Of course. Someone has to make sure this shoot comes in under budget." The director glares at her, but she smiles serenely. "Besides,

I wasn't sure what the deal was with that guy who just left. Something about him seemed a little off. Do I know him?"

Whether Cynthia knows him depends on how closely she watched the trial. I'll have to tell him to use a stage name, just in case. "I don't think so. Thanks for answering my call."

"Of course," she says. "Like I said, I was a little worried. But if you say he's going to be big—"

"He could go far, all right," I say matter-of-factly. "Listen, do you think you can get him under an exclusive contract? Something he can't get out of. I don't think he has representation yet, so it should be pretty easy."

She gives me a long look. "Oh. I see."

"Yeah. I'd like to look out for him. Supervise his career." I add meaningfully, "I think we'd do well to keep an eye on him."

"Say no more."

Cynthia will know what to do. Under her thumb, Carl will have nothing to complain about. He'll get parts. He'll make enough to live on. He'll be on TV. He'll get just famous enough to be on the outskirts of Cynthia's entourage. And no more famous than that.

"Thanks Cyndi," I say warmly. And then, thinking of Davis Q. Brown on TV and the wine-stained sofa, I add, as an afterthought: "I'll find a way to get you back."

For as long as I am involved in the development and production of Cynthia's show, I am contractually obligated to finish up my stage performances with a Betty monologue. I had representation when I signed that contract, so Cynthia made it worth my while. But she also made it clear that Betty was an essential part of the bargain. Like it or not, Betty is my brand.

The two of us are stuck together.

At some point during the second half of every show, I have a stagehand bring me the Betty wig, and I turn my back toward the audience, adjust the platinum thing on top of my now professionally styled brunette bob, and get into character. At first I did it because having the wig onstage the whole time was distracting—and not just to the audience. But Betty's entrance has become its own bit, something I do differently every time, so even fans who've seen me before feel like they're getting something new. I've experimented with different ways of stylizing the moment; I've had the wig tossed at my face from offstage or slid along the floor toward my feet. I've had it brought out on various chairs and divans, next to a glass of wine or a bullwhip; once it came out on a tiny litter borne by stagehands in Egyptian robes. Another time I had it draped over a Frisbee and dangled on wires around my head while a theremin made UFO noises in the wings.

For tonight's taping, I wanted something special but not too gimmicky or distracting. This time, I wanted Betty to feel real.

The North Door doesn't have a sophisticated enough setup for wires, so I hired a puppeteer to mount the Betty wig on slender rods and manipulate her from a few feet away. We practiced this in rehearsals, and although Sharla's puppetry is unimpeachable, I could never ignore her presence. But tonight is different. It's something about the lighting, maybe, or the crowd's energy, or perhaps what just happened to me in the greenroom, but Sharla's black clothes and the black puppet rods fade magically into the black background, and all I can see is Betty, marching up the stairs stage right and floating toward me just a little bit above eye level. I say "floating," but thanks to Sharla, who has watched me carefully when I'm in character, she seems to walk with Betty's cocky, bouncy gait, vibrant and alive. Her footsteps don't sync with Sharla's—someone else is doing them as a sound effect from offstage—which adds to the illusion.

When Betty first appears, the crowd cheers and claps obligingly. This is, after all, the moment they have been waiting for, the moment they are promised in every Dana Diaz show. It's very on-brand. "Everyone, this is Betty," I say. "Betty, everyone. Wave hello, Betty." The wig moves just slightly, as if Betty is flipping her hair back from her face.

But this time, coming off the Carl experience and with the creepily realistic Betty wig floating in front of me, something feels different. It feels like it's Betty, but how obvious is projection when you're doing it to a puppet? It's me who's different.

I slow down, lower my voice, and go off script.

"You probably know that Betty was inspired by someone I met about a year and a half ago." There's another round of drunken laughter; one person yells, "Free Amanda!" from the back, and there's a tumultuous round of cheers and boos. I wait patiently for it all to die down. "I know, I know. Y'all are an awesome audience. Thank you. But I want to get serious for just a minute, because you probably know that the person I'm talking about is in prison right now for murdering her ex-boyfriend, who was my boyfriend and best friend, Jason Murphy."

Dead silence. As I open my mouth to say the next sentence, I find myself shaking, perilously close to tears. The aftershocks of what I've just said aloud are hitting me with renewed force. For the first time since I brought the mic stand down on Jason's skull, I feel overwhelming anger for what I had to do, who I had to do it to, and how easy it was to pin on Amanda. Just on the other side of that anger is a grief so deep I can't yet face it. It's so much bigger than me. It's grief for Jason, who I lost long before I bashed his skull in. It's grief for me, for the me I could have been without a lifetime's worth of garbage dragging me down, and also for my mother and Cynthia and Kim and Ruby and Becca. But most of all, it's for Amanda, always Amanda, haunting my dreams at night, occupying the blank space just under the Betty wig, Amanda the true believer, the villain, the hero. My grief is too big, and I am going to spill.

"I'm sorry," I say, a sob hiccupping up through me despite myself. "Hang on a minute."

The audience waits, excruciatingly polite and pin-drop silent.

"So, I just want to say, intimate-partner violence affects everyone — men and women — everyone. In a very real sense, it ruined my life. And if your life is being ruined by it right now, please get help. We're going to put a phone number up after the show. And for those of you who may be standing next to your abuser right now — because it can be anyone —" I lose control again for a moment and take a breath. "I just want you to know, you're not alone. In memory of my fallen friend, I'm donating the full proceeds of tonight's show to organizations that work to end domestic and sexual violence."

Just like that, the silence transforms into a thunderous roar of applause. The audience members in the seated section rise, and the ones who are already standing begin stomping their feet and pumping their fists. Even the people dangling their legs through the staircase banister struggle to their feet. They believe they are clapping for Jason, and it's certainly true that he was killed by his partner — me. But it's Amanda's tormented face when I first met her, fresh out of an abusive relationship and still reeling from its effects, that I see.

Is this how Amanda felt after she got her hush money from Runnr? She had seen the machinery at last and manipulated it for her benefit. But then, when she was still figuring out how to be free, the wheel turned and brought another cog in the machine around to crush the life out of her. That cog was Jason. As she learned, and as I learned tonight, there will always be another Jason. You can move away and ignore him, or you can smash his head in with a microphone stand; it doesn't matter. There will always be another Jason. I saw it in the long line of Carls in the dressing-room mirrors, the endlessly reflected faces of abuse next to the endlessly reflected Betty wig on her Styrofoam head next to the endlessly reflected me. Even with Jason and

Amanda gone, it's as if the three of us are still locked together in a struggle that will never end.

Once you see that struggle, you can't unsee it. You can profit by it or get crushed by it, but you can't escape it. Even a terrorist like Amanda, who went crazy in the end and threw her body on the machine, was part of it. We all are.

But was Amanda crazy?

As the applause continues, wave after wave, I remember telling Jason, *She only stores things online when she wants other people to find them.* What she left online was the Neely video. Which incriminated her, not me. Even though the spyware recordings of me were useless at the trial, she could have uploaded them somewhere, left them to be found. But she didn't.

Amarillo. Drive. *Flash drive.*

Where did she hide it? Behind a picture frame? Inside my old jewelry box, tucked into one of the pink velvet ring holders? Probably it was somewhere outside, where she could find it if she went back for it—under a flowerpot, maybe, like a spare house key. Or wrapped in plastic and buried in the shade under the elephant ears. Somewhere in my mother's house or yard. It was right there, packed to the gills with incriminating evidence, the whole time I was recovering from the trial. She hadn't sent it to Carl. She'd hidden it somewhere safe—safe for *me.* And she'd sent me a signal. She'd told me where to find it.

I think if Amanda could have saved herself rather than me, she would have. But when she couldn't, she made the decision not to drag me down with her. She got my back one last time, and she did it for a reason.

As the heartfelt clapping subsides, I make my silent pledge to Amanda. *I'll do it,* I tell her. *I'll keep fighting. I'll do things differently than you would. I'm a standup, after all, and we're realists. I'll do it from the inside.*

I'll use power, not fear. I'll destroy them all, one at a time. The Carls. The Jasons. The Davis & Browns. I will listen, and I will destroy.

It's time to lighten the mood.

"It's hard to get back into dating when your last boyfriend got killed by a psychopath," I crack, as a transition. The audience laughs obediently. "But you know what? Betty never has that problem."

I slowly walk over to invisible Betty, duck under the wig, and let it settle into place, transforming myself into her avatar. Then I step back to my spotlight.

"Let me tell you about my weekend plans," Betty barks, and because I no longer have to be diplomatic, the story she tells is bloody, and ragged, and true. I know it will end, like all her stories do, with her taking matters into her own hands.

Acknowledgments

There are always many hands involved in guiding a book to publication, but this one required a small army. First and foremost, I'd like to thank my editor, Tim Mudie, for his patience, critical insight, and endless support during the writing and editing process. Without him there would be no *Good as Gone* and no *Last Woman Standing*. Thanks, as well, to my agent Sharon Pelletier for keeping me sane during the busiest two years of my life; to Lauren Abramo for supporting my books abroad; and to Helen Atsma at HMH for thoughtful commentary and encouragement.

For assistance in meeting deadlines while I had a newborn, I am profoundly grateful to have had help from more friends and family members than I can thank here. Alissa Jones Zachary was particularly heroic when I thought I'd never sleep again, much less finish a book. In a perfect world we'd each be blessed with one person who understands our work and its goals, one critique partner whose writing inspires us, and one friend who comes through with support in times of need. Alissa is all three.

ACKNOWLEDGMENTS

During moments of doubt, early readers Dan Solomon, Paul Stinson, Victoria Rossi, and Linden Kueck came through with invaluable advice, cheerleading, snacks, and rubber duckies. Thanks to the talented Andie Flores for her insights into the Austin comedy scene, and to all the other comics who make Austin funny. To my husband, Curtis Luciani, the funniest and best person in my life, I owe endless thanks for his endurance during this marathon year. To my son, Hal: thanks for learning to sleep through the night.

I feel endless gratitude for the readers of *Good as Gone,* who have supplied me with so much love and encouragement over the past two years. Many, including the funny and wise Kayla Lane Freeman, have shared personal experiences and insights that influenced my approach to this book.

This has been a year of brave women. Thank you all for being brave.